Acclaim for Caitlin Kittredge's Black London series

"Takes supernatural shadows to the next level. Kittredge knows how to create a believable world, and her fans will enjoy the mix of magic and city grit."

—*Publishers Weekly*

"Crackles with conflict and perilous magic...For those who love their urban fantasy hypnotically treacherous, this book's for you!"

—*Romantic Times BOOKreviews*

"*Street Magic* jumps right into non-stop supernatural action, taking urban fantasy fans on a wild ride."

—*Darque Reviews*

"This is a dark, visceral read that sucks you in and doesn't let you up for air. That is part of my intense love for this series... It hit all my buttons: ghosts, magic, demons, cemeteries, England, moors, fog, supernatural creatures, ancient deities. The way things ended, I am seriously anxious to see what is happening next. Go out and get this!" —*Night Owl Romance*

"Sensual and empowering." —*Romance Junkies*

...and the Nocturne City novels

"*Pure Blood* pounds along hard on the heels of *Night Life*, and is every bit as much fun as the first in the series. With a gutsy, likable protagonist and a well-made fantasy world, *Pure Blood* is real enough to make you think twice about locking your doors at night. A swiftly-paced plot, a growing cast of solid supporting characters, and a lead character you can actually care about—Kittredge is a winner."

—Jim Butcher

"I loved the mystery and the smart, gutsy heroine."
—Karen Chance, *New York Times*
bestselling author of *Claimed by Shadow*

"A non-stop thriller laced with a ferociously deadly menace. Count on Kittredge's heroine to never say die!" —*Romantic Times BOOKreviews*

"Kittredge takes readers on a dark adventure complete with thrills, chills, and a touch of romance. Well written…and impossible to set down." —*Darque Reviews*

"Fast-paced, sexy, and witty with many more interesting characters than I have time to mention. I'm looking forward to reading more stories in the exciting Nocturne City series." —*Fresh Fiction*

"Wow, I am still thinking about this book. The last time I reacted to a book this way, it was the first Mercy Thompson book by Patricia Briggs. If you are looking for a book that seamlessly blends a police procedural with a paranormal, go out and get this book."
—*Night Owl Romance*

"A tense, gritty urban fantasy that grips the audience from the onset." —*Mystery Gazette*

"Caitlin Kittredge just keeps honing her craft with each new book. *Second Skin* has some pretty creepy

elements and page-turning action. Readers who enjoy good solid urban fantasy will enjoy this installment."
—*A Romance Review*

"*Night Life* dived right into the action, and carried me along for the ride...If the following books are written with the same care and interest as *Night Life*, they will be a welcome addition to this fantasy genre."
—*Armchair Interviews*

"Kittredge's amazing writing ability shines through in this wonderful tale of murder, magic, and mayhem... The intriguing plot grips you from the very first page and takes you on a roller-coaster thrill ride with an ending that will leave you gasping for more."
—*Romance Junkies*

"If you're looking for a good paranormal mystery and enjoy reading about shapeshifters, give Caitlin Kittredge's work a try!"   —*Bitten by Books*

"Hot, hip, and fast-paced, I couldn't put [*Night Life*] down. Don't go to bed with this book—it will keep you up all night. It's that good."
—Lilith Saintcrow, national bestselling author of *Working for the Devil*

"Luna is tough, smart, and fierce, hiding a conflicted and insecure nature behind her drive for justice and independence, without falling into cliché...a lot of fun to read."
—Kat Richardson, national bestselling author of *Poltergeist*

BONE GODS

CAITLIN KITTREDGE

St. Martin's Paperbacks

This is a work of fiction. All of the characters, organizations, and events portrayed in this novel are either products of the author's imagination or are used fictitiously.

BONE GODS

Copyright © 2010 by Caitlin Kittredge.

All rights reserved.

For information address St. Martin's Press, 175 Fifth Avenue, New York, NY 10010.

ISBN: 978-0-312-38820-1

Printed in the United States of America

St. Martin's Paperbacks edition / December 2010

St. Martin's Paperbacks are published by St. Martin's Press, 175 Fifth Avenue, New York, NY 10010.

10 9 8 7 6 5 4 3 2 1

PART ONE

PURGATORY

My utterance is mighty
I am more powerful than the ghosts
May they have no power over me

—The Egyptian Book of the Dead

CHAPTER 1

The dead man lay in repose at the feet of Ramses II. His blood had dried long ago on the marble floor and left a rust-colored halo about his head. One of the dead man's hands stretched outward, his fingers curled like an oak leaf in the dead of winter.

Pete Caldecott watched the dead man from the doorway of the Egyptian Room. Early morning light lit the white-suited crime scene investigators and the somber blue-jacketed Metropolitan Police officers like a cluster of ghosts, even though every one of them was flesh and bone.

Involved in watching as she was, she jumped when a hand touched her arm. "Got you a tea," Ollie Heath said, passing over a cardboard cup. "Not that shite stuff we have down at the nick, either—posh British Museum tea." He swigged from his own paper cup, a bit of brown liquid dribbling out to land on his shirt.

"Cheers." Pete took a sip, noting in passing that the tea was, in fact, quite good. "What's all this, Ollie?

Your boys can't handle a bit of straightforward murder amidst the mummies?"

Ollie grimaced at the tea on his shirt. "Call came in at about five a.m.—body in the British Museum. Thought it was some kids taking the piss at first. 'S like something out of bloody Agatha Christie, right? Anyway, they kicked it to the DI in the rotation, I got the crime scene boys in for a look, and it was all going along fine until the medical examiner went to move the body." Ollie stopped talking, and Pete watched his usually flushed cheeks drain to pale. "She found, well . . ." He cleared his throat. "You need to see it for yourself."

Pete handed Ollie her teacup and ducked under the tape blocking off the Egyptian collection. It was eight in the morning, nearly. The museum would be wanting to open in a scant few hours, and Ollie's boys had been doing a fine job of getting things cleared away from view of gawking tourists, screeching schoolkids, and the odd homeless bloke until something had spooked them.

She accepted a pair of gloves and paper booties from the plod manning the tape as she considered that. Ollie was, outward appearance and broad Yorkshire brogue not withstanding, a good copper with a dozen years in the Met, half of those manning a desk in a Murder Investigation Team. He'd seen the worst people had to offer, all of the various permutations and perversions of death they could dream up. Pete didn't really want to know what could shake Ollie Heath so much he was hanging back like a first-year probie.

But since he'd called her, it was a fair bet that whatever had shaken Ollie and his team wasn't any of the usual murder, rape, and torture police counted as routine. If it were murder, rape, or torture of the garden variety, Pete would still be asleep. Murder of the freakish, occult variety—that would make Ollie pick up the phone.

Pete intercepted the medical examiner a few feet from the body. The woman was a new face since Pete had chucked her DI desk at the Met for the freaks, the occult, and the walking movie monsters, and she looked Pete up and down with an unreadable expression.

"Hello," Pete offered, along with her hand. "Ollie might have told you he asked me to have a look. I'm Pete Caldecott." The last thing she wanted to do was go treading on toes and starting gossip all over again about the crazy ex-DI who'd taken up with that crazy shite some New Age gits and mumbling schizophrenics called magic.

Which was all true, except for the part about it being shite. It wasn't, at least not completely. But Pete found that accepting that magic existed, that it was threaded all through their city as surely as roads and rivers and rail track, was the sort of hill most people weren't willing to hoof over.

"Of course." The medical examiner shook Pete's hand. "Dr. Annika Nasiri. Heath told me you might have some insight into the . . . condition . . . of the body."

"Might," Pete said. "Can't say until I see it."

Nasiri stepped aside. "Heard you used to be a detective. I trust that you know enough not to contaminate my evidence?"

"I'll try and hold back from smearing DNA all over him," Pete said, kneeling next to the dead man. She made a mental inventory of the victim, as if she were still a cop—white male, early forties at a glance, a little ginger hair up top and a lot on his chin, cultivated the sort of beard favored by adjunct professors and kiddie fiddlers. No injures apparent, aside from the gaping second smile in his throat, of course, and the blood pool under him, nearly as wide as Pete was tall, seeping into the base of the Ramses bust that glowered above her like an irritable graven image.

"You have a guess as to what they cut his throat with?" Pete asked Nasiri, out of habit. Perhaps she'd get lucky, and it would be as simple as a jealous colleague or a spat over a girl, or a boy. Nothing that needed a person familiar with sacrifice and ritual killing to pin the slit throat and the peculiar placement of the corpse as such.

The doctor consulted her tablet PC, screen covered in handwritten notes around an electronic diagram of a body, with the wounds picked out as shaded portions. "Some kind of single-edge blade, long and thin," she said. "Until I've made examination of the wound in my lab I can't be more specific, I'm afraid."

"Right then," Pete said, deciding that if Nasiri wasn't going to be forward, she would. "What's spooked you so much you won't come within three feet of the dearly departed?"

"When my crew started to move the body, one of them lost their grip," Nasiri said. Her throat bobbed as she swallowed, and her voice constricted down to just above a whisper. "The victim's shirt slipped open."

Pete leaned over and tugged aside the collar of the dead man's cotton Oxford. Her breath hitched in her throat. When she saw his flesh, she understood why Ollie had called.

Cuts covered the dead man's torso, slices and

slashes so precise and intricate they'd make Jack the Ripper weep happy tears. Lines and loops and circles, deep and shallow, cuts over cuts over scar tissue, inflicted over years. Newer wounds had been cauterized, the skin around them black with infection. The older scars grew together, twined like white, shiny vines in a fleshy garden.

The scarring and cutting interlocked to form symbols that had no heads and no tails, but were a continuous pattern over every centimeter of visible skin. They traveled from just under the dead man's collar, down his chest, and over his stomach, disappearing into the waistband of his trousers. They were nothing familiar to Pete, which was troubling in and of itself. Magical symbolism worked as a kind of shorthand, across all the various disciplines and religions contained within—a pentagram could be co-opted by hairy-legged hippies, true, but it was also shorthand for a white witch, to tell things from the nasty side of magic to step the fuck off.

These symbols were practiced and deliberate, and Pete couldn't make sense of them, except that they made her head hurt, deep down near the base of her skull. The power in the dead man's skin vibrated her back teeth, the power that the carvings gave off nearly palpable, like the stench of decay would be in a few more hours. No wonder Ollie and Dr. Nasiri were giving him a wide berth. You didn't need a talent to sense when something unnatural and rotten was in your psychic space. It was a simple human survival mechanism, to recognize the Other, and run from it fast as your two feet would take you.

Ollie's voice made Pete start, heart slamming against her rib bones before it began hammering again. "Well?"

Pete pulled the dead man's shirt open fully, exposing the spreading ruin of scar tissue, down both his arms and peeking out from his cuffs as well. "I think it's good you called me."

CHAPTER 2

Ollie took Pete outside, to get a breath of air he said, but Pete knew the real reason and she was just as glad to leave the oppressive web of black magic around the body as Ollie's subconscious was.

They stood on the steps of the British Museum, its long gravel lawn and the iron gates holding back the world, which passed beyond them without a care or a notion of what had taken place behind the museum's granite edifice.

Pete took her pack of cigarettes from her bag and lit up, waiting for Ollie to speak first so she could gauge his mood.

"So," he sighed after she'd taken a few drags. "We're in the shit with this one, aren't we?"

"Just a bit," Pete agreed, flicking ash onto the museum's steps.

"What, then?" Ollie said. "If it's cults or a serial bloke taking orders from the neighborhood Alsatian, I'd like to know now before the press come howling over my threshold."

Pete sucked on her Parliament to buy her a few seconds, but it didn't change the answer. "It's black magic, and fucking strong stuff. I could feel it all the way across the room. Beyond that . . ." She watched the smoke dissipate into the bright morning air. "I don't know, Ollie. I've never run into anything like this before."

"You can't, I dunno . . ." Ollie gestured in a vague circle. "Read the scene? Sense the vibrations of the ether or summat?"

Pete sighed. "Maybe if I were a bloody TV psychic, Ollie. I've told you, it doesn't work that way for me." *It* being a talent, and Pete's talent being even less use than a fake medium's in situations like the one inside. Murder wasn't something she could conjure an answer to, besides feeling the black magic seeping out of the museum even now, laying cold bony fingers on the back of her neck.

Ollie waved her smoke away from his face and fidgeted, the next bit not coming to him easily. "You think you could get your Jack to take a look? I've seen him do all the mumbo-jumbo stuff." He squinted at Pete. "You two didn't split up, did you?"

Pete dropped her fag-end to the granite steps, grinding it under her toe. Ollie was just fishing for a reaction. She was careful not to give him one. "No. Jack's not about anymore."

"Oh," Ollie said, sounding almost disappointed. "Well then," he continued, after a moment where Pete watched a valiant struggle not to ask for gory details play out in his florid face, "anything else you can give me about the dead bloke? Preferably something I can use to put a squeeze on whoever did him a bad turn?"

Pete breathed in, out, clearing her lungs of smoke

and her mind of the tight squeeze of emotions that Jack's name conjured up. As if she'd called his ghost into being, she swore she could hear his raspy laughter from just behind the next pillar, smell his scent of leather and stale tobacco and soap and whiskey, see a curl of blue across the air, the visible tinge of the magic that followed Jack everywhere he went. . . .

But she couldn't see it, not really. Because Jack was gone. And he wasn't coming back.

"Pete," Ollie said. "Hullo. Come back. I could use the assist. Hasn't been a banner year for clearing cases, since me brilliant lady partner shoved off for the private sector."

Pete rubbed a hand down the side of her face. She couldn't speak to the dead or even know by sight and sense what kind of spell she'd stumbled onto, but she could at least act like she had a brain in her head. "Give me his particulars. Maybe I can scare up his contacts or at least tell you what his poison was, sorcery-wise." She didn't have much in the way of a useful talent, but she could at least talk to the people who did, which was more than Ollie would get. He'd be lucky if he didn't get his heart pulled out, or at the very least his head stove in.

Ollie consulted his PDA, a blipping, annoying little device that Pete had always thought he put entirely too much stock in. "According to the museum's human resources, the name's Gerard Carver, he was an assistant curator of the Egyptian Collection, an excellent worker according to his boss (a Mr. Something-Egyptian-with-Ten-Thousand-Syllables), diploma from London City College, nary an enemy in the world as far as the museum was concerned." He scrolled through the notes. "Lives with his mum in Knightsbridge. Ah, shite, I'm going to have to be going there next." Ollie closed his eyes and sighed. Pete had all sympathy—telling someone their son was dead wasn't a task anyone should have to do with regularity.

"I'll find out," Pete said. "I'll need to get a few pictures of the marks. That all right?"

Ollie grimaced. "Officially, no, but go and be quick about it. Newell could have me out on my arse if he even knew you were here."

Pete nodded her thanks. Nigel Newell, her old DCI, was about as stolid and unimaginative an officer as any Channel Four procedural could have thought up. His last words to Pete before she'd left the Met had been *How disappointing you've let your imagination run away with you.* Not having to contend with Newell every day was one of the few upsides that Pete had found in quitting.

Before she could express her thoughts about what exactly Newell could do to himself if he found out Ollie had called her, a blond man came across the lawn, waving and shouting something Pete couldn't make out. She shaded her eyes with her hand. "Who the fuck's that?"

Ollie sighed. "Frederick McCorkle. New partner," he explained. "Useless as an armless lesbian with a box of dildos, that one. Freddy!" he bellowed, waving at the man. "You're bloody late!"

He descended the steps to berate McCorkle further, leaving Pete by herself.

She turned away and went back into the museum, across the broad modern lobby, past the glass case holding the Rosetta Stone, past the winged Assyrian statues arranged as they had been in their birthplace, as gates into a stranger world. It shouldn't sting that Ollie had finally gotten around to being assigned a new partner. She'd been gone from the Met for over a year. If she was going to come back, she'd be back. Ollie should be moved on, and the only sorrow she should feel was that Newell had saddled him with some baby-faced detective constable, still dazzled at the thought of being in plainclothes.

She walked past the smaller pharaohs—at least in relation to Ramses—and back to poor Gerard Carver's corpse. Whatever his proclivities in life, bleeding out on a cold floor was a hard end for anyone. But it wasn't as if he'd been a victim chosen out of a hat. Jack had at least taught her that the innocent and pure rarely got swept up in the undertow of black magic completely without their accord. People turned to sorcery for lots of reasons, most of them utterly mundane, and those people usually ended up exactly like Carver, plus or minus a few stab wounds.

Magic wasn't really so different from everyday life. People were petty, selfish, spiteful bastards no matter what side of the river you walked on. Pete took her mobile from her bag, tapped over to the camera screen, snapped a clear shot of Carver's exposed torso. She shoved the phone back into her bag before Nasiri caught her.

Again, this close to the corpse, she felt the vibration in the air, the spells that the symbols on Carver's body had woven when he was alive lingering as if a cluster of spectral flies still hovered above the dead man's carcass.

Jack would have known exactly what type of spell Carver's murderer had woven around him. He could see the fabric of spells, as clearly as Pete could see the dead man himself. Jack could have told Ollie what breed of sorcerer had cast the abominable thing, and likely what sort of biscuits he fancied and what pub you could find the bastard in. Jack had a sight that most people never opened their eyes to, least of all those with a talent as prodigious as his. Being magically and psychically inclined left you with roughly the same brain chemistry as a schizophrenic enjoying the world's most realistic acid trip. Jack kept himself together better than most, but seeing *everything* was far more than anyone could accept. There had been the drugs, the year-long blackouts, the suicide attempts, and the associated symptoms any normal person would tell Pete she was well rid of.

She couldn't argue, and she couldn't force herself to see things her mind simply wouldn't wrap around the same way Jack's did. She could only observe, and record, and try to solve her side of the mystery the old-fashioned way, with skills she'd learned at the Yard rather than from her talent.

Her talent didn't lend itself to exposing black magic, to fighting monsters and seeing ghosts. She was only a vessel for talent far greater than her own, like a transformer on a wire.

She backed away as the medical examiner's team, fortified against the markings on Carver now that Pete had gotten close and not burst into flame, laid down a body bag next to the dead man and prepared to roll him into it. Pete was done with Carver, and done with the knocking of his mutilated corpse against her psychic senses. She needed to be outside, away from the site of Carver's murder and the older, darker magic of the artifacts at rest around her. It was warm and amber, scented like honey, seductive as a warm pool of water that invited her to slip under and forget. . . .

Pete nearly knocked into a uniformed plod before she managed to exit the museum by the service entrance, where her red Mini Cooper was parked behind a phalanx of Met vehicles, Ollie's nondescript Vauxhall, and Nasiri's van.

She got in and turned the arthritic engine over—the car was older than she by an order of a decade. Her mum had left it behind when she'd done a runner, and Pete had been driving it since she'd convinced her da, DI Caldecott the elder, she was to be trusted with the keys. Mistakenly, of course—she'd used it to go tooling around country roads during weekends at university, and still had a sheaf of speeding tickets from local police she'd never told him about.

Too late now. Connor Caldecott was in the ground, just like Gerard Carver shortly would be. Just like . . .

Pete shut the engine off again and closed her eyes. She couldn't cry here. Not where the uniforms, Ollie, even that bloody scrubbed-faced McCorkle could see.

Her tears didn't care, and they still squeezed down her face. Pete had never believed that crying did a bit of good other than to waste time and give her bags under her eyes, but lately the tears had simply come, like blood comes when you slice skin with a blade.

Being on a consulting job, with magic flowing close to the surface in a way that it hadn't in months, not since Jack had disappeared, was too hard. She should have been smart enough to realize she wasn't ready for the feeling. Should have waited, until his disappearance was less raw. . . .

Except he didn't disappear, did he? Didn't pop out for fags and not come back. You know exactly where he went. Jack was gone, but it wasn't as if he'd slipped away in the middle of the night.

And she had to stop expecting him to appear and

solve every problem, furnish every solution she didn't have herself, work over every job that she couldn't finish on her own. She'd thrown herself into this shadow-life, where magic was real and you saw waking nightmares every day. She'd made the choice. With or without Jack, it was done.

She had to stop looking for him, and she had to stop seeing him. Had to get a grip on herself and make the empty spots inside stop stinging whenever she saw a familiar silhouette or heard the broad tone of a Manchester accent.

Had to face the truth.

She couldn't go to him when things got too hard.

Because Jack was in Hell, and he wasn't coming back.

CHAPTER 3

People who didn't feel and taste the ley lines of power running through it didn't realize London was a city of tides. The Thames Estuary swept seawater in and out, back and forth along the embankments and bridge pilings and bricked-over, secret places beneath the city. Underground rivers trickled through ancient waterways, and Joseph Bazalgette's Victorian marvel of modern sewage still crawled underfoot, sharing space with everything from medieval crypts to secret Cabinet rooms and bomb shelters from the Great War.

Beneath everything, the Black rose and fell the same way, ebbed and flowed against Pete's mind while she drove east, the current of life force as old as the first bricks the Romans had laid down in the city walls. Older. Older than brick, older than blood spilled upon this patch of ground just inland where the Thames finally turned calm. Old as earth.

But not of it.

At the places of low tide, the Black and the waking world sometimes intersected, creating spots where if you turned your head just right you'd swear you saw a thin alley, an iron gate, or a shadowed doorway out of the corner of your eye, a thing that vanished when you looked straight on.

Jack had showed Pete that such places existed, but he hadn't been particularly strict as to how one found them. She'd spent a memorable three hours wandering up and down Covent Garden in the rain, trying to find the break she *knew* was there. Magic vibrated on a frequency just like sight or heat or sound; it just wasn't a station most human receivers could tune in. Pete had heard all of the theories: magic was just another notch on the spectrum, beyond infrared and under ultraviolet. Ghosts were just electrons. Demons were just quantum disturbances that molded themselves into flesh.

That was where it fell down for her. Demons were real. She'd met a demon in its borrowed flesh and stood close enough to feel his hot, sour breath on her face.

She'd looked the demon in the eye before he'd taken Jack's soul, ripped it free of his body, and crawled with it in his teeth, straight back to Hell.

She found parking in Limehouse, and reluctantly left the Mini. Nobody drove in the city if they could help it, but Pete enjoyed it, being encapsulated in her own small world, with only shifting gears and red lights to mind, at least until she got where she was going.

The thin space called, even if she would have rather kept driving, straight out of London, onto the M-25, east until she got to the edge of the country at Dover. The Black couldn't be left behind, though. It simply was, and once you'd seen it, you couldn't look away.

Pete stepped into a gap between a newsagent's

and a pizza shop, and emerged into a Victorian street. In London, mid-morning approached, but here there was soft, fog-draped night. Gaslamps lit the way to the red door of a pub, through which drifted music and the occasional bout of laughter that dopplered from the brick row houses across the cobbles and back to her.

A black carriage thundered past, four horses with steam for breath and glowing red coals for eyes towing it on clockwork legs. The citizens of the carriage hid behind a red curtain, but Pete tasted black smoke on the back of her tongue as it passed, the taste of sorcery. She flipped the retreating end of the carriage the bird. Hadn't she had enough of fucking black magic for one day?

Once it was out of sight, she pushed through the red door and into the Lament pub, the one spot she could reliably locate when crossing. Time and place worked differently in the Black, and in many ways the whole of hidden London was as the East End under Victoria—dangerous, violent, and full of things that would gut you from stomach to neck for a shilling, or simply because they were hungry.

Except at the Lament. It was neutral ground. No fighting, no gambling, and no magic. Anyone who violated the rules found themselves promptly tossed arse over teakettle into the street by a brigade of immovable bouncers, who ranged from Takeshi the former karate champion to Dougie the bridge troll.

Dougie was on tonight, and Pete smiled at him. Dougie had lived under London Bridge until the early 1700s, when increasingly wheeled methods of transport made his habit of snatching livestock, stray cats, and wandering children and ingesting them somewhat impractical.

"Oi," he said to her, in a voice that was both high and soothing, for a towering, rock-skinned, web-fingered carnivore. "Haven't seen you in a while."

Pete tried to return the troll's smile. It wasn't Dougie's fault that she could barely stand to come here without Jack. "'M looking for the Green Knight," she said. "Is he here?"

"Came in about an hour ago," Dougie grunted. "Champion mood, as usual."

"Wonderful," Pete muttered. She hung her jacket on a hook, because the Lament was always warm and close, and because she didn't want the punters getting the idea that she had something to hide, and went to the bar. "Newcastle," she sighed. "And could I talk you out of a glass of water?"

"Sure, luv," said the bartender. She was tall, steel eyed, golden haired, and tattooed within an inch of her life. Valkyrie, Pete guessed. Or just a very, very fit former table dancer.

"Business not so great in Valhalla, then?" Pete said. She lit a cigarette while the publican poured out the ale.

"Your jokes need work," said the barwoman. "Or maybe a defibrillator." She set the Newcastle on the bar and leaned in to Pete, resting on her elbow. "Fair warning, Weir. I know who you are, and so did the gents who came in looking for you about half an hour ago."

Pete kept her expression blandly pleasant while she digested the information. She knew the Black at large gossiped about her—she'd be shocked if they didn't, really. She'd gossip about her, were she someone else. Pete Caldecott, Weir. The speaker for the old gods, one of the few of her kind still in existence. Jack Winter's woman, who could transform his not inconsiderable power into something that could turn the Black into ashes. Still, she didn't know that she'd ever get used to being openly stared at and recognized while she was buying a drink.

"They still about?" was all she decided to say. She felt the acute lightness of her belt, which used to hold pepper spray, a flexible baton, and sometimes a 9mm pistol. Right then she missed the pistol most of all.

"One went to the loo," the bartender said. "One's at the corner table, drinking coffee and taking up space." She sneered. "Won't even order a real bloody drink."

"I'm not here to start trouble," Pete said.

"They are," said the bartender. "I know nasty gits when I put eyes on them."

"Thanks," Pete said. "But I didn't come here for the nasty gits, even if they came here for me." She took the Newcastle and made her way to a round table in the center of the pub. She set the pint in front of the bearded man in a soft, dingy tweed jacket sitting there, smoking a pipe that would have given Gandalf a complex, and took the free chair. "Hello, Ian."

Ian Mosswood raised one eyebrow, and exhaled a stream of blue-green smoke. "If it isn't Petunia Caldecott. To what do I owe this dubious pleasure?"

Pete rolled her eyes. "I've kicked men square in the business for slinging that name about, you know."

Mosswood gave a snort. "I'd wager you've kicked them for far less. You've a changeable temperament, *Petunia*."

"Look," Pete said, shoving the lager at him. "I don't want to spend one more fucking second in this place than I must, and I've brought you an offering and everything, and I'm not even a druid. You don't have to be a cunt about it."

Mosswood raised the glass to his lips and took a healthy sip. "No. But I do have more fun this way."

Pete sighed. "Tosser."

Ian gave a small smile, more of a lip twitch, but with a being as capricious and powerful as a Green Man, you took what you could get. "What can I do for you, oh gracious and *most* serene Miss Caldecott?"

Pete pulled up the picture of Gerard Carver's torso and slid her mobile across the table. "You ever seen anything like this?"

Mosswood's pleasant expression bled away, as if a downpour had stripped all the leaves from a sapling. "Where did you get this?"

"A dead bloke in the British Museum," Pete said. Out of the corner of her eye, one of the gits the barwoman had pointed out got up from his table and joined his partner coming out of the gents'. They were a matched pair—dour, black coats and trousers, natty black hats of a style that was several generations out of date for the world Pete had come from, but perhaps not for theirs. They moved smooth and well, used to one another and used to violence, by the curve of their fists and the stamp of their boots. Mosswood's ale rippled as they approached. Pete weighed her chance of running and found it shite. The first move in a fight wouldn't land her any more favorably. Staying put was the winner, then. Maybe they simply wanted to chat.

Maybe she was Queen fucking Elizabeth.

"You must listen to me." Mosswood had carried on talking while she'd been distracted. "If this is what it appears to be, you must leave it—"

Pete felt a hand descend on her shoulder, then two hands, one for each git. "Petunia Caldecott," said the one who'd come from the gents'. "We wonder if you'd be so kind as to accompany us outside for a wee chat."

Pete rolled her eyes at Ian. "You see what you've done? Got every bastard in the place using that name."

"Please," said the other. His voice was posh, but he spoke English like he was kicking the hard consonants in the gut—German, Pete guessed, or from some other place where the whole language sounded like shouting and they ate a lot of sausage.

"This is a lovely pub," he continued. "I would hate for blood to get all over the floors and walls. Very unsanitary."

Mosswood inclined his head slightly in question, but Pete answered with a shake. She didn't need one of the oldest creatures in the Black to stand in her stead for a pair of knuckle-draggers.

"Very," she agreed, and stood, shrugging off Wee Chat and German Boy as she did so. They wanted her quiet and some place out of view, which didn't bode well, but when they touched her they didn't ping her radar as more than human, which did. Humans were low on the totem pole—breakable and fragile in all the usual ways, even with a talent behind them.

"Out the back, if you please," said German Boy, and he made a courtly after-you gesture that caused his long black coat to swirl.

Pete walked ahead of them, feeling the eyes of Mosswood and the barwoman and everyone else in the pub on her. Watching to see how Jack Winter's left-behind girlfriend handled herself. Watching to see if she showed them fear. Pete thrust her chin out and kept her face blank as she pushed through the kitchen door, past the loo and the storage closet, and out into the back alley, where it was still night and still foggy. At least out here, nobody was staring.

CHAPTER 4

"Right," Pete said, turning to face the twin gits as the pub door swung shut behind them. "You two from the Van Helsing fan club, or did your mums dress you like that?"

Wee Chat's mouth twitched. "I'm Abbot. This is Dreisden. And you, Miss Caldecott, need to come with us."

They wanted her to go somewhere, preferably in one piece. Things were looking positively sunny. Pete shook her head to Abbot's request. "I don't think so. You've got something to tell me, you can do it now or not at all, because I've had my quota of shadowy errands for the day."

Abbot sneered. "I wasn't offering you a choice, miss." He pulled aside his coat to showcase a truly impressive knife sheathed on his belt. Abbot made his point by pulling it an inch out of its leather casing, the pure liquid gleam of the silver blade catching the low light. Pete had seen knives like that before— silver over a cold iron core, repellent to Fae and to

most other things roaming the Black that would re-
quire a stab in the first place. Jack's old flick knife
had been similar, if a fuck of a lot subtler.

She called up Jack's face in response to Abbot's
show, in her mind's eye, his sneer and his screen of
contempt that let the rest of the world bounce off.
Hoping her expression at least managed to be unim-
pressed, she shrugged. "I guess you don't care if
everyone and their mum knows you're compensat-
ing, then?"

Abbot pulled the full length of the blade. It was
wickedly sharp, curved at the end to more effectively
hook on to flesh and organs, and wrought all over
with thread-fine engraving that danced and swirled
under Pete's gaze before settling.

Whoever they were, the Git Brothers knew their
way around spellcraft, and that negated all the posi-
tives Pete could find to her situation. Nobody was
going to stop Abbot from using her as a replacement
sheath for his great pigsticker, if he took the notion
into his head. Nobody but her.

"Look," she said, trying one last time to do as
Jack would have done and talk her way free. "I'm
sure you've got me wrong. I don't have anything you
want, and if I do, I'm sure we can work it so no one
ends up in hospital."

"Oh no, Miss Caldecott," said Dreisden, as Abbot
advanced, waving the knife like he was a small boy
who'd just discovered his own penis, "we know exactly who you are, Weir. Whore of the crow-mage."

Fuck. They did know who she was. And didn't
seem very happy about it.

"As to your condition, orders are to deliver you
alive," piped up Abbot. "Beyond that, we have no
further instructions."

So much for silver tongues. Pete managed half a heartbeat before Abbot lunged at her. He grabbed the front of her blouse and shoved her against the wall of the pub. Pete felt buttons give way.

"There you are. There's a good girl." The knife stroked the side of her cheek, perilously close to her ear. "Don't scream," Abbot hissed. "Be sweet to me and I'll be sweet to you."

He trailed off when Pete grabbed the hand holding her shirt and bent it backward, applying pressure to the wrist and the heel of the hand with her thumb and forefingers. She'd found the threat of a broken wrist at least made men, no matter how large, drunk, or enraged, reconsider whatever they were holding on to. Winning a fight wasn't about being big. It was about being mean, and Pete had no doubt that when it came to her bad day versus the Git Brothers, she cornered the market on meanness.

Abbot let go of her as Pete forced him loose. For good measure and perhaps a bit, she admitted, from spite, she put a knee into his bollocks. Abbot collapsed, and Pete kicked his knife out of reach before she turned on Dreisden. He was faster and less interested in her tits, and silver and iron appeared in his hand without missing a step. This time it was a straight razor with an ebony handle, more of the liquid spellcraft wrought into it. Dreisden clearly knew this dance, and he came in with a backhand slash that would have opened Pete from crotch to neck if she'd been any slower.

She was small, had always been the smallest in any given class or training during her Met days, and she used her size to duck inside Dreisden's reach, safe from the razor, pushing her arm into his elbow joint to break his stance and throw him off balance.

Pete hit Dreisden one sharp, short punch just under his sternum with her other hand, angling her fist up, and he let out a wheeze like she'd stepped on him.

She jabbed him once more in the hollow of his throat, and that was that. Dreisden fell to his knees, dropping the razor to attend to the pressing matter of not breathing. He looked up at Pete with bulging, accusing eyes as his mouth flapped like a trout's.

"Oh, calm down," she sighed. "You'll live."

Dreiden swiped at her with one hand, and Pete jumped back, out of reach. She raised her boot to put it into Dreisden's skull and convince him to stay down. Too late she felt the wind of movement on her back, and something cold and round and utterly too familiar press against the back of her neck.

A voice like carriage wheels scraping over cobbles said, "That's enough out of you, miss."

Pete stilled, putting her foot down and keeping her hands at her side.

"Good girl," the voice told her. To Abbot and Dreisden it snarled, "Get up!"

The pair got to their feet, Abbot standing bow-legged and wincing when he moved. "You didn't tell us she's some kind of fucking kung fu master, did you?" he mumbled.

"Shut it," the voice ordered. "A tiny little thing like her taking out the pair of you—you're a waste of my fucking air. Go back to the car."

The owner of the pistol grabbed Pete by the shoulder and turned her around. "I suppose you find this all very funny, Miss Caldecott."

Pete took in the new addition to the Git Family, and felt her stomach drop a bit. He had gray hair and matching gray eyes, two bits of polished steel. A face that wasn't quite craggy enough to be carved from stone, but would definitely put a fright into small children. Huge—not wide but rangy, his hand more than big enough to envelope the grip of the pistol with acres left over.

"It was a bit," she admitted, since with a gun in her face, her policy was generally the truth. "When I kneed him in the bollocks and his voice went all wobbly."

"Bitch," Abbot spat. "I should've cut you."

"Could've, should've," Pete snapped back. "Didn't."

"Car!" the man with the pistol bellowed. "Now!"

Abbot took his leave, grumbling invective that Pete was sure had to do with her heritage and proclivities. The git in charge stepped back, keeping the pistol pointed at her skull. "You going to give me any more trouble, girl?"

"Depends." Pete folded her arms. "You going to keep calling me pet names and trying to kidnap me out of pubs?"

"You're a lot of things, Miss Caldecott." The git in charge grinned. His teeth were very white and straight, like a row of standing stones. "But I don't think you're bulletproof."

"Look, who the fuck are you lot?" Pete demanded. "I was having a nice, quiet drink with a mate. You interrupted me, and you're rude. I don't see why I should listen another word you say."

The git lowered his pistol—it was a .45, Pete noted, with a nickle barrel and an ivory grip, both etched as his flunkie's blades were. A small cross in ebony was inlaid into the butt of the grip and it gleamed as the man put his weapon, carefully and lovingly, into a shoulder holster secreted under his black coat. "You're right, I was rude. Forgive me." He extended a hand in place of his pistol, encased in a black leather glove tight enough to be second skin. "My name is Ethan Morningstar. And I do need to speak with you, Miss Caldecott."

"Was that so hard?" Pete asked him. She felt she had a right to be peeved with the man. He'd had her dragged from a pub and nearly stabbed. "Why all of this needless crap with your hard men, Mr. Morningstar? Just talk."

"You'll excuse my men," said Ethan. "You have a certain . . . reputation for combativeness. My men were simply to ensure that the conversation remained civil. Their purpose was *not* to be lewd and lascivious, I assure you. Mr. Abbot will be disciplined." The way he said it made the small hairs on Pete's neck, the ones fine-tuned by years of Catholic schooling, bristle. Morningstar was hard like an old school East End gangster was hard—imposing, expressionless, and possessing roughly the same empathy as a tombstone. Abbot was a cunt and an idiot, but Pete didn't envy the remainder of his night.

"Maybe he's had enough," she suggested. "A boot to the nethers isn't something most gents forget with any speed."

Morningstar gave a humorless twitch of his mouth. "You are the expert in emasculation, I suppose." He gestured to a black BMW idling at the end of the alley. "Now, will you come with us of your own accord?"

Pete considered. It was rare enough to see cars in the Black, still rarer to see modern ones in good working order. Things with complex circuits and chipsets tended to get fouled up by the crossing over from regular London to the Black beneath—a fundamental shift in physics sent most post-1970s tech into fits. To be driving what looked like the newest in bul-

letproof, leather-interiored luxury, Morningstar must
have some powerful enchantments backing him up.
All that and a gun as well. Pete decided either it was
her bloody lucky day, or the gods were taking the
piss. Most likely the latter.

"No," Pete said to Morningstar. "I don't think I
will. You can tell me here or not at all."

Morningstar sighed, as if she were a child refusing
to eat her breakfast. "Very well. I'd hoped a show of
civility might convince you where force wouldn't, but
I can see I'm to resort to shock and awe."

He snapped his fingers in the direction of the car
and the back door swung open. A petite gray-haired
woman stepped out, her lithe small form and heart-
shaped face older and thinner but still undeniably
familiar to Pete as the features slowly lined up to fall
over a memory, like a tracing over an original.

Gold. The hair had been gold, when she'd gone
away. The shade that neither Pete nor her older sister
MG had inherited, thanks to Connor's black Irish
genes.

Pete felt her lips part, letting all her air out save
for what it took to say a word. "Mum?"

CHAPTER 5

Juniper Caldecott came over and stroked her palm against Pete's cheek once, then tucked a stray hair behind Pete's ear. "Hello again, Petunia."

Pete shut her mouth with effort, and thought it was frankly a miracle that she managed not to simply scream. "Mum, what the *fuck* are you doing here?"

Morningstar's eyebrows peaked. "I'll thank you to not use that language in front of your mother."

"I'll thank you to kindly fuck off back to your fancy-dress party, you gun-toting twat," Pete snapped, not taking her attention from Juniper. "Mum, what the Hell is going on? I haven't . . . *we* haven't seen you in bloody *years*."

"It was too long," Juniper agreed. "And I'm sure you have questions."

"Oh yeah," Pete agreed. "Questions, I have those. Just for instance, why'd you run out when I was eleven, never so much as pick up the phone, and let me and Da and MG think you were most likely *dead* for almost twenty fucking years?"

"Language!" Morningstar shouted, his coat flapping as if he were a bird and she'd chucked a stone at him. Pete turned on a glare on him.

"One more word and I'm going to *feed* you that hat of yours."

"I don't expect you to forgive me at once," Juniper said to Pete, "but do you think you could at least listen to me?"

"I don't think we have anything to talk about," Pete told her. Now that she'd stopped feeling like she'd been punched in the stomach, the things she'd imagined saying to her mother over and over seemed useless. Even the rage she'd expected was curiously void. Juniper was simply there, older like a piece of furniture that didn't fit in with the rest of the room. Juniper tried to reach for her and Pete backed out of range. She felt stiff, as if she were locked up behind her own eyes, watching someone else react as Juniper pleaded with her.

She could remember the suitcase Juniper had packed on the Saturday she lit out. It had hard plastic sides, robin's egg blue with a white handle. MG had cried. Pete hadn't. Connor had sat on the sofa, rolling a glass of whiskey between his hands, watching an Ireland-Scotland match on the telly.

Sometimes you just have to let go, Connor, she'd said with her hand on the front door of their flat.

And, *I have let fucking go, haven't I?* he'd snarled, and reached out to twist the volume on the set to maximum.

That was the last time Pete, MG, and their father had seen Juniper. Pete couldn't even find her through the Met's database to get in touch when Connor went into the hospital for pneumonia and didn't come out again, the lung carcinoma fed by thirty years of smoking like the copper he was eating him up in a little over six months' time.

"I got into a bad way with some bad people," Juniper said. "They wouldn't let me contact anyone. I had to get a new identity to get away. Ethan helped me with that. He's the one who got me free."

"So what?" Pete said acidly. "Ethan here doesn't believe in the telephone? He prefers family reunions in dank alleys?"

"I asked your mother along tonight because we all have something to say to you," Ethan said. "And I thought it would be easier to hear coming from someone who cares for you deeply."

"*We*?" Pete asked. "What *we* is under discussion, exactly? The Beatles? The Queen? The twats-in-coats collective?" She left the part about Juniper *caring deeply* for her alone. Morningstar was clearly delusional.

"*We* meaning the Order of the Malleus, Miss Caldecott," Morningstar said. "At this point, our interests converge, which brings you an opportunity to cease throwing your life away on sorcery."

Pete tried not to gawp stupidly for the second time that night. Along with her mother, the Order of the Malleus was a thing she'd thought purely theoretical, and probably gone for good, up until the moment. Non-magicians in the Black, crusaders for a set of ideals that had gone out of fashion with shoe buckles, the Order was something mages used to spook one another, any time somebody with a talent disappeared or died in a way that wasn't immediately explained. *The Order got 'im* was the Black's *'S true, my mum's cousin's boyfriend's seen Bigfoot and shaken his hand.*

In other words, utter shit.

"You're pulling my fucking leg," she told Morningstar. His brows drew together.

"I assure you, Petunia, I am taking this matter with grave seriousness, even if you are not." He straightened his coat and hat, the shoulder holster and pistol disappearing like a stage trick. "Murder may be an everyday concern to the scum that populates the Black, but we who are righteous still value human life, and I expect that you, as a copper, haven't lost your capacity for it just yet."

"What are you on about?" Pete demanded, though she had the sour feeling in her stomach that she already knew.

"Gerard Carver," Morningstar said, and confirmed it. "He was one of ours. Poor boy. He and we need your help, Petunia." He sighed and made a small sign in the air, not a cross but an older one that Pete recognized from her time with Grandmother Caldecott as a child, warding off the evil eye. With his shoulders slumped and his cannon hidden, Morningstar would look like any other old man stuck slightly behind the times, strolling down the street. Pete pitied the chav who tried to put the strongarm on Ethan Morningstar. Though not as much as she pitied herself, having to listen to him bang on.

"One," Pete told him, "stop calling me Petunia like you bloody know me. Two, I'm not brick stupid. Jack's told me all about the Order."

"Oh." Morningstar's mouth twitched. "Has he, now? And what does the great Jack Winter have to say?"

"He says you're no better than sadists," Pete returned. "Witchfinders, torturers, and frustrated Puritans who should've gotten snuffed out with King

James. If Carver was your mole, then he got what was coming to him, and I'll thank you lot to leave me the fuck alone from this moment forth." The stories she'd heard from some of Jack's mates about the order were toe-curling. Cotton Mather would have been best mates with every one of them, and probably nip round to the pub after a rigorous day of ducking, skinning, and raping mages and sorcerers and anyone else who found themselves even vaguely involved with the occult.

"Funny," Morningstar said. "I wouldn't think Jack Winter would have anything to say about the Order at all. Being as he's dead, you know." He grinned to himself at that, and he kept grinning until Pete slammed her fist into his teeth.

She felt skin give on her knuckles and her bones go out of place, but the *crunch* of Morningstar's perfect shark smile was satisfaction that overwrote pain.

"Petunia!" her mother cried, leaning down to help Ethan. "What is the *matter* with you!"

Morningstar spat out a tooth, but waved off Juniper grasping at his arm. "I'd hoped we could be civilized," he said, getting back to his feet. "But I see you're determined to find malice in any comment I might make."

"Is that what I did?" Pete feigned shock. "Because from here it looks as if I've told off a stupid cunt babbling about someone who's name he's not even fit to say aloud."

"The Order wants Carver's killer," Morningstar said. He hadn't even raised his voice, and Pete found that a bit worrying. Usually people were a bit more upset when you'd hit them. "It'll have them and you," he continued. "You can resist all you want, but the Order is the hammer of God. And God has chosen you to bring Carver's killer to us. Bad Catholic that you are, I wouldn't expect you to recall, but God has a way of dealing with those who ignore His summons, Petunia."

"Oh, sod off," Pete sighed. "Take your little sorcerous intervention and shove it straight up your arse."

"Oh, Petunia," Juniper hissed. *"Honestly."*

"You don't matter to me one drop," Morningstar told her. "I respect and care for your mother, and I'd prefer not to harm you, but you have knowledge and contacts that we don't, and you can either use them to deliver us Carver's murderer, or we will use further measures to show you the error of your ways in choosing to sin against God with your witchery."

Pete folded her arms, partly to hide her freely bleeding hand and partly to show Morningstar he didn't frighten her. "I would *love* to see you try, *Ethan.*"

"You live at Number forty-six in the Mile End Road," Morningstar said with maddening calm. "Fourth floor, front corner flat. Your laundry is sent out once a week and you shop for essentials on Saturday morning at the Tesco Express several blocks away. Your associate Oliver Heath could probably tell me even more, if I asked the right questions." He tilted his head, hat brim shadowing his stony eyes. "Need I continue, Petunia?"

"No," Pete said, throat tight and heart jumping. "You've made your point." *Do as we say or we'll hurt you and then move on to your nearest and dearest.* Not a particularly original threat, as threats went, but a damned effective one. Pete wished she'd hit Morningstar much harder when she'd had the chance.

"Good. I'll wish you a pleasant evening, then, and look forward to your findings on the death of the

unfortunate Mr. Carver," Morningstar said, turning
and going to his car.

"Mum," Pete said, grabbing at her sleeve when
Juniper made to follow him. "What the *Hell* are you
doing with those people? Do you know what they *do*
to people like me? They've *killed* friends of Jack's,
Mum. And done things so much worse it'd turn your
guts inside out. They're the fucking BNP of the Black
and you're in their fan club?"

"They saved me," Juniper sighed sadly. "They
could save you too, Petunia. If you'd only let them in."
She pressed a card into Pete's hand. "That's where
I'm staying. I know you're as stubborn as your father,
but if you ever want to have a real chat, I'd love it."

"I'll pencil it in!" Pete shouted as Juniper walked
away. "Set a date for it in that alternate reality where
Pete has a mother who's both sane and a gives a rat's
arse!"

The BMW revved up its engine and screeched
away in response, and Pete slumped against the alley
wall, finding a Parliament and lighting it with shaking hands. She exhaled three times before she was
able to bring her heart rate down to Regular from
I'll Bloody Kill You.

Dead men in museums, dead men made that way
by black magic, and now her mother, demanding she
bring the Order's brand of justice.

"Bloody wonderful," Pete said, stomping on her
cigarette butt hard enough to kill it, had it been
alive.

After she'd lit, dragged, and killed another Parliament, the door swung open. Mosswood stuck his
head out. "There you are. I was beginning to wonder
if it was time to drag the river."

"I'd be better off, probably," Pete muttered, watching the blue halo of smoke drift into the gaslamp light, dissolving like a ghost.

Mosswood cocked his eyebrow as he looked her over. "Your hand is bleeding."

Pete examined her knuckles. They were skinned, bruised from Ethan Morningstar's teeth, but not swollen, and she could move her hand with little enough effort that likely nothing was broken. "I'll muddle through," she said.

Mosswood took his pipe and a box of matches from his jacket, striking one on the brick wall. He sucked on the pipe, coaxing fragrant greenish smoke from it. "Care to talk about it?"

"No," Pete said, rubbing her second smoke out on the brick next to the scratch from Mosswood's match.

"Very well. As I was saying before we were so rudely interrupted," Mosswood said. "That photograph you showed me is disturbing."

"Yeah?" Pete felt a renewed interest in the idiot Gerard Carver. If Morningstar and the Order were searching for the killer of one of their own, she'd only be their first stop. Someone with more talent and less ability to defend themselves would be next, on and on like dominoes until Morningstar got what he wanted. Fanatics, be they dressed in street rags or thousand-pound suits, operated in much the same way.

Besides, she'd promised Ollie, and now she'd also put the Order of Malleus onto him, unknowingly. She couldn't very well back away now, even if she wanted nothing more.

"I haven't seen anything like those marks on your dead man for a long time," Mosswood said, quieter than his usual acerbic, professorial tones. "And for a Green Man, a long time is a very long time indeed."

Pete went for a third fag but found herself empty.

"Shit. Spit it out, Ian. You immortal types never just spit it out."

"You're very impatient, even for a human," Moss-wood said. "Has anyone ever told you that?"

"I've got a piss-poor temper, too," Pete said. "Get on with it."

Mosswood looked up at the sky, hazy and dark gold from the lamps of London, starless as the inside of a coffin lid. "They're very old, very powerful necromantic symbols, Pete. The magic they represent is the vilest the human mind can conceive, and I would not wish to meet the person attempting to use it face to face, if I were you."

Pete considered. Necromancy was not something people who wanted to live long, healthful lives got themselves involved with. More like people who wanted to live short, bloody lives and rise back up to feast on the family cat. "Attempted?" she asked Moss-wood.

He blew a smoke ring. "If they'd succeeded, I wager London would look a bit like the set of a cheap zombie film now."

"But you don't know?" Pete said. "I mean, what specifically they were trying to do, by killing Carver?" Other than get rid of a mole reporting their moves to his little club of god-botherers.

The Green Knight curled his lip back, showing his teeth. "I don't and never have dabbled in flesh-crafting, Pete. I don't know, and I don't want to know. And neither do you, if you want to keep on breathing."

"Well, haven't got a bloody choice, do I?" Pete said. Mosswood tapped out his pipe, and then carefully put it back in his jacket. He faced her, and put his hands on her shoulders. Pete saw the rush of green, great trees with roots down to the bottom of the world, trembling green buds passing into dry dead leaves that fell and rotted and gave birth to new shoots when they touched, the sting of electrostatic transference that allowed her talent, should she allow it, to siphon his power down like it was her own blood.

That was Mosswood. Life and sex and death. A druid like Jack respected his kind above all else. Except one. "You do have a choice, whether you think of it that way or not," Mosswood said. "I know what you're doing, keeping calm and carrying on, but in this case you mustn't. You're too valuable to necromancers, especially ones virulent as this. You and your particular quirk of talent."

"Jack wouldn't walk," Pete said. Jack never walked away, even when he knew better. Pete could at least give him that, prove that he'd taught her well now that he wasn't standing beside her any longer.

"My dear," Mosswood sighed. "Jack isn't here any longer. He belongs to Belial now, and if he *were* here, he'd say the same as I am."

Pete smacked his hands off her. "As if I'd forgotten that, you fucking bastard." It wasn't a memory like her memories of Juniper, but more like a series of grainy snapshots that flicked in front of her mind impossibly fast, too fast to ever be stopped and put away, with the other nightmares. The snowy white of the demon's pointed smile. The black, endless depths of its eyes as it dragged Jack to Hell. The snap and thump against her heart of two worlds vastly far apart shutting off from one another when they'd gone, leaving her standing in wet morning dew, smelling black smoke. Alone, as only those who'd seen and touched real evil, war zones and terrorist bombs and demon's smiles, could be.

Mosswood didn't reply, just went inside, door slapping closed behind him. Pete stayed, until the dizziness of memory and the sickness of seeing Belial's face faded enough for her to go back through the layers of hidden London to the one where it was still daylight, find the Mini, and drive home.

CHAPTER 6

The long, honey light of sunset had cast long shadows by the time Pete made it back to Whitechapel and parked in the alley next to Number forty-six. Jack's flat sat on top of a prewar building in the Mile End Road that had ceased to be crumbling and simply crumbled into four stories of brick, dry rot, cooking oil residue, and dust.

Still, for the last year, Pete had lived there with Jack. When he was there, with all his books and papers, his cigarette smoke staining the plaster, the repurposed record cabinet next to the sofa concealing the rotgut Irish whiskey that he insisted on drinking, it wasn't a bad place. Not at all. Now, she supposed as she climbed four flights of stairs and let herself in, it was as good a place as any.

Jack's piles of books and grimoires still existed just as he'd left them, on the worn built-ins and on the floor in tottering stacks nearly as tall as Pete herself. She'd rearranged some as she'd read through them, at least the stuff that wasn't in Latin or Aramaic or simply jotted down by someone with such terrible handwriting it gave her eyestrain, but she hadn't even attempted to organize anything to her liking. The books belonged to Jack, as did the specimen jars and decks of tarot cards, divination boards and talismans Jack had bartered, bought, or stolen on his various walkabouts to the darker corners of the Black. She left them, left his horrid, bachelor-flat furniture, and even let the old punk posters that curled at the edges to reveal the chipped, water-stained plaster hang.

Everything was just the same. Except for Jack.

Pete threw her bag and jacket onto the sofa and rooted in the ancient Amana icebox for a bottle of lager. She opened it and lit a fresh cigarette. The ashtray on the occasional table was full, but she couldn't be arsed to empty it just then. She rubbed the spot in the center of her forehead where a headache was brewing. It made the cuts on her hand open again and begin to sting. She sighed and looked at her distorted reflection in the lager bottle. "Aren't you a pitiful fucking sight?" she told it, getting up and going to the bathroom for antiseptic and bandages.

While she worked on her hand, she thought about what Jack would have done to Ethan Morningstar and his little group of elderly Goths when he'd found out what they'd tried to do to her. There wouldn't even be a word to describe the type of fury Jack would rain down on the Order.

Pete poured peroxide over her hand, watching the blood sluice away, leaving pink streaks on the porcelain basin. She'd met a husband and wife when she was with the Met, a pair who'd lost their son to a drug dealer with a temper when the kid was barely seventeen. Pete had told them all the right things, the things she was supposed to say—grief counseling, the loss would be difficult, but they would eventually get over it.

Six months later, the husband started their car in a closed garage and when the wife found his body she went into care. Pete saw the dealer who'd stabbed their son put into Pentonville. It hadn't helped.

Sometimes, there *was* no getting over it. Sometimes, you lived with the empty place inside of you until you imploded on it, loss as singularity, or until the empty place expanded and hollowed out the rest of you so thoroughly you became the walking dead, a ghost in your own life.

Pete wrapped her hand and taped the gauze. A faint halo of red droplets soaked through and stared up at her. Jack couldn't help her. He was gone and she was still here. And that was fucking that.

She shut off the water and put away the first aid kit, going down the hall to Jack's bedroom—their room, she supposed, now hers—and rifled through what had been his drawer of the wardrobe, tossing aside worn-out black denim, shredded socks, and Jack's favorite Dead Kennedys shirt until she found his address book. Shoving it into her pocket, she turned to leave again, but the scent was too much. The stale smoke, the mix of herbs and pot that clung to Jack's clothes, the supple creak of old, broken-in leather.

Pete picked up the shirt, twisting it between her hands. She pressed her face into it, allowing just one second. One second to imagine he was standing behind her, just out of reach. Then, before she lost her nerve, she pulled off her plain blouse and slipped the shirt over her head. It dropped off one shoulder and hung about her like a tunic over her skinny jeans, but Pete felt settled for the first time that day, as if she'd strapped on a stab vest rather than a ratty cotton shirt.

That done, she debated for a moment before she found her mobile and dialed her sister, MG, in Sussex.

MG and Pete hadn't been on what she'd call civil terms since Jack had shown up, the first time. MG hadn't taken kindly to her boyfriend stepping out with her teenage kid sister, and hadn't taken kindly to Pete for reciprocating the interest. Pete had always thought that considering all the New Age crap MG preached, she'd be able to forgive and forget, but it wasn't so, and they'd barely spoken after Connor had died. After a few rings, a voice mail box clicked on and continued the tradition.

"This is Morning Glory Caldecott. If you are interested in a tarot reading or having your chart done, please leave your name and details at the tone."

Pete massaged the point between her eyes. "MG, it's your sister. I saw Mum last night, and we need to talk about that. I'm at the same number still." She dove back into the bag for her Parliaments as soon as the call was done, and remembering she was empty, went to her jacket on the stand. She needed a smoke or, fuck it, a stiff drink after the morning she'd had.

As she passed under the flat's iron chandelier, possessed of only one working bulb to begin with, it blew out in a shower of sparks and glass shards. "Fuck," Pete muttered, snapping her lighter so she wouldn't trip over the piles of books and break her neck. Shadows danced away into all corners. Pete raised her lighter to pick her way between Jack's things to the fuse box, but movement on the ledge outside the tall windows in the sitting room made her pause.

The windows were ran nearly floor to ceiling, fat sills for sitting protruding into the room. In the grand tradition of straight men who'd spent their adult lives living alone, Jack didn't have any curtains covering the arched, bubbled glass. Pete raised the lighter, the small flame flickering in the draft. She'd met things come in from the cold before— *bansidhe* that Algernon Treadwell had sent after her and Jack. *Cu sith*, the hounds of the Underworld, sent to bring lost souls to their final rest.

Pete backed away from the glass. If she could get to the bedroom, she could find something made from cold iron, metal passed through fresh running water that would put a dent in whatever was trying to get in. There was no question that something was trying. Pete's entire scalp prickled and her skin was both icy and burning. Feeling the encroachment of magic was akin to constantly seeing something from the corner of your eye, with the difference that when you turned to face it, the thing would still be there.

She took another step back, ancient floorboards popping under her foot. If she could get to the bedroom, she'd be all right.

That was big fucking *if,* wasn't it? Humans ranked somewhere around three-legged cows in the food chain of the Black. Demons, poltergeists, Fae, creatures of the Underworld—all of them with a burning reason to wipe the slate on Petunia Caldecott. Really, the question wasn't if she could be faster this time, but when the next time would roll around.

She stopped backing up. Whatever was out there wasn't going to find her piss-scared and hiding under Jack's mattress. She shut the lighter and stood in the shadows to let her eyes adjust. The shape outside was small and gray, clinging to the limestone ledge with slender talons. The owl stared at Pete, umoving, wings flexing to keep its balance as the thin gray daylight turned it into a black silhouette.

"Shit." Pete shut her eyes and felt her pulse pounding in her temples as the claustraphobia of magic retreated. A bird. Just a bloody night bird, disoriented in the daytime. "You scared the Hell out of me, you nasty thing," she told it.

You should be scared, Weir.

Pete lost her grip on the lighter, and it clattered to the floor, skidding away to glint in the shadow under Jack's tatty armchair. "What the fuck do you want?" Not a bird. Something in the skin of a bird, a voice passed through the throat of a bird, but not a bird. The speakers came to her most often in her dreams, when she was more susceptible to psychic intrusion, but more and more her talent tuned her in when she was awake, hearing the voices of things that even mages like Jack couldn't normally discern.

The owl pressed closer to the glass, its pale eyes never blinking. *You know where your loyalties must lie, Weir. What binds you by blood. The guardian of the gateways will have her warrior, and when she calls you to the field of battle she wants you prepared.*

"I . . ." Pete shook so she could feel her fingertips fluttering against her jeans. No matter how many times it happened, how many of the old creatures of the Black spoke through her talent, it still made her sick and faint. "Why me? Who is it this time?"

You know, Weir. You've seen me, even if you didn't know me. You've been in my charge since the day you found the Black. A child of the crossroads.

Pete stared into the gold eyes of the owl. She'd never found owls unpleasant, quite the opposite. Their

faces and their thin handlike claws were comforting.
A small owl had lived in their back garden before Juniper had run off, and MG had painted a whole series
of mechanical owls, lit by coal and fire, for her art
levels.

But the eyes—those she'd seen before. The golden
eyes of the *cu sith*, the girl all in white who'd visited
Jack just before he'd lost his last fight against Belial.
The owl's eyes weren't the eyes of a night bird. They
burned like novas in outer space, ancient and only
now reaching a spectrum of human understanding.
"You were with Jack," Pete said, almost too quiet for
her own ears, never mind the owl outside.

I am the goddess of the gateway, it agreed. *The
Hecate, the three Fates of your life and every other.
And you feel it happening, Weir. How the Black is
changing. You feel the poison rising on the tide.*

"Yes . . ." Pete realized she sounded stoned, high
and dreamy. "I feel the tide." She was cold, couldn't
feel her fingers or face any longer, as if she were losing blood from a mortal wound. An insidious presence, the source of the cold, suggested the voice of the
owl was right. The Black had always been a dangerous
place for those like her, but now it was different. Necromancers were working spells in the open, murdering people without pause. Demons were snatching
souls out of the air like a hawk strikes a dove. The
dead were restless and awake. Jack was locked in the
vaults of Hell. "Yes," Pete said again, still echoing in
her own ears as if she'd chased a handful of Vicodin
with a cup of absinthe. "I feel the tide." She couldn't
move, couldn't even try to force a scream as the Hecate's voice and cold, bloodless presence filled the
reservoirs of her talent and held her in thrall like the
worst of the old silver screen vampires.

You must do what is required, Weir. Before the tide drowns all things, you must do what you were born to. Keep the seasons turning. The dead resting. The gateways impassable. If the gateways fall, the sea rushes in. This, you must never allow.

"What . . ." Pete swallowed, throat thick and her air slow. "What do you ask of me?" she mumbled at the owl, even though what she really wanted to do was chuck an especially heavy grimoire at the bloody thing and drop it in a heap down into the alley for attacking her with her own talent.

The owl spread its wings for balance, never blinking its gold eyes as it stared through her. *What has always been your born task, Weir. Kill the crow-mage. Stop the Hag.*

"I don't understand . . ." Pete started, but in a flash of silver feathers the owl took flight.

You will.

Pete came back to her own body as if she'd been thrown, going off balance and sitting down hard, her ankle twisting under her. "Ow!" she shouted. "Fuck me!"

The window ledge was empty. The light in the chandelier was buzzing happily on. Her Parliament had gone to ash in the tray, and her ankle throbbed like a small, determined rodent was gnawing it for sustenance. Pete put her hands on her face, still numb as her skull throbbed with residual power. She was chilled and damp, as if she'd just stood in a rain. She let herself be still for a moment, just feel the floor under her and the warmth returning to her skin.

The Hecate visiting her and smothering her in her own power certainly meant it was a serious matter, but as far as Pete was concerned she could jam her head straight up her own arse. Jack was already dead, and she had more important things to do. Like find out who'd killed a man whom everyone he knew had a reason to want dead.

She stood and hobbled to the sofa, where she opened the record cabinet and had her drink after all. A visit from a creature as old as the stones of the world warranted it. Pete toasted the empty window with Jack's whiskey. "Sod you," she told the Hecate, and drank the glass down in one go.

CHAPTER 7

Pete couldn't cross into the Black in Whitechapel. There were too many layers of psychic soot to allow any thin space to exist, caked up with murder and blood and the ashes of London's dead. Jack had loved the place, the way it dampened his sight down to nearly nothing, except for the passing of Whitechapel's own ghosts, trapped forever in the labyrinth of black magic and blacker deed that lanced through the narrow streets and leaning buildings like a parasitic nervous system.

Pete decided to walk, to clear her head of the talent hangover and also because it was near evening rush hour, and Hammersmith & City tubes would be packed. Near Tower Hamlets, she felt the pull again, the lessening of Whitechapel's static scattering her senses. Jack said the white noise helped him sleep. Pete likened it more to living under a constant, ominous thunderhead. The promise of rain and the crackle of excited ions, ever waiting.

She decided to call on Ollie first. If she were honest, she'd admit she missed the sounds and sights of a police squad, the routine of finding and solving misdeeds. Even after what had happened at the flat, and with bloody Ethan Morningstar and his brigade of thugs running on the petrol of Jesus. Piety and murder went so well together, like curry and rice, or, more likely with a bunch of self-important real English like Morningstar, sausage and mash.

Pete allowed herself to rationalize a bit, that not telling Ollie some behatted wanker in Christ had it in for him was the smart move. Ollie only half-believed on his best day, and he'd likely do something stupid like go round to Morningstar's and kick his door in, just to make a point. Then she'd be visiting Ollie in the intensive care ward, if not the mortuary.

She wasn't taking the case because of Morningstar. She was doing it for Ollie, and for the very real possibility that some idiot necromancer had bitten off more than he could chew and kicked off a carnival of the grotesque and homicidal with the spell he'd left on Carver's body. Demons and things of their ilk didn't need much of an invitation to kick open the gates of Hell. Usually a name was enough.

The CID unit for Camden, which included six detectives counting Ollie responsible for serious crime, was housed in a single cavernous gray room crowned with buzzing fluorescent lights at the Holborn police station. Pete bypassed the front, where a uniformed officer waved her on. She was still recognizable here, if not for her great detectiveing or her status as Connor Caldecott's daughter, then for the press coverage of her last case before she'd unceremoniously quit the force. Every law officer in Camden Town knew she'd been Ollie Heath's partner, the bird who dropped off the map and down into the dark side. The dark side, of course, being superstition and mumbo-jumbo, the one thing most coppers hated even more than shit coffee and national holidays involving pyrotechnics.

Pete found her way to Ollie's station, where she paged through the top of the snowdrift of papers that permanently occupied his desk. The Carver case had a fat autopsy report, and Pete flicked the cover open with her nail, looking at the large, high-res photos Nasiri had snapped before the cutting. The wounds on Carver still sent a spike straight through her head, even in 2-D form, and she flipped the file shut again.

"Snooping?"

Pete felt her heart fly up, slam against her chest, and fall back down. "Jesus fucking Mary Magdelene in a boat, McCorkle! Didn't your mother teach you not to sneak?"

"Sorry," he said with a shrug, settling himself at Pete's old desk and putting his feet up. "Think your mouth is even rougher than Heath's, you know?"

"I taught him his first dirty word," Pete said. "I'm like a proud mum." She looked pointedly at McCorkle's feet. His shoes were pristine, and she could see her elongated, glaring face in the toes. They'd get covered in shit and blood soon enough, and then she thought McCorkle might be a bit more tolerable. "Is Ollie in? I need to speak with him."

McCorkle dug out an evening *Times* from two days past and rattled it open. "He ain't here. Nipped out to get supper."

Pete bristled when she found herself facing rumpled newsprint, then reminded herself McCorkle was newly promoted and therefore arrogant. He'd learn. Or somebody would put their boot up his arse for being a prissy twat. "Did Ollie say he'd be coming back?" she said, giving McCorkle the same tone she used on the neighbor boy when he threw his transforming robot toys against the door of her flat.

"Might've," McCorkle said absently, turning the page. "You can wait, if you like."

Pete sat in Ollie's chair and took one of the biscuits from his righthand top drawer, crunching it just loudly enough to overshadow McCorkle rattling the paper. "Where'd you come over from, McCorkle?"

"Paddington Green," he said. "Missing Persons."

"They all get found, then?" Pete flicked her crumbs onto McCorkle's side of the desk. He looked at them as if they were live ants, then folded the paper away. In a stolid, Norse way, McCorkle was nice-looking, Pete supposed. His forehead was too thick and his hair was shaped vaguely like a blond wire scrub brush, but the crushed-and-reset nose and the bulky neck-deficient torso would do it for some women.

"You know," McCorkle told her, ruining any goodwill Pete might have allowed him by opening his mouth back up, "if even half of what they say about you is true, you have no business being in this room."

"Oh?" Pete wondered if she was going to have to punch somebody else in the mouth. Punching people got very tiresome. Sherlock Holmes didn't have to go around smacking skulls together.

"No business at all," McCorkle said. "I may not have a dad who was Supercopper, but I did the training and the time. And I sure as Hell didn't leak sensitive evidence to an informant and then quit the squad to avoid censure."

"Is that what I did?" Pete said. The rumor varied. Sometimes she'd bollocksed her last investigation, sometimes she'd joined a cult. Most times she'd simply quit because she couldn't hack finding four children catatonic and never catching the man who'd done it. Officially. The truth was somewhat more satisfying, but Pete wasn't going to try and explain hungry ghosts to McCorkle or anyone else in the Holborn nick. She didn't owe it to them. They'd talk no matter what.

"That's what you did," McCorkle agreed. "Makes you a shit cop. Always were one, to my way of thinking."

Pete forced an expression that was simply nothing, not anger and not agreement. "Why aren't you throwing me out, then? You too much of a saint to soil your good cop hands?"

McCorkle put his feet down and booted up his computer, scrolling over to the HOLMES database and beginning to type in case numbers. "Heath likes you, you get a pass. He's a good bloke."

"He is," Pete agreed, as Ollie backed into the squad room with two bags of takeaway. She leaned into McCorkle's half of the desk. "I wager you and I will see each other some day when Ollie isn't a factor," she murmured. "And then perhaps neither of us will have to be so polite."

McCorkle raised his nearly white eyes to hers. "Perhaps," was all he said.

"Oi, Pete!" Ollie said, dumping the takeaway on his desk. "Fuck you doing here? Homesick?" He pulled the wrap off his plastic fork and threw it at McCorkle. "Freddy, go eat at the kid's table or something. Pete and I need to have a talk."

Pete gave McCorkle a cheery wave as he grabbed his food and slumped away, pouting. Ollie sighed and opened his kebabs. "Fucking twat. Wasn't bothering you, was he?"

"On the contrary," Pete said. "He's a veritable ray of sunshine." She listened to the trill of phones and the click of keyboards, the inspectors and their detective sergeants and constables going about their day. "I'm making progress," Pete said, before Ollie could ask. He dabbed at a spot of brown sauce on his shirt.

"You close to telling me why this bastard got himself topped? Because his life is a blank fucking slate. Good schools, competent at his job, no dodgy tax shelters, bank balance not even enough for a night at the pub with a discount prozzie. Lived with his mum, for Christ's sake."

"That what you needed to talk about?" Pete said, helping herself to a cube of beef.

"Right," Ollie said. "It's a bit too perfect. Somebody that boring, you either expect them to do themselves in with Mummy's sleeping tablets, or have a dungeon full of Estonian teenagers hidden under the back garden. But I've turned up shit, and that bothers me, because shit means I've got shit on who'd want him killed."

"He was definitely arse deep in black magic," Pete said. "The symbols are necromancy, but for what I don't know yet. Beyond that, all I can say is idiots who dabble in that sort of thing often find themselves dead or otherwise inconvenienced. Since Carver was the first to go, I'm betting he had something they wanted, or had served his purpose. Not sure what the purpose was yet." Or his flesh-crafting friends had found Carver's dirty secret. Pete wondered about that. The death felt like overkill, even for a traitor. There was purpose behind it, rather than punishment. And the power dripping from Carver's corpse was something no socerer who wasn't completely addled would allow to go to waste.

Gerard Carver had died for something other than his penchant for deception. Pete wagered when she knew what, she'd know who.

Ollie tossed his empty takeaway container into his overflowing desk bin. "You're good, Pete. Always said, give you twenty-four hours and a cuppa and you'd solve the Lindbergh baby and the Ripper killings." He folded his hands over his stomach. "The better one of us, you were."

"Don't say that, Ollie," Pete told him. She stood and collected her things, being quick about it. "I wasn't a good cop. I quit."

"Do you ever miss it?" Ollie asked, as Pete made her move to leave. The CID room didn't feel welcoming and familiar any longer. Now she could feel the stares and hear the murmured conversations over the everyday sounds. She was a visitor, and an unwelcome one at that.

"All the time, Ollie." She turned her back and passed down the wide center avenue between the desks, which started at the door and ending at the big murder board where she'd put up her share of case notes. She turned her back to that too, and studiously ignored the stares of the working detectives as she left the station.

CHAPTER 8

Retrieving the Mini, Pete drove toward Kensington.
She passed the red brick edifice of the Victoria and
Albert Museum and the pavilion at the edge of Kensington Gardens, gold leaf gleaming in the late morning light against the nascent green of the foliage
beyond, which had just begun to show signs of life
after a winter that hadn't done anyone, plant or
human, any favors.

She picked up Bayswater Road and circled in
ever-widening loops through single-lane back streets
leading to tourist-choked main roads until she found
parking near Queensway. Threading her way through
the gawkers and well-heeled locals outside the tube
station, she climbed to Lawrence's flat and knocked.

Right now, Gerard Carver was the last thing on
her mind, but she had to think about him. Thinking
about her mother, or the Order, or what the Hecate
had said just made her want to curl up and never
leave Jack's flat again. Murder was the saner option.
Murder, she at least understood. Perhaps she could

even do what Morningstar demanded, though she doubted it. She was opposed to turning over the necromancer responsible just on principle, even though the git probably deserved it. Morningstar was a sanctimonious twat, as only old, white Englishmen with the Lord in their corner could be, and she hated him reflexively, far more at the moment than Carver's killer. But she owed Ollie answers, and needed something to leverage to keep him safe from the Order, so she hit the door again. "Lawrence! I know you're bloody at home. You never leave."

After a moment of locks scuffling, the door opened. "Your knickers on fire?" Lawrence demanded. "Why the fuss?" He blinked when he really saw her. "Pete!"

She managed to spread her hands and apply what she hoped was a charming expression. "Knew you were in. You're fucking agoraphobic these days."

Lawrence stepped forward and yanked her inside and into the fold of a bear hug. "You know where I live, you feel like stoppin' by. Why I need to go out?"

"Get some sun," Pete said, and poked his arm, which gave not an inch. "You're looking positively Caucasian, Lawrence."

"Fuck off," he said amiably, locking the door behind her and twitching a bindle of herbs and red thread back into place over the frame. "Glad you're here, you and your little razor blade for a mouth. Beginnin' to think you didn't like me."

"Been busy," Pete said, staying in the front hall while Lawrence went to his pocket-sized kitchen. In point of fact, she hadn't seen him since the day Jack had gone. She'd wanted it that way. Lawrence was Jack's best friend—which was no mean feat, considering the rapidity with which Jack alienated almost everyone he crossed paths with. Lawrence was as replete with memories as Jack's flat. Plus, he was a decent bloke and a decent friend, and in the way of decent people would want to commiserate, give and get sympathy. He would want to remember Jack, and Pete didn't have the strength to heap on any more memories.

Lawrence came back with two tumblers full of thick, viscous green liquid and held her at arm's length. "So. Miss Petunia. You blown back to my door—for what?" He grinned at her crookedly, teeth white enough for an advert. "I know you never be without trouble riding on your shoulder."

Pete decided blunt was best. Lawrence was at least too polite to throw her out. "I need you to tell me whatever you know about necromancy."

The smile and the warmth went out of Lawrence's face, a candle covered with a jar. Taking a seat on the leather sofa, he drained his tumbler and offered Pete the other. She caught a whiff of something dead and sea-borne and crinkled her nose. "Fuck, no thanks. What is that shit?"

"Seaweed," Lawrence said, as if it were a natural thing to pour down your gullet. "Your loss. Might improve your mind, so you don't go around askin' about black deeds that'll get you dead." He took a joint from the mellowed ivory box at his elbow and offered it to her once the end was a cozy orange. Pete inhaled and passed it back. Like the Newcastle for Mosswood, it was a gesture of hospitality, the handshake of Lawrence's mostly white witchcraft and Pete's talent, which was no color she could discern.

Lawrence dragged like a movie cowboy on a handmade cigarette and let the pleasant murk fill his sitting room when he exhaled. "Now," he said. "I've gotta ask: Why a smart girl like you messing with necromancers?"

"I didn't mess with anyone," Pete said. "They killed a bloke and left him in broad view in the center of the fucking British Museum, so they rather brought this on themselves." She dug out her mobile and called up the photo. Lawrence's hand-tended and magically coaxed pot at least blunted the edges enough that the damn thing didn't give her a migraine, but she still held the mobile gingerly as she passed it to Lawrence.

He whistled, and smoothed his free hand over his forehead. Lawrence was generally unflappable, but his pupils flexed as he examined the photo. He handed it back and took a quick, nervous drag. "This ain't somethin' you want, Petunia."

"I just need to know what they mean," Pete said, snatching the fag back. "What kind of spellcraft they're designed for. Who'd know enough about necromancy to carve them into a bloke's torso in the first place."

"You think *I* know?" Lawrence barked a laugh. "I'm flattered you think I run with that kind of crowd, but truth? I'm a white witch. I stay clear of the boneshaker's business and gods willin' they stay outta mine."

"Yeah, yeah, you're strictly ballroom," Pete said. "But you did spend twenty years being Jack's best mate, Lawrence. Don't take me for an idiot. You at least know who *can* tell me, if you're concerned for your virtue."

Lawrence tipped his head back against the sofa. "Maybe I don't wanna tell you because I know you'll get yourself a whole lot more than trouble if you keep pushin' this."

Pete set the remains of the fag in Lawrence's ashtray and mimicked his pose, pulling her legs under her. "Maybe I'll sit here, smoke all of your good shit, and generally make myself a nuisance until you change your mind."

"Fuck me!" Lawrence put his hands over his face and groaned. "You gonna get yourself killed just as dead as that dead bastard on your screen, you keep this up, Pete."

"Duly noted," Pete said. "Who, Lawrence? You know I can tell." She pointed to his jittering knee and giggled once. She wasn't immune to the effects of a good garden witch's product. "You're a terrible liar."

"Normal people be thinkin' that's a good thing," Lawrence muttered.

"Yeah." Pete stretched, lying out on the length of Lawrence's decadently squashy armchair. "But you're not fucking normal, Lawrence. Neither of us. So you gonna tell me, or am I going to park in your sitting room for the evening?"

He lifted his head and glared at her before he sat up and rooted around in the occasional table that held the box. "Might know a bloke has the cipher to your nasty little drawings. *Might*. I ain't promisin'."

"Wasn't so hard, was it?" Pete asked him. She lit a Parliament to chase the sweet, sticky resin from her lungs and blew a blue halo. "More necromancers, then? When you're a Jet, you're a Jet all the way, sort of thing?"

"No," Lawrence said, looking at the scrap of vellum in his hand before passing it over. "They worse."

"Now I'm intrigued," Pete said. "Worse than blokes

who skulk about in the night buggering corpses for a thrill. How disappointed their mums must be."

"Listen," Lawrence said. "When Jack and I were much younger an' less bright, he met this bloke who was . . . an antiquarian, I guess. Kind of a collector. Except not of anything you'd want business with. Things from the Black, books and worse. Makes Jack's little cabinet up in his flat look like a set of fuckin' dollies." Lawrence rose and went into the kitchen again, but this time poured a dark rum from an umarked bottle into a jam jar and sat back down, swallowing the drink in one go. "Jack traded him for a medieval grimoire, I think, nothin' special. It was the collector. He were a spook show. Wanted to write down the things Jack saw when he went off into the never-never, when the sight took its hold." Lawrence looked into his glass as if he wished it would fill of its own accord. "Wanted his . . . visions, he called 'em, even though you ask me, were just Jack talkin' his usual brand of bullshit." He put the glass aside and rubbed his palms, resting his head against his hands and not looking at Pete, or indeed anything in the actual, visible dimensions of his flat. "Found out later he was an Antiquarian, capital A. They beings of—they're made up of memories, you understand, eat 'em and use 'em to maintain. Collect memories and visions and grimoires and nasty bits in a place called the lost library. Not many souls, even on the black side, think it's a real place, see? Supposed to be a collection like you ain't never seen. Holding every manner of dark evil thing that any dark evil man has lost through history, includin' their minds." He extended the square of paper toward Pete, and she saw it wasn't a scrap but a piece of stock, worn round at the endges. "Antiquarian gave Jack this," Lawrence said. "*In your time of dying*, he told him. Wanted his memories and his spells. You call on him with that."

"And the Antiquarian," Pete said, taking the card and turning it. "He'll help me?"

Lawrence folded his shaking fingers into a tent. "If you call what those things do *help*. Yeah. He do that, and gladly for you, I'm sure."

"Good." Pete looked at the card. The lettering was faded to a mellow brown, nearly unreadable, and the words weren't in a language she understood. "How do we get in touch?"

Lawrence took the card back. "If you're really serious about this nonsense, I do a bit of divination with the cantrip on this here card and we meet when they say we meet." He tossed the card on the table and got up, opening the door. Pete took the hint, stopping on the threshold to touch his arm. "Thank you," she said. "I wouldn't ask if I didn't have to."

"One thing in return for all this, I ask," Lawrence told her, folding his opposite hand over hers. "I'll be with you when you talk to these bastards."

"Oh no," Pete said immediately. "Lawrence, I couldn't ask you . . ."

"Listen." Lawrence shrugged her off. "I made Jack a promise. I promised him that I always look out for you, and I take that serious. A promise to a mage on his deathbed about as serious as they come." Lawrence's mouth quirked. "'Course in Jack's case, I made it in the loo at Paddington Station . . ."

"Lawrence, that's sweet and all," Pete said. "But this is my problem. The last thing you want is necromancers calling at your door."

"I made Jack a promise," Lawrence insisted. "You either go with me, or I'll burn that divination up right now and you won't be goin' at all."

"You're a stubborn git, you know that?" Pete said. Still, it wouldn't hurt to have backup when she went chasing after a clutch of necromancers who'd already proven they were willing to slit one throat, and Lawrence was large, imposing, and motivated backup to boot. "You can come," she allowed. "But you don't flip your lid if you hear something you don't like, yeah?"

"Yeah," Lawrence said. "Doubt you gonna show me anything Jack hasn't already."

"Very well," Pete said. "You call me when you've got something." She descended Lawrence's untrustworthy stairs, boards groaning under her boots.

"You tell trouble," he called after her, "he comes around, just keep his ass right on movin'."

"Right," Pete muttered, shouldering through the front door and back into the rush and hum of the world. "I'll be sure to pass that along."

CHAPTER 9

The city mortuary at Wapping was plain and practical, with nothing haunted or ethereal in its makeup, and Pete appreciated that fact. Ghosts were easier to deal with if they appeared among steel refrigerators, faded by fluorescent bulbs.

She found Dr. Nasiri in one of the autopsy rooms, working over a skinhead with an impressive sector of his skull cracked apart like a clay flowerpot.

"Hello there," Nasiri shouted over the whine of her Stryker saw. "Put on a mask and booties, will you?"

Pete did as she asked. "I'd hoped to get another look at Mr. Carver," she shouted back. "And possibly some closeups of his wound patterns."

"Sure. I'll get you copies when I'm done here," Nasiri said. She put the saw aside and lifted out a section of the skinhead's ribcage, the way Pete would lift the top off a plastic tub. The Y-incision and the thin line of the saw blade bisected his blurry hand-done tattoos and a ragged white scar over his left nipple.

Pete had gotten past the reflexive throat clench sometime during her probationary year at the Met, but she didn't return Nasiri's smile as she set the rib-cage aside in a metal tray and worked to remove and measure the internal organs, slapping them onto the scale with the acumen of a butcher.

"Know what did this naughty boy in?" she said in a bright tone, as if she were a professor asking question.

"Zombies?" Pete offered, pointing to the hole in the man's head.

"Stupidity," said Nasiri. "Tried to rob an off-license and the owner slammed him in the skull with a cricket bat when the guy called him, quote, a curry-stink Paki bastard and then foolishly turned his back. Apparently his favorite vodka was on the high shelf."

Pete moved a step away from the steel table. "Tick a box for Darwin, then." Her head was beginning to throb as Lawrence's hospitality wore off, and the smells and sights of the mortuary weren't mixing in a way she'd call pleasant, or even tolerable.

"Stupidity is the leading cause of death in the United Kingdom," Nasiri said. Her hands kept moving, weighing the man's heart even as she stared at Pete across his chest cavity. "But not for your Gerard Carver, is it?"

"You're asking me?" Pete said. Her mask pressed against her mouth, a sterile papery kiss, and the air conditioning in the mortuary had made her mouth dry.

"Aren't you the one with the *spooky* psychic powers?" Nasiri said, her cheeks twitching. "Aren't they why Heath has you coming in here on the sly, telling me to slip you autopsy files, and getting evidence from you in turn he couldn't possibly use in a court trial? He believes in your uncanny visions from the other side?"

Pete pulled her mask off, the itchy paper all at once suffocating. Nasiri was taking the piss, and she knew better than to argue with a skeptic. She'd been one for too long to think there was any merit to it.

"I'm not psychic," she said, crumpling up the mask and tossing it at the bin. She missed.

"At least you can admit it to me," Nasiri said. "I mean, bored housewives saying bodies will be found near water, I at least understand. They're attention seekers. You I don't get at all."

"I'm not telling Ollie I can wave my hands and make a killer appear," Pete said. "I'm not a fake and Ollie's not an idiot. Not like this is the Yorkshire police and Peter Sutcliffe. It's one man, and I really can help Ollie close his case. Wondering whether you think I'm full of shit or not isn't going to keep me up nights."

"You used to be a DI," Nasiri said. She packed the organs back into the skinhead's chest, plopped the ribcage back into place, and covered the table with a paper sheet. "You used to be a *good* DI. And yet you chucked it to chase spirits. If you're not psychic, you must believe there's something else out there. Or else you're a complete nutter and hide it very well."

Pete removed her paper booties and threw them into the bin at the same time Nasiri pitched her gloves and paper scrubs. "Are we going to have the conversation about how you're a woman of science and you'll expose me? Because I tell you, I don't fancy it."

Nasiri stuck her forearms under the pedal sink and coated them in soap, scrubbing vigorously. "I'm not trying to be a bitch, Pete. I've never seen any-thing like what was done to Gerard Carver. I'm will-ing to buy you might have insight, if not the power to pull a unicorn out of your arse. You don't drag Ol-lie into the mumbo-jumbo and I won't grill you too much about what exactly it is you're into when you're not being a good fairy for the Met."

Pete wasn't used to having someone else look out for Ollie, and she wasn't sure she liked it very much. "I'm just trying to make sure Ollie knows what he's dealing with," she said.

"Then we won't have a problem," Nasiri said. "I'm not a nonbeliever, Pete, all cold dead flesh and electron microscopes, but I'm not big on blind faith."

"Finally something we agree on," Pete muttered. Nasiri went a short way down the corridor to a set of offices, leading Pete to the one with her nameplate.

"It's too bad we didn't work together. I think that would've gone well." She unlocked her office from her keyring. "I'll just get you those photos."

Nasiri disappeared into her office, and Pete leaned against the wall, wondering if anyone would noticed if she smoked. As if her tête-à-tête with Mc-Corkle hadn't driven the stake in far enough, Nasiri had made sure. This wasn't her world any more. The Met thought she'd gone over to the side of kooks and crime scene ghouls, and Pete couldn't even explain herself without sounding like exactly that. What would she even tell the rational and the plodding of London's finest? *Magic is real and your nightmares have teeth*? That was a fast trip to a psychiatric ward if she ever heard one.

Pete stuck a Parliament in her mouth and tongued the filter, but didn't light it. Overhead, the fluores-cent tubes buzzed, an insect heartbeat, flickering off and on, creating a shadow pulse. What the Hell was taking Nasiri so long?

Far away a door banged open and shut, and gurney wheels clattered on tiles. Pete felt the small part of her mind that sensed the tides, the flow and flux of the Black, unfold and send trembling fingers forth.

The hall lights snapped on, off, on, and Pete watched through the open door of the autopsy bay as they gave the skinhead's lumpy form under his sheet dimension and life.

Snap again, and when Pete's eyes adjusted to the light a shadow stood in the door of the autopsy room, no shape really, just a thin slice of darkness the size of a man, whose presence sent needles of ice through Pete's mind. The thing peered at her from a tear in the Black, a bleeding intersection of the daylight world and what lay beneath.

She didn't stay frozen, like she had when the owl fixed its gaze on her. Pete snatched her pepper spray from her bag and aimed a concussive stream of it at the figure. "Come on then!" she shouted.

The hall lights snapped. The pepper spray spattered across the tile floor. The doorway was empty.

Nothing waited for her, just on the other side of the Black. The lights stabilized, and the mortuary hallway remained bland and sterile as ever. Pete felt her heart drumming at a thousand RPMs, and her blood was rushing so loudly in her ears it came in like a radio station. She didn't hear Nasiri until the doctor tapped her arm.

"Everything all right?" Nasiri extended a plain brown envelope, inter-office mail for the Wapping police station. "You look a bit startled."

Pete shoved the pepper spray into her back pocket and took the envelope in one smooth montion. The last thing she needed was Nasiri thinking she saw things. Her opinion, and that of the entire CID, was already low enough. "Just thought I heard someone back there in the autopsy."

"The bodies don't generally get up and walk about on their own," Nasiri said. "Though if they do, you'll be my first call."

"Cheers." Pete walked slowly leaving the mortuary, keeping her face calm and trying not to let the throb of her heart vibrate her. She hadn't imagined the thing in the doorway—her skin was still prickling with the fever of close proximity to the dead, and not just the dissected skinhead on the table. Whatever had tried to push through had been of the Underworld, and it had wanted her badly enough to manifest in broad daylight, inside a building full of steel and computers, anathema to ghosts. Wanted *her*, not just whatever member of the living it happened on first. Pete wagered that whoever they were, Gerard Carver's killers knew she was in the mix. It took her until the tube station to shake off the cold.

CHAPTER 10

Lawrence didn't call the next day, or the next, and Pete had begun to think he never would. She was set on going into the city for a few hours and trying to finish off some more of Jack's unfinished business— bills, council taxes. The transfer of the dubious deed to his flat would have to wait until he was declared legally dead rather than simply missing. And for that, Pete would have to file a report. Have to explain why she'd waited six months. Have to have a reason and for that reason, make up a lie her brain simply didn't have the capacity for at the moment. English property law was nearly as complex as the symbols that marked Gerard Carver's corpse, and Pete could wait until she, too, had shuffled loose the mortal coil to deal with Jack's estate.

Her mobile trilled at last while she was at the DIY shop finally buying new bulbs for the sodding chandelier. Pete shoved the mobile between her ear and shoulder as she handed over a tenner to the store clerk. "It's about bloody time, Lawrence."

"Who the *fuck* is Lawrence? And what the *fuck* do you mean, "you've seen Mum?"" Pete's sister MG screeched.

"And hello to you too, Miss Morning Glory," Pete said. "Been into the ceremonial gin, have we? You sound a bit pissed."

"Nobody has seen Mum for *years*," MG shouted. "And why you, out of everyone we know? Why London? She *hates* London."

"I don't know what to tell you," Pete sighed. She stopped on a corner of the pavement, letting the Whitechapel Road crowd flow around her, coming and going from the pubs and money-changers and newsagents next to the Whitechapel tube. "Don't have to tell me you two were the fast friends, MG. You think I didn't notice Mum didn't bother with me if she could help it, even before she took flight on her broomstick?"

"She called me a few months ago," MG said. "Babbling shit about reconciliation and Jesus bloody Christ and probably John fucking Lennon for all the sense she made, but actually *dropping in* on you? What the Hell is going on, Petunia? I'm so upset by all this I haven't even been able to do my normal readings, never mind communicate with my spirit guides."

"What happened to Cthulhu, or whatever tentacled horror that commune of yours worshipped?" Pete asked. "Thought they frowned on strapping on a scarf and reading tarot for the locals."

"Oh, fuck off," MG sighed. "The commune was rubbish. I've been living in Sussex for five years. My boyfriend Gil owns an esoteric shop, and I do readings. I'll have you know it's very lucrative."

"I'll be sure to send Gil a congratulatory bou-
quet," Pete said. "Did Mum say anything specific to
you? About the reconciliation?"

"Who could make sense of that closeminded
Jesus 'n' friends shit?" MG said. "And you—are *you*
still a bloody fascist copper, goose-stepping in good
order like Da?"

Pete lifted her eyes for a moment, asking whoever
might offer it for patience, and then tried to sound
happy. "Lovely talking, MG, but I'm afraid I've got
more pressing matters, like dropping a frying pan
on my foot. If I see Mum again, is there a message
I should pass on?"

"Why *you*?" MG said again. "You said it yourself. She didn't even *like* you."

Pete made her free hand into a fist. "Goodbye,
MG. Blessed fucking be."

She leaned against the outside of the DIY shop
and took some theoretically relaxing breaths. So her
mother was serious about the Order, serious enough
to call up her sister and try to engulf her in the fold.
Pete didn't know why she was surprised—MG had
been Juniper's favorite from the get-go. Which wasn't
hard, since she was older, and interested in all the
things Juniper thought girls should be interested in,
namely boys and looking pretty to catch one. Pete, in
that respect, had been a grave disappointment.

Her mobile trilled again and she nearly pitched it
into the path of an oncoming bus, except that Lawrence's name came up on the screen. "Please tell me
this is good news, because otherwise I'm going to
start kicking small, fluffy things," Pete said.

"I got a place," Lawrence said. "You close?"

"I can be," Pete said. "I'm near the tube."

"Okay," Lawrence said. "Meet me at Kensington High Street, but make it quick. These types, they don't linger for long. They do the damage and move on."

"I'll be there," Pete insisted, shoving her way down the steps of the tube station. Once, she thought she'd been followed by another man in a black coat, but he got off in the city and Pete rode the rest of the way to Kensington alone.

She met Lawrence on the high street, a place Pete had always considered London as the outside world thought of it. Narrow streets, uneven pavement, quaint shops full of posh artifacts, begging for Hugh Grant or Colin Firth to pop out from amongst the antique books and obscure oil paintings and sweep you off your feet, into a charming adventure full of eccentric side characters with amusing accents. As far from the real city as one could get and still be in it. Lawrence waited in front of one of the few closed-down shops in view, jiggling his left foot and habitually checking his watch. Pete figured from the stares of the well-heeled passersby that she looked out of place as he felt. Neither of them belonged to storybook London, and unless they were rock stars looking to snap up a row house, nobody in Kensington wore army boots, black canvas pants, and a Penetration shirt with the neck cut out. Pete returned the stares of a pair of helmet-haired biddies with a snarl before she reached Lawrence.

"This is not where I'd expect some kind of shadowy memory-eater to hang his hat. Its hat. Whatever."

Lawrence shrugged, a bit jerkily. He was nervous as a scalded cat, and Pete wished he'd listened to her and just stayed home. "This is where they say to go, this is where we go. Or we could just forget the whole thing. Like I been sayin' we should."

"We've come this far," Pete said. "What's a little divination between friends?"

Lawrence mumbled something that could have been either a prayer or an impressive string of curses, and jerked his thumb over his shoulder. "In there, then."

The closed shop's window held a globe painted with drawings of constellations, a dead and mummified fern, and an impressive amount of dust. The fading gold script across the glass read simply CURIOSITIES.

"Remember what we discussed, and keep your trap shut," Pete said. "You're jumpy enough without chatting up a storm."

"Fine by me. We go in there, I blind, deaf, and mute. Don't want none of what he's selling." Lawrence hunched inside his army coat, managing to look small even though he had a good half a foot on Pete.

A bell chimed, musical and out of place when they entered. The interior of the shop was as musty and cluttered as the window was bare. It wasn't a comfortable sort of clutter, to support the cultivated air of the mysterious that so many antique shops in Kensington worked to maintain, but the books cramming the cases and cascading across the dust-covered counter were the genuine article. "Fuck me," Pete murmured. "Are they all grimoires, then?"

"Most," Lawrence said. "Bloke who ran this place dropped off a few years ago. Inland revenue. But he were a twat before, and I ain't surprised he dealt with the Antiquarians."

Pete picked up the plain cloth volume on a display stand and opened the front cover. Plain black print declared, with frightening practicality, *Malleus Maelificarum*. Even though the book itself was utter nonsense and Cotton Mather was a sexually repressed twat of the first order, the thin paper and running ink, and the many notations in the margins on effectiveness and practical results, made Pete drop the thing again and swipe her hands on her trouser legs. She banged on the counter bell instead. "Oi! Anyone home?"

Lawrence stayed as close to the door as he could without being outside on the pavement, hands shoved in his pocket, boot tapping. Pete tossed a paperback pulp at him, cover depicting a heaving-bosomed blonde tied to a cross, menaced by faceless figures in crimson robes. *The Demon's Bride*. "Will you cut that out? You look like we're in here trying to cop."

"Aren't we?" Lawrence muttered. "In one fashion or another?"

"Oh, for the sake of all the saints." Pete chimed the desk bell again. "*Hello.*"

The door to the back room of the shop rattled, and a figure wrapped in tweed that had to be as old as some of the books in the shop appeared. He blinked at Pete through round spectacles, greasy silver hair falling in his face. "Ah. Here you are."

"Here we are," Pete agreed. "Waiting."

The man extended a hand, silver rings to the knuckle on each finger, but Pete didn't bite. The Black wasn't the place for friendly handshakes. You never knew what you might be touching in addition to skin. "Tyrell," he said, dropping the hand back. His eyes flicked over Lawrence. "You're the man?"

"Hell no, I ain't your man," Lawrence snorted.

"She's the one who wanted this. Far as I'm concerned, you can crawl right back into that hole you oozed out of."

Tyrell blinked, and then smiled at Pete, slow and crooked as if a rock had rolled back from the entrance to a cave. "How lovely," he said. "A damsel in need of rescue."

"Let's keep the bullshit down to a dull roar, shall we?" Pete suggested. Tyrell's tongue flicked out and back in, and he grimaced as if the air tasted bad.

"Whatever you say, my dear," he said at last. Lawrence was staring a hole in her over Tyrell's head, but Pete kept herself reserved and stony. She was willing to be polite, but she wasn't willing to play the courting games so many creatures of the Black demanded. She'd always been crap at being obsequious, and she wasn't going to lick Tyrell's boots just so he could maybe, possibly but probably not give her a scrap or two of new insight into Gerard Carver's death markings.

"That is what I say," she agreed. Drawing out the folder Nasiri had given her, she fanned the photographs on the counter, dislodging dust that was likely older than she was. "You know anything about this?"

Tyrell coughed and waved at the air in front of his face. "Not *here*," he said. "Are you stupid as well as unpleasant?"

"Oh, I assure you," Pete said, shoving the photos a bit closer, "we haven't even scratched the surface of just how unpleasant I can be."

"Pete," Lawrence said, and gave her a hard squeeze on the arm. "We know how it works," he assured Tyrell. "But we wanna be sure you ain't wastin' our time."

"I dare say there isn't much you could do to me if I was," Tyrell said, with the peculiar glee of small children who enjoy stamping on fluffy things. "You, after all, are the ones who need something and I am the one who has it."

"I don't need it that badly," Pete assured him. "I'm not a prissy white witch you can run in circles. If you can't help me, then piss off and let me find someone who can."

"Oh, my dear," Tyrell said. "You think you frighten me, with your rough edges and your empty threats? I am an Antiquarian. To collect for the lost library, I've bargained with things far worse than a kitchen witch and the whore of a dead mage."

Pete felt all the joints in her hands and arms tense, and she forced them to relax one at a time. She wasn't going to give Tyrell the reaction he was fishing for. Wasn't going to shout and cry simply because he'd called her a name. That was the game, and she wasn't playing any more. Jack might have risen to every invitation to smack someone in the gob, but she was better than that. And if not entirely, at least better than some cackling creature who looked like a goblin had mated with a Jim Henson puppet.

Tyrell wilted a bit under her glare. "Far be it from me to judge," he said, clapping his hands together. "The terms are blood, spellcraft, or trade. Judging by your general air of poverty and the fact that you aren't a sorcerer, I suppose it'll be trade." He traced the marks across Carver's torso, finger leaving an oily streak on the photograph. "I'll search the archives and you'll give me a little something to store in them in return, yes?"

"Pete," Lawrence said at once. "Don't do it. Don't give anything you got to an Antiquarian."

"Witch, kindly shut the fuck up before I disengage your jaw from your skull," Tyrell said, eyes gleaming. "The young lady and I are engaged in bartering."

"All right, all right," Pete said. "No need to open your trousers, boys." She tapped the photo with her fingertip. "You've got yourself a deal, Tyrell. You better be worth it."

"I think you'll find I'm worth my weight in gold," he said, drawing the photo away from her and folding it into quarters. "Now, shall we take a look through the archive and see if we can't find a match to your dead bloke?"

"Get on with it," Pete agreed. Tyrell came from behind the counter and wound through the stacks toward a narrow back hallway. Lawrence began to follow him, but he shook his head.

"You're too pure and bright to deal with the likes of me. The lady and I are in a bargain, not you."

Lawrence flicked him off. "Where she goes, I'm goin'."

Tyrell bared his teeth. "Then you're not going far, are you, boyo?"

"It's all right," Pete said, to head off Tyrell getting a boot through his teeth. Lawrence growled in the back of his throat.

"You don't know how far from all right this is."

"Lawrence." Pete felt a headache spring to life behind her eyes and tried to massage it away. "I know this isn't what you'd do, but you do trust me, yeah?"

His jaw ticked, but he nodded. Pete leaned in, so Tyrell wouldn't be privy. "Then trust I know what I'm doing. This isn't my first shady old man in a dingy shop."

"Jack ever heard about this, he'd wring my fuckin'

neck." Lawrence sighed. "Anything happens, I'm in there."

"At the very least, avenge my death," Pete told him. She joined Tyrell and let him lead her into the back room. It wasn't much, just a slant-roofed space that had once been a coal shed, filled to the rafters with paper mountains even more vertiginous than Jack's. Pete's boot clanked on something, and she saw a metal door, more of a hatch really, set into the floor.

"Tea?" Tyrell cleared papers away from a kettle encrusted with green minerals sitting on a burner that gave off a blue spark when he flicked the switch.

"No," Pete said. Tyrell grunted as he rooted in the drawers of a narrow apothecary.

"Suit yourself. Tea makes it go down easier."

"What?" Pete said, drawing back as far as she could without starting an avalanche of ancient books and papers onto her head. Smothered in circulars from before Churchill was in office was not the way she'd imagined kicking off.

Tyrell held up a small brown bottle. "You're not a sensitive, am I right? You want a look at the archives, you take this."

"Like Hell I'm drinking something out of a bottle some skeevy old man brandishes at me," Pete said.

Tyrell coughed, or perhaps he was trying to laugh and not making much of a go. "My dear, you're so generous." He showed his teeth again. "Calling me a man."

He busied himself finding a pair of cups and an ancient tin half-eaten by rust, measuring the tea into the strainer by hand. Pete felt her gaze slipping to the front of the shop. She'd lost sight of Lawrence, even though she could hear him rustling around and the sounds of the street outside. Not far at all, but she had the distinct feeling that if she made a break for the door, Tyrell would spring like a great insect and wrap his skinny limbs around her.

He wore his human skin poorly, as far as things disguising themselves as men went. It sagged around his face, and his hair was matted and greasy, as if he'd climbed inside a homeless man and hadn't bothered to clean up. His eyes burned too bright, and whatever his real shape looked like hadn't quite mastered blinking. Tyrell displaced just a little too much air for his size, the thing living under his skin larger than his concentration camp limbs and cavernous face.

"What should I call you instead?" Pete said.

"Whatever's your pleasure." Tyrell brushed his fingers against hers when he handed her the teacup and added a drop from his bottle.

"Don't do that," Pete warned. She sniffed the tea. It was gave off musty steam and smelled rather like the inside of a pensioner's purse, but not like poison.

"I'll do what I like," Tyrell said, downing his own cup, sans potion. "You wouldn't be here if you didn't need me, desperately, and I don't think you're really in a position to boss me about." He clinked his empty porcelain against Pete's. "So drink up, Alice, and quit pretending you're not quivering with anticipation."

"Fuck off," Pete said, and tossed the tea back in one long swallow. Tyrell banged his cup down.

"That's the spirit. Give me a hand with this." He wrenched at the wheel of the hatch in the floor and hauled the rusted, creaking thing free. Pete peered over the edge and saw a pitted metal ladder leading down into night.

"After you," Tyrell said. Pete didn't argue. He had

her number—she didn't have another bright idea if the Antiquarian wouldn't help her. As she descended her center of gravity shifted, as if she'd passed through a sheet of running water. By the time her feet hit brick, she was seeing everything with a bleeding edge and hearing sounds down a long, convex tunnel.

"Dammit," she said. Her own voice came across like a wax record, warped and tinny. "What did you give me, Tyrell?"

"Opened your eyes," he said. When Pete looked at him from the corner of her vision, something much thinner and taller was in his place, and when she looked full on, he was the same grotty old man she'd cross the street to avoid.

"I asked for help, not . . . not this," Pete said. She reached out, grabbed at chipped concrete. "Where the Hell are we?"

"Down the rabbit hole," Tyrell said, and passed a hand across her neck with a chuckle. Pete felt claws, long multi-jointed fingers that could search through pages, or bones, with equal alacrity. An elongated jaw, yellow teeth made for slurping and grinding living flesh. Robes made from dirty grave winding cloth that concealed a body with more legs than two, with eyes that stared from between Tyrell's rib bones, and soft insides that pulsed wetly behind an exoskeleton. Vast, unblinking hunger, but not for Pete. Tyrell wanted something much more, was trying to touch not her skin but the talent underneath, searching and seeking like a needle hunting a vein.

Pete became aware that she'd fallen over when she tasted blood from a cut cheek and felt the cool of brick against her face.

"See anything you like?" Tyrell crouched, and looked at her with his head twisted halfway round.

"What are you?" Pete mumbled, feeling her face. Wet on her fingers, but her nerve ends were blunted. Her face was completely numb. She remembered the few times she'd tried acid in school, how her dirty laundry in the hamper had turned into a crowd of black, flapping things and the paint had begun to bleed and reform on the walls of her room into scenes from MG's tarot cards. That had been dreadful, and this was ten times worse.

"I told you," Tyrell said. "I'm an Antiquarian." He scuttled down the curved corridor ahead. Bare bulbs in cages hissed and spat above his head, and he stopped at a second metal door. "Coming?" he said, casting a look over his shoulder.

All right, Petunia, Pete said. *Get your arse up. You've had worse.*

She couldn't remember when, but she got herself on her feet, and tried to ignore the ship's-deck feeling of a bad trip rocking under her feet. "Where are we?" she said.

Tyrell pointed to a faded seal on the metal door. Pete saw it was from the War Office, decades out of date. It also kept moving, skating from one side of the door to the other. "Bomb shelter," he said. "Thin here. Lots of fear, lots of people all shut up together, feeding off one another." He spun the hatch. "A bit of the lost Black, for the lost library."

"I can cross into the Black," Pete insisted, knowing she sounded as if she'd drunk an entire pub's worth of lager.

Tyrell extended his hand to pull her through the door. "Not like this."

Pete ignored the gesture. Even wasted out of her skull, she knew better than to willingly touch Tyrell. She stepped through the hatch, and the bottom fell out of her stomach. The Black closed over her head, intractable as freezing water. Her head felt as if she'd left her skull floating a meter away, her brain flopping uselessly. The connection, to the currents and tides, was gone here. The Black was a bubble, trapped under glass, and Pete quivered under the psychic feedback.

"I do enjoy this place," Tyrell said. "The world rushes to and fro, and the Black creeps into every crevice like tar, but here . . ." He inhaled, nostrils flaring white. "Here, it bends to the Antiquarians."

Pete pressed a hand over her mouth, hoping the pressure would keep her together. Sweat chilled all over her bare skin.

"If you're going to vomit," Tyrell told her, "kindly do it in the corner and not near me."

"This isn't right . . ." Pete managed. All around her, the Black was screaming, rent open and bleeding magic into the void. She'd gotten sick the first time Jack had brought her over, but nothing like this. Something larger and more powerful than any single mage had torn a rip in the fabric of the Black here, and it was clinging to her mind, sinking in a million tiny needles that made all of her senses scream. For the Antiquarians to do such a thing, they were far worse than Lawrence had imagined. And she was here with them alone. Brilliant.

"Breathe," Tyrell said, taking the folded photo from his vest with a clipped motion. "If I can stand it, so can you."

Pete forced herself to focus on anything except her irregular heartbeat and the roar of the Black all around. The feeling wasn't any worse than when they'd run suicide drills during her police training, back and forth in the rain and muck, until a cadet either passed out or chucked up their guts. "Hurry," she mumbled at Tyrell, loathing the fact he'd made her beg. "Please."

Tyrell pressed the photo to his lips, mumbled something Pete couldn't understand, and then dropped it to the floor.

Blue flame crept in everywhere, over the walls, across the floor, through Tyrell's hair, caressing his face and hands. Pete watched it raise the hairs on her arm, but she didn't scream. It wasn't really fire; it was power, bleeding out of the Black and into the physical realm. Jack could do the same trick.

Tyrell panted slightly, and while the witchfire crept over every surface, Pete felt more than saw something vast and fathomless open before her. This sliver of the Black bumped against another, connected, slippery as soap bubbles. "The archives say they know nothing," Tyrell said presently. "I'm sorry, my dear."

"Piss off," Pete said. She could feel a bit of herself again, enough to know that she'd be miserable with bruises by the next day. If she even made it out here without her brain turning into cauliflower. "Try again."

"I'm sorry." Tyrell crumpled the photo between his fists. "The archives have spoken. If they don't know, it's not there to know."

Pete pulled herself to her knees, and then, using the wall, stood up. She felt her knees wobbling, but she locked them and favored Tyrell with a glare. "People don't just do this for a laugh. There's a reason he's dead."

"Humans want to ascribe reason to everything," Tyrell said. "It's a failing of the breed." He made for the door. "Our bargain is void, of course. I'm sorry that I, as an Antiquarian, could not be of service." His awful caved-in mummy's face composed itself into an expression that actually seemed contrite, but Pete pointed a finger at him.

"I'm desperate. You're right. But I'm also not an idiot." Her arm was too heavy to do anything but hang, so she let it. "You know something."

Tyrell tugged at the door. "That's odd."

"Tell me," Pete said. "Whatever it is. I can take it."

"No, Miss Caldecott," Tyrell snapped. "You can't. Because you're human, and like a human you will try to rush in and change things, push and shove them into your image of what the world should be." He gave the door a kick. "Bastard thing. Enchantments are as dodgy as a knockoff watch."

Pete inserted herself between Tyrell and the door, even though a fresh wave of dizziness crested and crashed over her. "Tell me," she snarled. "I have even less patience than the average human, Tyrell."

Tyrell worried his hands, nails clacking. "It's not a death spell, all right? It's not a spell at all. The carvings are Babylonian and a sort of necromancy, yes, but not in the narrow way you think. Not simply calling or repelling the dead. This thing that was done to this flesh—it has no order and no sense. It's as if someone who didn't speak the language wrote a book in Chinese, yeah? Nothing can come of it."

"Clearly somebody thought different," Pete said. The carvings had power. What she'd felt in the museum wasn't simply psychic soot, deposited by the normal passage of the Black.

"Perhaps. I don't know. I don't care. Antiquarians do not concern themselves in the affairs of the Black," Tyrell said. "Far more pressing is the fact that I cannot open the door."

Pete stared dumbly at him for a moment. "What?" It was certainly her day for asking obvious questions.

"The Black has been torn," Tyrell said. "Shredded and remade, just now. It has pressurized us here, as if we were submerged deep under the ocean." He shrugged. "Something massive is passing through, and we are feeling the ripples."

Pete slid down the wall, until the floor of the small metal room met her bottom. "Dear lord. I'm going to die in here. With you."

"It will pass," Tyrell said. "These events are more regular than creatures like you realize. The Black is fragile and full of things that can cause such an event. Most are simply too old or too terrible for your kind to believe they still exist, or ever did. The wave will recede eventually."

"How soon is eventually?" Pete said into her knees. *Don't panic,* she ordered herself. *Don't breathe, don't vomit, don't lose your head.* Easy to tell herself, hard to put into practice. The effects of Tyrell's toxic tea were wearing off, and she was nauseated even without being trapped in a sliver of the Black she couldn't access or escape on her own.

"Minutes," Tyrell shrugged. "Decades."

"I hate you," Pete said.

Tyrell tested the door again. "Ah," he said as it swung free. "Miss Caldecott." He presented her a card with sleight of hand, a much cleaner and newer version of the one the long-ago Antiquarian had given Jack.

CURIOSITIES, the card read in bold script, and below it, MEMORY, ANTIQUITIES, & DREAMS, ALL TRADES CONSIDERED. The flip side contained the same gibberish chant.

"We'll be in touch," Tyrell said. "Good hunting, miss."

The door slammed, and Pete was left alone to find her way back to the surface world.

CHAPTER 11

Pete bent double on the sidewalk outside the shop, breathing deep, trying to quell the roiling sickness in her guts.

"I ain't a fan of sayin' I told you," Lawrence said. "But I did. That Antiquarian, he's a no-good snake." He rubbed a hand between Pete's shoulder blades. "You gonna sick up?"

"Not if I can help it," Pete mumbled, trying not to move her jaw. The passing posh crowd was casting increasingly alarmed looks, and it would only be a matter of time before someone called the police on the large black man and the skinny white woman acting as if she'd just come off a fortnight heroin binge.

"You get anything useful, at least?" Lawrence said. "Make this worthwhile?"

"Walk," Pete said, even though the pavement looked as crumpled as velvet to her eyes. She grabbed Lawrence's elbow, and they made their slow way down the high street. "Yes," she said, when they'd left the stares behind. "Babylonian. Necromantic. Not a death spell. Beyond that, it was all a babbling brook of bullshit."

"Antiquarians love bein' smarter than you," Lawrence agreed. "Smarmy cunts."

Pete thought the rumbling that enveloped them, along with darkness, was her own blood in her ears for a moment, until Lawrence jerked her under the awning of a sweet shop. A moment later, a flashbulb went off across the entire sky and the heavens over London opened, pissing down cold spring rain that filled the gutters and caused a taxi to nearly jump the curb, wipers flailing madly against the windscreen.

"Just what we bloody need, eh?" Lawrence said. The thunder drowned out anything else, and nerves of lightning lit the skin of the iron-gray clouds that had collected in the space of a few footsteps.

"Never seen a storm like this," Pete said.

"My old nana used to say a storm like this could wake the dead," Lawrence said.

"I'm sure if your grandmother was aware of how annoying folksy wisdom is, she'd've kept that to herself," Pete said.

"Oi," Lawrence told her. "Just because you in the grumps doesn't mean we all gotta be."

The rain abated after a few more moments, not much but enough to run for the tube. The scarcity of people on the high street was the only reason Pete noticed the man all in black standing near a close, watching her from under the dripping brim of his wide hat. Pete tugged on Lawrence. "Hold it."

Dreisden tipped his hat to Pete with a chipper grin, and turned and slipped away before she could take more than one step toward him. A taxi blared, and Lawrence jerked her back. "What's the matter?

Now you looked good and riled, in addition to wet and hungover."

Pete glared at the spot where Dreisden had been, then dug in her bag for the card Juniper had handed her outside the Lament. "What's the matter is I don't like being fucking threatened."

Lawrence didn't answer, but he did follow her, which Pete didn't argue with this time. She was through being menaced by Ethan Morningstar, and he'd pushed enough. If Lawrence could help her push back, so much the better.

*   *   *

The Order of the Malleus didn't reside in any sort of posh modern flat near Canary Wharf, or a sinister, brooding Victorian narrow house watched over by iron gates crawling with ivy and Gothic sensibility. The address was on one of the side streets running up to the south side of Regent's Park in Marylebone, a nondescript row house with a blue door and two small granite Chinese dogs guarding the steps.

Pete ignored the devil's-head knocker, slamming on the wood with the flat of her hand. "Open this fucking door!" She used her best copper voice, and it rattled back from the row of flats opposite. Curtains twitched aside up and down the street.

Five seconds, then ten, then thirty went by without a response. "Oi!" Pete resorted to kicking, the steel of her boot leaving an ugly black wound in the door. "Morningstar! You know why I'm here, you creepy bastard!"

"Maybe we should . . . do something that isn't this," Lawrence suggested, from where he stood on the pavement. Pete cast around, then picked up one of the dog statues and walked back to the shiny black BMW parked in front of the row house. She swung hard and deliberate, letting the weight of the stone carry itself.

Windscreen glass exploded into the street, and the car's alarm began to whoop. "Ethan," Pete shouted. "Get your arse out here!"

The car alarm cut off, and the door of the house opened up. "Petunia Caldecott!" Her mother appeared on the stoop, arms crossed. "What on earth do you think you're doing?"

Pete tossed the statue aside. "Nothing that concerns you, Mother." She pointed at the house. "I know he's in there. What's wrong, he can't come himself? Has to send his overdressed rent boys to be the hard men?"

Juniper threw up her hands. "Oh, Petunia. You always had a flair for being overdramatic."

"You'd know about dramatic entrances and exits," Pete said. "Listen, Mum, you can prance about with these fuckwits all day long, but I want to talk to Ethan and I'm going to carry on smashing things that belong to him until he comes out." She folded her arms. "Is that dramatic enough for your taste, Mother?"

"You'd think somebody nearly thirty would have learned not to be such a disagreeable little brat," Juniper snapped, her serene Mother Superior composure finally wearing thin. Pete was gratified that she still had the temper that had caused her to bawl out MG for staying away all night and chuck the occasional lager bottle in Connor's direction when he snapped at them once too often because of his job.

"It's all right, Junie," said a voice from the dark of the doorway. Morningstar appeared, a deal less imposing without the vampire coat and hat, but still with a glare and craggy hands that could crush Pete's skull into shards. "We weren't expecting you so soon, Miss Caldecott," he said. His eye drifted to the smashed car and he sighed. "You know, you might have simply rung."

Pete gave him a tight smile. "I don't work for you, Ethan. We had this talk."

Morningstar guided Juniper back over the threshold. "Go inside, dear." He came into the street, picked up the statue, and set it back on its pedestal. "As I recall that conversation, we agreed you *did* want to do something for me, Miss Caldecott. If not for your sake than for your dear friends." He tipped a salute to Lawrence. "Here's one of them now."

Lawrence made a move to Pete's shoulder, but she waved him off. "He's a bigot with fancy dress," she told Lawrence. "This, I can handle."

"Not him I'm worried about," Lawrence muttered. "Your mum's a lot scarier."

"Fuck off," Pete said, and mounted the steps. Morningstar gave her one of his knife-edged smiles.

"So kind of you to stop by."

"Believe me," Pete said. "I'm not having kind thoughts, Mr. Morningstar."

"Ethan," he said, shutting the door behind her. "Call me Ethan."

Morningstar's house was furnished in the same bland, vaguely classical style as the outside. Persian rugs muffling the floors, furniture with feet, and dour portraits of a man who looked like the genuine witch-burning article hanging in the front hall. Morningstar flicked a finger at one. "Sir Percival Morningstar, a several times great-grandfather of mine. Disposed of seven sorcerers in his day."

"Must have been the toast of his inbred village," Pete said acidly.

"I don't hate you, you know," Morningstar said gruffly. "Nor people like you."

"Love the sinner?" Pete guessed.

"And burn the sin," Morningstar agreed. He led Pete to the rear of the house, unlocking a door with a skeleton key he took from a ring in his pocket. "The Order of the Malleus is not what you think, Miss Caldecott. Despite your unfortunate first impression, we're here to cure, not to torture. We kill as a last resort, to protect the Order."

"Yes, well," Pete said. "Some of us manage it without killing at all. 'M not going to pat you on the head."

"How many people have you killed as a law officer?" Morningstar asked. "And how many do you think Mr. Winter caused the demise of before his misdeeds finally caught up with him?"

"We've been over this ground," Pete said. "You found it full of pitfalls, remember?"

Morningstar gestured her through the open door but Pete balked. She wasn't sure Morningstar wouldn't simply shoot her in the back if she annoyed him excessively. "After you," she said.

"Paranoia is an unfortunate side effect of magic on human brain tissue, you know." Morningstar took a seat behind the sort of desk the headmaster of a snooty prep school would use. It suited him. Pete stood rather than use one of the straight-backed chairs facing Morningstar, as if she were a bloody truant. The office was surprisingly spare and far less grim than the rest of the Order's house. One row of books paraded across the shelf behind Morningstar's head, and an arty black and white of Hadrian's Wall was the only decoration. ·Definitely a man's office, a man spare and hard through all his deeds. Pete all at once didn't feel so right about smashing his car.

"I'm careful," she said. "And I learned that a long time before I admitted the Black was real."

"Even so." Morningstar put his feet on his desk. "The human mind was not meant to contain the energies of the Black. I strongly urge you to pull back before you do yourself permanent damage, Petunia." Morningstar took a cigarette from a silver case at his elbow and lit it, but didn't offer one to Pete.

"You're one to talk about permanent damage," Pete said, yanking Nasiri's remaining photo from her bag and tossing it on Morningstar's desk. "No need to send your boy, Ethan. I was coming for a chat anyway."

"Oh?" Morningstar exhaled thin twin streams through his nose. "Regarding?"

"Let's cut the shit, shall we?" Pete said. "Carver got killed working some nasty magic, yeah, but these cuts were made over years. And it wasn't death magic being worked on him, it was something worse. He was arse deep in necromancy and you knew. What happened, Ethan? Did your dog break his chain?"

Ash grew on the end of Morningstar's fag, forgotten. "You've learned a lot in a short time, Petunia. I'm impressed. But Gerard's proclivities don't concern you. He was one of us, sinner or not."

"Did you know what he was doing?" Pete said. "Tell me the truth or I swear to your musty old god I'm going to break a lot more than your car."

"I very much doubt that," Morningstar said. Pete gritted her teeth. Morningstar didn't seem the slightest bit uncomfortable that she was in his house. If anything, he appeared bored, smoking and loosening his tie as if she were a problem he wouldn't have much trouble solving.

"I can't help you if you won't help me," she tried.

Morningstar stubbed out his fag-end in a saucer. "I had an idea, yes. Gerard was a deep cover member of the Order. He had a talent. He had to use it occasionally. And necromancy . . . it's seductive. So yes. I knew about his usage. What I don't know is why he was killed, and that's a concern. For you as well as for the Order."

"I don't mess with necromancers," Pete said. "So really, I think I'm safe and sound."

"All I want to do is help," Morningstar said, slamming his hand down on the desk. Pete jumped. He stood, jabbing a fresh fag at her. "You, Gerard, everyone who's gotten caught in the web. Who got tricked into believing in magic. You must get out before it burns you alive, Petunia. Your mother . . ."

"Leave my mother out of this," Pete snarled. "You've already brainwashed her—is that not enough? You want the whole set of Caldecotts? I'll have you ring up my sister, if that's true. She'd let you sell her the Tower of London if you told her it was constructed by benevolent elves from outer space."

"Goddamn it, this is not a fucking joke to me!" Morningstar bellowed. "I'm saving the good people of the world. They may not see it, but in the end, they get on their knees and thank me in their prayers."

"Please," Pete said. She turned to leave, because being ignored wore on men like Morningstar a thousand times more than defiance. "Preach it to someone who doesn't know what's really out there in the dark."

"You think I don't know?" Morningstar said. "You think I'm a fanatic who condemns from the outside?" He sank back into his chair, and jabbed out the cigarette viciously. "I've seen, Miss Caldecott. I've seen . . ." He ran a hand down his face. "My sister's name was Charity. Even though we were brought up God fearing, magic denouncing, as all members of the Order should be, Charity fell in with the Black. Through our research, she met them. The mages and the sorcerers, the unclean things that crawl below the skin of this city, and she fell . . ." Morningstar's jaw twitched. "She died. Nearly thirty years gone, now. I spent nights down there, looking for her." He shook his head. "She still slipped away. I knew enough about necromancy to bring her back, Miss Caldecott. But I didn't. I redoubled my dedication, and I found the lost souls when I could, and led them to the light. And that's why, when I found Gerard Carver, I knew I had to save him. And when he died, I knew that something terrible was stirring in the Black. Because I know my enemy, Petunia, and I know that we've precious little time left to stop him. Can you say the same? About anything?"

Pete hadn't expected a bastard like Ethan Morningstar, with a view narrower than a chimneysweep's arse and sermons to match, to ever make her feel like shite. Still, she felt her stomach tie in knots as he stared at her, waiting for her reply. She thought about all of the nights looking for Jack in his various drug squats, the hellish week when he'd been detoxing, and knowledge ever after that he was one bad day or bad vision or Hell, stubbed toe away from using again, and she'd have to do it all over. There was never any question of whether she'd go after him when he slipped back down into the Black. She had to. Jack was the one thing she could never be clean of.

"Gerard Carver didn't deserve what happened to

him," she said. "But he was into some nasty fucking magic, and it's going to take some time to unravel it all. Meanwhile, may I suggest you stop following me and stop making these little chats necessary?"

Morningstar scrubbed a hand across his eyes. "I assure you, Mr. Dreisden was there for your protection. I meant what I said. The Black is out of balance, and what information Gerard passed me was troubling. Necromantic rituals that haven't been used since before Christ, cropping up again. Horrible stuff. Feisty as you are, Petunia, it would eat you alive."

All at once, Pete saw Morningstar with perfect clarity. Perhaps it was the absence of the Black at last, after the oppressive weight of the lost library. With her senses quiet, she saw Morningstar as a man past his prime, exhausted furrows writ into a face that was really too young to hold them, at least so deeply. Back bent from stemming a tide he knew would surely drown him, with the next wave, or the hundredth—it was only time, as his strength ebbed and the Black continued to flow just as it always had.

"I'm not doing this for you," Pete said. "Let's just get that straight. I'm doing it so you'll leave me and mine alone. Permanently."

Morningstar lit his second fag. "I'm going to be honest with you, Miss Caldecott: We've been seeking you out ever since you sought the company of Jack Winter, what is it, two years ago now?"

"It was two years," Pete agreed softly. "Just about."

"Like I said," Ethan sighed. "We are not ignorant to the movements of the Black. You have a prodigious talent, and you could use it to do so much good."

"All due respect, Ethan," she said. "I'm doing good. You and your Order are doing precisely shite that I can see but sit around wringing your hands."

She opened the door to the main hall. "I can see myself out."

"This mystery spell that killed Gerard," Ethan said, wagon-wheel voice serving to stop Pete in her tracks. "Wouldn't happen to be Babylonian, would it?"

Pete knew she'd gone stiff, from the pang in her shoulder where she'd landed on it badly years ago, chasing a shoplifter along the Camden locks. "How did you know that?" She had to be careful. She was alone with Morningstar, a big man with a gun who wasn't afraid of or even adverse to violence. If she accused him of having a bit more of a hard-on for spellcraft than was officially accepted by an upright outfit like the Order, she had no doubt Morningstar would put her through the nearest wall.

"Wipe that look off your face," Morningstar said. "I told you. It's a sign."

Pete stayed still, but she did him the grace of turning around and not saying anything snide. There was a window behind Morningstar, but it only faced the brick of the next house. She probably couldn't break the glass without a running start. The front door was far away. At least Lawrence would eventually call Ollie if she didn't come back out.

"A time ago, when I was searching for Charity, I happened across a book." Morningstar produced a key and used it to open a small compartment in the wall. He pulled out a small volume and opened it with great care. "It was just a scribbling, a transcription of a Babylonian grimoire that some speed-addled mage had set down while he was high and touching the face of Ishtar," Morningstar murmured. "But I know it's the truth. Thirty years, Miss Caldecott. I've built my life around this page, right here."

"Brilliant," Pete said. "Care to share so I can get on with my day?"

"*The serpent winds the world*," Morningstar read. His voice was so soft that Pete had to step closer to hear it, overshadowed by a ticking clock and someone moving about in another part of the house. "*The serpent devours the world. The bone gods dance in dreaming. The serpent becomes the world.*"

Morningstar shut the book and placed his hand on the cover. "Nearly three thousand years ago, someone in Babylon predicted the end of days, Miss Caldecott. And it's here. It's all around us. And you—you're right here. With us."

Pete found her mouth was dry when she tried to speak. "That doesn't mean anything. There's hundreds of prophecies back in my flat, in Jack's books. You can set about as much stock by them as by some bloke on a street corner yelling about the lizard men."

"It's true," Morningstar said, "and some part of you believes it, or you wouldn't have come straight here."

"I came here because you're irritating me," Pete said. "And I'm working the Carver thing because I have to. You or any of your trenchcoat brigade come at me again, and I will take it personally. You read me?"

"You're going to get in over your head unless you let me help you," Morningstar insisted. "And for that, you need to accept the truth of those words."

Pete jabbed a finger into Ethan's chest when he got inside her personal bubble and tried to do the soothing hand-on-the-shoulder move favored by teachers wanting too badly to be liked and perverted older men playing on daddy issues.

"I don't need protection," she said. "I'm not a shy

baby bird left helpless because I don't have the great Jack Winter watching me. I don't need another set of minders. And if I did, your psychotic mouth-breather brigade would be the very last I'd ask."

Deciding she'd probably said enough to cause Morningstar to want her dead, even if he hadn't before, Pete turned around and left.

"Petunia, I'm serious . . ." Morningstar started, but she held two fingers over her head.

"Sod off, Ethan!" She slammed the front door on him, cutting off the oppressive silence of the Order's headquarters for the buzz and hum of the street.

CHAPTER 12

Ollie rang just as Pete was running a bath, and she shut off the water, sitting on the edge of the tub. "Yeah, Ollie?"

She unlaced her boots, cradling the phone and letting the steel toes thump to the tile.

"Tell me you have something for me," Ollie muttered. He sounded as if he were muffling the phone. The gentle hum of the incident room was missing, and Pete heard water trickling.

"Ollie, are you in the loo?"

"Newell found out," Ollie said. "Tore me up one side and down the other. Pete, just tell me you found something before I'm out on my arse and back in Yorkshire, writing traffic citations to combine harvesters."

"Yeah," Pete said. She peeled off her damp, sweat-encrusted blouse, trousers, and bra while swapping Ollie to speaker. Her head had begun to throb as soon as she left the Order's house, but she'd braved it until she was in the flat and could ride out the hallucinogenic hangover in peace. Her cheek was cut deeper than she'd thought, and blood had trickled down her jaw on the tube. On the upside, she'd gotten an entire bench on the Hammersmith & City train to herself. Hospital was out of the question, but she'd need to at least glue it shut if she didn't want to look like she'd been attacked by a werewolf. "Shit," she muttered as fresh blood oozed down her cheek when she prodded.

"You found shit?" Ollie barked. "Pete, don't bloody do this to me!"

"Wasn't talking to you, was I?" Pete sighed. "Look, the markings on Carver weren't a killing spell, they were some musty old Babylonian ritual, and I haven't found much else yet. That bit mean anything?"

"Might," Ollie said. "Carver worked with Babylonian and Egyptian antiquities. If it was within a thousand miles of the Fertile Crescent, he had his paws on it, is the word from his boss. And we've found some irregularities with his customs manifests, now that the tech wanks have poked a bit. Seems old Gerard wasn't so squeaky as he appeared. May have even been selling off odd bits of history on the side. His mum has a *very* nice little terrace for a pensioner who thinks her next door neighbor is a German spy."

"I'd really love to get another look at the room he died in," Pete said. "I mean, if you're going to go to the trouble to carve someone up, wouldn't you do it in private? Why dump him like an exhibit, unless it meant something to you?"

"I might be able to get the curator to let us have another go," Ollie said. "Assuming Newell doesn't fire me when I get back from taking a piss. Can you meet at the museum after closing hours?"

Pete gave up trying to stanch the gash with a washcloth and reached into the cabinet for peroxide. "Yeah. Around eight?"

"Eight it is," Ollie said. "And you better pull a rabbit out of your hat that sings fucking Morrissey, because Newell is apoplectic."

"No pressure for me to have some sort of clever day-saving plan, then," Pete muttered.

"You're tops," Ollie said. "Cheers."

"Fuck you," Pete told him, but he'd already rung off. She tossed her mobile and went into the bedroom to retrieve Jack's half-arsed first aid kit, which consisted of a crumbled box of Band-Aids, gauze, Super Glue, and a fifth of whiskey.

Daubing the wound with antiseptic was the worst part, although she supposed she could count herself lucky that it was real peroxide solution and not something cheap and ninety-proof that Jack had pulled out of some dank cabinet in his terrifying excuse for a kitchen.

Pete hissed as the blood stained a collection of cotton wool pink. She irrigated the wound with a bit of contact lens solution—poor man's saline—and dabbed Super Glue along the lower edge, careful to keep it off her fingertips. Once the skin had knit, she slapped on a piece of surgical tape and took a quick gulp from the whiskey bottle before shoving the whole mess out of sight under the basin.

She'd gone her entire Met career without being stabbed, and it wasn't until she'd seen Jack again that grievous bodily harm became the order of the day. This wasn't a bad wound, but it was a bad reminder of both how lucky and how completely stupid she'd been, drinking down the Antiquarian's potion and diving into the whole Carver mess, necromancers leaving corpses strewn all over the city and Carver's living friends itching to shove her soul in a box for their tally.

Jack would have been smart. He'd have found a way out of both ends of this by now, and he didn't need any sodding poison tea to open his third eye. This was Jack's life. Pete slipped into a nightgown hanging on the door of the loo and then went into the bedroom and let herself drop onto the mattress, boneless. Jack's life. But she the one left living it. Pete had no idea how that was fucking fair, but there it was.

Her nightgown was another of Jack's shirts, soft from wear and washing until it was nearly transparent. She'd run it through the laundry, but the fabric still smelled faintly of him. Whiskey, cigarettes, and sweat. Jack, in one breath. Pete was relieved she was too tired to have to stop herself from crying, and that her mind was too cluttered to relive the touch of Jack's hands against her bare skin. She curled up on the mattress, pulling the blankets over her head to shut out the daylight, and was asleep before she even realized she was falling.

CHAPTER 13

Ollie met Pete at the freight entrance to the British Museum, and together they walked through the back hallways to the silent, dark exhibits. The head curator, boss of Carver's boss, was a little woman named Matthews who giggled at everything Ollie said whether it was funny or not. She led them to Gerard Carver's office, buried deep back in the maze of the museum not open to the public. It was a shabby little office that fit the shabby little man Carver had been in life. Pete shifted the journals and printouts around a bit, seeing if she could catch a glimpse of either of his other lives—fanatic witch-finder or sleazy necromancer—until Matthews cleared her throat and drew her bushy brows together.

"Sorry," Ollie told her. "Miss Caldecott sometimes forgets where she is."

"As I was telling you on the telephone," Matthews said. "Now that we've examined the manifests Mr. Carver signed for more carefully, there are several glaring inconsistencies. It's terrible. Really terrible. All of our employees pass a thorough background check."

"You think he was sellin' the stuff?" Ollie said. Matthews put a hand to the collar of her fuzzy pink jumper, as if Ollie had asked what her sign was.

"Well, I wouldn't know anything about that, Chief Inspector. I don't deal on the black market. I believe antiquities are for the world to appreciate, and they should be preserved."

"And nothing says preservation like hacking them off the side of the Pantheon, does it?" Pete said, shoving another stack of magazines just to take the piss.

"The museum does a service for the *entire world,*" Matthews snapped. "Our methods were not always sound but we take the greater good into consideration, and if Gerard was selling these items to private collectors, then he's violated the most sacred trust a curator is given."

"It's just Inspector," Ollie injected. "I'm a DI. Can you account for what's missing?"

"Oh, yes." Matthews brandished a printout as if she'd been challenged to a duel. "Here's a complete list. Five items, mostly Babylonian funerary items. Nothing that was terribly valuable, which is how they were overlooked. Gerard signed them out for cleaning and simply never signed them back in."

Ollie skimmed the list and then handed it off to Pete. The manifests contained a few lines of description, a log of the object's activity once it entered the museum, and who'd signed it out. "Idols?" she said.

"Oh my, yes," said Matthews. "The Babylonians in particular attached enormous importance to their idols. They believed their gods and heroes resided simultaneously in their stone and ethereal form. Great care was taken with them."

Pete pointed to the last item. "And this?"

"A jar, I believe," said Matthews. "Just a house-hold item but very nice. We would have used it for the rotating exhibits—life in the Bronze Age, you know. The sort of thing schoolchildren enjoy."

"Yeah," Ollie said. "Always liked that, at school. We got to go to a recreated Roman village once. Thought that was tops when I was a kid."

"The jar was the last thing to go missing," Pete told him. Carver had signed it out one day before his death, in fact, and hadn't bothered to jot down an excuse.

"Maybe he fancied it," Matthews said. "You do get attached to your objects, as a curator. They're pieces of the world, the bones of history that we build on. You see?"

"Think I'd rather have a cat," Pete told her. "You got a picture?" If Carver was stealing antiquities, Pete would lay even money that it was only partially to fund his side activities of fiddling with the dead. Magic objects had a way of slipping between the cracks, turning up in junk shops and attics, until someone with the right radar happened on them. Jack's flat was a prime example.

"Somewhere in the database, of course," Matthews agreed. "I'll have to look it up via inventory number and then I could mail it to DI Heath, if he'd be so kind as to give me his e-mail address."

Ollie cleared his throat and scribbled on the back of one of his cards before handing it over.

"How lovely," Matthews beamed. "I'll do it straightaway in the morning. Now I'm afraid I must be going—I don't care to be walking the streets after nine p.m. It's not safe. Of course you understand."

"It's a veritable Wild West out there in darkest Bloomsbury," Ollie said. Matthews batted her pale eyelashes at him once more before taking her leave. Ollie started to follow, but Pete caught him and shook her head. She pointed down the hallway to the public area.

"I'd like to get one more look," she said. "See if I can't figure out why they left him there."

"Just make sure that bloody woman doesn't pop 'round the corner," Ollie muttered, beating a hasty retreat after her.

"You going to take her out, then?" Pete said. "I bet her knickers match her jumper."

"Fuck off," Ollie told her. "You think you could have slagged her off any more? She's a witness, and I have to deal with her now."

"I think one look at that chiseled jawline and manly chest you're sporting and she'll forgive you anything, Chief Inspector Heath," Pete said.

"You're a horrid person and you're going straight to Hell," Ollie informed her.

Pete didn't really feel her good humor, but she allowed herself to punch Ollie on the shoulder rather than cringe. Being with Ollie was a good distraction—she could fall back into their familiar rhythms and not think about necromancers, the Order, or her bloody mother.

She got out her pocket torch when they reached the Egyptian Room, a cavern of shadow on shadow in the faint light coming from the outside. The floor had been scrubbed clean, a scrape of roughness under her boot the only sign that blood had lain there long enough to soak into the marble. The leaking power from around Carver's body had gone, but she could still feel the threads of magic here—worn and frayed, drifting among the artifacts, and more recent, sharp and grasping, like a nest of thorny vines.

"Why here?" she said, flashing her light over Ramses II. Ollie scratched at his temple.

"Psychiatrist would say he's making a statement, wouldn't they? Telling us something from dumping the poor git here."

"Or he's bragging," Pete said. *We know where you sleep and work. Even here, among the oldest magic on earth, you're not safe.*

"Or he's a lazy sod who couldn't be arsed to drag the body the rest of the way down to the trash compactor," Ollie said.

Pete clicked the light off. "Thought maybe this would make one of us clever."

"Clever's your bit," Ollie said. Pete looked down at the spot where Carver had lain. In the dark, it was easy to imagine his slumped shape, imagine whoever had dragged him here, tugged on his hair to bare his throat, and done him in with one clean slash.

And then . . . tossed the knife in the bin and fucked off down the pub?

"Ollie, did the security tapes get anything?" Pete said. He snorted.

"You think I'd still be here if we'd caught anything on CCTV?" He gestured at the corners of the room. "State of the art, but someone using Carver's login shut 'em off through the mainframe. Fancy stuff. Security guard who found the body said he'd heard noises—you know, our old friend, suspicious sounds. Beyond that, whatever he was up to in here before he died is between him and his god."

Pete thought of the bloody marks on Carver's

torso, fresh and red and dripping when Nasiri pulled his shirt aside. "He was there," she told Ollie.

"Yeah," he said. "Wait. Who?"

"The Pope. The guy who did Carver, Ollie." Pete scuffed her toe across the spot. "Carver killed the cameras because Carver wasn't expecting to die. He was expecting to carve himself up and do a ritual, sure, but I'm thinking he found out that a human sacrifice was the bonus behind the curtain."

"And that didn't sit well, so he kicked up a fuss," Ollie said, looking toward the main lobby of the museum. "The guard interrupted 'em."

"It's not finished," Pete said. "Whatever Carver was doing, it's not finished."

"Good, I think," Ollie said. "Trying to work dodgy spells amid a bunch of mummies never ends well in those programs where the girl kicks high and stakes the vampires."

"Not good," Pete said. "Because if they didn't finish with Carver, they're going to finish it with someone else."

Carver hadn't been working death magic because he hadn't expected to die. But any spell worked in flesh and carried out with funerary relics wasn't something that was going to cause pink unicorns and toffees to rain from the sky. "I think we need to look at Carver's house," Pete said. "And I think I need to find out who his friends were off the clock."

"You can't come along to his house," Ollie said. "Newell will shit his own testicles. But if you were to take it upon yourself, as a good citizen of my fair city, to make discreet inquiries, well. I'd be obligated to follow any leads, as an officer of the law."

"Cheers," Pete said. Ollie started to reply, but his mobile went.

"Heath," he grumbled. Then, his breath hitched, and Pete's stomach twinged. She knew the pause, knew the slack absence of expression that caused Ollie's jowls to bag. She saw it in more than enough faces to memorize during her Met days, when she appeared on doorsteps, delivering bad news.

"Where?" Ollie bit out. "Fucking when?" A few seconds of silence and then, "Right. I'm coming now."

"What is it?" Pete said. Ollie's face was blank as she'd ever seen it, and he gripped his mobile in his fist so that it chirped as his grip mashed the buttons. "Ollie," Pete said, running to keep up with his broad stride. "What's happened?"

Ollie breathed in, out, and then stopped, pressing his forehead against the corridor wall. "McCorkle," he said. "He's dead."

CHAPTER 14

Ollie didn't ask Pete to come with him, but he didn't say anything to the contrary when she followed him to his Vauxhall. Ollie didn't say anything, full stop, until they were over the river and heading into the crawling ant-farm roads of South London.

"Said his landlady found him. Christ, his fucking *landlady*. Not even a girlfriend . . . Hell, boyfriend. Not even *me*."

"Ollie," Pete said, watching his meaty hands turn pink and white as he gripped the steering wheel hard enough to dent it. "This is not your fault."

"He was *my* partner," Ollie said. "I was meant to be looking out for him."

"We don't know the details," Pete said. "Could have been anything. Could have slipped in the loo, completely accidentally." Of course, the officers from Ollie's own station, miles from the crime scene, wouldn't be calling him if that were the case. Accidents that happened to coppers who worked CID, especially on an MIT, weren't even always accidents. Connor had written off a few suicides in his day, gun-cleaning incidents, slip and falls, that sort of thing. Pete knew it and Ollie knew it, but offering him a ray of hope was just the thing to do.

McCorkle lived in Brixton, and Ollie crawled along Coldharbour Lane, past a mom-and-pop market and a pub, a café with its gate down for the night, and an upscale vintage shop.

"Place has changed a lot," Pete said, to say something. Sitting with Ollie and yet being completely silent wasn't natural. "My dad was in the '81 riot, you know. First year on the job as a PC." Ollie didn't tell her to shut up, so she kept on as lights from patrol cars flared in the distance, gathered outside a pair of Victorian homes that had been chopped into flats, estate agent's sign still hanging in a front window. "Never talked about it much. Imagine it bothered him, being an Irish kid forced to smash other kids with a truncheon unless he wanted to be done in himself. Think it put him off the job forever, in a way. He was never the kind of copper who talked about being the line, acted as if he were doing some great service."

Ollie parked illegally near the phalanx of uniformed officers milling outside McCorkle's flat, smaller bodies orbiting the two marked cars and the ambulance. "Stay here," he said. "I'll be back in a moment."

Pete waited a respectful thirty seconds, until Ollie had found a plod who seemed to at least have enough brain cells to give him relevant details, before she joined him on the pavement. "What's going on?"

"Trying to determine that myself," Ollie said, hands twitching like he wished they were around the plod's neck. "Listen, you—either let me in there or I'm walking over you. No real decision on your part."

"Heath?" A tall figure wrapped in a blue coat cut through the uniforms and came to Ollie's side. He was as trim as Ollie was wide, and together they cut an odd pair, even more so given the new bloke's immaculate navy suit and shined shoes, even at the late hour. Dark curls slicked back from a high forehead, exposing delicate features, but Pete wouldn't have crossed him. This one walked like the coppers Connor had detested—as if he were the sheriff of all he surveyed, protecting the villagers from the wolves.

"Who the fuck," Ollie said, summing up Pete's feelings, "are you?"

"DS Patel, from Lambeth," the tall detective said, extending a hand. "I caught your man's call-out."

Ollie ignore the hand, so Patel turned it to Pete. "You're Petunia Caldecott," he said, snapping it back to his side when he recognized her. Pete was so used to the reaction from cops she barely let it rile her. Patel frowned. "Heard you went Section 8."

"Do I look like I'm bloody Section 8?" Pete demanded. Patel considered, tilting his head.

"Felix Patel," he said finally. "Pleasure's all mine. I trust you'll be fine to wait here while I allow DI Heath a look at the scene. Ask one of the plods to bring you a cup of tea."

Pete opened her mouth, but she would have been speaking to air. Patel had already measured and dismissed her. His eyes were back on Ollie. "It's bad, Heath," he said. "I'm sorry to say it. Very bad."

"I've worked MIT," Ollie grumbled. "I can take it."

"It's not a murder," Patel said, gently as he could. Pete watched Ollie's face go from bulldoggish to kicked in the space of a breath.

"You sure you're ready?" Patel said, putting a hand on Ollie's shoulder. Ollie tucked his chin down into his collar, a gladiator tucking into armor and preparing to take a bad hit, and glared at the spot where Patel touched him. "Right," Patel said. "Come along."

"I'm coming," Pete said. She moved to Ollie's shoulder, so he could feel her there.

"You're not a DI any more," Patel said. "And even if you were, you've no jurisdiction on this side of the river. I'm doing DI Heath a courtesy for his partner's sake."

"For fuck's sake, Patel." Ollie's voice was rough, echoing off the concrete entryway of the flat block. "She's likely a Hell of a lot more well trained than your fresh-faced schoolboys here."

Patel locked eyes with Pete for a moment, and she stared back, unblinking. She got it—Patel was a DS, probably looking to make his name. A cop suicide was a dodgy enough matter. If he let the Section 8 former DI wander around his scene, his halo would aquire a little tarnish.

Patel surprised her, though, by sneering and then nodding. He led them up the steps of the Victorian on the left, up another set on the inside, to the top floor. McCorkle's flat was the entire attic, the grand house carved up into smaller spaces on the cheap. Fresh plaster hit Pete's nose when they crested the stairs. McCorkle's door stood open as the white moonsuited figures of crime scene techs went about their business within his living space.

Former living space. McCorkle wasn't living there any longer, at least in his own skin. The moment Pete came within a few feet of his door, though, she could tell that *something* was still very much present in McCorkle's flat. It started as vague unease, prickles like she felt before a storm broke over the city, all of the ions in the air cycling against her skin, and the pressure got faster and stronger as Patel lifted the tape for Heath, speaking to the crime scene unit but paying her no mind. Pete scrubbed at her forehead. She was just bruised a bit on her sixth sense, that was all. First the Hecate and then the lost library. She was uneasy being here, in the remains of the life of a man she hadn't liked much in the first place. That was why she felt fingers on skin, the lightest of touches on her other senses, whispers through the Black just out of her hearing.

Patel stopped her at the tape and gripped her arm hard with a set of pincer-like fingers. "You touch anything, say anything—you *sneeze* while you're inside this room—and you will need a team of specialists flown in from Norway to remove my boot from your arse."

Pete looked at his hand on her, back at him, hoping the suggestion he should mind his personal fucking space came across clearly in her withering glare. "Don't you worry, DS. I leave the brilliant deductions to Batman."

"I know all about you," Patel said, low. "None of that psychic bullshit, gone to a better place, messages from the back of beyond here. Heath's lost his man and doesn't deserve that."

"I've got a message for you," Pete said. "I know Ollie far too well to think he'd ever believe that shite, never mind want it. Now get your fucking hand off me or I'm not going to fucking smile about it."

Patel grimaced, an abortion of the smug smile he'd

no doubt been saving for the grand finale of Pete's place-putting. "Heard about your temper. Figured they exaggerated."

"Absolutely," Pete agreed, as he let go of her. "Sweet as custard cake, me." She didn't pick up an impression from Patel, just a general sharpness, like he'd been made of metal and sealed off. Jack had said some blokes had more natural defenses against magic than others—the uber-normal, as it were. That was probably just as well. Patel wouldn't embarrass McCorkle and by extension Ollie. He'd close it up quiet and quick, all the loose ends accounted for and the right paperwork filed, and the legend of Freddy McCorkle would become a ghost story to tell at closing hour down the pub.

"Oliver," Patel said, at once all conciliatory smiles and low, soothing tones. "Let me take you through the timeline."

Pete didn't need the narration of Patel's clipped private school accent. The blood told the story, and there was enough of it to paint every inch of her skin.

McCorkle's body was in the center of the flat's tight sitting area. The crime scene techs had put a plastic sheet over it, but one hand protruded, fingers splayed like a flower. A few inches away rested the kind of short, blunt all-purpose kitchen blade that held a serrated edge, also painted with blood spatter.

The biggest pool of blood was under the corpse, but an arterial spray had hit McCorkle's sofa and dribbled down the front of his flat-screen telly, which was still playing a rerun of an international match between two countries whose flags Pete didn't recognize.

"TV was on when first responders arrived," said Patel. "Landlady came up to ask him to turn it down.

She claims she didn't touch anything, but, well . . ."
Patel shrugged. "You know how little old women
can be."

Patel knelt down and twitched back the sheet.
Pete saw Ollie flinch, but he hid it after a split second, his impassive, cowlike nonexpression in place.
"One cut," Patel said. "Pulled the knife all the way
across before he passed out. Hit the carotid. I know
it's probably not a comfort, but he didn't feel it for
long."

Ollie passed a hand over his face. "Forced entry.
Something. Freddy wouldn't just . . . wouldn't just . . ."

"Not that we can see," Patel said. "Of course,
building's not secure, and it is Brixton. But no, he's
been alone all evening according to his landlady.
This was . . . this is unfortunate, Heath. I'm sorry."

"I called him a twat," Ollie said. "He'd misfiled
some papers on the case we were working."

"Heath, you really can't look for blame or reasons
in this sort of thing," Patel said. "Trust me. It'll drive
you around the bend."

Pete watched as Ollie visibly reined himself in,
pulled up his spine, got back into the skin of the unflappable copper. "He wasn't depressed, since I know
you'll ask. Wasn't anything, really. Didn't socialize
much, always rushing off end of shift. I thought he
had a girlfriend, or maybe he was gay and he didn't
want his new nick finding out . . ." Ollie hunched
again, took a breath, and deliberately turned his back
on the corpse. "I don't know why this happened."

"Can be anything," Patel said. It was a line, but
Pete was glad Ollie was too far gone to see that.
"Don't blame yourself, Heath." He carried on with
his guided tour of the scene, Ollie moving with jerky,
numb motions beside him.

Pete turned her back on them, once Patel's eyes were off her. The thread was still there, the tremble through the Black. McCorkle's flat telescoped into a claustrophobic hallway that peaked into an A shape as the builders ran out of room next to the roof, closet on one side, bedroom and en suite on the other. The bedroom was still neat, free of blood, the bed crumpled on one side with a dent from McCorkle's head still in his pillow.

Above the bed was a giant print, one of the generic street scenes of Paris you could buy from an IKEA, and the whispers in Pete's mind rose to shrieks, from a great distance, across a vast and windy plain.

Not bothering with her shoes, Pete climbed onto the bed and grabbed the print by the edges, lifting it off the hook.

The blood was fresh enough that it gleamed in the low bedroom light, and it had dribbled down McCorkle's bland coffee-colored walls in slow rivulets. The lettering was a bit bigger than Pete's hand and she nearly fell at the onslaught of black magic on her senses. The message, though, was a simple one.

THE SERPENT BECOMES THE WORLD

CHAPTER 15

Patel was less than pleased with Pete's discovery. In fact, she'd wager she'd never seen a detective from the Met get quite so volcanic, quite so quickly. She could still hear him cursing at Ollie in the other room, shouting at what a mess this was, since *clearly he didn't get up again after slitting his own throat and write us a fucking note.* A uniform watched Pete with the stern glare of a young but earnest school-teacher.

"Oh, calm down," Pete told the plod. "Be grateful he's not screaming at you, just because he can."

"He's a twat," the officer said, clearly desperate for a sympathetic third party to relay that bit of information to. "Nearly got me fired last month because I had to go take a piss and left my partner alone at a perimeter."

Pete looked back at the letters in McCorkle's blood. She'd ended up here as a favor to Ollie, and the simple hope that if she tried hard enough to move on, to finish a job and find a bad apple without Jack, she'd be able to actually do it. To have *closure*.

But now . . . now they'd made it personal, and they'd killed someone to do it. Jack would never have let it go this far. He would have known what he was looking at the moment Carver's body turned up in the museum. Wouldn't have thrashed around in the dark for days and let McCorkle end up skewered. It had to be her fault. The necromancers who'd nearly happened on her at Wapping had decided to take a more direct route and reach her and Heath in one swift stroke. *We know where you live. Even here, in the bosom of your copper's sanctuary, you are not safe.*

"You all right, miss?" said the constable. "Stuffy in here, ain't it?"

"I'd murder a glass of water," Pete said. "Could you be a love? If I go out there I think Patel's liable to rip off my face and spit down my neck."

The constable snorted a phglemy laugh. "Sure, miss. You wait here like he said though, yeah? I need this job."

Pete sighed. If this was the caliber of soul populating the new, young Met, the criminal underworld should be throwing a fucking soirée.

As soon as the constable vanished into the en suite, Pete went for McCorkle's drawers. She could explain McCorkle topping himself, miserable bastard that he'd been, but not the writing—word for word what Morningstar had read to her from his bloody book, hidden in a place that the crime scene techs wouldn't have found for days, if not weeks— plenty of time for McCorkle to be filed as a suicide and the file to be pushed to the bottom of Patel's pile. Plus there was the small matter of whoever had orchestrated this little abattoir choosing McCorkle in the first place. He had no history with occult crimes and even less history with the Black.

Morningstar could conceivably have had time to do it—he could have sent Dreisden and his razor after McCorkle—but she'd been in his study, within strangling distance, and he'd let her walk out again. Besides, Morningstar wasn't about knives in the back. He was a shock-and-awe type, assaulting the wicked with the righteous fury of his own self-importance.

And neither Morningstar nor the Order explained the black magic. The necromancer who'd gone after McCorkle wanted something from her, had practically painted her name on the wall along with the phrase.

Pete didn't put stock in prophecies, and for all she knew the phrase about the serpent was as well-known as "Mary Had a Little Lamb" among necromancers. There was a plethora of serpents in Revelation, even, the fan fiction of religious texts: *And the dragon fought and his angels.* Slithery things were all over magic texts, from Babylon to the Golden Dawn. But if the necromancer was reaching out to her with the tip of his blade, then what, exactly, was the message Pete was supposed to receive?

Jack would know. Pete tossed the drawers faster, hearing the water shut off and the constable begin his plodding return to the room. Jack would know, which was no bloody help to her, because the necromancer hadn't reached for Jack. He'd reached for her.

The power in the flat was still up. Small ice picks in the base of her skull told Pete that magic was here, and her talent whispered to her to let it in. It would fill her up, consume her, *drown* her in power, but what a sweet death it would be, suffused with all the power the Black had to offer. Pete bit down on the inside of her cheek, hard. Pain could usually pull her back when things threatened to get hazy, and she yanked open the last door, hearing Patel snap a question at the plod and the plod answer—*Just wanted a cup of water.*

She's a fucking menace and it's a murder scene now, Constable. Get back in there.

Any other time, Pete would have been flattered that Patel held her in such regard, but now she was merely beginning to sweat. If anyone saw her, Patel would toss her in lockup. He was an intractable bastard and Ollie had already had to convince him not to arrest her simply for finding the writing.

McCorkle didn't have much in the way of possessions—no box of keepsakes, no photos, not even an awkwardly hidden stash of porno.

The drawer refused to close when she shoved it back, and Pete rattled it, keeping one eye out for the constable. A gurney had arrived to take McCorkle on to the Lambeth mortuary, and she heard Patel snap an order before his footsteps started down the hall to the bedroom.

"Shit," Pete hissed, jamming her hand into the thin space between wood and wall. That was one benefit of being petite—she could reach the tight spots. Pickpockets and coppers, Connor had said. The two trades that rewarded quick hands and devious minds.

Her fingers brushed a bundle attached to the underside of the wardrobe with DIY tape, and Pete snatched it. It was a plastic Tesco bag, wrapped round and round something that smelled like a cross between a dodgy restaurant and rotting orchids. When she touched the plastic, the Black flared again, a veritable flash flood of power cascading over and around her mind, clawing with small fractious fingers to be let inside.

Pete shoved the mess into her jacket, kicked the drawer shut, and leaped across the room to a sitting position on the bed, just as Patel burst in.

"I hope you have something damn impressive to say about all this, Miss Caldecott, because otherwise I'm going to arrest you right now."

Pete looked up at him. Patel's cheeks had flushed to a deep magenta, and his regal nose flared with every breath. She considered for a moment, keeping her arm clamped to her side to hold the bundle against her stomach. "Nothing comes to mind."

"You think I'm fucking about? I'll have you," Patel snarled. "You were a liability on the force, and now you've apparently fucked off 'round the bend with the fortune-tellers. I don't care who your dad was—I'll have you. Conspiracy to murder. Start talking."

"Felix, bloody Hell, it's my fault," Ollie said. He was also red, hands trembling and sweat breaking out on his temples. Some might mistake it for anger in a man of his size, but Pete knew Ollie, and Ollie was scared.

"Don't cover for her, Heath," Patel said. "You're just going to make it worse than it already is." He sneered at Pete. "Outside consultant, my arse. Whose cock did you suck to stay out of jail thus far?"

"Your mum's. Disappointingly small." Pete stood. "I'm leaving. You can charge me if you have the balls."

She left the crime scene, feeling curiously numb after the flashover of rage. The thing in her pocket prickled her skin and she drew her hand away. She'd be furious at Ollie for dragging her into this if he weren't as fucked as she. He'd probably lose his job and his pension, if Newell was in a foul enough mood. Not to mention that in under an hour she'd managed to both get McCorkle killed and make an enemy of Felix Patel, the sort of hard-nosed bastard who'd probably harass her with traffic citations and littering charges until the end of time, just because he could.

"Arse," Pete said, though Patel was long out of earshot. She hated being out of her element, hated that she was a tourist in the world of the Black with no talent of her own besides being filled to the brim and possibly burned alive any time she came in contact with sorcery. Hated that she couldn't find her feet, solve the problem. All she could do was walk to the fucking bus stop, sit and wait to be taken back across the river, a lost soul riding the steam and neon of London back to the underworld.

So what are you going to do about it, then? That was Jack, all smirk and permanent halo of smoke. *Not like you to just fuck off and moan about your sorry lot, luv.*

Pete hunched into her jacket inside the bus shelter. This late, it'd be nearly an hour before she could catch a night bus.

She didn't have Jack's talent, nor his twenty-five years of living, breathing, and dreaming the Black, but she had his books and she had Lawrence. She could moan forever, knocking about the Black like the sad old bastard who wants to sit beside you in pubs and talk about the war, or she could admit she'd cocked up, climb back on top of the problem, and start over. She could still find the why and who of Gerard Carver's last ritual. Fuck it, if she found that, she'd likely find who killed McCorkle.

It all seemed like a brilliant plan, until the thing

in Pete's pocket began to whisper, rushing tides of the Black cascading over her mind, as if she were hearing snatches of esoteric radio out the windows of the few passing cars.

Pete cast her eyes into the small patch of unlit park across the street. A darker piece of nighttime stood among the bare oaks. It was the same thin figure that had tried to accost her at the mortuary. Eyes gleamed in the dark, picking up the streetlamps.

The figure smirked at her across Coldharbour Lane, standing perfectly still for a moment before he took a step toward her, then another. Pete looked up and down the street. This late, she could hear the thump of bass from a club a few blocks down, but there was nobody else on the pavement. The bus shelter didn't offer any protection and the alleyway beyond even less.

The figure picked up speed, long, loping strides closing the distance between them with frightening alacrity. Pete felt the thing in her pocket prickle, coming alive at the onslaught of the figure.

Necromancers could call a lot of things— poltergeists, zombies, and worse. Pete decided she wasn't going to wait until the thing made it across the street to find out exactly what it was, although the loping, bowlegged stride and the long, narrow sliver of face she could see under the streetlamps bore out her theory that it wasn't a human thing.

Pete ran straight toward it, dodging at the last moment and causing the thing to stumble and wheel about. It hissed, and she heard the scrape of claws on asphalt as it chased her. The Black was rising, filling the empty spaces around her as Pete bore for the park, the musty stench of something long dead breathing in her face.

The park across the street bore stern warnings that it was closed from dusk till dawn, but she grabbed the rusty iron gate and heaved herself over. Metal bit into her hand, but she kept running.

The thing vaulted the gate on spindly legs, closing fast, and Pete bore down. She'd been smoking too much and running too little, and her lungs scissored with every breath, but she ran. Magic dogged her every step, the moon slicing light and shadow out of the ground. The green space ended in someone's garden wall, and she scrambled up, feeling wetness on her palm as it scraped across brick. The thing chasing her landed on top of the wall, crouched like a spider for a moment as it roved to catch her in its gaze, and then gave a hiss like an enormous kettle as it sprang back to the ground and kept chasing.

Pete burst from between the narrow buildings onto Atlantic Road, feet nearly going on the uneven pavement. The vista there was even more deserted, National Rail tracks bordering the street on one side and dark windows on the other. Fingers, or perhaps claws, snatched at the back of her jacket; she didn't look back to find out. A newsagent a few doors down was still lit, and she poured her last ounce of oxygen on.

She made it halfway across Atlantic Road, and then thing caught her, wrapping too-long fingers around her thigh and pulling her off balance. Pete fell and rolled once, the thing on top of her, its hand going around her neck.

It hissed at her, and Pete had the feeling it was talking to her, or perhaps cursing, in its own language. The hair on its head was matted, stitched into place with red thread, and Pete saw why it couldn't speak—its blue, swollen lips were stitched as well.

Zombie. Of course. Just her bloody luck. Zombies

were like poltergeists, except where poltergeists were dead things, stripped down to anger and cruelty and honed like a blade, zombies were the same thing, summoned into corpses prepared for the purpose. The mouth was stuffed with ritual herbs, and the eyes were crossed out with black thread. Zombies weren't bright, but they were relentless and resilient. Pete pounded ineffectually at the thing's chest, skin cool and pulpy under her fists, like a rotted orange.

The zombie scrabbled at her clothes, overgrown nails tearing holes in her shirt and raking at the skin beneath. Pete kicked and struggled as much as she could. Screaming was out of the question, with the thing's hand around her throat. Zombies were strong, fueled by the rage of the ghost bound inside their flesh, and she wouldn't have been a match even if she hadn't just run a fucking forty-yard dash.

It stared down at her with its eyes crossed by thick black stitches, hissing and scratching as if it were an enormous, furious housecat and Pete was the mouse.

She didn't really mean to use the last of her air on a spell. She wasn't even very good at magic, at least that sort, when she was focused and calm and not being set upon by a corpse with a bad attitude. Still, the word came to mind and flew from mind to tongue with minimal intervention. It was the simplest of hexes, one Jack could throw out pissed and standing on one leg, but Pete had never been able to simply grab a handful of power and fling it outward in the same way. She gasped rather than spoke with any authority, her vision starting to spin as her last breath went. *"Sciotha!"*

The Black rippled around them, as if she'd cast a stone into it, and Pete felt a small tug on her chest.

The zombie lurched, as if he'd caught a limb in a bear trap, and then fell to the side, twitching like a squashed insect.

Pete gasped for a moment. The newsagent, who'd been closing his shutters, was on the pavement a few yards away, staring. Pete met his eyes, and the man held up his hands and retreated. In Brixton, they clearly knew not to get involved in street fights involving a petite woman and a hulking hellbeast.

Her throat burned, and her shoulder and knees throbbed when she got up and started going through the zombie's pockets. It was wearing a polyester suit, cheap and unidentifiable. It didn't have any marks of being embalmed, and it wasn't decayed overmuch. Pete would lay money the body's former owner had been murdered specifically to bind the ghost inside him. She went through the suit's pockets with fast fingers. The paralyzer hex didn't last forever, even when it was thrown by someone who knew what they were doing. The zombie's legs began to thrash, and he bucked under her like an excitable pony.

"Why you following me, eh?" Pete said, holding him by the neck as he'd pinned her. "What're you after, you scuttling piece of shit?"

The zombie's cloudy eyes rolled back in its head and it made an enraged sound, low and guttural. Pete found nothing in the pockets except a dry-cleaner's receipt and a few pennies. The zombie made a feeble swipe at her as she tossed the items aside, and she caught sight of a faded mark, not from ritual but from ink. An ace of spades nearly hidden in the webbing of the man's thumb, the sort of thing they stamped on your hand at clubs that washed off in a few hours.

"I don't know if you understand any of this," Pete said, standing as the zombie began to twitch more violently. "But if your masters send you after me again, I'm going to chop you into firewood and douse you in petrol. Right?"

The zombie hissed.

"Right," Pete said, and took off running before somebody called the police.

CHAPTER 16

She rang Lawrence from an all-night café in South-wark, after she'd walked and doubled back enough times to satisfy her throbbing heart and twitchy nerves that no one and nothing was follwing her.

Lawrence mumbled, "I know you're nocturnal, but some of us ain't."

"Fucking zombies," Pete said. "Fucking zombies after *me,* Lawrence. Within full view of a bunch of Met officers. These bastards have got balls the size of the O2."

He yawned. "Who's got zombies?"

"Whoever killed the bloke we asked the Antiquar-ians about," Pete said. "I'm bloody angry now, Law-rence." Bad enough to top McCorkle, bad enough to try for her at the mortuary—a host of sorcerers against her was something that never would have hap-pened six months ago. Morningstar had been right, much as she was loath to admit it—the Black was changing, and the nightmares were getting bolder.

"You need me?" he said. "Where are you?"

"South London," Pete said. "And no, it's fine for now." She started to ring off and then put her mobile back to her ear. "Lawrence, you know of any clubs in the Black use a hand stamp? Ace of spades?"

"Not in the Black," he said. "But there's one on this side, down on your side of the river. Moves around a lot—ain't exactly got a bar license. Called Motor. Why?"

"You have a last known?" Pete said.

"Got a number," Lawrence said. He banged about for a moment, read it off, and then disconnected without a goodbye. Pete wrote it down on her arm. It was a Southwark exchange, but she couldn't very well go bursting in without any sort of preparation. Besides, she was exhausted and cut up and bruised in seven colors. She had to at least stop at home and clean up. And get her pepper spray and her baton, because if the men responsible were sending zombies, she was going to have to send back something more than wits.

Pete caught a bus and managed to doze a bit on the way, but by the time she was back in Whitechapel she was mainly acutely aware that she'd taken a hard fall. Her hand wasn't cut as badly as she'd thought, but it was a mess of purple where she'd slammed it into the iron fence, and she couldn't close it very well.

Just what she needed—to go about for the next two weeks looking as if an irate boyfriend had tossed her down a flight of stairs. She tried not to whimper as she climbed up to the flat, but even slight movement awoke fresh aches. She needed aspirin and a hot bath, preferably filled with whiskey.

The first sign something was amiss in the flat was quiet. The building was never quiet—the neighbors shouted, the noise from their tellys drifted down the hallway, and the small neighbor boy who was constantly in the hall conducting elaborate battles with his Transformers shrieked and made laser sounds.

Deserted, silent except for the buzzing of the overhead lights, the hallway outside the flat looked like something out of an ancient, elegant ghost story. The stamped tin ceiling and heavy wood doors were caked with decades of grime, and the scarred wood floor creaked under Pete's feet.

She stopped outside her own door and splayed her fingers against the wood. The protection hex that lay over the flat like finest cobweb still hung there, undisturbed. Still, Pete couldn't shake the niggling feeling that something was off. Never had her neighbors been so dead silent. Never had the air in the building been so still, as if lightning had just struck, or was just about to.

Could be she was paranoid. Felix Patel certainly thought she was off her rocker.

Could be, but she still inserted her key slowly and turned the lock soundlessly, entering the flat with her back easing up to the wall.

Everything was just as she'd left it. Faint silver light of morning was creeping through the windows and picking out motes in the air. Pete realized her heart was hammering, and she kicked the door shut, letting the crack put the lid on that. She'd had a hard night and she was exhausted, and magic would fuck with your brain chemistry quicker than any drug. That was all.

She slung off her jacket, which was covered in

dust and road muck, kicked off her shoes, and made it a few steps into the apartment when the curse wrapped around her from foot to head, cold and unyielding as chains. She fell hard, choking, icicles of magic jabbing into her skin. After all the abuse she'd endured in the past few days, one more bruise didn't make much of a dent. What worried her more was that she couldn't breathe. Or more accurately, she could, inhaling ice and exhaling knives.

The owner of the curse moved into her field of view, backlight from the window turning him into a featureless man-shape, as if he were a figure on a church window, calling up a sharp memory of mornings in mass at the Catholic school Connor had insisted she attend: kneeling in her illicit fishnets, the nylon leaving hash marks on her knees, Pete squirming against the sting while the stone floor chilled her down to the bone.

She was blacking out. Her air was going. Her mind jumped and twitched as the curse fought with her talent, and won handily. Pete wondered almost idly as the man walked over to her and nudged her with one shined Oxford shoe, if he meant to kill her or only scare her. If it was the latter, she hoped he'd let up soon. The pain was causing her to make odd, gasping noises that sounded as if she were drowning. Sooner or later, the curse would kill her nerve endings, and then her ability to breathe, and finally her brain cells, magic dissecting her into so much blood and bone.

The curse-thrower twitched up his soft gray wool trousers and crouched, cocking his head to look in her face. "Hello, Pete," he said, and smiled. He had the sort of smile that could stop traffic. If you didn't know that in his private moments he was a murderer, a sorcerer, and a sadist.

Pete tried to say *Nicholas fucking Naughton*, but managed a feeble sort of squeak. Naughton chucked her under the chin. "Don't get up. I know you're not being rude."

Nicholas Naughton was a necromancer. That made a bit of sense. She'd been looking for a necromancer, hadn't she? The kind of nasty cunt who'd carve a man up and leave him for the world to see. Nicholas Naughton was precisely that kind of cunt. He'd nearly gotten Jack killed when he'd sent Pete and Jack to put down a poltergeist he'd lost control over. His own brother's ghost, which he'd tortured to the point of madness.

"I do love this flat," Naughton said, straightening up. "It's a piece of shit, but it's got excellent bones. I'd shovel out the esoteric crap. Paint it white. Something tasteful yet respectful of the lines." He passed his hands over the things on the coffee tables—Pete's laptop, the ashtray, an empty teacup, a snowglobe she'd bought Jack when they drove to Brighton. "Wondering how I got in?" he cocked his eyebrow at Pete. "Wondering how I got here in the first place?"

He sat on her sofa, arms out, ankle over knee like he sat there every day. "Imagine my surprise when my zombie shambles home and informs me he met a feisty little mage in Coldharbour Lane. A feisty little female mage using *Fiach Dubh* magic that *I* was under the impression had died with the *last* soppy little wanker who tried to throw his weight around and found himself wanting."

Fuck you, Pete tried for, but she couldn't even croak this time. She was at the edge of unconsciousness, and she heard her blood rushing past her ears like a flight of birds, light and feathery as her heartbeat faded.

"But then I remembered." Naughton leaned forward and helped himself to a fag from the pack on the table. "That soppy wanker had himself a sweet little lady friend, who's exactly the sort of persistently nosy bitch who'd be hanging around a dead policeman's flat. And I found you in no time at all." He sat back, lit, and drew a cherry on the end of his fag, and all at once Pete felt the curse lift. "You're looking very well," Naughton said. "I'm sorry for your loss."

Pete stayed still. It wouldn't do to move too soon. Taking a body-bind curse was like taking a cricket bat to the kidneys—blunt and stunning, until the magic had ebbed. She focused on breathing first, in and out, the sweet, stale air of the flat and Naughton's cigarette. Moving would come in good time. Naughton wasn't going to off her straightaway. He'd had his chance when she'd walked in like she was strolling down fucking Oxford Street. He might still torture and kill her, but right now he was going for maximum theatricality. He wanted to frighten her into something, so she had a little time.

"World's dangerous these days," Naughton told her. "Can't trust a bloody soul. Looks like your friend McCorkle discovered that rather more abruptly than most." He held out his hand, beckoned with his palm. "I'll have what you took from his flat."

"Fuck you," Pete said. It came out quite loud that time.

Naughton set his fag down with precision on the edge of the ashtray, and then walked up to Pete and kicked her hard, once, in the stomach. "Don't think you fool me," he said, patting her down efficiently and finding the bag. "You're so scared your poor little breast is heaving." He sat back on his heels, unrolled the crumpled plastic, and dropped the object wrapped in red thread into his palm.

Feathers and a bundle of black herb protruded, and Pete felt a thin spike find purchase behind her eyes, just a flit of power, a solar flare that died quickly as it rose.

"Not much juice left in it," Naughton said. "Still, would be awkward if the police put it in one of those neat little baggies and eventually, by dint of the thin gleam of light making it up to their head through the crack of their arse, discovered what this little beauty is for." He retreated, picked up his fag again.

Pete tried putting a little weight on her arms and found she could sit up, though everything swam into trim more slowly than she had. No heroic kung fu moves, then. "You knew McCorkle?"

"Only as a thief and a brigand," said Naughton, tossing the little bundle in his hand.

"Jesus Christ, who says *brigand* anymore?" Pete said. She drew her legs under her, pulled herself to sit on the low table, and got her own fag. Kept everything slow and easy, not because she didn't want Naughton getting the wrong idea but because she still felt as if she might pitch face-first into the carpet if she went too quickly.

"Freddy McCorkle bought something from Gerard Carver, something that belonged to me," Naughton said. "He was as dirty as a fucking ha'penny whore's twat, a bent copper, whatever you want to say. You think it's fate he attached himself to Ollie Heath like a barnacle? With Heath comes you, dear

Petunia, and occult artifacts would have bought Mr.
McCorkle a lovely terrace in Highgate to live out his
days."

"You kill him?" Pete dragged. Breathed. Watched
Naughton's every twitch.

"I planted the seed," Naughton said. He tapped
the bundle once against Pete's nose. "It's just a bit
of hoodoo magic, whispers in your ear, makes you
think perhaps this life is a bit too much to take."
He shoved the thing into his pocket. "Peasant shit,
but I thought I was rather clever. And before you
ask, I had no direct hand in the untimely death of
Gerard fucking Carver."

"Wasn't going to ask that," Pete said. "Just wondering if you were going to be leaving any time
soon, or should I call for some takeaway?"

"Did the police find something in McCorkle's
flat?" Naughton asked.

"They found a lot of somethings," Pete said.
"Mainly blood, from where poor Freddy decided to
carve himself a new smile with a bread knife." She
stubbed her fag out, put weight on the balls of her
feet. She could be up and moving if she had to, and
that would have to be good enough. "You wouldn't
be thinking of a Babylonian funerary tablet, would
you? The kind Carver was nicking from the museum?"

Naughton clapped his hands together. "Oh, very
good. Always the detective, even when she's not.
No, my dear. That was not precisely what I meant.
But I do thank you for not stalling and trying for
doelike innocence. I'd hate to have to take a hand to
that sweet little face."

"I'd hate to see you after you tried," Pete said.
"Anything else?"

"We're finished, I think," Naughton said. "Obligatory advice: Stop poking at my business. Gerard got exactly what was coming to him. Next time, it won't be one lousy zombie."

"I'm not scared of you," Pete told him. She waved the pack of Parliaments at him. "You owe me fags. And a new protection hex."

"Get somebody who halfway knows what they're doing in next time," Naughton said. "That one was a bit embarrassing."

"Leave," Pete told him. "You can come in any time you want, I'm not safe in my own home. Point fucking made. Kindly let me be."

Naughton picked up his leather coat and slid into it like a snake retaking its skin, broad shoulders flexing under oily black. "Just this, Petunia: You're quick and brave and all the things a Weir should be, but when it comes right down to it, you're a receptacle for mages. Not even a magical pussy, or any sort of that feminist claptrap. A rubber lying in the gutter. You catch the leavings of magic. And your mage is dead, and the Black isn't the place of heroes and cowboys any longer." He opened her door and fished a pair of sunglasses from his coat. "Don't push me. I'll fucking gut you."

Pete didn't move for ten minutes after the door shut, and when she did, all of her blood equalized with a feeling like plunging off the first drop in a roller coaster. Her muscles felt weak, kittenish, and she stumbled to the front door, throwing the deadbolt, the second lock, and the hasp at the top of the jamb, which she didn't think Jack had bothered to lock, ever.

She watched her fingers shake for a moment, clasping the old iron. The curse was gone but the cold was still with her. Nick Naughton had come into her home, into her fucking flat, and he'd paralyzed her without so much as a word. He could have done anything—raped her, killed her, made her rise again as one of his spirits like his brother, Danny.

He hadn't, but he'd known she'd think of it later, and know he *could* have. And that would be worse.

Pete checked the locks on all the windows, especially the kitchen window that looked out onto the fire stairs, and then she got the bottle from the cupboard and poured herself three fingers of whiskey, which she gulped down with two fast, hard swallows.

Her hands still rattled the glass as she set it down, and pulled her knees up to her chest on the sofa. Her heart continued to thrum until she'd poured another inch of whiskey into herself. She was scared of Naughton—anyone in their right mind would be scared by an unstable necromancer breaking into their flat—but she wasn't afraid of him. Petty thug-level threats meant she'd scared him, too.

At the very least, his line about Gerard Carver was a load of crap. If Naughton hadn't held the knife, he knew who did. He'd set up McCorkle, and he knew what spell Carver had been meant to work. He knew it all.

Pete went and put her glass in the kitchen sink, working her fingers on the porcelain edge until she was sure all the feeling had returned. Lawrence and probably even Jack would tell her to leave it, let Naughton think he'd won, and back the fuck off before she found herself with a sliced throat or worse.

But he'd come into her home, threatened her. She doubted Morningstar would be dissuaded by the tale, either. And if Pete was honest with herself, Nick

Naughton had royally trampled on her toes, and she'd relish the opportunity to do a bit of stomping in return.

She wrote down the number Lawrence had given her for Motor, and then went to bed, burrowing under the coverlet until the last of the cold disappeared.

CHAPTER 17

Her first stop that evening, after she'd dealt with her new crop of bruises and cuts and found clothes that covered the worst ones, was a council block in Peckham, some of the new construction, very neat and tidy, with a geranium sprouting in the front window of number thirteen. Pete knocked with the flat of her fist. "Denny!"

A curtain twitched, and a moment later the door was thrown open. "Fuck off!" Denny Pendergast told her. "I'm clean, and you ain't even a cop any longer."

Pete folded her arms. "At least half of that is bullshit, and anyway, I'm not here in my former professional capacity."

"I should fucking hope not." He sniffed. "Considering the only job you'd have nowadays that'd allow you to knock on my door would be mail girl or prozzie."

"I'm a private citizen and that means I can put a steel-toed boot in your crotch with very little repercussion," Pete told him. "Let me in, unless you want to conduct business in the breezeway, all smiling for the CCTVs. Somehow I don't think you've been out of Pentonville long enough to show off."

Denny grumbled and pulled the door wide. He knew she couldn't do fuck-all about anything she saw inside, and he was grinning as her eyes roved over the stacks of newspapers, the broken-down sofa facing the high-end gaming system and LCD television, and the pair of plain black gun safes that comprised Denny's sitting room.

"I need a pistol," she told him. Denny's skinny sharp-boned face split in a wary grin.

"You're pulling my leg."

Pete pointed at the cut on her face, which had gone from bloody gash to angry red line. She wasn't sure which was worse. "Do I look like I'm pulling your bony leg, you tosser?"

Denny considered, and then went to the safe on the left and punched in a combination. "What sort you need?"

"Sig Sauer?"

He snorted. "In your fucking dreams. Copper wants a copper's gun. There's a shock." He gestured at the safes. "I've revolvers from the stone age, Steyer knockoffs out of Russia, and if you're considering an upgrade, couple of fucking pristine Winchester Model Sevens. For you, I give the civil-service discount. Cash up front, no refunds, no exchanges."

"I just need something small I can shove in my jeans," Pete sighed. "And that takes ammo enough to do some real damage with the first shot."

Denny raised a finger. "My stock's not classy enough for your kind of person, Former Detective

Inspector Caldecott, but I did take something in trade last week. Wait here."

He returned with a pistol wrapped in cloth. "It's a fucking antique but it'll get the job done."

Pete hefted the little Walther and tucked it into the waistband of her denim, smoothing her jacket over it. She might as well have been concealing nothing at all. It wasn't slick and nickle plated like James Bond's, but she wasn't about to get picky over aesthetics. "It shoots?"

"'Course it shoots." Denny pulled an offended face. "I'd be out of business pretty fucking quick if I sold ornamental shooters."

"Fine," Pete said, taking the gun out and testing the weight and balance. It was a good little piece, and deceptively heavy. "How much?"

"On the house, provided you never, ever come back here again," Denny said. "It's a showy piece, high-end. I sell it to some fucking street hustler, he shoots some fucking boy over some drunken fight, the cops find the original owner and through that whiny little ponce find me. Doing me a favor." He handed her a box of bullets. "Hollow point. You'll tear a bloke up with those."

"Cheers." Pete secreted the box in her bag and the Walther back in her waistband. "Bye, Denny."

"Oi," Denny said, when she was on the stoop. "You never did tell me what you want an untraceable piece for, Caldecott. Always figured you were a regular straight arrow. Charged into battle with your baton and a prayer."

"Me?" Pete smoothed her shirt over the gun. "No. Straight arrow is something I don't have the luxury of being any longer."

Denny started to say something, but he changed it midstream to, "Where you off to?"

Pete stepped into the breezeway and zipped her coat against the chill that came with sunset. "I'm off to see a man about a corpse."

CHAPTER 18

Whatever else happened, Pete felt calmer having decided on one thing—if Nicholas Naughton came near her again, she was going to put two bullets between his eyes. The sick stomach and itch on the back of her neck she'd felt since Naughton had broken into her flat finally calmed a little.

She saw the owl sitting on a lightpost soon after she got off the tube in Southwark. It stared at her, unblinking. Pete flicked it off and approached a boy on the corner, shiny red and gold windcheater and iPod marking him as the kind of hustler she needed. "Oi."

He looked up at her with bright, speed-contracted pupils. "Wot?"

"You know a club called Motor?"

The hustler blinked rapidly at her. "Sure I do, but it ain't the kind of place you want."

Pete had dressed the part, black army jacket, boots, black denim. No copper signals from her. The hustler's reluctance was, as far as she was concerned, just being contrary. "Why not?"

"Ain't for straight folks," the hustler said. "Now, you want something to taste, I gots crystal, hash, pills, morphine . . ."

"Regular little underground Boots, aren't you?" Pete said. She pulled out a tenner and folded it between her fingers. When the hustler grabbed for it, she snatched it back. "Motor. Where?"

"Your funeral, ain't it?" the hustler sighed. He pointed to an abandoned building at the end of the block. "Down in the cellar. You won't get in, though. Need a password, like one of them skeevy sex clubs."

"Thanks for that," Pete said. "*Time Out* should come 'round and interview you, really."

The hustler dialed his iPod back up. Pete walked, and the shadow of the owl flicked over her face as it glided away beneath the streetlamps.

The Hecate could send all the omens she wanted. Pete wasn't biting. She had far more pressing issues, like how she was going to talk her way into Motor. And trying to ignore the nerves, telling her it was a bad fucking idea in the first place, that she wouldn't learn anything new, and might get the shit kicked out of her besides.

A cross faced her when she reached the door the hustler had pointed at, covered over with several layers of racist graffiti and concert posters advertising bands that had last come through London several years previous. OUR LADY OF GOOD COUNSEL had been painted across the facade, but the letters been defaced to GOOD CO N.

The neon underneath the facade crunched beneath her boots, shattered, and the burn marks spelled out

REPENT TO THE LORD, FOR ONLY IN HIM WILL YOU FIND SALVATION.

The basement level, at the bottom of a narrow set of brick steps, appeared to have staved off vandalism, in the form of a heavy fire door that looked as if it could withstand an IRA bomb. Pete pressed the buzzer. The Black was thick here, gathering in what had once been a sacred place, profane as a swastika across the face of the Virgin Mary. The energy wasn't friendly, as much as the Black was ever friendly. Pete felt it tighten against her skull, trying to worm its way inside and fill up her reservoirs. She shut her eyes and breathed short and sharp through her nose. Pressed the buzzer again.

Thunder cracked somewhere close, and a smattering of rain fell on Pete before a slot in the door slid open, and an eye regarded her. "Yeah?"

"I'm . . ." Pete started, ready to flirt, threaten, or lie her way inside as the occasion called for. She knew enough names to chat a good game, at least until someone more intelligent than a door minder got involved.

"Pete Caldecott," said the eye's owner. "Hang on."

Pete composed herself in the few seconds it took the fire door to unlock itself and roll open. She'd never thought her name would get her anything in the Black except grief.

The eye belonged to a bouncer, and the bouncer was, contrary to gravelly growl and shaved head, a woman, half a foot taller and probably twice as wide as Pete. "You're not much, are you?" she asked Pete.

"You look like enough for both of us," Pete said. The bouncer stepped aside and clapped her on the back hard enough to realign her vertebrae.

"Have fun, little girl."

Motor started out in a long, oppressive hall that seemed to vanish into an event horizon, painted as it was in jet black with white, light-reactive graffiti over the entire length that faded as the dark encroached again with the slamming of the door.

Music flowed through the walls, up through the soles of her boots and into her bones. Hard, percussive, post-apocalyptic music that made you want to put a fist through someone's face. She caught the tail end of "Ace of Spades" before it switched over to an old track by Slayer.

A beaded curtain parted before her, and a couple stumbled out, girl and boy attired almost identically in studs, denim, and blunt, face-breaking boots. Pete gave them a berth, as their clothes were already starting to come off.

She pushed the curtain, sticky with nicotine residue, aside, and stepped into the club proper. There had been plenty of shady dives in her days following Jack's band around, but none made her feel quite so much as if she'd stepped into the Wild West.

The music emanated from an ancient, scarred Wurlitzer that dominated one wall, red lights rotating over the gathering of faces in a gibbous, arhythmic pattern, like living blood spatter. PA speakers grew from snaking cables and sprouted over the pit like cubist flowers.

Gleaming white paintings continued over all the walls, flaring and fading as light hit. Giant eyes, inverted pentagrams, all of it just a bit too sharp and real to be random graffiti. Motor might have been a club on the daylight side, but Naughton's fleshcrafters had been busy decorating.

The club consisted of a bar, blocked in with razor wire except for a few small gaps through which a bartender roughly the size and shape of a lorry pushed pints, the pit, and a stage. The stage was empty, but the pit was full, flashing metal and flowing ink over skin, the crunch and thud of flesh and bone connecting, hard.

Pete joined the crowd around the bar, taking an inventory of the locals before she did anything foolish, like open her mouth. If Naughton had really been serious, somebody would find her and scold her soon enough. The song changed again, and the rhythm of the pit increased, bodies heaving like corpses on a tide.

Arms shoved her, and a bloke with a mohawk held stiff by orange spray-paint knocked into her, moving her away from the bar and toward the edge of the pit. Pete turned around and shouted "Oi!" but the mass had their backs to her, focused on shouting orders at the bartenders. "Fucking Hell," Pete said. Her bruises reminded her to be more careful about being shoved while she studied the crowd. No faces popped out. What had she been expecting? A sinister backroom where all of Naughton's secrets would be revealed? Dark rites conducted in the VIP lounge? The reality was a grungy, passé club full of metalheads and smells she could just as well do without.

Another body brushed against her, and Pete's foot skidded over the edge of the pit. Just enough to put her off balance, and she felt herself going over. It wasn't a far drop, less than a meter, but she fell badly and landed on the shoulder the zombie had already scored with. The crowd pressed in above her, as if she were lying at the foot of a row of gravestones, granite angels watching her with pale, sightless eyes in the flicking strobe light.

The music turned to indecipherable feedback

through the antique PA as a boot landed in her gut, then another. Pete curled to protect herself, but there were feet and hands from all directions. The floor shook as one, then another, then a herd of the spectators dropped into the pit and crammed it even more. Another boot, a steel toe, connected with her shoulder blade and a cry escaped her lips, lost in the static and the screaming speakers.

Dancers paid her no mind, their movements changing from pogos and flying elbows to a concentrated orgy of blunt force that began at the foot of the stage and rippled out. She saw a woman grab the man next to her and pull his head down to connect with her knee. Two other men began bashing their skulls together, the sound of bloody meat going straight to her gut.

Around Pete, the air changed, as if the storm outside had wormed its way in. The insidious cold that she'd learned the hard way to associate with necromantic spells crept across her face. She fumbled for her pistol, attempting to protect her midsection and breasts with her free arm. She didn't know what good, exactly, a handful of bullets would do her, but she wasn't bloody well going to kick off on the sticky, ale-scented floorboards of a shitty metal club.

The violence rose as if a toxic tide were sweeping the pit, and Pete felt a warm spatter of raindrops across her face. Her tongue tasted of iron. A woman in leathers jumped on the back of a shirtless skinhead, gnawing at the Aryan tattoos arrayed across his shoulder blades. A pink-haired girl, even smaller than Pete, shrieked in time with the wordless whorl of sound as she beat her spiked bracelets against her own temples.

Feet and bodies impacted with her, buffeted her,

lifted her up and slammed her back down. Pete felt a sharp, hot pain in her side and wagered a boot had cracked one of her ribs. Bodies pressed too close to allow her air, never mind space to crawl away. All around her in the pit the dancers screamed and flung themselves on one another.

A hand closed on the back of her jacket, and strong arms yanked her free of the throng, as it howled and spat and gouged at one another's eyes. Pete railed against the arms for a moment, until she realized they weren't groping or clawing, simply wrapped around her torso, holding her flush against a warm, hard chest heaving with its own breathlessness, encased in a black cotton shirt scented with whiskey, tobacco, and magic.

Pete twisted her head, in the low stuttering light of the club, and felt her body drop away from her heart. "Jack?"

PART TWO

THE UNDERWORLD

When there is no more room in Hell,
the dead will walk the earth.

—Dawn of the Dead

CHAPTER 19

Jack stared down at her for a pair of heartbeats. Pete stared back, unable to think of a single thing to say. The pain all over told her she was awake; the warmth of his body told Pete he was alive. She wasn't dreaming. He wasn't dead.

"Haven't lost your talent for finding big fucking trouble, I see," he said at last.

Him speaking let Pete move again. She drew back her hand and cracked Jack hard across the mouth. "You fucking bastard! I thought you were fucking *dead*."

"Christ and fucking Christmas," Jack yelped, stumbling away from her. "What happened to *Thanks very much, Jack*? I saved your courageous little arse just now."

"You *left* me is what you *did*," Pete hissed. "You fucking *left*."

"Well, I'm here now!" Jack said, swiping at his lip. "Dammit to Hell, do you have to play so rough, Petunia? At least give me a chance to explain meself."

"Go piss up a fucking rope," Pete snapped. "And then do me a favor and hang your lying arse with it."

In her dreams, when she saw Jack again, she'd never shouted at him. Of course, in her dreams, they'd both been dead and the reunions had a very different cast.

Jack had let her think for more than half a year that he was gone for good, let her toss sleeplessly over him, shove all of his memories into cardboard boxes in the back of her mind, where they couldn't paralyze her, and he was fucking *smirking* at her like he'd just done a particularly clever trick.

He stared at her for a moment and then the smirk bloomed into that infuriating grin. He ensnared her in his embrace again and pulled her against him hard enough to make her cracked rib scream. "Fuck, it's good to see you," he said against her hair. "Really bloody good."

"Sod you, Jack Winter," Pete responded, shoving at him until he took a hard step back from her force and nearly fell. "You don't get to ramble back here smiling as if you've just landed from holiday."

"Fair enough," Jack said. "But let's move the heartfelt speech of righteous indignation elsewhere. This isn't the place for nice girls like you, Petunia." He gestured at the pit, floor slick with black, shimmering blood. "Point of fact, it's not the place for naughty boys like me, either."

"If you think," Pete started, "that you can just reappear from the bloody dead and start ordering me about, you've got another fucking thing coming, Jack. In fact . . ."

He grabbed her hard by the shoulders, and Pete felt the pinpoints where his fingers would leave round bruises under her clothes. Jack's mouth closed over hers, hard and warm, depositing the taste of whiskey on her lips. Pete sought his tongue through no accord of her own, her fingernails digging into the warm, tattooed skin of his forearms as she gripped him. She couldn't breathe, couldn't hear, couldn't feel. Nothing except him.

"What the . . . what the *fuck* is going on? What was that?" she demanded, when she trusted herself to make whole sentences again.

"It's an orgy," Jack said, tugging her past the bar and down a back hall that led to a closed door and a pair of loos that stank of bleach. "A blood orgy. You know, like sex 'cept with smashing faces instead of fucking?" He patted down his pockets, drew out a fag, and touched his finger to the end. Smoke curled up to tangle in the rancid air of Motor. "About *that* . . ." He gave her that smile again, tongue flicking across his bottom lip. "Told you. It's good to see you."

"How did you even know where I was?" Pete said. She desperately wanted a cigarette of her own, but her pack was smashed, just tobacco and shredded paper, after her encounter with the pit. She tossed it away.

"Followed you," Jack said. "And I have to say, I was a bit disappointed you didn't spot me. Though you've been busy. It's understandable."

Pete cast an eye back toward the club. The violence was slowing down, going to ground, bodies twitching and choking out on their own fluids and internal bleeds. A few figures intertwined, their grunts audible above the noise of the music.

"It's a cantrip," Jack said. "Musty Babylonian chanting to get you in the mood. Sounds like cats fucking in an echo chamber, don't it?"

"You *followed* me?" Pete put her eyes back on him. She could scarcely believe it was really happening, that he was here, in front of her, as if she'd wished him there. Without meaning to, she put out a hand and squeezed him on the shoulder. He was solid, there. More solid than she remembered, really. Jack had always erred to skinny and mean rather than meaty. "For how long?" she said.

He shrugged, ash falling off the end of his fag. "Couple of days, I suppose. Which reminds me, I own Lawrence a smack right in the teeth for letting you anywhere near the Antiquarians."

"*Days*?" Pete felt the heat in her breast rise again. "I'll fetch *you* a smack. Jack, I thought you were fucking *dead*."

His face closed up, all of the lines she remembered coming into relief. He shrugged off her hand. "I was dead, Pete. For a nice long while. Now I'm not. Do we need to make more of it than that?"

"Jack . . ." Pete ground her fingers into her temples. The howling, pulsing music was creeping into her, up through her feet, making her pulsate with it everywhere that hurt. "Jack, you can't just be *dead* and then *here* . . ."

Jack picked up her hand again, put it against his face, and pulled her close with his free arm, pressing them together from her waist to her breasts. "And yet, I am. You can put me off if you want." He put his mouth against her neck, breath hot when he spoke. "You're right. I've been a cunt."

His skin, where it touched hers, bare to bare, closed a current that Pete's body had ached for since the first time Jack had touched her, back when she hadn't known any man could touch her like that. "No," she managed. "I'm giving you a pass. Just this once."

"Fan-fucking-tastic," Jack growled, and his fingers curled in the waistband of her trousers, searching and tugging at the fly button and zipper. Pete shoved his hands away, and felt a twinge low in her stomach when their skin lost contact.

"I . . . I can't . . . ," she managed. "We . . ."

"Come on, luv." Jack attacked her neck again, then her earlobe, tangling the fingers of his right hand in Pete's hair to expose more flesh. "Being dead's like being in jail. Shit food and no women. 'Specially not ones hot as you."

"Jack, stop it!" Pete shoved him again, putting her back into it. The shrieking music made any conversation besides screaming or lipreading impossible, but Pete put her mouth near Jack's ear and tried. "This noise is mucking with your mind!"

Jack blinked once, and then rubbed the heel of his hand into his temple, a gesture Pete found so familiar she felt as if she'd been kicked in the stomach all over again. "Sorry!" Jack shouted. "I told you we needed to get out of here!"

"After you!" Pete said. Jack took her hand, but before they could get far the blank door at the end of the hall opened, and a man in a black suit emerged. He pointed at Pete, and then at Jack, and beckoned.

"Yeah, don't think so," Jack mumbled, tugging her along. Pete fetched up when two more figures appeared at the other end of the hallway, blocking the way to the front door and bottlenecking her with little choice but to turn around.

"Do you know these gits?" Jack whisper-shouted at her as the trio herded them toward the blank door.

"Yeah," Pete said. "You're not going to like it."

She'd expected something in keeping with the rest of Motor, lots of leather and rivets and maybe some light BDSM decoration, but what lay beyond the door was a blandly modern office filled with ASDA furniture and an LCD screen flickering between grainy CCTV images piped in from the larger club.

Nick Naughton sat behind the glass desk, rocking his chair back and forth. "Now, this is confusing. I recall telling you only this morning to stay the fuck out of my business."

Beside her, Pete felt Jack stiffen. "You twat," was all he said. Naughton regarded him, one eyebrow up.

"Mr. Winter. I was under the impression you were no longer with us."

"Check your sources," Jack suggested. "If you have time before I come over that desk and wring your neck."

"All right, all right," Pete said, snatching Jack by the arm before he could get himself wrapped in a curse like the one Naughton had thrown at her. "No need to measure. We all know you're the big man, Naughton."

One of the suits patted her down and took away the Walther. Naughton shook his head as if she'd disappointed him, and nudged the gun away from him. "Mind telling me what you think you're doing in my place of business?"

"Business?" Pete jerked a thumb at the door. "That's what you call that out there?"

"Don't be cute," Naughton said. "Or I might not be so calm. Why are you here?"

"I think you're a fucking liar and you broke into my flat," Pete said, deciding any excuse but the truth would just get them run through a wood-chipper and scattered in someone's garden.

Jack twitched again at the mention of Naughton

in the flat, and Pete dug her fingers into his arm. He'd definitely put on muscle—he was hard in places where he'd been stringy, and his skin was hot under her fingers.

"Hmm," Naughton said. He shoved his chair back and stood up. "Bring them here," he told the suits, who hustled Pete and Jack through a door in the rear of the office and through a closed-down kitchen. Water dripped and roaches scuttled out of Pete's way.

"I can't say you're making my life easier," Naughton said, "but it appears you may be the solution to an intractable problem." One of the suits opened a rust-rimmed door to a walk-in freezer, and Pete nearly slipped on the damp floor when she saw inside.

"He's giving me the silent treatment," Naughton said, brandishing a finger at Ollie, who was tied to a chair and sporting a cheek and eye that were swollen and starting to go blue. "I don't fucking appreciate it."

"Ollie . . ." Pete went toward him reflexively, to insert herself between Heath and Naughton, but one of the suits hauled her back and slammed her into the metal wall. Her skull connected with a dull *bong*.

"Naughty," he said, and kept his hand on her breastbone, pinning her as if she weighed no more than an insect on a display card.

"There's absolutely no need for this," Pete said. "Please. I'll never bother you again. Just let Ollie be."

"No, don't think I will," Naughton said. He squeezed Ollie's swollen jaw between his thumb and forefinger, forcing a whimper from Heath. "This fat bastard is being remarkably uncooperative. I think he fancies himself a hard man." Naughton let go of Ollie and backhanded him on the bruised side of his face, reopening a cut under Ollie's eye with his thick silver ring. "That right, hard man?"

Ollie sucked dried blood between his teeth. "Your mum seemed to think I was a hard man when I bent her over," he said, tongue thick from the earlier beating Pete could read all over his face.

She bucked against the suit's hand, but he pressed down harder, so she couldn't do anything except breathe with ease. "There's no need for that!" she shouted at Naughton. "You've no quarrel with him."

"I beg to differ," Naughton said. "I've got quite a persistent quarrel with Inspector Heath, seeing as how he's repeatedly refused my very simple and reasonable request." He moved his gaze between Pete and Jack. "However, your intrusion does give me an idea."

Pete looked to Jack as well. He stood very still, a pillar of black cloth and pale skin, hand loose at his side. He didn't return her look, just drilled his glacial eyes into Naughton as if he wanted very badly to slice off his face and make it into a hat. She was on her own as the rational half, then. That really wasn't any great leap from when Jack had been alive. With her. She'd think over the proper phrasing later. Pete put her attention back on Naughton. "Can't wait to be dazzled with your brilliance, Nicky."

"You'd get a lot further in this life if you at least pretended not to loathe the entirety of the human race," he told her. Naughton removed a cloth rag from his jacket and wiped Ollie's blood from his ring. "I'm proposing that I pass the recalcitrant inspector's task to you, and he will stay here, receiving my hospitality, until such a time as I'm satisfied."

Naughton was a reptile. Not in the sense that Pete would have gladly kicked him in the teeth and called him a bloody snake if she got the chance, but in that he had cold blood and cold nerves, the kind of sociopathic politeness endemic to gangsters and professional soldiers. He was a camouflaged monster, walking and wearing a man's clothes, buying groceries and smiling at pretty girls, until the skin shed, and the dead eyes and venom-filled mouth underneath showed themselves. All that did was make Pete more likely to acquiesce to him, not less. Naughton was a legitimately scary bastard. Pete didn't make a habit of getting on the wrong side of those, especially not when they had her best friend tied to a chair. "Fine," she told Naughton. She lifted her hands and pointed at the suit. "I'm agreeing to be civil. Could you possibly ask your Pomeranian here to quit groping me?"

Naughton waved his hand and the suit stepped back, giving her a smile that revealed that he had the sort of hobbies where teeth were knocked from his head with regularity. "Gerard Carver," he said. "We want him back."

"Back?" Pete said. "Isn't that more your department, Nicky?"

"His corpse," Naughton said. "Gerard Carver's immortal soul can be chewed, swallowed, and shat out the arse of Dagon for all I care. But his corpse, I would very much like returned."

"I'm sure you've already thought this through," Pete said, hoping that Naughton wasn't even further around the bend than she'd guessed. "But can't you, er . . . retrieve Carver yourself? 'S not like the Wapping mortuary has a posse of ninjas guarding the door."

"I'd like to," Naughton said. "But I can't." He patted Heath on the cheek. "Do be quick, Petunia. I think the inspector's already rather homesick."

"Why do you want Carver now?" Pete said. "He already fucked you and got himself made dead. Seems a bit moot."

Naughton twisted his ring. "I'm not finished with him," he told Pete. "That will be all," he said to the suits, and they hustled Pete and Jack back through the crush of fucking, fighting bodies and out the front door. It slammed behind Pete, and the quiet of the night street replaced the vacuum.

"Well, *that* was fifty kilos of fun in a forty kilo sack," Jack said, acid etching the words. "I'd murder somebody for a fag."

Pete sat down hard before she fell down, making even more of an arse of herself.

Jack sat next to her, and wordlessly she gave him a cigarette. "You've had a bit of a makeover," he said, lighting it. "Gun-toting, playing nice with necromancers—you're a regular dangerous type these days, Petunia."

Pete lit a fag for herself. "You've been gone awhile, Jack."

"True enough," he said.

"So, are we going to talk about this?" Pete said. "Or am I supposed to accept coming back from the dead as a part of your inscrutable mystique?"

"You just found yourself agreeing to steal a corpse from the police at the behest of a circle jerk of bastard necromancers, and you're worried about a little resurrection?" Jack tsked. "Priorities, Petunia."

Pete fetched him a punch on the arm, hard. He yelped and lost his cigarette. "Are you bloody five? That hurt."

"You're going to tell me the truth," Pete warned. "As soon as we have this sorted. You get me?"

Jack rubbed his arm. "Never said I wouldn't. Fuck me, you've got bony hands."

Pete pointed herself in the general direction of the tube station. "Mortuary's closed this time of night. Station's running a light crew."

Jack shoved his hands into his pockets. "Really think that fool's errand Nancy Naughton gave you will be that easy?"

"Of course not," Pete agreed. "But it's not as if I have a choice, so let's get on with it."

CHAPTER 20

Southwark to Wapping was a long ride, longer when you were trying not to shout everything that came into your head at the person who was taking the trip with you. Pete tried not to stare at Jack under the harsh fluorescent light of the train car, either, but she admitted by the time they rattled past Bermondsey station it was a lost cause. They were alone, this late in the evening, except for a few sleepy wage workers and a bored transit officer looking off into space.

Under light, Jack didn't look as good as he had in the club. His skin was pallid. She could see veins, how his blood moved through his body, the stark, shining whiteness of the scar on his cheek. Twin half moons had taken up residence under his eyes, as if they'd always lived there, deep and purple, fading away into the lines she remembered.

She voiced the least offensive thing she could think of. "You look tired."

"Yeah." Jack rolled his neck back and forth. Small bones popped. "Being alive will do that to you."

The train ground to a stop at Wapping, and the doors hissed open. They walked in silence the rest of the way to the mortuary. Pete couldn't think of another topic that didn't involve *So, Hell. Hear it's lovely this time of year.*

"Right," Jack said, when they reached the stern brick edifice of the mortuary, boats hooting on the Thames as if warning of their approach. "So I assume you've got a plan all worked out."

"Of course not," Pete said. "It's a city works building, and there's CCTV all over the bloody place, not to mention, you know, police officers."

Jack grimaced. "Fuck. Stealing corpses in Thailand was much easier."

"Unfortunately, Naughton seems set on this particular corpse," Pete said. "Any actual helpful idea would be shockingly appreciated."

"Whole thing stinks," Jack said. His entire body was wire-tight, and if Pete didn't know better she'd swear he was back on smack and jonesing hard, from the way his fingers played the air and his eyes darted from side to side. Pools of dark beyond the lamps in front of the station revealed nothing.

"Cheers, Captain Obvious," Pete said. "Necromancers demanding you steal a corpse is rarely a harbinger of unicorns, rainbows, and candy-filled shopping trolleys."

Jack laughed. "So sharp, luv. Don't tell me our brief separation has turned you into a bitter spinster."

"Not in the least," Pete said, "though our brief reunion has caused me to entertain the notion of shoving my boot up your arse." She discarded the idea of the main door at once. It was locked at this hour, requiring a desk officer to buzz you in, and a camera across the street pointed directly at it. She walked down the close between the mortuary and the next building, back toward the museum on the history of the Thames patrol and the modern marine support building. Jack followed her.

"Are we actually going to give this dead bloke to Naughton? Because I have to say, I don't fancy it."

Pete jiggled the handle of the delivery entrance, keeping her face shy of the CCTV camera. Locked. "You're actually asking for my opinion? You really have changed."

"Heath's your friend," Jack said. "And in spite of being a rotten, nasty pig, he's not a bad sort. I won't kick up a fuss if you do exactly as Naughton asks, but I'm on record as saying it's a shite idea. Your call, Petunia."

"We'll have a better chance during the day," Pete said. Ollie wasn't going to stay in one piece if she got rash and found herself locked up by Patel, who'd think Christmas had come bloody early if he nicked her absconding with evidence.

Jack nodded. "Morning, then."

"Don't be too overjoyed," Pete warned. "Because when we get home you're going to tell me why you're really back here."

CHAPTER 21

When he stepped into the flat, Jack paused with one toe over the threshold and one still in the hall. "Protection hex is shot. Lawrence should have laid it again."

"He's not on call for me." Pete tried taking off her jacket and immediately regretted the attempt, all the way down to her bones. Her shoulder throbbed and there were ink-blot bruises already turning purple up and down her arm. She'd have them on her stomach, too, and felt a dull twinge every time she breathed. Her cracked rib chimed in with a gleeful jab.

"Fucking layabout, is what he is," Jack muttered. He went into the kitchen and rattled around in drawers, returning with a black zip-up bag. "Where's me chalk? Used to have enough to run a school."

Pete spread her hands. "Do we really have to do this now?"

"In case you haven't noticed . . . ," Jack said, curling his lip in the way Pete hated. It meant he was about to impart Great Knowledge to her, the mundane who knew fuck-all about magic. "The Black isn't the friendliest of places these days."

"Don't know what you're talking about," Pete said. "Since you've been gone, it's been a regular tea party."

Jack flopped down on the sofa, dropping the bag. "I'm done in, Pete. Fucking wrung out. I don't want to argue or have a meaningful conversation. I just want to clean up the mess and then get pissed and go to sleep for about a month."

"Oh, it's my mess, is it?" Pete said. "All of this shit cropped up like flowers in horse manure after you made your little devil's bargain and left me to fend for myself?"

"Pete . . ." Jack warned, but she cut him off.

"Sod you, Jack. It's your flat, and you're welcome to stay here, but you can sleep on the sofa and I don't need your fucking condescension disguised as a helping hand."

She slammed and latched the bedroom door, but the force wasn't enough. Pete unlaced her boots and chucked them against the far wall. They chipped the plaster with a satisfying crash, but the noise didn't lessen the aches in Pete's chest. At least not the ache that wasn't from a boot landing in her flesh.

Jack was the one person who could assure her that everything was going to be all right. Except he wasn't doing it, and Pete wouldn't have believed him now if he did. She dropped backward on the bed and pressed a pillow over her face, letting out a scream. She couldn't give Naughton Carver's body, in spite of Ollie's bind, and she couldn't expect Jack to pull her out of the oncoming freight train's path. Not this time.

He had to be finishing the spell. That was the

only reason. Carver had tried to go freelance, and now Naughton was back in the game. He couldn't have Carver's corpse. Nicholas Naughton was an evil man, and evil from men was the most insidious sort. Whatever Naughton was playing at, she couldn't let him get to the endgame. She had to at least try and pretend she had a spine and a plan to make everyone and everything she'd set into the sights of Naughton's wrath all right.

The owl landed outside the bedroom window with a thump, staring at her with gold, unblinking eyes. Pete shoved the pillow under her head and turned her back on it. "Leave me alone," she muttered.

You know I can't do that, Weir.

Pete felt her breath stop. In the place of the owl sat the woman, small and clad in white, gold eyes and dark hair, skin the same shade as moonlight. She put her hand on the glass, pointed black nails leaving score marks on the pane.

"I don't want this," Pete said. "I don't want you."

Still you have me, Weir. You who are marked as a servant of the crossroads. Whether you desire my ministrations is irrelevant.

Pete sat up, deciding that if the Hecate wasn't going to shut up it was just silly to pretend she wasn't there. The woman watched her. Like the owl, she never blinked. *You allow that abomination to slumber one room away. I told you what to do.*

"I think you're forgetting we're not on the orders given and received system, you and I," Pete told her. "Whatever your problem is with Jack—it's not my problem. Far as I'm concerned, you can float away back to whatever musty corner of my dreams you came from and give me some bloody peace, because I'm not doing it."

You're wrong, you know, the girl whispered. *The crow-mage rides at the head of a bone army, borne on a river of red death. Forget your memory of the man, Weir. The thing he has become must die, or the world dies, and wind will scatter its ashes.*

"I've lost Jack once and it was bloody enough for this lifetime," Pete said. "I won't hurt him. He's not a threat to you, and if you've got a grievance with his patron goddess, maybe you two ladies should hash it out over a cup of tea and stop bothering humans with your spats."

He's not the Jack you know, the Hecate whispered. *The Jack you know could not crawl from Hell unscathed, no matter your faith in him. And you know this is the truth, even if you will not speak it. What has returned in Jack Winter's skin and bones is not Jack Winter as you knew him.*

Fingers of cold spread away from where the Hecate touched the glass, creeping over Pete's skin, down her throat, choking off her air, and the glowing gold eyes filled up her vision, until all she could see was the flame burning at the center, flame that spread out and consumed the walls and the bed, until everything around her was ashes.

She came awake gasping, and it took her a moment to realize she could breathe, she wasn't freezing or burning, and she'd fallen asleep with the pillow jammed at an awkward angle under her neck.

Pete swiped a hand over her forehead. It came away with a sheen of sweat. Her shirt was damp as well, even though the air in the room was cool enough to catch her breath and turn it white. Shivering, she burrowed under the duvet and lay very still, trying to calm her throbbing heartbeat.

She'd had apocalyptic dreams for as long as she

could remember—of Jack, when she'd thought he'd died the first time; of the Morrigan, his spectral, dark-winged goddess; and now of the owl-eyed woman. It was part and parcel of being the Weir. She was an antenna for disturbances in the unseen, and her brain was a projection screen for any and all signals slithering their way through the Black.

This was different, though. Before, she'd known they were dreams. The visions of the Hecate, though—she couldn't pick out the dream from the waking. Those with a talent who couldn't see the Black and the daylight world for what they were had a nasty habit of going insane, or simply chucking themselves into the path of an express train to end the constant, blurring carnival of horrors the Black paraded before them.

The bedroom latch clicked and the door swung ajar after she'd lain there for twenty-four minutes by the glowing clock numerals on the bedstand, and weight settled on the other side of the mattress. "You awake?" Jack said, voice faded to a rough whisper.

"Yeah," Pete said, not bothering to complain at him for using his talent with locks on her privacy. She didn't turn toward him as he settled, but the dire cold finally shook off her bones.

A lighter snapped and flared in the dark, and she listened to Jack drag and exhale before he spoke again. "I think I was a bit of a cunt back there."

"A bit?" Pete did face him then. "That's kind."

"It's so . . . cold . . . here," Jack said. "I feel like I'm in my skin, behind a glass wall. Everything's rushing around me, too fast, and I'm out of step. I . . ." He inhaled on the fag sharply, and Pete watched the ember flare. "I want to tell you. I want to spill my fucking guts, but I can't."

"Can't or won't?" Pete said.

"Can't as in can't bloody remember," Jack said. "I remember . . ." He trailed off, coughed harshly, and stubbed out his fag. "I remember snapshots. Ends of film reels, a few frames here and there. And then I'm waking up next to some bins near Aldgate, and an Iranian fellow is shouting at me to get away from his restaurant. I found you, I followed you when I realized you were in fucking deep shit, as you usually are, and you know it from there."

She wanted to scream at him, hit him with the pillow and say that was no sort of fucking answer, and if he was going to keep dying and reappearing he might as well just flit off permanently. But she swallowed down the scream and reached out, brushing her fingers down his bicep. She swallowed all of the whispers that the Hecate was right and that Jack coming back and not remembering how wasn't a boon, it was a warning, and simply held on to Jack, because he was warm and there and she couldn't bear to have him gone again. "I guess that's enough for now."

He stubbed his cigarette out in a saucer on the bedside table. "Cheers." He started to rise, but Pete tightened her hand on his arm. All at once, she didn't want him out of her sight. If he was close, she'd know he was really there. And her dreams would stay quiet. Jack acted as sort of a psychic buffer, and if she touched him while she was asleep and her defenses were down, he soothed her talent so that it would allow her to rest.

"Stay," she said. Jack sat back down, the line between his eyes deepening.

"You sure?"

Pete nodded and yawned at once. She hadn't really slept in days, and what sleep she'd gotten since Jack had gone had been fitful and fleeting. Plus, she'd had the piss kicked out of her and couldn't have shifted Jack off the bed even if she'd wanted to.

Jack kicked out of his boots and undid his belt, dropping the pyramid-studded strap to the floor. When he swung his feet onto the mattress, Pete saw his socks had holes in both big toes. "Landed in the same clothes I left in," he said. "You'd think Belial would have at least fitted me up with one of those posh three-button jobs he's always gadding around in."

"So you think it was him?" Pete said. "Belial?" A demon who let the soul he'd chased the longest simply stroll back from the jaws of death. Not very demonlike. And certainly not like Belial, who reminded Pete of an obsessive bloke who might spend years chasing a rare stamp. So Belial had sought Jack. And found him. And pinned him to the fucking page. "Jack?" she said, when he didn't answer.

"I told you everything I know, Pete," he mumbled. "When I know more, I'll pass it along."

Pete edged toward the window to give him room, but he stayed close to her. Jack had nearly a foot on her, and his frame easily curled around her body. His arm, with its new weight, lay across her waist.

Breathing against the back of her ear, his words tickled. "All right?"

Pete nodded, and let herself relax against Jack, back to his chest. Whatever else happened, Jack was here. And she knew, even when the Hecate and Pete's own meager knowledge of Hell and all the senses her talent gifted her with said differently, that this was the way it should be.

Jack stroked his fingers down her back, over the

thin material of her shirt. "Been raiding my wardrobe."

"Didn't think you'd mind," Pete mumbled, squirming as Jack's fingers slipped between her denim and the hem.

"Not a bit," Jack said. His finger slalomed between the bones of her spine, until he reached her rib cage and found the side curve of her breast. "All right?" Jack said. Pete bit her lip as the callused tips of his fingers skated against her skin, raising gooseflesh.

"I'm not . . ." Pete shivered as Jack ran his hand down her bruised stomach, gently enough that he just grazed her skin, and found the button on her jeans. "I'm not really in shape for that, Jack."

"Relax, luv," he said, wriggling her jeans over her hips. "I'll be gentle."

"Jack . . ." Pete gasped when his hand dipped into the crevice between her thighs, Jack letting out a contented sigh as his fingers found purchase against her clit.

She didn't need flashing neon to tell her that this was a bad idea. Jack popping back up from Hell with no memory and no marks, fresh and new as if he'd been remade, wasn't a miracle or even, likely, a good thing. The last thing she should be doing, Pete told herself in her stern, Inner-Connor voice, was letting him stick his hand inside her panties.

Jack licked the line of her shoulder, up her neck, and landed back against her ear. "Pete, don't tell me that. Please."

If she told him no, he'd stop. He wasn't a bastard. But he made an excellent point, Pete thought, as he rubbed her more insistently, his other hand sliding under her ribs to bring his shirt over her head. She didn't want to tell him no. She could explain it any way she liked—in the copper way, that told her they'd both suffered a trauma, and were projecting, or even in the plain common sense way, that said hopping back into bed with Jack would net her nothing but headaches. Jack wasn't reliable under the best of circumstances, and these were far from them.

Pete knew she wouldn't throw him out. After six months of thinking she'd never smell him or see him or touch her hand to his skin again, he was here. How and why could be saved for a few hours.

She rolled over, dislodging Jack's hand and fumbling at the fly of his pants. He made a gravelly sound in the back of his throat when she drew out his cock, stroking with both hands between their bodies. "Thank you. . . ." Jack muttered, face in her hair, but Pete shook her head.

"Shut up, Jack. Please just be quiet and fuck me."

He pulled her down to his mouth, hand knotted in the hair at the nape of her neck, and Pete felt him nip her bottom lip. He kissed her as if he were starving until he had his fill, then took Pete by the shoulders and put her on her back, kneeling above her.

"You're so fucking beautiful," Jack said, just a hairsbreadth above a raspy cigarette whisper, and then ducked and lifted Pete's thighs over his shoulders.

She grabbed for his hair when he lowered his mouth onto her clit, taking long, slow strokes that made Pete tighten her fingers in the bleached strands. Jack grunted but didn't lift his tongue, the insistent flicks against her getting quicker and rougher.

"Fuck," Pete gasped, lifting herself to press closer against Jack's mouth. The motion sent a stab through her abused abdomen, but she didn't, at that moment, particularly care. Being with Jack pushed her straight over the edge—there was no slow, no tender with him. He made her want nothing except him, and what he could do to her, and Pete spread her fingers across the top of his head, urging him on. "Please . . ." she managed. "Jack, I'm . . ."

She felt his fingers dig into her bruises, sharp hot pain contrasting with the slow, trembling contraction of her core. Pete let out a small, involuntary cry when she came, Jack running his tongue against her until she had to fall back on the mattress, boneless.

Jack stood for a moment, wordlessly stripped all the way out of his denim and pants, and climbed back into the bed, turning Pete onto her stomach. Her heart rate was finally coming back toward regular, and Jack stroked her back again as he nudged her knees apart, mattress sagging under his weight. "Not hurting you, am I?" he asked, urging her hips off the sheets with his hands.

"No," Pete muttered, muffled against the pillows. Her aches and bruises protested no matter which way she moved, but she wasn't about to cry off because of a little pain. Jack slipped one finger, then another, into her pussy.

"Good," he said, free hand running across her arse to hold her hip, fingers pressed into the hollow next to her stomach. "You all right to be fucked?" he said, curling his hand inside her. Pete felt a residual rush of nerve endings from being eaten out and squirmed, pressing back into Jack's hand. He chuckled. "I'll take that as a yes."

He replaced his fingers with the head of his cock, guiding it slowly until his pelvic bone pressed against Pete's arse, Jack inside her to the hilt. "Fuck," Jack groaned. "This'd drive lesser men mad, you know that?"

Pete felt a giggle escape her into the pillow. Jack rocked back, then forward. Pete wrapped a handful of sheet in her fists, held on as he fucked her. The worry had gone, and all she really cared about at that moment was Jack's breath heating the back of her neck. He bent over her, put his forehead on her shoulder, and thrust into her twice, jerkily, before he came.

Pete lay still for a moment while Jack went to the loo and cleaned up. He came back and wrapped his arms around her. Pete tried not to whimper when he pressed into her bruises, and just focused on the fact that he was there, and that he'd still be there when she woke.

Jack didn't say anything else to her before he fell asleep.

CHAPTER 22

She only slept, really slept, for a few hours—it was six a.m., glowing and red in her face, when her eyes snapped open. Jack's breathing quickened almost as soon as hers did, and he opened his eyes. "Back to the bone-shaker's errand, then?" he said, voice husky from smoke and sleep.

Pete sat up and tried to work the kinks from her neck. "Suppose we have to." Despite her resolve not to give Naughton more ammunition for whatever sort of wickedness he was up to, she couldn't think of another way to keep Ollie from ending up like poor McCorkle.

"You hungry?" Jack asked. "Stealing on a empty stomach's no good."

Pete shook her head. "I haven't been hungry since Naughton showed up here and gave me the hard line, like the scary bastard he is." She found her shirt and panties and slipped them on, feeling her skin prickle when the air hit it. A scrim of frost lay on the window and the street outside, just starting to stir and growl at this hour of the morning. The radiator in the corner of the bedroom kicked on with a hiss and a clang.

"How about you?" she said after Jack spent a quiet few moments both getting dressed and studiously avoiding her eyeline. "Hungry? We could stop on the way."

Jack dug in the wardrobe and pulled out a clean shirt, rolling it over his torso. "Nah. 'M fine, luv. No appetite. Let's go."

Pete pulled her jeans on and took the hint. He wasn't talking about the sex and she wasn't going to be that sort of woman, the one who interrogated everyone she happened to take a tumble with.

She got her bag and added the usual inventory—mobile, lighter, wallet. "I'd just gotten that pistol," she told Jack. "Hope Naughton's enjoying running about like he's in MI6."

"Meant to ask you about that," Jack said. He pulled on his old leather and let out a sigh. "Hello, gorgeous."

"You weren't here." Pete went to the lift. "It's not as if I can shoot fire from my fingertips." She started to tell him about the zombie and the paralyzer hex, then thought better of it. Best case, Jack would laugh at her. Worst case, this Jack with no memory and no marks on him would know she could throw hexes. Pete couldn't be that kind of lovesick fool, even when she wished she could. When Jack came up with more than a blank spot in his memory about walking out of Hell, she'd tell him about the hexes.

"Don't think we'll need a gun, though," Pete said. "Assuming she hasn't changed her mind, the ME's a friend."

"Always did like the bossy detective side of you,

luv," Jack said. He placed his hands on her waist, swaying slightly as they waited for the lift. "Are you sure we have to go poach Carver right this minute?"

Pete lifted his hands away from her. "Jack, that is not going to work."

"No?" His bottom lip protruded. "Not even a quick tumble? Take pity on me—being locked in Hell makes a bloke horny."

"Keep your pants on," Pete said, walking ahead of him to the lift. "I mean it." Jack didn't get to pretend everything was normal between them, normal in bed and normal as they walked to the tube, and find his way into her knickers any time he liked. Pete could admit that she'd made a mistake ever letting him touch her, at least with so many uncertainties. That Jack was all right. That he'd really forgotten how he'd clawed free of Belial's bargain.

That he was still Jack.

Pete let the tube ride pass without saying a word, and when they reached the station, waited across the street under the awning of a café until a familiar curly-haired form entered the front door, messenger bag slung over her shoulder. "That's Dr. Nasiri. Let's go."

Nasiri had disappeared down the hall to the autopsy theater by the time Pete caught up with her, but she walked on, ignoring the NO PUBLIC BEYOND THIS POINT sign and nudging open doors until she saw Nasiri shrugging into a lab coat in front of a locker stuffed with street clothes.

She spun when Pete stepped into the room, her eyes widening at the sight of Jack. "What in the—this is the women's changing room, Ms. Caldecott."

"Yeah," Pete said. "Sorry about this."

Nasiri simply stared at her. "Never thought it'd be

you," she murmured. "Wanted to think you were better than that. Stupid."

"Look," Jack said, flexing his fists and blocking the door with his bulk. "We just want—what's the bastard's name?"

"Carver," Pete supplied.

Nasiri looked between the two of them. "You don't want to do this," she told Pete. "Whatever they've promised you, you have no idea what you're about to do."

"They didn't promise me anything," Pete said. Nasiri's calm and her lack of expression weren't jibing. She should at least be furious, if not scared out of her wits. "What I'm doing is nothing you need to be concerned with." She took Nasiri by the shoulder of her coat and steered her to the door. "I'm sorry to say this, but I'm going to have to get rough if you make noise or don't cooperate. Let's go. Get him out of the fridge."

Nasiri shuffled into the hall with Pete's prodding, head down. "All right. If that's the way you're going to be." She glanced back at Pete with each step as they walked to the cold room. The arctic air flowing from the vents above ruffled the plastic sheeting that lay over the corpses, transparent shrouds that did nothing to hide their last wounds and grimaces. Aside from the dead, the room was deserted.

Jack shivered next to her. His eyes were nearly white, and she knew the dead in the tiny, metal-lined room were troubling his sight. She nudged Nasiri. "Just give us Carver and we'll be out of your way."

Nasiri began checking the dead's ID tags. "You still have to get out of here with him, you know."

Pete cast her eye on a pair of jumpsuits hanging on hooks by the door. "Nobody will notice one more body wheeling in and out, Nasiri. You know as well as I do the dead spook the holy Hell out of most decent sorts."

The doctor stopped at Carver's corpse, double-checking the metal tag holder affixed to his body. "Then I suppose you've thought of everything. I won't try to talk you out of this terrible choice again."

"That'd be nice," Pete agreed. "Get his paperwork, too." Nasiri was entirely too calm. If someone had snatched Pete and forced her to hand over a corpse, she'd at least give a try at bashing them in the teeth.

"All right," Nasiri said sadly, and turned to move among the carts to the wall where a row of clipboards with intake paperwork for the dead resided. Even in the arctic chill, Pete felt sweat on her palms. Her aches were a hundred times worse after having a few hours to set in, and dizziness was coursing over her in waves. At any moment they'd be discovered, by another pathologist or simply a hapless mortuary assistant going about their morning routine. Jack could take care of that. She just had to focus on getting Carver. Get the corpse, and she'd have leverage on Nick Naughton.

She wasn't terribly surprised, still, when Nasiri swung the metal clipboard holding Carver's paperwork in a wide parabolic arc, slamming into Pete's injured shoulder. The clipboard came back and smacked Pete across the temple.

There was a flash, like a camera in her face, and Pete was on the floor. The cool tile pressed against her face, leaving a crosshatch of marks.

Nasiri's foot, in its plastic mule, came close and nudged Pete, who decided it was best to simply stay still. Above her, Nasiri picked up something from a surgical tray and pointed it at Jack. "I'm a doctor, crow-whore. I know how to cut a man so he bleeds. Get down there next to your woman."

Jack stayed where he was, the animal stillness that came over him when he faced something unexpected freezing him in place. "How'd you know who I am, luv?"

"You people assume everyone around you is a blithering idiot," said Nasiri. "You assume we think about takeaway and telly and football, and that we don't see." She went to Jack, grabbed him by the neck of his shirt, and yanked him to his knees, pressing the scalpel against the soft part of his neck, beneath his jawbone. "I see you, crow-whore. I see those bony, bloody wings across your back, and I can taste the ashes in your mouth."

Pete's temple had started up a rhythmic throbbing, and she felt blood trickling down the edge of her eye socket and following her cheekbone. It cooled almost as soon as it hit the air. Another damned head wound for her collection. "Leave him alone. This was my idea."

Jack shook his head as he got down on all foors, and then touched his stomach to the floor, keeping his chin up. "She's not just an especially observant sawbones, luv."

Nasiri narrowed her eyes. "And psychic visions on top of it. Aren't you a bright lad?"

Pete risked raising her head. Nasiri, from below, was a terror, her coffee-cream skin and wild black hair crackling like a storm cloud, while her eyes knifed directly into Pete's. Not to mention the knife in her fist, sharp as the cold air and big as a house. "Whatever you think's going on here, it's not," she said. "I'm not a necromancer." The Nasiri of before, the skeptic, was long gone, and Pete felt monumentally idiotic for taking the act at face value.

Nasiri flicked the knife toward her. "You and this piece of demon-chewed flesh here are going to give Carver over to the same bastards that sliced off pieces of him in the first place, to save your own arse. That about cover it?"

"Not mine," Pete said quietly. "Ollie Heath's."

Nasiri's stony expression twitched at that, but she tightened her fingers on the scalpel. "You're a lying bitch."

"No," Pete said carefully. "I wouldn't be here if they were only on to me. Ollie got pulled in because of things I did." She raised her head, and tried to sit up. Her spinning skull gave her mixed results. "He's innocent in all of this. I'm just trying to fix what I put wrong, Nasiri. I swear."

"Then why are you here with *this?*" Nasiri snarled, and moved the knife to Jack. Jack met her eyes, a smirk playing across his lips.

"I know what you are now." He raised a finger and pointed it at her like a gun. Nasiri took a step forward.

"Don't fucking move, either of you!"

"Half-breed," Jack said. "You've got a bit of dirty old human in your veins, don't you?"

"You shut your gob," Nasiri snarled. "You know nothing about me. Your blood is just as filthy."

"Filthy, yeah," Jack said. "All of us humans are filthy and wicked. Didn't find that out, pretending to be one?"

Nasiri's lips peeled back and her limbs went stiff. She was going to cut Jack, and Pete made a decision. She didn't bother trying to leap and disarm Nasiri with her hands, but lashed out with her boot, steel toe connecting with Nasiri's knee. The joint went *pop*, and Nasiri crumpled, bringing her face to face with Pete.

"*Fuck*." Nasiri's face was pale. "You broke my fucking knee."

Pete knocked the scalpel away. It rattled across the tile and came to rest under a rolling gurney holding the corpse of the skinhead Nasiri had been working on. "You all right?" Pete said to Jack.

"I'm aces, luv," he said. "No thanks to this crazy cunt."

Nasiri clutched her knee. "You're filth on my boot. That's right—sludge at the bottom of the Black. Sewage."

"Enough," Pete told her. "I don't care about your refined sensibilities, Nasiri. I just want Carver's body."

Nasiri levered herself up with difficulty, clutching the edge of Carver's gurney and holding her leg in a lame crook. "You really have no idea what's going on here, do you? What these men are doing to the Black?"

"Unrest, black magic, blah fucking blah," Pete said. "I don't care about that. I care about Ollie."

"No," Nasiri said. She twitched the sheet back from Carver's face. "I mean *him*. This poor bastard. I heard you talking to Heath in the museum. I know you don't have a clue what happened to him to bring him back here."

"And you do?" Pete said, folding her arms. "I find that unlikely."

"Listen," Nasiri said. "Just give me five minutes to explain. I like you, Pete. I'm trying to help you."

"Why should we trust a fucking word that comes out of your mouth?" Jack said, folding his arms in a mirror of Pete's gesture.

"Because unlike you, crow-mage"—Nasiri sniffed—"I don't lie whenever my lips move."

"Fine," Pete said, forestalling Jack with a hand from smacking Nasiri. "You have thirty seconds. Speak."

Nasiri reached for a mop leaning against the wall, using it as a makeshift crutch. "You didn't have to work me over," she told Pete. "I wasn't going to really hurt you. I'm on your side."

Jack gave a laugh that echoed off the tiles, over the giant's-breath roar of the refrigeration unit. "A thing like you, on our side?"

"Didn't say *your* side, did I?" Nasiri snapped. "On Pete's."

"Oi," Pete said. "Get on with it or I'm going to take that stick away, smack you in the skull with it, and wheel Carver out of here."

"You know the carvings are Babylonian, right?" Nasiri said. "The things in his skin?"

Pete sighed. "I got that bit. Babylonia or Brighton, makes no fucking difference to me. All necromancer's dirty tricks, isn't it?"

"Well, you should care," Nasiri said. "Because this isn't a spell. Not a hex or a curse or anything that's usual in the Black. I've never seen it." She passed her fingers over Carver's cheek. The knife cuts had puckered and widened as his skin tightened with slow decay, and the edges were wrinkled as if he'd just stepped out of a bath. Nasiri sighed. "There's a long, old word for it. Translated simply, it goes something like *soul cage*. A binding that tethers a soul to a corpse, but doesn't animate. Not a zombie or a ghoul. More like . . . a lure. An anchor for something much larger than a human ghost."

"Fuck me," Jack said softly. He pulled off the sheet and examined Carver more closely. "This poor sod is a bloody mess, in more ways than one, but a soul cage? Those are campfire stories."

Nasiri snatched the sheet and smoothed it back. "You, of all people, should know that most ghost stories start out being true."

"What's Naughton going to do?" Pete said. "Roll him out at parties to impress the ladies?"

"A soul cage is the most ancient of necromancies," Nasiri said, almost reverently. "The first act taught to the bone-shapers by their dead gods. The man transformed is a soul but not a soul—a soul stripped bare and screaming. It's more than a lure, really—an offering, a torch in the darkness of the Underworld. The necromancer that did this . . ." She shook her head. "Well, he's a bastard you don't want to meet up a dark alley, that's for bloody sure."

"Figured that out for myself, thanks," Pete muttered.

Jack rubbed his chin. His fingers made the sound of match scratching over matchbook. "You're so smart, Doc, what's the payday? Who's this bloke being dangled for?"

Nasiri kept her hand on Carver. "I know the dead, crow-mage, but I'm not a necromancer. I don't get involved with their sick little hobbies."

"Oh, I wouldn't be so kind, luv," Jack said. He showed Nasiri his smile that was like a knife in the kidneys—sudden and sharp. "You've got the stink on you, the death stain."

Nasiri's nostrils flared and she backed up against the gurney as Jack invaded her space, but she didn't blink. Pete had to give Nasiri credit for nerve. Staring at Jack's blazing blue gaze was like putting your skull inside an oven. His magic flowed from his pores like sweat, and it could drown you.

"You smell like funeral pyres," Jack whispered. "Like smoke and ash. So don't pretend you're so holy, Doctor. You know the dead as well as old Nicky Naughton does."

"I know the dead enough not to twist and deform them," Nasiri said quietly. "I know the dead through my blood, not my lust." Her knuckles went pale on the mop handle. "Now back up to a polite distance, Mr. Winter, before I jam this in your arse."

Pete thought it was really too bad that she and Nasiri stood at odds. She was beginning to like her quite a lot.

"Leaving that aside," Nasiri said. "The necromancer in question made a bollocks of this, since Carver ended up here instead of a vessel for some tentacled beast from beyond time."

"She's right," Jack said. "His soul is still here. Hasn't been made an offering. Faint, though. This kind of death should make one bastard of a ghost. I should be screaming."

Pete looked at Carver, and though she would have rather shoved her hand into a bin full of hypodermics, she reached out and put a hand on his chest. His skin felt like marble after a rain—hard and cool, but also oddly slippery, like some kind of alien life still pulsed under his pulpy muscles, rigor come and long gone.

She couldn't see, as Jack could, the dead, but Carver gave not a twitch to her senses, not a trickle of power into her mind. "So what's Naughton going to do when he finds out his offering is a pile of scrap?" she said.

"Not going to be dancing, I'd bet," Nasiri said.

"But he could still recall Carver's soul and sacrifice him again, if he's good as he seems. Carver's out there somewhere, not crossed over and not bound. Waiting for the first clever bone-shaper to pick him up and use him. Your man Naughton's got his work cut out, but it's possible."

"I'd really like to know what he was supposed to be an offering for," Pete said. Naughton wouldn't ask for a worthless corpse. He'd have a plan. A backup, a workaround, because he *was* a clever bastard. Much cleverer, Pete had to admit, than she currently felt.

"Soul cages are made for nothing nice and cuddly," Nasiri said. "Take my word on that."

Pete took her hand off Carver. She looked at her feet, her plain ordinary boots that had the same plain ordinary scuff on the left toe and the same broken lace she'd knotted at least fifteen times rather than replace it. The tile beneath was still spotted with her blood, and she stooped and wiped it up on her fingers. Jack had taught her not to leave her blood lying around. The less friendly citizens of the Black could have a party with the blood of a Weir, the kind that ended with her naked body in several dozen pieces.

"I can't give this to him," she said, realizing rather sadly and anticlimactically that she couldn't simply do the quickest, easiest thing to get Ollie out of harm's way and take Naughton off her back.

"Pete," Jack started, and when she turned to him with a hard look he tilted his head at the door. "Can we talk about this?" he murmured.

Nasiri gave a grunt. "My office is a lot warmer," she said. "And I've got to go find a medic and have this knee looked at before it's the size of a melon. I won't rat you out."

As soon as the door to Nasiri's cramped office

shut behind them, Jack turned on her. "What the Hell are you playing at?"

"I can't," Pete said quietly. "If half of what Nasiri says is true, I'm sorry, but I can't let Naughton even have a chance at finishing his ritual. It'd be like handing a vial of anthrax to a disgruntled mail worker and telling him to throw a bloody party."

"Oh," Jack said. "You hear a spooky story and suddenly you're Joan of fucking Arc? Ready to ride into battle?"

Pete sank into Nasiri's chair, unable to keep upright any longer. Her head joined the throbbing chorus of her body, and the dizziness hadn't abated. "You're being a cunt."

"*I* know what men like Naughton are capable of when you try and make them blink," Jack said. "And so do you. You weren't half as heroic a few months ago. What's changed?"

"I found out you'd sold your soul and then you got your arse hauled off to the pit." Pete prodded her head, feeling the pulpy spot where she'd grow another bruise. "Kill or be killed. That's the rule *you* gave me, Jack, before you fucked off to play with your good friend Belial—"

Jack's snatched her by her front, lifting her out of the chair and slamming her backward into Nasiri's sagging shelves of medical references and bulging files. An avalanche of A4 slithered down on Pete's head as the wind went out of her. "You know *nothing* about Hell," Jack hissed. "And you know fuck-all about what happened to me while I was there. Fucking got it?"

Pete felt that her eyes were wide and her expression slack, in the liquid moment when she could only stand frozen. She hated that split second, the one that let a crack of pain show through the stone-carved nonexpression she'd cultivated over a hundred dead bodies and a thousand unpleasant encounters with live men. Because this wasn't simply another drunken hooligan or pompous DI who thought a shaft and balls gave him automatic reign. It was Jack, and he was looking at her as if she were a complete stranger.

The falling feeling in reality lasted only a heartbeat, and then Pete's blood sped up, and she wriggled free and hit Jack in the nose with her closed fist, not caring if she broke him or herself. Jack cursed and lost his balance, knocking into Nasiri's desk and sending her laptop to the floor. "Fuck!" he shouted. Blood dripped down his face, landing on his chin and soaking the faded fabric of his shirt.

"You bastard," Pete told him. "You think I had an easy time of it alone? You think I was welcomed into your old circles with open fucking arms?" She grabbed up a handful of papers and flung them at Jack, crippled birds that landed in a snowdrift around his boots. "You fucking *abandoned* me, you piece of shit, and I'm supposed to put up with your crap now because you're what? Lazarus with fucking post-traumatic stress?"

Jack snatched at her hand and Pete yanked it away. If he touched her she was going to scream. "I can't imagine what happened to you there," she said. "But you didn't even *fight*. You just let him *take* you, and . . ."

The wet on her face wasn't blood, and her eye stung. The room blurred around her. "You didn't let me help you," Pete said desperately. "You didn't *do* anything . . ."

Jack grabbed her again, by her upper arms, and

Pete didn't fight him this time. Jack pressed his lips against hers, hard enough to pulp her own lips, and Pete's hands clutched his shirt. She tasted Jack's blood, and shared his breath as he reached up and grabbed the back of her head with one hand, tangling her hair.

"Pete," he said finally, barely a rasp of air. "Pete . . ."

She broke it off, knowing if she touched him for one more second, she could never stop. Would never be able to survive if he were gone again.

Jack let go and pushed a hand through his hair. "What could I have done, you know? I'm just a man, Pete. And not even a very good one."

Pete smoothed her shirt where Jack had popped a button off. "I shouldn't have said that."

Jack got a handful of tissue from the box on Nasiri's desk and pressed it against his nose, red still flowing. "Suppose I had that coming," he said through the baffle.

"What happened to you?" Pete blurted. "How did you come back?"

Jack pitched the bloody wad into the bin. "Pete. We've been over this."

"I meant in Hell," she said, not wanting to look at him. If she looked at him, she could never ask the question. "Before you came back. What did Belial do?"

"We're on to you now," Jack said, and Pete didn't miss the stiffness in his voice and body. "I'm telling you, you don't want any part of some noble scheme to save the fucking world. Not now. Just give them Carver, get Heath out of hock, and walk away."

"I can't," she told Jack, and he threw out his hands. "Of course you can't. Because you're Pete fucking Caldecott, defender of all that's good and true. Dragonslayer to the last."

"I'm not any of those things," Pete said. "But if you think I'd let a sweatstain like Naughton get exactly what he wants by threatening my life and my friends, you really have forgotten a lot about me, Jack."

He sniffed blood, some catching on his upper lip when he smiled. "I never forgot you, Pete. Not once, in all the time I was in Hell."

Pete felt the same pain she'd get, just above her gut, when she'd see something that unexpectedly reminded her of Jack these six months past. The difference was, he was here and it still hurt. And the Hecate's voice was in her head, always, unceasing as a tape loop. *Kill the crow-mage.*

She couldn't do it. Jack might not be Jack, and the Hecate might do terrible things to her when refused, but if she could foil Naughton, she could at least go with her head up.

Jack wiped the last of the blood off on his jeans and tilted his head toward her. "Suppose you'll need some help dispensing justice and protecting damsels, then," he said.

Pete squeezed his hand. Jack squeezed it in return, and for the first time since he'd pulled her from the pit, he looked like the man she'd watched walk away from her. "Thought you'd never ask."

CHAPTER 23

"I hope you're happy," Pete said as they left the police station. "I'm never going to get a lick of help out of the medical examiner's office, ever again. Nasiri will blackball me from here to Liverpool."

"Eh," Jack said. "Ifrit are touchy. Territorial. Plus, I think she fancies me a bit. She'll get over her bashed kneecap."

"That's what she is?" Pete headed for the tube station, taking them through the gates and to the platform.

"Yup." Jack rubbed the back of his neck. "Nasty little soul-suckers. Good thing she's got some human blood. Otherwise she probably would've just gnawed on our limbs until she felt better about her life."

"Better question," Pete said. "What are we going to do about Gerard Carver? Seeing as we don't actually have him?"

"That corpse isn't what Naughton's after," Jack said. "I'd bet you a quid."

"Carver's soul," Pete said.

"The one that should still be with his body, but is not," Jack said. "It's a mystery. Let's call Scooby Doo and have done."

"Naughton could raise him," Pete said. She didn't know why she even gave the idea voice, because it was insane. "Why couldn't we?"

Jack favored her with a crooked eyebrow. "What?"

"We could summon him," Pete said. She never would have suggested such a thing even a month ago. She put it down to being desperate, dizzy, hurting, and out of ideas. Between the Order, Naughton, and Ollie being locked in a freezer waiting to get fitted for a bucket of cement around his feet, she didn't see any way out that didn't make her the villain even without resorting to necromancy. "Not raise him back into his corpse, but bring back his ghost. Summon him, like those gits tried to summon Algernon Treadwell last spring."

Jack paused near the bus stop that would return them to Whitechapel. "Have you lost your bloody mind?"

Pete lifted one shoulder. "Like they say in America—go big or go home."

Jack looked hard at her for a moment, and Pete became interested in a wad of gum near her toe. Jack had his brushes with black magic, but Pete had the feeling that her being the one to bring it up was breaking some sort of silent contract between them, Pete the innocent and Jack the mage, who'd seen every unspeakable thing that crawled through the underside of the Black.

"Even if you weren't talking about something that could get both our intestines ripped out through our arseholes by Carver's hungry ghost, it wouldn't work. He's still tied to his flesh. He's not crossed into the Underworld, like that woman Nasiri said. Carver's in-between, and there's no ghost, just an echo in the flesh. His soul is in the thin spaces, wandering hither and yon. Really, it's just a question of who gets him first—the Bleak Gates, Naughton, or some nasty like Nasiri scavenging the in-between for lost souls."

Pete stepped aboard the bus as it squealed to a stop at the curb. "Soul, then. What if we were the ones to recall Carver's soul? Be one definitive fucking bargaining chit with Naughton." Not to mention it would both solve her problem with Morningstar and prevent Ollie from having any fingers lopped off.

"Finding a wandering soul isn't like picking up loose change off the street," Jack said. "And putting him back in that body is still necromancy, Pete. I know I ain't always been the one on the bright and shining path, but black magic like that is going to leave a stain."

"Then I'll do it," Pete said. She climbed to the upper deck of the bus and took the front seat, London passing beneath her feet. "I'm past caring, Jack. This isn't like other things we've come up against. This is . . ."

"This is worse," Jack said softly.

Pete pressed her forehead against the bus window. "What's happening, Jack?" she said, in the same tone.

"End of the world," he said. "End of the Black. Who knows. Been coming a long time, this storm. The smart ones, they realized. I was the stubborn sod who ran out in the rain without my umbrella."

"And now?" Pete said.

"Now I don't know what I am," Jack said. "Trying not to let it bother me."

"Help me," Pete said. "You can't stop whatever's happening in the Black but you can put a collar on Naughton once and for all." She faced him. "You know I'm right," Pete insisted. "We can't hand Carver over and we can't walk away unless we do. This is the only way."

Jack scrubbed a hand across his face. "Not going to be easy. Black magic is always the trickiest. Like playing catch with nitroglycerine."

The bus jerked Pete as it stopped and started, and she gripped her seat. "If it were easy, Jack, I wouldn't be asking you for help. I'd have solved it already."

His mouth curled and for just a moment, he looked like himself, before the veil dropped down again and he said, "Suppose you would."

They rode in silence after that, disembarked in silence, and walked down Mile End Road in silence. Pete was content to keep things that way until they reached the flat, but a black shadow standing eerily still and ramrod straight on the front steps changed her mind. She plucked at Jack's leather, stopping him a dozen meters or so from the flat.

"Law?" he said, taking in the rangy figure and his black coat and hat.

"Worse," Pete said. "Self-righteous cunt." She closed distance and jabbed her finger into the man's chest. "What are you doing here, Ethan?"

"Miss Caldecott, really," he said, backing out of range and brushing at the front of his coat. "I don't have endless patience, you know. So here I am, Daniel bearding the lion in her den."

"Please," Pete said. "You're about as much a man of faith as Graham Norton is a Cub Scout."

"My faith is as vast as my wrath," Morningstar said, with that small, calm smile that seemed to constantly play across his crooked mouth. Pete wondered how many different times Morningstar had gotten his face bashed to make him quite so asymmetrical. "Have you what I'm looking for?" he said. "Or am I going to be forced to use more direct persuasion?"

"Sorry, Ethan," Pete said. "You've been bumped to the back of the line as far as threats and menacing." She pulled out her key and shouldered past him to open the door. "But do take it up with Nick Naughton down in Southwark. In fact, I think you two twats would get on famously."

Morningstar grabbed the collar of her jacket and yanked her back down the steps to face him. "I'd really hoped I'd talked some sense into you last time, but I can see there's only one thing you'll understand." He reached inside his jacket, but before he could draw his pistol Jack spoke.

"Fuck me!" He pointed at Ethan. "Was trying to place those enchantments you've got riding on you, but you're the real article, aren't you, mate?" Jack extended the point into a poke, prodding Morningstar's arm. "Petunia, look. A witchfinder in the flesh."

"We've met," Pete said, struggling against Morningstar, who still held on to her as he would a naughty puppy.

"Oh, top notch," Jack said. "Never thought I'd see one of you blokes up close. Thought you died out about the time we stopped putting leeches on sick folks and tossing villains in the stocks."

Ethan drew his spine straight. He had a few good inches on Jack, and thickness as well, but amusement was no longer crawling across his face like a snake across furrows of earth. "You lay a hand on me again, Mr. Winter, and I guarantee I'll take your filthy index finger off and carry it home for my mantlepiece."

Jack grinned at Morningstar, showing all his teeth. "Now *that* is impressive. No magic, nothing but a commanding presence and a dashing hat, and you've got me pissing in me knickers." He clapped Morningstar on the shoulder, and Ethan did pull the pistol from his coat then, holding it down in the fold so that passersby would never notice it.

"One warning, Winter," Morningstar rasped. "That's all I give. Petunia here still has a shot at salvation. Maggots like you are beyond hope. Go back in the gutter with your junkies and perverts and heathens, before you press my good nature any further."

"You did," Jack agreed. "You did warn me, mate. You were very clear." In the next moment, Pete heard the familiar *snick* of Jack's flick knife, and the silver was in his hand. His other grabbed a fistful of Ethan's coat, backing him into the brick wall of the flat hard enough to dislodge chips of paint and a shower of brick dust. "Now let me tell *you* something," Jack said, in the same pleasant and oily tone. "You ever come near Pete again, you so much as look at her crossways or think about her during one of your little tent-revival wankfests, and I am going to shove your own balls so far down your throat you'll think you've immaculately conceived the second coming of Jesus Christ Himself."

Jack pressed the blade into Ethan's cheek, leaving a dent in the fat of his jaw that Pete watched trickle a little crimson. "I've never seen a witchfinder, but I've seen what they leave behind," Jack said. "Their fucking so-called morality that does nothing but put the facade of God's will on your torture squads and your hate crimes. I wager you've probably put the screws to a few friends of mine, mate." Jack turned the knife, so the point pierced Ethan's skin and blood flowed in earnest. "And unlike you," he said, "I never had any good nature to speak of, so why don't you jog on before I decide I'm not really in a forgiving mood?"

Ethan managed to smirk, and Pete had to be a little impressed. Even with a knife at his neck and Jack glaring at him with witchfire behind his eyes, Ethan wasn't even sweating. "You wouldn't cut my throat on a street full of people in broad daylight, Winter. You've got an ego the size of Westminster but you're not stupid. The Order's got files on you that would curl hair."

Jack leaned in, mouth almost against Morningstar's ear. "Then you know," he breathed, and Pete had to lean forward to hear, "that I know so, so many ways to make you hurt that won't leave a single mark."

Morningstar paled at that, blood startling crimson against his sallow skin. "If you kill me," he said, tone measured, "there will be no corner of the earth safe enough. My brothers in the order will track you and crush you."

Jack stepped back, spreading his arms. "Then come find me, darling. You seem to know right where I am. I'd delight in leaving a few of you bastards twitching and pissing themselves in my wake."

Ethan straightened his coat, and produced a handkerchief to dab at the blood on his face. He put his pistol back in holster with a smooth motion and then looked at Pete. "I'm sorry you've chosen this,

Miss Caldecott. Your mother will be, as well. We'll pray for you."

"Do me a favor and save them for yourself, Ethan," Pete said, making a shooing motion. "My soul's no concern of yours."

Morningstar sniffed, as if the pair of Pete and Jack were unreasonable children, then turned on his heel and left, holstering his pistol.

Jack took Pete's chin his hand, turning her face from side to side. "You all right, luv? Did he hurt you?"

"Him? Fuck, no," Pete said. "He might eventually bore me to death, but he's never put a hand on me."

Jack nodded, nostrils flaring as he watched Ethan retreat, coat flapping like an ill omen as he cut a swath through the crush of Mile End. "Good," he said. "That's good."

"You . . ." Pete chewed on her lip for a moment. "You seemed to fancy Morningstar about as much as I do."

"Eh, necromancers and Jesus freaks aren't so bloody different," Jack said. "Fucking fanatics, whatever colors they fly. Frothy-lipped, glaze-eyed tossers, the lot of them."

Pete let herself in and held the door for Jack. "Thank you," she said, after she'd shut it and heard the lock click. At least Ethan hadn't also violated her home. If she'd come back to find his Puritanical silhouette darkening her threshold, she simply would've had to move.

"Nobody touches you," Jack said simply, and mounted the steps to the fourth floor.

Upstairs, Jack surveyed the flat slowly, while Pete took off her coat. "Hadn't really looked around yet.

You didn't change anything," he said with surprise. Pete threw up her hands.

"Where to begin? It's the fucking Mount Kilimanjaro of paper in here."

Jack wagged his head. "You couldn't bear the thought of it nice and tidy in here, could you? It's unnatural."

Pete dropped her eyes. "That's it," she said, the words more acid than she meant. Now that he was here, flesh and blood and warm and smelling how he always had, she felt pathetic. Keeping his things. Not even changing the furniture around. His clothes still in their drawers and closets, even the vintage dirty magazines he didn't think she knew about in their box on the high shelf in the bedroom.

She was worse than any of the victims' families she'd seen. She'd turned the place into a fucking tomb, simply because losing one more bit of Jack would have pushed her past the point of no return.

Jack dropped onto the sofa, and put his foot on the ottoman. A little stuffing oozed out. "I'd murder a drink."

Pete picked up the bottle from the side table, where she'd left it, and Jack took a pull. "Carver," she reminded him.

"Yeah, like I said, pulling a soul from the in-between isn't an apprentice-level trick." Jack wiped his mouth with the back of his hand.

"Counting on your brilliance," Pete reminded him. "I'm just the magical spittoon, remember? There for the filling."

A line drew between Jack's dark brows. "Don't say that," he told her. "You're not just some dumpster for whoever wants you, Pete. You know that."

"Yeah? You being gone certainly seems to have raised the notion in some of the finer denizens of the Black. I'm becoming downright paranoid every time I leave the flat."

"Paranoia's good at keeping you alive," Jack said. "Take the insomnia and the facial tics as bonuses."

Pete smacked him on the arm. "I do not have facial tics, you wanker."

Jack got up and went to his books, running his fingers reverently over their battered spines. "Thought I'd never be back here again. Truly."

"Me, either," Pete told him. She hadn't meant to, but it made Jack stop moving, hold on to the shelf with one hand until his knuckles were white.

"I'm sorry, Pete."

She shrugged. "Let's just figure out how to get Ollie out of his mess, shall we? We can cry and fling things later."

"Or never," Jack said. He lit a cigarette and dumped out a box he found on a high shelf onto the floor. Odd bits and bobs of crystal and feather landed in a heap, along with what looked like a round game board, painted with an unblinking eye at the center and tiny boxes, barely larger than Pete's thumbnail, each inscribed with a character that may have been part of a language once, many thousands of years ago.

"You can scry for lost things," Jack said. "Never looked for a soul before. What a grand new adventure I'm on." He grabbed up a handful of the other things in the box, a flat black stone and a ragged gray and silver feather.

"Thought you needed a map to scry," Pete said. She didn't particularly like looking at the board. The lines were too close and many, imbued with a sense that they might simply crawl away at any moment.

"That is a map," Jack said, banging it onto the low table by his elbow. "Of Hell." He went to the kitchen, fishing in drawers until he found a roll of DIY twine.

Pete traced the lines with her finger. The top of the board was curiously sticky, as if the varnish on it wasn't quite dry. She decided she didn't want to know. "Of course it is. Silly of me to wonder."

"Just because you can't see it doesn't mean there's no rhyme and reason there," Jack said. "You know how demons love routine and regimenting." He sat down at the table across from Pete, letting out a sigh as he crossed his legs. "We really need some more chairs in here."

"Awfully domestic of you," Pete said. Jack fixed the stone and the feather to the twine. The stone was perfectly round with a hole drilled in the center. It swung free when Jack let the twine unfurl from his fingers, like an eclipsed moon hovering above the concentric circles that made up the maps of Hell.

"Fuck domestic," Jack muttered. "Pushing forty is too old to be sitting like a bloody hippie."

Pete had seen Jack scry before, though never with such conventional media. Once, memorably, there had been a severed head involved. He stretched out his arm, letting his eyes fall closed. The string trembled a bit and then fell still. Pete watched him, feet tucked under her. Jack had been skinny the entire time she'd known him, but he'd sprouted wiry muscles since she'd seen him last, blue veins standing out against his pale skin.

As she watched him, Pete saw something that made the air catch in her throat. Jack's forearm was pale, pristine, and unmarked. But not just his ink had vanished. The track scars that had stippled his skin like a black constellation were gone. Even his wrists were bereft of the thin white lines that ran up the inside of his arm, neat and precise in the way only a razor could mark your flesh.

Before she could look and see if he was different in any other way, Jack's eyes popped open and he let the stone fall with a thunk. "No joy. I can see him a bit but he's a slippery fuck. That bone magic Naughton threw on him feels like taking a power drill to the skull."

Pete put out her hand. "Let me try."

Jack blinked at her. "You serious?"

"Please, Jack." Pete let her eyes roll. "It's not as if I haven't seen it done enough times."

He handed over the stone, lips quirking. "Look at you. Necromancy, scrying—soon you'll be throwing me over and pushing out Naughton at his own game."

"That isn't funny," Pete said.

"It is a bit," Jack said. "Remember when you thought magic was something gits in top hats did on a stage?"

When Pete took the stone, their fingers touched, and Jack's were icy cold. The prickle of his talent this time felt like a static shock, not like the usual warm awakening of nerve endings his touch brought to her talent. The owl-eyed woman's words jumped into Pete's head. *He's not the Jack you know.*

"You all right, luv?" Jack said. "I really was just taking the piss. I know you're not a sorcerer."

"I'm fucking exhausted and my best friend is being held hostage by necromancer," Pete told him. "Forgive me if I'm not turning cartwheels."

"Pete . . ." Jack said, but cut himself off, his jaw ticking. "Forget it."

Pete let the stone dangle from her fingertips, holding her arm steady, breathing in and out through her nose to still her pulse and her nerves. She felt the Black tugging on her, trickling through the conduit in her, a warm and yet frozen prickle all up and down her skin. Under her, the stone began to swing, the twine tugging back and forth against her fingers.

Quickly as it had come to her, it was gone again. When she'd hexed the zombie, she'd grabbed hold of the magic, dug her fingers into it and scraped furrows from its flesh. Now it was as if she were trying to scoop a live goldfish out of a bowl of grease.

"Shit," she muttered. Jack's fingers brushed the back of her neck, resting on the nape. He'd moved behind her, his body bringing no warmth with it. Pete shivered.

"Relax," he murmured, his breath on her ear. Whiskey and cigarettes permeated her nostrils. "You have it," Jack murmured, his fingers grazing her skin. "You're so close."

Pete felt the floor drop away from her. Touching Jack was usually enough to make her dizzy. Touching him when the magic was up filled up her reservoirs to overflowing and started an enormous pressure against her brain. The Weir knew what needed to be done, even if Pete didn't in her waking mind, and it wanted to drink Jack dry.

The pendulum swung in concentric circles, the twine burning her fingers with friction. Pete shuddered, Jack's proximity and his fingers on her skin raising goosebumps.

She shouldn't be so close. She shouldn't be letting his talent fill her. When mages and Weirs allowed each other too close, terrible, terrible things could happen.

Yet she couldn't pull away, and she began to see, as the pendulum swung, the lines on the board move and change under her gaze. They crawled and twined back on one another, formed dragons and thorns and twisted thickets of spellcraft, writ small on the board. They reached out for Pete, psychic feelers inviting her to pick out the hidden picture in layer after layer of ink and varnish. She saw, with Jack's power feeding her, and watched the layers of the Black peeling away before her. There was London, stinking, screaming London full of its smoke and rivers and the iron veins of the tube deep beneath the earth. The grave-yards and the forgotten souls, passing through the thick yellow mist of the Thames.

Still she watched, more and more filling in before her gaze, the ghosts and the things beyond the psychic clamor of the city, the slithering black spaces between the worlds. She saw what Jack saw and she spun onward, weightless, chasing a bright ember in the blackness populated only by screaming, clawing spirits that had lost their way between the Black and the land of the dead, sucked into the singularity of nothing that was the in-between.

Gerard Carver's soul was on fire, and as Pete drew closer she could hear him scream, over the howl of the Black. Before him rose the great iron gates of the Underworld, their spires poking into an orange sky, a sky reflecting the flames of Hell.

The Bleak Gates. Pete had never been so close, never felt their overwhelming draw. In the darkness around her, things were moving. They winked across Carver's soul like owls across the face of the moon. Pete reached out, sure that she could touch him, and then the darkness closed in, and she felt herself fall. Toward the Bleak Gates, toward the Underworld, a living soul bright amidst the silver contrails of the dead drawn to its magnetic pole. Past the Bleak Gates, past the dead, and straight down to the lowest realm, where the demons waiting beyond the turrets of Hell welcomed her living flesh with hungry cries.

She came back with a scream, realizing she was flat on her back, staring up at the flat ceiling. Jack leaned over her, pressing his fingers into her neck. "Breathe, Petunia."

"I saw . . ." Pete tried. Her throat was raw, parched dry, and she swallowed hard. "I saw Carver." The desert dryness was still on her skin, the barest kiss of the air of Hell, and Pete brushed herself all over, as if she were trying to rid her skin of a swarm of insects.

Jack pulled her up and onto the sofa, putting a glass of whiskey in her hands. Pete drank it down, and the hot burn of the cheap liquor finally helped the trembling in her hands subside. "We have to stop doing that," she told Jack.

"Scrying?" he said, taking the bottle for himself. Pete shook her head.

"Touching."

Jack grimaced. "If that's what you'd like, luv, try wearing shirts with collars for a change."

Pete let the remark pass without fetching him a slap. She was wrung out. "Carver was somewhere dark near the Bleak Gates. Full of screaming." Those screams echoed in her head, and would echo for a long time, Pete had a feeling, whenever she shut her eyes at night. They were the screams of the lost, of minds ripped so far asunder they could never be put back together.

"Thin spaces," Jack said. "The places where things that fall through the cracks end up." He set the bottle down. There was barely an inch left. "The good god-fearing types call it purgatory."

Pete shivered. "I can still feel it all over me."

"If Carver's close enough that you saw the Gates, we've got precisely shit for time," Jack said. "Won't be long before something or other snaps him up, or he gets caught up with the dead and the things that live beyond the Gates tear him to bits. They don't take kindly to trespassers."

"And Naughton's got to have others looking," Pete said. "I really doubt he'd put his faith in me."

"There's only a few ways to visit the thin spaces," Jack said, "and the only one that makes sense for something flesh and bone is to be near death. I doubt Naughton's brigade of matched thugs is keen to mess with that sort of acid trip."

Pete didn't ask if Jack had visited the howling void where Carver resided during any of his near-death experiences—she had a feeling if he had, it probably wouldn't be a topic of conversation that'd win her any favors. "We're fucked, aren't we?" she said instead. Jack killed the whiskey bottle and set it on the carpet by his boot.

"Likely." He seemed content to let that sit, but Pete stood up, pacing the track that usually belonged to Jack, when he was thinking or simply too wound up to sleep.

"I guess we just have to be game for it," she said. "The thin spaces." She'd never thought it would really work, but she owed it to Ollie and her mum to at least try and break them out of what they'd gotten into. If taking a return trip to that place was in the cards, Pete supposed it would be a deal easier than attending Ollie's funeral.

"No," Jack said instantly. "No. I went along with

this until we found where he was, but I'm putting me fucking foot down hard. Nobody who wants to keep on breathing in this world goes to that one, at least alive."

"Oh, very well," Pete said. "Since you have all the answers, then, how else do you propose the two of us wrest Ollie back from the bosom of a dozen necromancers with bad attitudes and prevent Nick Naughton from turning this city into something out of the Book of Revelation?"

Jack slammed his hand on the table. "Do I *look* like I have all the bloody answers, Petunia? Is that what you think?" He sat back and rubbed the spot between his eyes furiously. Pete recognized the telltale sign that Jack's sight was bothering him. "Look," Jack said. "I like Heath well enough. He's a good bloke, and I'll help him any way I can, but I'm not starting another ritual that ends with you, me, Ollie, or the whole bloody Kingston Trio of us in A&E or more likely, on a fucking slab."

The patience Pete had held on a tenuous tether snapped, and she shouted. "What then, Jack? Give up? Ask Naughton nicely to please repent and change his ways? Or roll over and let him do what he likes? Because that's not on my list of options."

She went to the front door of the flat, jabbing her arms into her jacket, wishing she could drive her fist into wall, slap Jack—something. "You stay here and mope if you like. I'm going to find someone who can actually help Ollie."

Jack jumped up from the sofa. "Pete, wait."

She ignored him, snatching up her keys and unlocking the deadbolt. Jack closed the space between them and slammed the door shut again, barring it with his arm. "I said wait, goddamn it! I'm not finished talking to you!"

Pete rattled the door, which did precisely no good against Jack's new bulk. "The time has well and truly fucking passed, Jack. I'm done talking."

"You still don't get it, do you?" he asked her. "The Black isn't like the daylight world. Things don't always work out like they should. Bad things happen to good blokes for absolutely no fucking reason at all, and it's shit, but you pick up and you get on with things."

Pete stopped trying for the door, and slumped against it instead. Standing was still a dodgy proposition. "That's my world, too, Jack. If you'd spent any time in it you'd realize that." She spread her hands. "You said near death is the easiest way to find Carver. What are the others?"

"Oh no," Jack said. "That's not an option, trust me."

"I'm not stupid enough to swallow a handful of pills and hope for the best," Pete said. "So spill it, Winter, 'fore I beat it out of you."

Jack shoved his hand through his hair, but he let go of the door and conjured a fag, lighting it before he talked. "There's a flower, a kind of orchid, that puts you under, down deep to near dead. Very Timothy Leary, lick the face of Jesus type of shit, but it will put you in the twilight long enough to dip into the thin spaces."

"Brilliant," Pete said. "I'm in."

"Well, if it were that simple, every git with long flowing hair and a book on Wicca would be doing it, wouldn't they?" Jack said. "Your soul leaves your physical form, Pete. You're vulnerable to anything floating in the in-between, and if you don't have the correct words to bring yourself back, well . . ." He made a *poof* motion with his hands. "You're so much dust on the boot of the universe, aren't you?"

"Don't come if you're scared." She tossed it off lightly, but she felt the ball of unrest grow in her stomach, the one that had led to nothing but trouble in the past. But what was her life these days except bad luck and trouble? Doing the ritual and downing some toxic flowers couldn't make it any worse.

"Right, I'm warning you off tripping to the brink of both physical and psychic death because I'm scared of the boogeyman." Jack's lip curled up, and the flash of smugness made him look a bit like his old self before it faded. "I've been dead before, Pete. It's not one of the things that scares me at the moment." He reached out and ran a thumb over her cheek, bringing his new cold with him. "'Sides, who's going to help you out of trouble this time if I don't ride along?"

"Lawrence," Pete said.

"*Lawrence?*" Jack barked a laugh. "Luv, Lawrence would piss himself at the very thought of what you're asking me. He's a good little boy."

"He's got more balls than you do right at the moment," Pete said. "I'm doing it, Jack. You can come along or not." With that, she did open the door.

She heard Jack sigh "Fuck me all the days of my life," and then he was walking beside her to the lift.

CHAPTER 24

They crossed into the Black and found the Lament, but Jack hesitated at the door. "I think you should do this bit alone."

"For the love of all that's holy," Pete said. "Have you got bloody stage fright?"

Jack grimaced. "My little sojourn to the pit hasn't exactly made me popular with people like these, in case you didn't realize." He pointed at the door. "Look, just go in and tell Mosswood I need to talk to him. He'll understand."

"Maybe we should fit you for a giant nappy," Pete said. "Perhaps warm you a bottle."

"Will you just fucking get this over with?" Jack demanded. He wasn't smiling, not on his mouth and not in his eyes, which stared daggers of ice through Pete.

She ducked her head. "Sorry. Not like anyone's making you be a twat," she muttered, pushing the pub door open. The Lament, never a rowdy place, fell dead silent as the punters caught sight of her. She saw Mosswood at his usual table, glass halfway to his lips. Taking a step forward felt like stepping into an electrical storm. The magic in the Lament was up, and it wasn't friendly. Everything on Pete that could prickle stood on end. She kept her chin up and her shoulders square, passing quickly through the tables to Mosswood. A storm of whispers and muttering grew up around her, a rising tide of hostility that held an almost physical weight. If she'd still been a copper, she would've called for backup, but her backup was skulking outside, smoking and too much of a twist to come in himself.

"Hello, Ian," she said. She started to sit down but Mosswood shot up, grabbing her by the wrist and pulling her within kissing distance.

"Are you completely insane?" he hissed.

"Not that I know of," Pete said. "But I suppose if I have gone insane, I'd think everything was normal, wouldn't I?"

Mosswood didn't smile. "I know, Petunia. Where is he?"

"Outside," Pete said. "For *some* reason he got the notion he wouldn't be welcomed with open fucking arms."

"Idiot," Mosswood snarled, not clarifying whether he was referring to her or Jack. He made for the door, still holding her. Pete was forced to follow him or have her arm dislocated.

"Oi!" Pete shouted, digging her heels in. "You're hurting me, Ian."

Mosswood stopped walking and let go of her, causing Pete to slam into him. "You stupid bint!" he shouted. "How dare you come in here as if everything were up in roses!" Lower he muttered, "Keep walk-

ing if you want to get out of here alive. You have no
idea what that fool Winter has let you in for."

Pete gaped, but she forced herself to keep going,
throwing a few more token curses for show as Mosswood hustled her outside and then distanced himself, fixing his cuffs and collar and shaking himself
like a cat with its fur going the wrong way.

"I've seen some displays of rampant stupidity in
my time," he told Pete. "But that one nears the top of
my list."

"I'm still not seeing why walking into my local
was so offensive," Pete told him.

"You walked in knowing full well you were with
him." Mosswood jerked his chin at Jack. "And that,
my dear, is not a tenable place to be at the moment."

"Ignoring my popularity contest," Jack said. "I
need to speak with you, Ian."

"I should hope so." Mosswood sniffed. "Though
it did take you long enough. Jack Winter, the man
not content to cheat death once, but a matched pair
of miracles. Can't even be bothered to drop in on his
old mates. I see how it is."

"Need your help," Jack said. Mosswood rolled his
eyes heavenward.

"Of course you do. Why else would you turn up,
unless you wanted something, Jack?" He pressed his
palms together and pointed them at Pete. "I implore
you, whatever he's tangled you in this time, back
away. You've enough trouble on your own head as it
is, getting into that spat with Nicholas Naughton."

"Nicholas Naughton can fuck himself with his
gran's tea service for all I care," Pete snapped. "I *need*
your help, Ian. *We* need your help. I know you've seen
what's happening in the Black, and if you think a

bunch of necromancers coming out in the lead will help things, well. Maybe you've been sitting in that pub for too many centuries."

Mosswood drew himself up, his presence all at once outgrowing his sad tweed jacket and raggedy trousers, dark eyes flaring with power. "I will not be cajoled to throw down my gauntlet on any side. I don't concern myself with a rumpus between a few humans slinging magic they don't understand."

Jack let out a laugh, short and gravelly as a smoker's cough. "You and I both know that's utter shit, Ian. Before you went soft and poncey and started dressing like Harry Potter's creepy uncle, they used to sing songs about your . . . *involvement* . . . in mortal affairs."

"Even if I were inclined to help you, Jack," Mosswood said, "I can't. This isn't my fight. When the dust clears, and the smoke's gone, and the blood has soaked back into the earth, I expect I'll continue on much as I have." He made a motion to go back to the pub. "You, on the other hand . . . you've never been one of the survivors, Jack."

Jack muttered a string of curses and then kicked the side of the Lament, hard. "Forget it," he told Pete. "He's just another Fae fuck cowering behind his mystique. See how he likes a world made of cinders, with all his bloody trees—and followers, for that matter—a pile of ashes."

"Lovely imagery," said Mosswood. "If you're quite through with your speech, I was in the middle of a pleasant evening."

"You really think you can just sit in your pub while this storm passes you by?" Pete asked Mosswood. Her voice bounced off the alley, rolled back and forth through the ripples of the Black. "You think that you're going to walk back out of that bloody pub after Naughton finishes what he started and the world will be exactly the same?" She took Mosswood by the shoulder and turned him to face her. "It won't be. I've seen it in the daylight world, you know. Not magic, but drugs and guns and gangs. Naughton's the tip of the iceberg. Under the water, there are other things. Dark days are coming, Ian, and you won't be immune. Not you or any of your kind. Not Jack and certainly not fucking me. I'm not the type to lie down and die. With or without your help, I'm still going to try and stop this from happening."

Mosswood gave her a withering glance. "Take your hands off me, Miss Caldecott."

"I think you're afraid that what I'm saying is absolutely true," Pete told him, "and that when the blood and the dust settles, you'll be just as dead as the rest of us."

Mosswood stared at her for a long time. His eyes were dark and green, the color of a deep forest where no light could penetrate and ancient things without eyes slithered beneath the roots of trees. "By staying with Winter, you've signed your own death note," he said at last. "He's not the man you think he is, Petunia. He never has been."

"You'll either help us or you won't," Pete said. "You can bang on all day, but I don't have to listen."

Mosswood dropped his chin to his chest. "Dare I ask what it is you even want from me?"

"Nightsong orchid," Jack said. "I'd get it from my usual supplier, but my lines have dried up. Me being dead and all."

Mosswood pointed at Pete. "You know what nightsong orchid is used for, I take it?"

"She does," Jack said. "This whole fucking circus is her idea. And that's the other half. You bringing me back when I've gotten what I went under for."

"Oh, is that all," Mosswood said. "I'm going back inside."

"Please, Ian!" Pete said. She didn't dare grab him again, but she went after him to the pub door. "It is my idea," she said. "It's the only one I've got. I'd make excuses as to why, but know you don't care, so will you help us or not?"

The green man took his hands off the door. "I suppose I'll never be able to live with myself if I don't at least see how badly this turns out." He gestured to the alley, pulling his sport coat around him. "Lead the way, Miss Caldecott, to our damnation."

CHAPTER 25

The shop Mosswood led them to was the only lit window in a deserted close, golden lamplight spilling in a slow burn on the dark cobbles outside. The buildings around it were ramshackle, window glass destroyed, in one case merely a pile of rubble. Far off, Pete thought she caught the wail of a siren before it faded into nothing.

Time and memory were fluid in the Black, and she thought she'd never really get used to walking from a nineteenth-century pub to Blitz-era London in the space of a few blocks.

Mosswood knocked, and they waited. Several heartbeats went by, Pete's breath misting the chill air. Now that she had a moment, in the stillness, with Jack standing silent beside her, all of the doubts she'd shrugged off in the heat of Jack reappearing came crawling back, like rats and roaches after the lights went out.

She didn't stand a hope against Naughton. He was a necromancer and a psychopath to boot. She didn't stand a hope of hiding from the Hecate, even if she was never going to carry out their bloody orders. And even if she somehow got one over on Naughton and managed to evade the owl-eyed woman, Ethan Morningstar would be waiting for her with open arms and a pair of pliers.

But there was still Ollie. Still Jack. And because of them, she had to at least try. If she went down kicking, it at least wouldn't be a bad death. Better than her father's, pale and wretched in a hospital oncology ward. Better than Jack's, being led into the fold of a demon while it whispered in his willing ear.

She straightened her spine as the door opened, though she realized she needn't have bothered, because the woman before them was so stooped Pete had a good six inches on her. Pete wasn't tall by anyone's standards, including her own, so the crone was verging into comical territory.

"What?" she demanded crossly. "Can't you read?"

Pete noticed there was a small notecard jammed crookedly in one of the door's panes: HRS 11–7 DAILY. SHUT HOLIDAYS.

"Now, Irina," Mosswood said. "Is that any way to talk to your dear friend?"

"Friend?" The woman peered up at him, lip curling back to reveal an impressively white and sharp set of dentures jammed into her wrinkled red lips. "You're no friend of mine, Green Knight, any more than the Inland Revenue or the bloody clap."

Jack let out a snort over Pete's shoulder. "I think I like this one, Ian. Ex-girlfriend?"

Ian shot Jack the sort of glare Pete had seen often as a teenager, when she'd tried to sneak in late and

Connor had caught her dressed in short skirts and smelling of lager and smoke.

"*You*," Irina said, catching sight of Jack. "You're no better, are you? Just the crow hag's rent boy, bringing bad black trouble like rot wherever you go."

"To be fair," Jack said. "'M more like a high-priced escort. Talent like mine's too good for street-corners."

"Go away," said Irina. "The lot of you."

Pete, seeing she was about to slam the door, said the phrase beloved of pushers the world over. "We can pay you."

Irina hesitated, peering up at her. Her face was framed by a red scarf, as if she were merely an over-grown doll. Her eyes, surrounded by crow's feet, were nearly clouded over. Irina was blind as a bat, but she moved with the alacrity of a school-aged athlete and snatched Pete's wrist.

"Ohhh," she cooed. "So we've brought a proper good and true vestal virgin with us to sweeten the pot, have we?"

"I'm not very good," Pete said. "And I'm hardly a virgin. Sorry to disappoint."

Irina carried on stroking as if Pete hadn't spoken. "Her," she said. "You two wait out here."

"Like Hell we will," Jack said.

Pete put a hand on Jack's chest, feeling angry breath under the scarred leather. "I'll be fine," she said. "It's not like this is my first time on a buy."

Jack's jaw ticked, but he only favored Irina with a glare. "Anything happens, you won't have a corner black and secret enough to hide from me."

Irina muttered something that sounded as if it were Russian and defintely derogatory before dragging Pete inside. "Your man seems to think he's in charge." She chuckled.

"He often does," Pete said, and yanked her hand free of Irina's grasp. "No offense," she said, when the old woman's face crinkled. "You're a bit clammy."

Irina began pulling sacks and boxes from one of the overflowing shelves on the shop wall. "What you need? Love potion? Fae nectar? We got some hydroponic hash my son Mikel grows. Mellow and sweet. Keeps you dreaming even when you're awake."

"If I wanted pot," Pete said, "don't you think I'd find an easier way to get it?"

Irina stopped throwing her merchandise around. "Let's see your money, then."

"Let's see if you have what I'm after," Pete countered. The first rule of illicit transactions was not to appear eager. Don't flash your cash. Don't look vulnerable, or strung out, or more trouble than you're worth. Above all, don't act like a cop.

"All right, all right," Irina said, flapping her skirt and settling into an armchair at least as old as she was, and twice as decrepit. Her accent went from being raspy East End to a carefully educated diction, her syllables a bit too round to be native to British soil. "Obviously, you're not here to waste my time. I'll bring the usual dance to a halt, and you tell me what's so important you bring the Green Man and *that* to my door."

"Fair enough," Pete said. "I'm after nightsong orchid."

Irina sat forward, painted eyebrows wiggling. "That's hardly a gateway drug."

"I'm not a gateways kind of girl," Pete told her. "Can you get it or are you wasting *my* time?"

"Of course I can." Irina sniffed. "But I'd dearly love to know why you want it."

"I'd love to know why you pretend to be a crusty old Romany with a Cheapside accent," Pete told her. "But I'm polite enough to figure out it's not my fucking business."

Irina started to laugh. "A little thing like you can't afford to be acting like she's tougher than a coffin nail," she said. "Somebody's going to cut that smile right off your pretty face."

She rose and went to the beaded curtain that hid the back room from Pete's view. "Harvesting what you want is specialized. Wait here."

Pete did as she said, and when the curtain clacked closed, she took the opportunity to look around the room. Aside from the tarot spread—in no particular order, just all of the most terrifying of the Major Arcana arranged to scare customers—there was the usual jumble Pete would expect from a second-rate magic shop. But it seemed like so much clutter carefully obscuring the face of something else, like a stage set. Irina's outrageous costume alone would tip off any respectable mage that the place wasn't worth their time.

She went to the shelves, moving things aside until she could see the wall. The plaster was scarred and carved with black markings, and Pete moved more boxes and clutter. A cigar box full of gris-gris, resplendent with beads and feathers, bounced off her foot and scattered its contents across the boards.

"Shit," Pete muttered. The markings were clear now. They weren't the harsh symbols that covered Gerard Carver, but they weren't pleasant to stare at either. Pete couldn't shake the feeling that she'd seen the swooping marks and lettering somewhere before. They matched a silver-tongued language, one that humans in the Black steered well clear of.

"It's Fae." Irina came out of the back room holding a bell jar, within which rested soil and a tangle of green stems topped by one perfect silver flower.

"Is it?" Pete said. Of course. She'd read in one of Jack's books that Fae language was never spoken aloud by men, in hopes of avoiding the sort of curse that got you a donkey's head or napping for a hundred years.

"If you're looking for Fae orchids, you knew that already," Irina said.

"I've seen it before," Pete admitted. "Not quite this much. What is it?"

"You ask a lot of bloody questions," Irina fussed. "You a cop?"

"Used to be," Pete said. "Now, I just want to take my silly plant and go."

Irina went to a set of apothecary drawers behind the shop counter and gestured her over. "You sure you know what you're about, tripping on this shit, little woman? You really think you can swim back out of whatever dark cave it is you're diving into, when you're done?"

Pete spread her hands. "What I do with it is my business."

"And I suppose you being tangled up with Jack Winter hasn't got any bearing on you wanting this little darling whatsoever," Irina said. It was casual, but there was bite behind the words. She drew out a baggie, the sort expensive markets kept out for measuring spices into, and a pair of delicate surgical scissors with tips like silver fangs.

"Jack is also my business," Pete said. She knew it was bad form to smack an old woman, but she had a feeling perhaps this time she'd get a pass.

"I am indentured to a Fae," Irina said, as if it were the most natural thing in the world. "I traffic their plants and whatever else they care to have humans imbibe, and in return they protect the shop and its neutral ground for anything nasty. Really, a very snug arrangement. I wish I'd had it when I was a girl living in Dolgoprudny. The monsters there were men, but monsters all the same."

"This is fascinating," Pete said, "really, but I'm in a bit of a rush."

Irina handed her a pair of sound-dampening earphones, the sort you'd wear to stand by a jet engine. "The song can drive you insane," she said. "If you're not someone it knows."

"It knows us?" Pete looked suspiciously at the orchid under the bell jar.

"Knows me," Irina said. Pete clamped the apparatus around her ears and watched Irina coo as she lifted the jar off. Pete didn't hear anything, just the beat of her heart, but she smelled the scent, far too sweet with an undertone of something rotten. She could choke on it, as Irina stroked the stamens of the orchid, lips moving, almost as if she were distracting the thing before she put the scissors against the stem and lopped the flower neatly off.

She waved at Pete, and Pete removed the headgear. She was glad to see Irina package the flower with the acumen of a chemist, taping it shut and cutting off the scent before Pete passed out. "There," she said. "I'll even give you the police discount."

"How kind," Pete said, as Irina accepted her wad of notes and rooted below the counter for change.

"Not really," she said. Pete watched her rise with a pistol in her petite, knotty fist.

Pete lifted her hands slowly, so that Irina wouldn't get the wrong idea. "Something I said?"

"If you think," Irina gritted, "that I'm letting you walk out of here and give the crow-mage the power to walk between worlds, then you're sorely fucking mistaken, miss."

"You've got the wrong idea," Pete said quietly. "Jack isn't the one . . ."

"Winter is an obscenity," said Irina. "A whore of the blood gods that would tear the Black to shreds and suck the marrow from its bones. I might serve the Fae but I would never serve them, and never allow him the power this holds."

Pete had always been crap at negotiations. The whole diffuse the situation, calm the hostage taker, win/win situation shite had never been her forté. If she wanted insanity and confused rambling, she'd call her sister.

"Gun's a bit pedestrian, don't you think?" she said to Irina. The old woman grinned at her.

"You're not made of stone. Or Kevlar."

"That I'm not," Pete had to agree. "Look, why don't we just back this up, you'll listen this time when I tell you this orchid is not Jack's doing, and we'll part ways with no harm done?"

Irina sneered. Her wrinkled forearm was bare from holding out the gun, and Pete saw an Orthodox cross tattooed to the inside. It rippled when her wasted muscles flexed. "The harm's already done." She took the safety off the pistol. It was a nickle-plated .22 with a mother of pearl grip, a lady's gun. Exactly the sort of piece Pete would expect from a crazy old woman running a magic shop.

"I don't know what you think you know," she told Irina, keeping her voice calm and steady, just like in her training. "But it was my idea to get the orchid, and my idea to go to the Underworld. Jack's innocent."

"Jack Winter is *not* innocent," Irina told her. She looked as if a gust of wind would snap her in half, but her grip on the gun never slackened and her aim never wavered.

"Who among us is?" Pete said. This had all gone pear-shaped. Irina wasn't budging, and the utter lack of feeling in her face told Pete she'd shoot her if it came to that. Irina was a hard old bitch, and whatever dusty Russian mafia uncle had taught her had done a bang-up job.

Pete made the decision to finish this at almost the same moment the hex was on her lips, and she felt the peculiar tug in her gut as it sprang across the space between her and Irina. "*Sciotha.*"

It didn't work like it had with the zombie. Nor like when Jack did it, flinging his talent in a wide, sharp arc to wrap around his target and take them to ground. Irina's own magic, or perhaps the Fae writing all around them, caused the hex to run wild, smashing a row of the apothecary jars behind Irina's head. It did snatch at the woman's gun arm, though, and Pete relied on the fact that she wasn't eighty and a raving nutter to do the rest.

She jumped the counter, knocked the pistol down to Irina's side, and put her fist hard into the old woman's face. Cartilage crushed under her knuckles and the small, gravelly *crunch* was nearly drowned out by Irina's scream.

Pete tried to shake the pain from her fist as she watched Irina roll around on the floor behind the counter. She went for the pistol again, but Pete kicked it out of the way. "Give me the fucking orchid," she said. "And I'll be going."

Irina stopped thrashing about and went limp. Blood dribbled from her nose. Pete crouched and twisted her head to the left. "Don't choke on your own blood, you stupid bitch," she sighed. Irina curled into a ball, spitting more Russian curses. Pete left her where she was and plucked the orchid from the countertop, shoving it inside her jacket. Ollie better appreciate what she was going through for him. Punching old ladies in the face was above and beyond the fucking call of friendship and cameraderie.

She was nearly to the door when Irina spoke up. "His living again has made things so much worse. We thought we might be safe when Belial took him, but now . . . you have no idea."

Pete rubbed her forehead. The stuffy shop and the flower smell were coming at her in waves, urging her to simply lie down and sleep for about a decade. "And what are you? Fucking Batman?"

"The Fae see things that mortals never will," Irina rasped. "I keep my company with them, with other things older and wiser than humans, and all said the same—it's a blessing the crow-mage is dead. And when he came back they told me something else."

"What did they tell you?" Pete asked, though the knot in her stomach knew the answer.

"They told me that the end times are coming," Irina said, voice thick with blood. "And that the crow-mage and his Weir the cause."

CHAPTER 26

Pete shut the door softly behind her when she exited Irina's shop. Her fist hurt, and her head was throbbing. How many hours had she been awake? Too bloody many to bother counting. It would only depress her.

Jack flicked away his fag when he saw her and lifted himself from the spot where he'd leaned against the derelict flats, the half-wall behind him showing a little bit of pinkish London night sky. "Old woman talk your ear off?" he said.

"We had a difference of opinion," Pete told him. She shoved her scraped knuckles into her pocket.

"We should go," Mosswood said. "Having that bag of Fae foulness is like having a duffle full of hundred-pound notes. Every thieving thing in the Black will be down on us." He walked to the end of the close and ducked through a ruined doorway.

They emerged from the Black across the road from the Smithfield Market, its ornate tri-colored iron gates shut, streetlamps on either side spitting in the

mist. The Smithfield Market was a working meat
market, and if you were an early riser or a tourist,
you could wander among the bloody slabs of beef
and barking vendors in the predawn light, the scent
of blood and flesh curling up in your nose along with
fog and damp. Pete saw a shadow detach from the
gates as she, Jack, and Mosswood turned toward the
Farringdon tube station, long coat and slouched hat
making him little more than a memory of a shape in
the fog. She flicked two fingers at the Order thug
and kept walking.

Jack and Mosswood had two topics of conversation
on the tube ride and the walk to the flat—whether
Mosswood was a twat and whether Jack knew what
he was doing. "You're really going through with
this?" Mosswood asked Jack for what had to be the
tenth time.

"Fuck me, again?" Jack said. "Ian, I've had expe-
rience with both tripping and dying, so please, just
sit yourself over there and make sure nothing hid-
eously violates my comatose body."

Mosswood settled himself on the sofa with a
grunt. "For the one who dragged me into this, you're
not being very hospitable."

Pete caught Jack's eye over Mosswood's head and
said, "Tea, Ian?" When Mosswood nodded, Pete gestured Jack into the kitchen. He wasn't going to like
her question, had dismissed her before, but Pete had
begun to feel a weight on her, the sort she'd get at the
Met when a case was about to go sideways. She'd
spent enough time among liars to realize when she
was being lied to, and she lit the burner under the
kettle and then faced Jack. "Aren't you going to ask
me what's wrong?"

Jack shrugged. "Is something?"

Pete slammed the mugs onto the countertop. "You know damn well, Jack. Ever since you rose from the fucking grave my life has been nothing except death threats and sinister figures nipping at my heels." She met his eyes. Jack's eyes were devoid of life, flat as a stagnant pond, as they'd been ever since he had returned. They were victim's eyes, soldier's eyes, witnessing the same trauma over and over again, knowing it was coming but unable to look away.

"What happened?" Pete said. "I know I said I wouldn't ask, but if we're doing this, we might not make it back. At least not me. I need to know if you really don't remember, Jack. How you came back." *Why you came back. What happened in Hell to make the Hecate order me to murder you on sight.*

"I'm not talking about this." Jack picked up a mug and rooted in the cabinets for the tea. "Not now and not ever. Not with you."

Pete grabbed his arm, and turned him to face her. "No. You tell me what the fuck is going on." She voiced what she'd seen in his face. "Something that you're not telling me is under there, and whatever it is, I want to know. Now, please."

Jack looked down at her hand, back at her face. "Unless you're planning a quick jerk before the festivities, get your hands off me."

His voice was cold, and Pete felt a stab low in her gut at the fact that his expression never even changed. *Jack Winter is not the man you knew.*

"What happened to you, Jack?" Pete whispered. "Who are you?"

He put his hand against her face, tender for a split second and then his thumb and fingers tightened along her jaw, pulled her close enough to almost brush his lips with hers, and Pete felt her flesh twinge where his finger-pads would leave marks come the morning. "You don't want to know," Jack whispered, as the shriek of the kettle overtook Pete's senses. "So for your own continued good health, stop asking."

After a moment of sharing breath, Pete brought her hand up and smacked Jack hard on the cheek. "You arse. Let go of me." He did, and Pete felt her cheek where she'd have finger-shaped marks. "That really hurt."

"Life hurts," Jack said. "Surprised you haven't figured that out by now. Or do you save your brilliant insights for things you know nothing about, like my time in Hell?"

"Oh, very well, fuck you," Pete snapped. "When I've gotten Ollie out of harm's way, you can just pack up and move along. I don't want your shit piled on me."

"Then maybe you should stop opening your legs and pining after me," Jack said. Pete grabbed the mug from his hand, resisting the urge to spill it on his crotch, and dunked a teabag for Mosswood.

"Don't worry. As soon as I've got Ollie back from Naughton, you and I are done." She moved to take the tea to the sitting room. "You're not the same. You never would have said that to me six months ago."

"I've been to Hell, Pete," Jack said. "You try it, and see if you're still a ray of fucking sunshine."

Pete took Ian his tea rather than respond. Jack had a lot of enemies in the Black, people who'd breathed easier when he was secreted away in the pit. They couldn't be happy he was back, and they would spread any rumor that would get more of the Black wanting him gone all over again. Like Irina, with her stone expression, and the Hecate, with her incessant, unchanging order. Pete couldn't ignore the signs, no matter how badly she might want to.

Something was wrong about Jack, and his coming back hadn't been a reprieve. His appearing back in her life wasn't fortune. Quite the opposite. Jack's secret, whatever it was, had the Black in an uproar, and because of that, Pete knew it could only be a few things. Not possession, but perhaps something else. Belial wouldn't need Jack's body if Jack gave his soul over voluntarily.

Had he cut a deal with Belial? Here on a demon's errand, tempered and remade in the fires of Hell into the one thing the old Jack would have spit on without a second thought? Jack as a sorcerer was a terrifying enough thought. Jack as a sorcerer with powers gifted to him by one of the generals of Hell didn't even bear contemplating.

But right now, Ollie came first. He couldn't defend himself. Pete could handle Jack Winter. And if she couldn't, at least nobody else would be dead because of it.

"You should probably lie down," Jack said, coming in behind her, as if nothing had happened in the kitchen. Pete's face was still hot where his fingers had gouged her, as if she'd stood too close to a fireplace.

"On the floor?" she said. She couldn't remember the last time she'd swept the sitting room.

"Either that or keel over where you stand once you've dosed yourself." Jack stretched out on the carpet. "Your choice."

Pete stripped off her jacket and lay down next to him on the threadbare Persian, foot to head. Jack sat up and chalked a crooked circle around them, into the pile. "Bit of binding, he said. "So our souls don't fly straight up the fucking chimney." He handed the chalk to Mosswood. "Anything dodgy happens, you close that bastard and pull us straight back. Not more than a few hours in any case. This shit will eat holes in your brain."

"I have done a ritual before, you know." Ian crouched stiffly next to Pete. He pressed a clump of the sticky silver flower into her palm. "Chew, and spit it out before you go under," he said. "Don't choke."

"You do realize this is completely fucking mad," Jack said, before he shoved a clump of the stuff into his own mouth and chewed.

Pete bit down on her share of the orchid. It didn't taste like much at first, as if she were outside on Guy Fawkes and had breathed in a taste of cordite from the fireworks. A cold tingle stole over her tongue, and Pete tasted rusty iron that spilled over into the taste of blood, and down her throat with a grasp like freezing water. She managed to turn her head and retch the vile thing out, as Mosswood had instructed, before blackness crawled across her vision, and her heart roared in her ears like a tube train passing by.

Pete felt as if she were stripped of skin and muscle and bone and only her nerves were left, throbbing. Her heart thudded like she was still running suicides at Hendon with the other PCs. She could almost smell the mud, her own sweat, breath razoring in and out in time with the *thump-thump-thump* of her heart as her boots dug into the peat and her own cold sweat wet down her clothes. Could almost see the weak dawn light that cast everything cold and blue while she and the other recruits ran the course. Could feel the sharp stab of exhaustion in her side, letting her know she'd vomit the moment she stopped running.

Pete felt every inch of her body begin to turn numb. It started in her fingertips, as if she'd gone outside on a cold day and forgotten mittens. The numbness crawled straight to her heart, and Pete felt her pulse slow to nearly nil.

Just before her vision bled to solid black, she felt Jack's fingertips touch hers, a tingle of power that rippled up her arm like electricity. She squeezed his hand, and it was the last thing she felt before the Black reached up with its great dark hand and pulled her down.

PART THREE

DEMONS

They are fatherless creatures, and their whole ancestry is hidden in a past of demons and ghosts.

—Beowulf

CHAPTER 27

Pete had never died before. She'd been stabbed, when Jack and Algernon Treadwell had their dust-up over his body, but she'd never seen the Bleak Gates.

She opened her eyes to the flat, the same stained ceiling and Moorish chandelier. The same wrinkled rug under her back. For a moment, she thought the nightsong orchid hadn't worked at all. She sat up, fuzzy headed, the walls pulsating slightly when she wobbled and grabbed the sofa for balance. She felt like nothing so much as tremendously hungover, mouth dry and eyes aching as the light from outside streamed through the shutters.

"Jack?" She was alone, the candles at the head and foot of the circle burnt down to nubs of wax that cascaded across the wood like lava flow. The flat was dark, bulbs in the lamps burnt out in their sockets. Mosswood and his tea had vanished from the sofa. "Jack!" Pete shouted. She took a step outside the chalk marks. Her boot crunched down on a fine grit across the floor. She bent and rubbed black, oily smut between her fingers.

"Soot," Jack said from the kitchen archway. Pete felt her heart convulse inside her ribs at the sound.

"You fucking sneak!" she told him. "Scared me half to fucking death."

"It's soot." Jack gestured at the black coating over every surface of the flat. Pete brushed her hand on her denim.

"Did it work? We're in the exact same spot."

"It worked." Jack massaged his forehead. "Sight is going insane and I feel like I just drank enough whiskey to fill the Thames. That's a nightsong trip, by the fucking book."

Pete pulled the shutters open, squinting against the light. London was covered over by black smoke, clinging to the rooftops and obscuring the flash of the Thames in the distance. Their usual view was wreckage, all of the post-Blitz buildings vanished: in their place were blackened bricks and crooked chimneys. The windows of the flat were cracked and in a few cases shattered altogether, letting in the sounds of the street, the clatter of cars seventy years past their prime, and the wail of an occasional air-raid siren.

"Is this coal smoke?" Pete said, coughing as more of the stuff wafted inside. Under Victoria, the miasma got so thick it would sometimes fell infants and those with weak lungs, giving London the undesirable nickname of the Smoke. Victorian London, though, didn't have cars, or klaxons, or their 1920s flat block.

Jack pointed east, to where the smoke thickened to obscurity, blotting out the horizon into a blurry line. "They're burning their dead," Jack said.

"Who?" Pete stared at the spot, discerning blue-white flame dancing at the horizon line. "There's nobody out there," she said. No footprints disturbed the soot and ash on the street below. All the noise came from far off, the empty city acting as a giant echo chamber.

"There's an eternal fire at the Bleak Gates," Jack said. "The souls who don't pass or won't stay in the fire forever. East is the Land of the Dead." He closed the shutters. "We're not going that way."

Pete re-examined the flat, covered in the ashes of the damned souls trapped at the Bleak Gates. "Fine by me," she said, trying again to swipe the oily stuff off her hands.

"We should move," Jack said. "We're a fucking homing beacon for anything hungry out here. Live souls don't come along every hour." He peered into the hall before stepping out, moving tight, eyes always roving.

"So, what will get us first?" Pete said, sticking close to his shoulder, a stagger pattern used by incident response teams. Of course, in incident response there were more than two people, and they had stab vests and rifles rather than jackboots and ragged denim.

"Damned souls. Scavengers. Demon on a day trip up from the pit," Jack said. "Take your pick."

A single bulb flickered in the hallway, and when they reached the street, Pete was assaulted by the dry, crackled scent of the funeral pyres and the flicker of shadowed, winged figures passing through the smoke overhead.

"I thought it would be more . . ." She looked at the ruins of the Mile End Road, the UNDERGOUND sign outside the tube station hanging by its wires. Far below them a train rumbled, whistle screaming as it ran on without stopping. The asphalt was pitted, down to the brick below in most places, and Pete stumbled. "More . . . otherworldly," she finished.

"Think of the thin spaces like shared hallucinations," Jack said. "We're both pulling bits, things we've seen, psychic impressions, painting it onto the nothing out there. That's what it is, you know. Sucking nothing. We stay too long and we'll forget the street ever looked any other way."

"It looks more like I imagined Hell," Pete said, boot nudging aside burned and cracked bones. Human or animal, she didn't care to stop and be sure.

Jack's mouth tightened. "This is a far fucking cry from Hell. Trust me."

Pete decided to ignore his black expression. "How do we get Carver back?"

Jack patted himself down for a cigarette, and then cursed. "Of everything in my pockets, you'd think I'd at least carry over the fags."

Pete checked her own pockets experimentally. Her mobile was missing, along with her wallet, but her crumpled pack of Parliaments was still in evidence. Her clothes had changed as well, and she realized that Jack wasn't wearing his black shirt and denim from before. "What the fuck?" she said, gesturing at him.

"This is what your soul chose to dress itself as," Jack said, snatching the Parliaments from her hands. "Which is lucky, because I've seen blokes cross over starkers more than once."

"You're actually not complaining that I'm not naked?" Pete cadged a fag back and lit it.

"Not the time or place," Jack said, and exhaled a cloud of blue. "More's the fucking pity."

"Certainly not," Pete said. She passed the White

Hart, her and Jack's favorite pub on Whitechapel Road, and saw that it was burned out, twisted forms of metal lying in the wreckage. "I didn't think I had anything in my head that was quite this apocalyptic."

Jack flicked his fag away after a single drag. "Well, 's not my fault. I was thinking about a Tahitian beach full of topless backup dancers when I went under." He glanced up at the shapes moving through the shadows overhead and took Pete's hand. "We should pick up speed. It's going to be *Mad* fucking *Max* here in a few more minutes."

Pete checked herself over as they walked, realized she was back in the clothes she'd been wearing the day Jack died. *Thanks so fucking much for that. See Petunia. See Petunia's dysfunctional subconscious. See Petunia have a nervous breakdown and be taken into care.*

Jack, for his part, looked as he had the first time Pete had seen him at sixteen. Shredded Sham 69 shirt, denim that fit him like his skin, and the jacket that let him look bigger than he really was. Jack wasn't the sort of man most sensible people would fuck with, but he definitely wasn't going to win dust-ups on pure mass alone. The jacket was his old one, hammered with silver pyramid studs, drawn on and scraped up, the Dead Kennedys armband stained with something that was either curry sauce or blood: Pete had never asked. Subtract the lines from his face, add a little height to the bottle-blond hair, and it was Jack a dozen years ago plus change. Before he'd gone away and come back with the flatness in his eyes.

Pete focused on not turning her ankle on the pitted pavement rather than contemplating what she had to admit was true—Jack was different. How different, she didn't know. Whatever Belial had done to him, though, she'd bet the admittedly anemic balance of her savings account that she'd find out soon.

"Stay with me," Jack told her when she got a few paces behind him. "Nothing's real, and nothing's to be trusted."

"You can die here, real enough," Pete said, not letting it be a question. The shapes overhead were more, and lower, and she could hear the hiss of man-sized wings through the smoke-shrouded sky.

"You can die a lot of places," Jack said. "This one just happens to be slightly more unpleasant than a gutter, or a grave." He glanced upward at the shadows. "If you die here, you stay here. These bastards are sharper than I thought. We'd better get inside."

He led the way into the burnt shell of the White Hart, mounting the creaking stairway to the upper floor. "Carver's got to be close by." Jack lit a fag and dragged on it. His wrist flashed free from his leather and Pete noticed that the white lines on his forearm were back. In her memory, Jack still had scars.

Pete settled herself by the window. The glass was just jagged teeth, mostly gone, and it caught on her elbow as she shifted. "Ah, dammit. You think we'd imagine someplace that wasn't quite so sharp."

"That's the Black," Jack said. "Putting sooty little fingers all over your third eye. You start bleeding," he said, pointing to her torn shirt, "we're fucked." He came over to her and leaned out the window. "They aren't after us yet, but live blood will light us up like Las Vegas. They're looking for him."

"What are they?" Pete watched slow-descending fireworks blossom as the air raid klaxons wailed on. Billows of fire erupted where they fell to earth, a meteor shower sprung from a human hand. Juniper's mother had lived through the Blitz, as a teenager,

and in the few years that Pete had been old enough
to pay attention before she passed, Nana Morrow
still refused to go into tube tunnels and hated any
noise above pleasant, thoroughly British conversation. She'd been a far cry from their Grandmother
Caldecott, whose father had been an IRA fighter
and who, when Connor stepped out for a fag during
their summers in Galway, had told Pete and MG
stories about the fuckin' Black and Tan bastards what
dragged him away when she was a girl.

"Heard a lot of theories," Jack said. "Lost souls.
Things that don't have souls. Grim reapers, if you
want to get Judeo-Christian about it. They're from
the Underworld, but not welcome in it. They feed on
the ones that fall by the wayside, don't make it to the
Bleak Gates. Anything that passes through. Human,
demon, it doesn't matter. They're never short of new
meat, though usually the meat's not stupid enough to
waggle itself under their noses."

Pete watched the shadows' passage as they drifted
to the south over Limehouse, dipping low out across
the river like ink drops, ever changing and shifting,
until they dropped out of the smoke to alight on the
diseased, sewage-choked water.

"There," Jack said at her shoulder. "They've caught
the scent. As it were, since it'd take a fucking miracle to smell anything in this place except burned
bones and shit."

Pete backed away from the window. "South?"

"South," Jack agreed. "Down to the banks of the
dirty river we go."

CHAPTER 28

While they walked, things solidified. Pete stopped feeling as if her mind were two steps ahead of her body, and the lines of things no longer blurred when she moved her head too fast. She wondered how long she'd been under. How much pull the Bleak Gates exerted as the orchid slowly killed her.

"This is strange," she said to Jack.

"We're in fucking purgatory," Jack said, as if she'd stated that she had black hair.

In the next step, before Pete could take the opening to air her feelings that nothing about this vision of the thin spaces was right or proper, nothing like when she'd seen a brief snatch while bleeding from Treadwell's stab wound, nothing that was going to help them, a bank of floodlights snapped on and sliced across her face.

"Fuck!" Pete hissed, as her corneas flexed painfully.

"Stay still," Jack told her.

Pete shielded her eyes with the flat of her hand, discerning shapes behind the blazing klieg lights but not much more. "Scavengers?" she said to Jack.

"No bloody idea," he said. "But no, if it was, we'd be a meal by now."

"At least somebody's got their head twisted on straight around here," said a voice from behind the lights. The largest of the shapes chopped a motion, and slowly the spots pointed at the ground rather than Pete's eyes.

"Don't know what you think you're doing," Jack told the voice. "But we're not sticking about long. We'll turn one way and you turn the other. How's that sound?"

"I've not turned stupid just because I'm dead, you twat," the voice growled. Pete could nearly place it—she'd heard it before, using the same scornful undertone.

"You lot aren't from this place," it said. "You're living and breathing, and you've got flesh to go home to." The figure stepped forward, backlit by the lights.

Pete squeezed her eyes shut as she saw the thick neck, bifurcated by a ragged cut, and the bottle-brush hair. "Shit. McCorkle, is that you?"

"What's left of me," he agreed, teeth pulling back from his lips. His face was a corpse's face, blue and swollen on one side with livor mortis. Clad in tattered leathers, he looked more like the zombie from outside his flat than a thing that had ever been alive.

"Who the fuck's McCorkle?" Jack said out the side of his mouth. "Boyfriend?"

"Naughton made him kill himself," Pete replied in kind. "He stole some kind of musty artifact Naughton needs for the ritual. Him and Carver both."

"Brave man," Jack said aloud. "Stealing from a necromancer. But I see you learned the hard way, it's ultimately idiotic."

"I didn't believe in magic," McCorkle said. "Thought I was buying a relic, not a fucking piece of the fabric of Hell."

"Freddy," Pete said. "We're just passing. We're looking for your partner, not you."

McCorkle reached out and pulled her close by the front of her clothing, until their faces were less than an inch apart. He smelled dead, too sweet, and slimy, and she could see the bilious black marks creeping under his skin. McCorkle was caught decaying, eternally falling apart while he was stuck in the thin spaces. If this was what McCorkle had seen, it was no wonder Naughton was able to convince him to carve his carotid like a Christmas ham. "Freddy's not here any longer," he told Pete. "And I know exactly what you want. Which is why I think you'll be spending a little time with me instead."

Another few of the decayed ghosts came forward and grabbed Jack, who moaned and grabbed at his temples, nails leaving long furrows, when they touched him.

"Please," Pete said. "He's a sensitive."

McCorkle grinned at her, gums black. "Then you'd better hope I decide to let you go before his brain's about as useful as a raw turnip, hadn't you?"

He hustled her with him into the tunnel of light, and Pete didn't resist, because it was that or be left alone in the thin space, with nothing but shadows for company.

CHAPTER 29

The gang took them to a rotting pier with a rotting warehouse piled on top, stretching out into the Thames. The Docklands before they'd been reinvented as the shining jewel on the breast of London—dirty, rat-infested, and full of cutthroats.

"Jack?" Pete said as what had been McCorkle prodded her along with his swollen hands. She hated the note of panic in her voice, hated that she was turning to him instead of trying to get out of this mess herself, but she looked to Jack and hoped that she wouldn't see the same panic reflected in his face.

Jack tried to reach out for her, but the things jerked him away, three of them. The largest had a truncheon, and he slammed Jack across the back of the knees to still his struggling. Jack buckled. "Fuck! Fuck you straight up the arse, you poncey putrefied bastards!"

One of the three stuffed a greasy kerchief into Jack's mouth, muffling his yells. "What should we do with 'im?" it asked.

"Chop him up!"

"Throw him in the river and let the naiads pick his flesh!"

McCorkle tossed Pete down to the splinter-ridden wood of the pier along with Jack. "How about you brain-rotted morons shut your gobs?"

"Ey," the one who'd hit Jack leered. "You wait a bit longer, bright boy. Yours'll rot like pudding as well."

Jack mumbled something around the gag, and McCorkle jerked his hand. His nails were long and spotted with graveyard dirt. "Get the crow-mage out of my sight. He doesn't have any wisdom for us."

The other ghosts hauled Jack away, and McCorkle crouched, lifting Pete's chin with his fingertip. That nail dug into her, pricking the tender spot under her chin. She pulled back. "Look, Freddy, I'm fresh out of shock and dismay, so why don't you just exposit and threaten, and we'll take it from there?"

McCorkle tried to grin. In the light, Pete could see his upper lip was bifurcated by a stray knife slash, exposing his full gums. "You're a mouthy bitch, Caldecott. Anyone ever tell you that?"

"Enough times that if I had a quid for each one, I'd be rich enough to buy myself a life without things like you in it," Pete said.

McCorkle's hand tightened on her. "You snark again and I'll rip your tongue out of your head and swallow it whole." He sat back on his heels and waited. Pete stared at him, refusing to blink first, but she kept quiet. Ghosts were the worst bits of you—rage and pettiness and fear—and McCorkle had hated her more than enough in life to do everything he'd threatened.

"I don't know what you're doing here." McCorkle

leaned in so he was almost whispering in her ear. "I'm just glad you came." He lifted a finger toward the half-caved in roof. "You see those things up there? The carrion birds of the Underworld? They scavenge us like meat." He snorted, and a bubble of bloody snot grew on one nostril. "Suppose I am that. Meat. But now . . ." He petted the spot under Pete's chin where he'd cut her. "Now, we've got something live to feed them. Had me a snake when I was a boy, used to swallow mice that trembled just the way you are now. Predators love live meat."

Pete stared into McCorkle's sunken face. She realized that the lack of panic probably meant her mind had simply said "fuck it" and gone into standby mode until she could have a proper breakdown. She had to put that off as long as possible, preferably when she wasn't a hairsbreadth from her eternal reward. "Naughton killed you," she said. "Those others as well?"

"He's been at it for a while," McCorkle said. "Carver was very impressed with his old boss man."

"But not you," Pete ventured. The old scenario— distract the mad bastard until she had time to come up with something clever. Distract herself so she didn't simply start screaming.

"We were schoolmates, Gerry and I," McCorkle said. "Brain on that bastard was big and squashy, but he was a klepto even then. Mum used to beat the Hell out of him, and sweets and cigarettes would pop out of his pockets while he mewled and whinged."

"So naturally when you became the very brightest of the dirty coppers, you turned to your mate with all of the best scratch," Pete said.

"He didn't want to sell me that thing, but his obese whore of a mother needed some hip wotsit.

Could have told her fat arse to lay off the Guinness and chips and gotten the same result," McCorkle said. "Then I start getting harassed. Sods in suits, jabbering about witchcraft. It was fucking comical. Thought so right up until Gerry got himself sliced. Thought so even as I did the same."

"I could've told you not to trust a spoiled public school brat who mucks about with corpses," Pete said. "Honestly, McCorkle, that shouldn't have been a hard one even for someone like you."

"I don't have to justify myself to you, you fucking Irish twat," McCorkle said. "Someone tells you you've bought a reliquary for a dead god, you tell them to fuck off and stay on their meds. Don't pretend you were so open-minded, before you spread your legs for all that nonsense."

He drew a hunting knife out of his belt and waggled it in Pete's vision, huge as Nelson's column. "The only thing I need from you is to decide whether I gut you and leave you for the crows before or after I fuck you senseless."

Pete's heart sped up, even though she shouldn't have a heartbeat at all in this place. The orchid trance was tipping over into actual death, and her only hope was that Mosswood would pull her out before McCorkle carved her up. But that would leave Jack behind, so she forced herself to stop shaking, reach up, and close her fist around the blade of McCorkle's knife. "Don't talk your power-and-control rapist shit at me, you poncey little cunt. You're not the worst nightmare I've seen. Not by fucking far." The blade slid into her hand as though her flesh were warm and buttery, and her blood was hot when it dribbled down her forearm. The pain of severed nerves came more slowly. Pete ignored it. Pain was tertiary.

"The only thing you can do to me," McCorkle snarled, "is beg not to be alive when I violate you like the little Catholic whore you are."

"First of all," Pete said. "I haven't been inside a church voluntarily since I was thirteen. Second of all, if you were going to do it, you'd've done it by now. Not your fault. I imagine at some point, your balls rotted and fell off." Pete didn't think about her bloody hand, the cool steel in her grip, Mosswood or Jack or any of it. McCorkle was all that mattered. He was standing between her and Carver. Between her and getting back to the daylight world with her soul.

McCorkle tried to pull his knife back, but Pete grabbed the hilt with her other hand, closing her fingers over his slimy digits. "I can help you," she said, not blinking. If she blinked, or thought, she'd go mad with terror. Fear was the only sane response to something like McCorkle, to being in the thin spaces and so close to death at all.

"Help me? Do you realize where we are?" McCorkle barked a dead man's deformed laugh, born from collapsed lungs.

"I know that you can't leave again, unlike me," Pete said. "I know it was Naughton who fucked you in the arse and sent you here. All of you. All I want in return is Carver."

McCorkel's face twitched spastically, his nerves running wild. "And what'll you do for me?"

"I'll send Nicholas Naughton down here in my place," Pete said. "And him, you can do whatever you like with."

She watched him with all her copper instincts, trying to pick a hint off of his mangled face. McCorkle sniffed deeply. "Why should I trust you? Naughton's sent near a dozen of us down here, trying to cage his bloody demon or demigod or whatever it is. You won't do any better against him."

"I'm not like these sad things." Pete pointed at the other ghosts, clustered a little way away. "As for Nick Naughton—I hate that bastard more than Hitler."

"You'd slice him cold-blooded, for me?" McCorkle grinned and slowly released his grip on the knife. "I think I'm in love."

The blade clattered to the boards, and Pete tucked her hand under her T-shirt, trying to sop up the free-flowing blood. It felt like she'd pressed a poker against her palm, red hot and prickling.

"Give me Carver," she said, "you get Naughton. Soul for a soul. Even you can do that math, Freddy." She got to her feet and raised the index finger on her good hand. "Oh, and Jack's leaving here, too."

"No," McCorkle said at once. "The crow-mage stays."

"Fine," Pete said. "Then you might as well get on with the cutting and the raping, because Naughton is far too clever for the likes of you. You'll be here until the crows out there suck you dry like a milkshake."

"For a good little girl, you do seem to love sticking your fingers into the fires," McCorkle said, and then bellowed gutturally. The trio of ghosts reappeared, dragging Jack.

Pete narrowed her eyes, a black sense of unease crawling up from the pit of her mind, where her talent lay. "What's that supposed to mean?"

"He hasn't told you?" McCorkle said. "How he crawled up out of Belial's charnel house, like the snake in the garden of Eden?"

"I don't care what Jack did for Belial," Pete told

McCorkle. It was none of his bloody buisness. He was a ghost. She was allowed to lie to those sorts of creatures.

"Belial?" McCorkle's tongue flicked in, out. "No, I don't think it's the Prince you have to worry about. I'd wager it's the Hag."

"Jack's a servant of the Morrigan," Pete said. "It doesn't mean a bloody thing." She turned to go, but McCorkle snatched her arm. Jack extricated the kerchief from his mouth and started for them.

"Get your fucking hands off her."

"Don't think I will," McCorkle told him. "You hear things, out here in the nothingness. Echoes from the Underworld, from the Hag herself, and the army she's gathering at her feet. We hear the dead whispering, from inside the wall. So unless you want me to tell your little flower here what I've heard . . . you be sweet to me, crow-mage."

Pete expected Jack to curse, sneer, and possibly set McCorkle on fire with his mind. She didn't expect him to freeze, an expression close to panic on his face.

"Don't," he told McCorkle. "Or I'll . . ."

"Or you'll what, crow-mage?" McCorkle snarled. He let go of Pete and spread his arms. "I'm a piece of flesh and soul trapped in the maw of Hell, Winter! Do your fucking worst!"

Jack closed distance and took Pete's hand. "Come on," he said quietly. "Let's get the fuck away from here."

"Go!" McCorkle crowed. "Carver's on Blackfriars Bridge. He's waiting for you, Petunia Caldecott. And so's the truth!"

Jack yanked her along and they were clear of the

warehouse and the horrid mortuary stink of the Thames. "Move it," he said. "You're bleeding like a pig and the crows'll be thick as flies."

Pete shrugged free of his grasp and stopped walking. She knew that McCorkle hadn't been lying, at least not completely. She knew with the certainty that her talent gave her, that certain events were inexorable and fixed, and that the truth couldn't be buried. "Are you?"

"I'm not running on demon fuel," Jack said, too quickly. "I'm still flesh and blood. You should know after what we did."

Pete shut her eyes. *Don't look. Don't let him put the lie in your mind.* "Are you who you were, Jack? Did the Morrigan do something for you? To you?"

Jack didn't answer her. He only started walking again, and Pete was left to either follow or be left alone in crumbling, poisoned London.

CHAPTER 30

In Pete's waking life, Blackfriars Bridge was a cluttered span of taxis and people, the red wrought iron appearing too delicate and lacy to support the load of London's populace. Now it was sooty black and canted to one side, pilings groaning as the black tide of the Thames rushed around it.

At the center, where the river ran deepest, a single lamp was still lit, flickering like a firefly in a jar. Under the lamp waited a man, or at least a man-shaped shadow.

"Spirit," Jack said, rubbing his index finger against his temple as if his brain itched. "Not a ghost. That's a soul. At least that McCorkle wasn't a liar on top of a great pasty twat."

"Carver?" Pete called, cupping her hands around her mouth. "Gerard Carver?"

The shadow didn't move, except to raise a hand and lower it again.

"Careful," Jack said. "You stay here long enough

when you're not all the way dead, you get as crazy
and vicious as those scavenger souls."

"I think I'm tipping over," Pete said. She could
feel the mist now, the cold on her skin, every inch of
her nerves and blood, as if she were really here as
opposed to only visiting. "I'm smaller and I took the
same dose. We need him before Mosswood pulls us
out."

"Fine, then," Jack said. "What was that? Go big
or go home?" He started straight for Carver, paying
no mind to the holes in the road bed.

Carver looked better than he had in life, wearing
a tweed suit and a midly interested expression, ginger beard neatly trimmed. "I knew someone would
come," he said. "You're not any of Naughton's."

"Should bloody hope not," Jack said.

"He did send us," Pete said. "He wants you back.
You cocked up his ritual."

"Nicholas cocked up his own ritual," Carver said
viciously. "Tried it without the reliquary, in what
might as well have been broad fucking daylight.
Hated that arrogant bastard."

"Yeah," Pete said. "Ethan Morningstar is big into
the hatred, from what I've seen."

Carver blinked at her from behind his wire-
rimmed spectacles. "I might have known Ethan would
hire on sorcerers. Always did have more drive than
sense, God bless him."

"Oi, you ginger cunt," Jack said. "God's not here.
Never has been."

"You cannot return me to my flesh," Carver said,
expression slipping into terror. "You don't know what
Naughton's tried to do."

"Reliquary, necromantic ritual, human sacrifice,"

Pete said. "It's a summoning, isn't it? Some big nasty burrowed down in the muck of the Underworld."

"So much worse," Carver said with a laugh that sounded like ashes. "I'm not going back. I'll stand here until the ashes have burned down and the dragon has wrapped himself around the world. That will be my final service to the Order. I'll repent for all my necessary sins at last."

Pete cut a glance at Jack, who rolled his eyes heavenward. "Madness sets in quicker for some," she said.

"He's not mad," Jack said. "He's just spouting that thirdhand apocalyptic crap. Jesus freaks and necromancers, I told you. And this bright lad is both."

"Crow-mage," Carver said, "you of all people should know that I'm speaking the truth. That's why you're here, isn't it?"

"He's here with me," Pete said. "We're taking you with us, so I suggest you don't kick up a fuss."

Carver smiled, and his mouth was a black slice in his pale face, his skin pulling back into a wide mockery of joy. "Winter's not here with you, little one."

"Shut up," Pete told him. "I don't need to be riddled by dead men."

Carver stepped into the light. His eyes were pure black, the eyes of a ghost, seeing countries and dreamscapes far beyond living sight.

"The crow-mage isn't your man, Weir. He's come through fire. He's changed."

Pete waited for a rebuttal, but there was silence from Jack, and Carver began to laugh. The sound was like a nail in Pete's skull. She became aware Jack was out of her eyeline, standing just behind her and to the side, looking down at his boots. "Jack?"

she said softly, the plunge in her stomach having nothing to do with the cant of the bridge.

He said nothing, didn't move, and Carver continued to laugh.

"You crawled out of Hell, you came through fire, and she didn't find that suspicious?" He shook his head at Pete. "You stupid, stupid bitch."

Pete pointed a finger at him. "You, shut your gob. Jack, what is he talking about?"

Jack finally raised his head. "You didn't know what it was like there. In Hell. I was there for good. I belonged to Belial."

"Jack . . . ," Pete started. "You didn't . . ." Jack had never believed in destiny, any more than Pete had. The Morrigan had marked him as her own, but to Jack it didn't mean anything more than his sight and a mildly irritating nickname. Jack detested his patron goddess even more than Belial. He wouldn't have.

"She came to me at my lowest, and she explained what I'd always known, really. She'd put her mark on me, named me as the crow-mage for this moment, when the Black is in flux, dying and coming up from the ashes. Who's standing when that happens is up to her. She's the Hag, Pete. She's the raven of war, the bedmate of death."

Pete's throat tightened as Jack went on in a flat shell-shocked tone barely audible over the rush of water. "There is a storm sweeping over the Black, and when it clears the shadow of the crow will reach across every face in it. It's the Hag's time, and the crow-mage stands at the head of the Hag's army of the dead. Not the necromancers, not the Hecate, and nobody else. I'm her walker, Pete. I'm the hand of death. And I'm sorry. I'm so, so sorry."

He stepped forward, stretching out his hand to Carver. "Gerard Carver, I bind you soul and spirit to your earthly flesh, life after death, until my word says otherwise. My will is your will, living and dead, ashes and dust."

Pete felt the flare of magic, dark and sooty as the air around them. Black magic always felt like a needle, loaded with a drug and primed straight into her senses. It was hot coals and glacial ice, the stench of decaying flesh and of the fires of Hell, all at once. Jack shivered as the incantation passed through him.

Carver kept grinning. "You wait," he told Pete. "He's not finished."

Pete couldn't stir herself. She thought another bargain with Belial would be hard enough to take, but *this* . . . this told her that Jack had well and truly been broken. Hell had taken the one man she'd thought unbreakable and snapped him in two. He was the crow-mage now, truly, and he was to the Morrigan what she'd sworn she'd never be to the Hecate.

"Jack," she said at last, "just let go." She grabbed his shoulders and faced him toward her. "I don't care. I know why you did it, and I would've done the same. I was wrong to say those things about you. I couldn't survive Hell. I'm sorry, Jack. But you can walk away. You're not the Morrigan's slave. You don't have to help her burn the Black."

The Hecate hadn't been wrong. That was the worst bit. If she'd killed Jack, the moment he'd come back, none of this would be happening. The Morrigan wouldn't have her walker and Naughton wouldn't have a shot at Carver, because Pete never could have done this ritual herself.

If she'd killed Jack, she'd have also killed Ollie,

and let Naughton get away with two murders, at the very least.

There was no *if* for her, though, right as the Hecate was.

She never could have done it. She'd still be standing right here, because much as heroin and adrenaline were Jack's drugs of choice, he was hers. The only thing she could never kick. The only person she'd ever needed, in the way of aching bones and desperate, clawing craving.

All she could do now was show him that was the truth.

"Just come back," Pete whispered. "Don't let her, Jack."

"You are a servant of the Morrigan, Gerard Carver," was all he said. "Bound to serve the crow-mage and only him. So it is now, so it is forever until you pass or the world does."

"No . . . ," Pete told him. "No, Jack, we have to bring him back. Ollie will *die* . . ."

"I'm sorry," Jack said. He looked at her and then his gaze darted out to the water. "But this is my price, Pete. This is my task. Deliver the necromancer's offering to the Morrigan, to use as she sees fit. Or she'll give me back to Belial and we can never . . ." Jack drew a breath. "I can never go home again." He reached out and put his hand on her cheek. "I had to betray you this time, Pete, so that I can be beside you the next. When the storm breaks. Please, just say you understand me."

"I *don't* understand *any* of this!" Pete shouted. "How could you, Jack? How could you?"

Jack moved his hand from her, and shook his head. "At least now I'll have a little time to try and explain it to you."

Pete heard the shriek of scavengers, and Carver snapped his head up. "If your Hag wants me, crow-mage, you better take me now. Otherwise you and I will be standing on this bridge until the Black burns down around us."

Jack shook his head. "I'm sorry, Pete. I hope you can forgive me."

He put his hand on Carver, and the spirit flick-ered. The power rose around Pete like the ions in the air before a lightning storm.

"No," Pete said. "No, Jack . . ." Before she could say anything else, there was a sharp tug in her chest, as if she'd been slapped with the business end of a cricket bat. Her head went light, and her vision screwed. "I'm not ready!" she shouted at Mosswood. "Damn it, Ian, not yet!"

Things went black, the slow swirling black of suf-focation, and then Pete's eyes snapped open and air rushed into her lungs. She saw the ceiling of her flat and smelled tobacco and incense. The honks and rattles and shouts of living London reached her ears. She lurched sideways and vomited, gasping until there was nothing left. Sticky black bile crept across the floorboards.

"All right." Mosswood shoved her hair out of the way. "You're all right, Pete."

His hand on her skin started a feverish fire and Pete retched again, feeling the battered sensation of pulled muscles in her abdomen.

"You hang on," Mosswood said. "I haven't fini-shed with Jack yet."

Jack . . . Jack watching her with those icy eyes that were not his own, Jack stealing Gerard Carver's soul.

Mosswood moved away from her and crouched

by Jack's head, touching a finger to his brow and murmuring a few words. When he was finished, he blew out the black candle at the head of the circle.

Pete forced herself up, hands and knees, then only knees, and then, using the sofa as a pulley system, to her feet. The flat swayed and pulsed around her as the remnants of the psychotropic danced through her system like ice water and hot coals at once.

"You shouldn't be up," Mosswood said sharply. "I haven't opened the circle yet. Anything could have come back."

Now that she was awake, it seemed so utterly simple to Pete. Jack hadn't come back for her. He'd come back at the behest of the Morrigan. He'd never intended to help her stop Naughton's murdering. He'd just used her to get to Carver, from the moment he'd pulled her out of the pit at the club.

She'd been a fool.

Jack came awake when Mosswood removed his hand, choking and letting some of the black stuff dribble down his chin. "Feel as if I've been hit by a fucking lorry," he gasped.

Mosswood said something to him, but Pete couldn't make out the words. She felt like kicked shit, her cracked rib still throbbed, and her head was muzzy from the orchid, but she couldn't be in the same room with Jack any longer.

"Pete?" She felt his shadow drop over her, and she smacked Jack's hands from her.

"Don't you fucking touch me."

"Can I explain, Pete?" he said, swaying when she shoved him back. "Can you at least give me that?"

"You've explained enough, I think," Pete said. She pointed to the door. "I'd like to leave now."

"Petunia," Jack said, low. "She would have sent me back. She would have given me back to Belial and this was all she asked. As long as it's not Naughton doing the ritual . . ."

"No," Pete said. "It's not. It's the Morrigan, Jack. I'd ask you who exactly that ritual is supposed to call, but it doesn't even matter. All she wants is death. And you're helping her do it."

"Helping to keep you safe," Jack mumbled. "If I'm in Hell, I can't be with you, Pete. I can't protect you from what's coming."

"Fuck me," Pete said. "You really have changed." She wanted to smash her fists into him, scream at him for lying to her. Not that Jack had made a habit of the truth, but to do it so casually, so smoothly, as if she were just another mark in the crowd at a conjure show. "You used to know I didn't need your fucking protection. I needed *you*, Jack. Not . . . not whatever you are."

"You want to tell me I'm weak," Jack said. "Go right the fuck ahead. I am weak. But don't tell me you don't understand why I did it."

"Ollie's going to die," Pete said. "I might die, you might die—the whole fucking Black is going to collapse in on itself if that bitch goes through with Naughton's ritual, and you're licking her bloody boot." Pete jabbed her finger into Jack's chest. "I don't think you're weak, Jack. I think you're a pussy."

He snatched her hand, pressing it against her and shoving Pete backward into the wall. Her head knocked the plaster, and dust and paint chips rained down. "You don't fucking *know*," Jack snarled. "You haven't been to Hell."

"Then tell me," Pete whispered. "That's all I ever wanted."

Jack dropped his head to her shoulder, nuzzling his lips into her neck. "It's constant screaming. It's your life, over and over and over again, until you can't take it for one more second. He broke me, Pete. He shattered every bone in my body. He flayed my skin off by inches. And when he'd gotten tired of hearing me scream, he put me together with thread and stuffing, and he started all over again."

Jack let her go and stood back, passing his hands over his face. "You think this is the first time the old gods have gotten their back up? I'll do what the Morrigan has been chasing me for since I was fourteen fucking years old, and things will carry on much as they have."

"You don't believe that," Pete said. "You would never have believed something like that, Jack."

"Doing a hitch in Hell makes you believe a lot of things you never thought were possible," Jack said. "There's no room for showy heroics in this story, Pete. We're giving Carver to the Hag, and Naughton can deal with her. Heath will probably be all right. And if he's not, I'm bloody sorry, but that's how things must be."

All at once, hearing it from his lips, Pete's confusion and grief hardened and tempered into rage. She cocked her fist back and slammed it into Jack's jaw, hard and sharp, following through with all her weight.

Jack stumbled, his legs buckling. "You cunt!" he shouted. Blood trickled from the corner of his mouth.

"I'm not the cunt in this conversation," Pete snarled. "Not by a long way."

Jack struggled up to his feet. He'd already sprouted a bruise. "I did what I had to do, Pete. That's all I can ever say about it. I know it wasn't right. I fucking know that. But I had to. For me, for you. I could have stood the pain, but knowing you were alone—that, I couldn't let stand. So yes, I'm the servant of the crow. And I'm not sorry."

She wanted to draw back from the expression on his face, the cold, inhuman flatness in his eyes, but she steeled herself and moved nearer. "Just give me Carver. We can find a way—"

"I told you no," Jack said. "Now will you listen this time, or do I have to slap a hex on you?"

"Don't bother," Pete told him. "I'm leaving." She jerked the door open to find a gang of black suits and pale faces that crowded her back into the room. "No sudden moves," said one, whom she recognized from the back room of Naughton's vile club.

Three all together, like all bad things, and they moved straight for Jack. "Fuck me," Jack muttered, backpedaling. "Boys, let's talk about this, shall we?"

"Mr. Naughton says you're out of time," the one closest to Pete told her. "Do you have what we want?"

Pete jerked her chin at Jack. "He does."

"Oh, yes. Lovely," Jack said. "This is a terrible idea, mates. Trust me on that."

"Don't think so," said the hulking one. "You've fucked with the big dog, my son, and now he's going to bite your arse. Come along."

Pete checked the sitting area, but Mosswood had gone, through some inscrutable method of his own. One less problem, but one less body for backup when things inevitably got ugly. She eased open the door of the entry table, scrabbling for the heavy torch she kept there for emergencies, but one of Naughton's men saw, threw her to the ground, and stepped hard on her injured hand. Pete felt small bones go and let out a scream.

"Naughty, naughty," the necromancer told her, and tilted his thin face toward Jack. "What do you say, Winter? You'll come quietly for your little slice of heaven here?"

"She's not worth it to me," Jack said, and if Pete could've flinched any harder, she would have. Jack had a hard face, always, the kind of mask everyone who'd grown up poor and smacked around in a dirty factory town manufactured. But it had been just that, a mask. Not like it was at that moment. "You're not going to coerce me, gents," Jack said, "and you're not going to scare me by roughing up some poor girl half your size, so why don't you just toddle on home?"

The big one raised a hand. "How about instead we hex you and drag you back there boots-first?" He didn't wait for Jack's response before he threw the hex. Jack batted it aside and cracks blossomed in the plaster walls of the flat. The necromancer didn't play about—the next thing he flung wasn't a simple hex but a curse that turned the air to ozone and filled Pete's nostrils with the scent of burnt rubber.

Jack went down hard, and the necromancer's next effort bounced off a shield hex that rippled into being before his body. The feedback screamed through Pete's skull, and she knew it would be ten times worse for Jack, letting his talent flow and his sight absorb magic unchecked.

The necromancer hit again, and again, and the entire flat shook. The high windows exploded, and in the kitchen Pete heard glasses and plates popping like firecrackers. Sharp-edged snow rained down to pepper her bare skin.

"You want me?" Jack sneered at the necromancers. "You want that sad little excuse for a soul cage for your boss? Come and get me." He stepped back, slung his leg over the sill of the shatttered window, and dropped from view.

The trio of necromancers rushed to the window while Pete stared. "Fuck me," said the one who'd stomped her hand. "Four stories straight down."

"Demons juiced him," said the big one. " 'Least that's what I heard."

"Nah," said the rat-faced one. "Heard he bedded down with the crow woman, got his powers the old, bloody way, like fucking Cù Chulainn or some shite."

The rat-faced necromancer jerked his thumb at Pete. "What about her?"

"Pick her up and take her with us," the big one said. "Let Mr. Naughton decide what to do."

CHAPTER 31

Nick Naughton stroked his thumb over Pete's cheek. She flexed her hands, the broken one knifing up her forearm. Naughton's thugs had tied her well, with plastic zip ties that bit into her wrists. "I suppose you think you've very clever, playing the holdout game, waiting for your mage to save your arse."

"Fuck off," Pete said. She wasn't in the mood for creativity, and Naughton didn't deserve it anyway.

Naughton heaved a sigh. "Sean, get those off and hold her up."

Sean, the hulking necromancer, looked at Naughton with wide eyes. "What if she, yanno, sucks all me talent out of me head? She's a Weir."

"She weights a hundred and ten pounds soaking wet, you great frilly girl," Naughton sighed. "And it's not as if she's a bloody superhero."

Sean cut the plastic with his flick knife and hauled Pete up, pinning her arms behind her back.

"So, Petunia," Naughton said. His thumb stroked her lips. Being touched by him was like being touched by something drowned and dead—slimy, with the scent of damp, mossy places that had never seen the light of day. "What are we going to do about you?"

"You could let Ollie and me go," she suggested.

"It's good to keep your sense of humor." Naughton's hand dropped to her clavicle, the tips of his fingers skating under her collar. "But you and I have a mutual goal now—we both want what the crowmage took from us. Why don't you stop treating me as an enemy and go convince him to hand it over. Use your winning smile, and tell him nobody else will get hurt." He grinned. "I mean, that part's a lie. I rather like hurting people. But it sounds better that way."

"I know what you're doing," Pete told him. "Carver. The reliquary. Why you tried to sacrifice him."

"We *succeeded* in sacrificing Carver," Naughton said. "That arse McCorkle thought he could rob me, and some unfortunate circumstances—they buggered the *ritual*, not the sacrifice. Well, to be more precise, one circumstance buggered the ritual. His name was Henry, and Henry is no longer with us. Isn't that right, Sean?"

Sean gulped. Naughton patted Pete's cheek. "You have nothing more than some thirdhand Babylonian legends and muttered rumors from a few mages scared of their own shadow. You don't know, Miss Caldecott. You don't even comprehend the scope of what's coming up through the layers of the worlds below ours. What changes he will bring with him. But if you want to survive long enough to take a gander, then you're going to do as I ask."

"Or I could tell you to shove your poncey new world order right in your arse," Pete said. Naughton considered.

"I suppose you could."

"I think I am."

"And I think you simply don't understand the gravity of our situation," Naughton said. "Perhaps you and I should go somewhere and have a more private chat."

"The serpent winds the world," Pete said, blurting out Morningstar's prophecy. Anything to stop Naughton touching her. "The serpent. Whatever it is, that's what you're calling. That's what the reliquary belonged to. That's what the soul cage is for. It's not a spirit at all."

Naughton narrowed his eyes at her and was quiet long enough to let Pete know she'd touched some kind of nerve. He snapped his fingers like a pistol shot. "Sean."

"Yes, guv?"

"Take Miss Caldecott into the kitchen. She's so eager to see her fat friend, put her in with him."

"Right." Sean snatched Pete by the arm. "Come on, then." He dragged her to the walk-in, thrust her inside, and slammed the door. Pete heard a chain clatter through the handle on the other side.

She patted herself down for her lighter and flicked it open. "Ollie?"

"Pete?" She felt a hand swat her, and then close around her arm as the flame flared to life. Ollie's face was drawn and covered in stubble, but he looked healthy, and he grabbed her and gave her a hard squeeze. "Was beginning to think you forgot about me."

"Never," Pete said, thumping him on the back. "Who'd be around to eat half of my curry and harangue me that magic isn't real if I let you kick off?"

Ollie'd been untied, but the spindleback chair was still the only furniture in the old freezer. The rest was full of boxes, musty and old as the hills, and Heath settled on the ground, his back against them. "Fuck me. Been sleeping on this floor for a decade, feels like."

Pete took a seat next to him, careful to keep the lighter from the rat-gnawed cardboard. "I'm sorry. I really hoped this would be a rescue."

He patted her knee. "Shit rescue, but it's all right, Caldecott. Sooner or later that stiff bastard Patel will notice I'm not around for him to shout questions at, and he'll send some plods looking for me."

"We might not last that long," Pete said. "Not that Naughton's going to off us, but London might not be in the same shape by the time Patel catches on."

"Fuck me, you're a ray of bloody sunshine, aren't you?" Ollie grumbled.

Pete fingered her pack of Parliaments and found it was empty. "They been treating you all right?"

"Aside from cramming me in this rat-infested shit trap? It's been like a weekend in Blackpool," Ollie said. "At least the takeaway that cunt-faced wanker Sean brings in isn't too dodgy."

"Sounds better than my day thus far." Pete flung the empty pack into a corner.

"What about your boy Winter?" Ollie said. "Setting aside for a moment his trick act of showing up alive. Any chance he'll be making a grand entrance?"

The mention of Jack forced a few tears from Pete's eyes, unexpected and hot as fresh blood. "Jack and I aren't together right now, Ollie. Not about all this."

"Always said that bloke was miles beneath you." Ollie sniffed. "You two have a falling out?"

"He's a fucking liar," Pete said. "I don't want to talk about Jack, Ollie." She shut the lighter since it was just the two of them and some junk in the dark, not worth wasting fluid on.

"Should we plot and scheme on how to bust out, then?" Ollie asked. "Or do you want to tell me what ridiculous bit of Doctor Who shenanigans that pasty lot out there is up to?"

"Necromancers," Pete said. "Summoning something inhuman and horrible, likely. Sacrificial rites toward same. Cryptic prophecies. That sort of thing." She could keep herself together for Ollie, but being shut up in the freezer was already making her twitch. Especially since she knew neither Felix Patel nor Jack would find them in time. That Jack would not come at all, until he'd done what the Morrigan demanded of him.

Pete wasn't angry with him any longer. She simply felt like the greatest idiot in all of England for trusting Jack in the first place. He'd nearly gotten her killed when she was sixteen. He'd let her think he was dead once before. He'd lied about his deal with Belial, until the demon snatched him from under her nose. Jack Winter had never given her a single reason to trust him. And yet, her chest was still tight when she thought about the casual way he'd turned on her this time. *The last time*, Pete vowed.

"Necromancers," Ollie said at last. "You know, Caldecott, eighteen months ago I would have put you in for a psychiatrist and a few weeks in the country. Now, I really don't have a better explanation for all this crap." Boxes rustled in the dark as he fidgeted. "Things are bad all over. Murders are up. The schizophrenics are screaming even stranger shite than usual when we get called out. You don't have to be bloody magic to see that something's slid out of tilt in this city."

Pete nodded. "Way out. Out past coming back, I think."

Ollie grunted. "How bad is it going to be?"

"Bad," Pete said softly. "Worse than the bombs. Worse than the fires, maybe. It's a fundamental shifting, if we all just sit back and let it happen. If we do, I don't think we're going to crawl out of our safe little holes to the same world."

"Full-tilt zombie robot apocalypse." Ollie snorted. "And me without my freeze-dried rations, machete, and girl in a leather bikini."

"Do you think I'm an idiot?" Pete asked him. "For not just riding the tide and waiting to see where everything comes down once the storm's gone?"

"Somebody's got to be on the side of the angels," Ollie said. "And I think you're a good pick, Caldecott. More than you credit yourself with."

Pete let herself slide down until she was on her back on the floor, staring at the sliver of light through the exhaust port in the freezer's ceiling. "That makes one of us thinking that, I suppose."

A shadow flicked across the port, and she sat up. The owl landed, its passage causing the vent fan to spin, casting slices of light and shadow across Pete and Ollie.

I warned you, the Hecate whispered, as the owl tilted its head and stared down at her with glowing yellow eyes, perfectly round and fathomless as the sun.

"Just what I bloody needed," Pete muttered. Ollie shifted in the dark, and Pete knew he was probably looking at her with suspicion.

"What are you on about?"

Kill the crow-mage, the owl whispered. *I told you what you must do and you steadfastly ignored me.*

Now you've reaped the fruits of the poisoned tree. You should have cut it down and salted the earth.

"Sod you," Pete told it. "I don't run about stabbing people in the back." She massaged her throbbing forehead, the proximity of the thing sending bright stabs of pain through the Black. "There's got to be another way now."

You don't believe that, said the Hecate. *But it doesn't matter. You failed, Weir. You allowed the Hag an opening to release her army, not just into the Black, but into the daylight world. Death is walking because of you, Petunia Caldecott. Are you pleased?*

"'Course I'm not fucking pleased!" Pete shouted at it. Ollie started, but she could explain her seemingly abrupt descent into chattering at birds later.

And neither am I, the Hecate said. The owl spread its wings. *This is the end of all things, Weir. Now all that is left to me is punishment. Not recourse. Not bargaining. Not mercy. The Hag has banished those things as she encroaches. All I can look forward to is blood.*

The air crackled around Pete, and every inch of her skin prickled. She heard Ollie say, "What in the—" before blackness dropped across Pete's eyes and the worst pain she'd ever felt gripped her. It felt as if her consciousness and body were being yanked in opposite directions at roughly the speed of a bullet train, and that iron hooks had pinned themselves into her brain, spiking deep down into her talent. She heard herself scream, or maybe it was just the scream of wind past her ears, and then as quickly as the feeling had started, it stopped, and white light burned out Pete's eyesight.

Blinking furiously, tears sliding over her cheeks,

she reached out for anything, anything at all, but there was nothing but cool wind and wet droplets plastering her skin. Her knees buckled and falling down seemed like an extraordinarily good idea, so Pete did, landing on something soft that smelled of green and dirt.

Do you recognize this place? The Hecate, no longer the owl but the girl with the long, narrow face and the yellow eyes, placed her hand on the nape of Pete's neck, pulling her close.

Pete, for her part, gulped and tried to assess whether she was still alive, and if alive, whether she had all her bits attached. "What did you do to me?"

Crossed you, said the Hecate. *Through the gateways. You're with me now, Pete. To do with as I see fit.* Her slender fingers and their blunt nails tightened. *Now, do you know what you see?*

Pete tried to focus her eyes, tears drying cold on her cheeks and leaving salt trails like nerveless scar tissue. She sat with her legs akimbo at the top of a green hillock, looking down on a white clapboard cottage with a leaning chimney, surrounded by an untidy garden and a path that led down to a dirt road. Far away, over the humps of the blindingly green hills on the other side of the valley, Pete could glimpse the sea.

Pete knew the place. She hadn't been in nearly fifteen years, but she knew it well enough to be able to pick out every missing brick in the garden path and avoid them.

Well? The Hecate stared at her. The wind running off the water ruffled her straight brown hair, spun it around her face like a spider's web.

"It's my grandmother's house," Pete said. Her

throat was raw from screaming and her voice came out a rasp that blended with the breeze and the shriek of gulls overhead.

Very good, the Hecate told her. She gripped Pete's arm. She was even smaller than Pete, but her fingers were like iron and she hauled Pete to her feet as easily as you'd toss an empty chip sack into the bin.

"I don't understand," Pete said. It couldn't be anything good. Some part of her had always known that when she went to the thin spaces, not by design but by death, this was what she'd see. The ramshackle little house and the endless verdancy of Ireland, bound on all sides by salt and sea.

The Hag has her patron, said the Hecate, *and I had mine. And she has failed me. So here you will stay, Petunia Caldecott. Not alive and not dead. At the crossroads of all worlds, buried for your sins until I see fit to release you. Or until the world burns down around you. It's a toss-up at this point, I think.*

"Wait!" Pete said as the Hecate started to walk away. "That's it? I don't turn to murder because you snap your fingers and so you just leave me here to rot?"

Not to rot, said the Hecate. *Your body will be in what your friends will call a coma, and your soul will be here. Some day they may reunite, but by then you'll be quite mad.* She lifted her face to the weak sun peering through the wispy lace curtains of mist that floated across the hillside. *Perhaps you and the gulls will learn to speak to one another, in the creaks and croaks of your ruined throat.*

The Hecate turned away again, and Pete raced after her up the hill, feet sinking into the mucky peat. "Fuck you, you glassy-eyed bitch! You don't own me! And if it was so important that Jack and Naughton not get Carver, you should've left me there to get him back!"

Pete could see only one of her glowing eyes and the razor edge of her child's profile as the Hecate glared at her. *You still don't understand. Even on the brink of death, you maintain that the world will go on. And I do own you, Petunia. As the Hag owns Jack Winter, and as his dead god owns Nicholas Naughton, you are an avatar. You are one of the touched, the people who in the past would be saints and madmen.*

"So then tell me what I've missed!" Pete shouted. "Give me a chance to fix it, if I'm your bloody chosen child!"

There is no chosen one, the Hecate hissed. *There are the touched, and you are replaceable. I owe you nothing.*

"Oh yeah?" Pete folded her arms. "Then why are you so angry?"

The Hecate sighed. The wind kicked up and raked fingers through Pete's hair and over her chilled skin. *Because you are a good person, Petunia Caldecott, and you should not have let the Hag and her general with his dead man's eyes drag you into the mud.*

"Just tell me what's coming," Pete said. "And I'll find a way to stop it. Don't just leave me here. I'm listening now. Please." She refused to believe the wetness on her face was more tears. "I was wrong," Pete whispered. "Tell me what's going to happen."

The Hecate came back to her. She placed her palm against Pete's cheek and stared into her eyes. It was such a human, mothering gesture that Pete nearly recoiled. Gentleness should not come from a being that didn't even understand the concept of compassion.

You really want to see what I see? the Hecate whispered. *You truly desire?*

Pete nodded wordlessly. The Hecate turned her around to look down the other side of the valley, where the ground sloped inland to eventually end in the motorway that lead into Galway proper.

There are triads in the Black, and there are triads before the Black, life and birth and death, stretching back to the beginning. At one time we were separate, and at one time we stood joined.

Below Pete, clouds blacker than any soot crawled across the valley, and crimson droplets spattered against the back of her hands and her cheeks. She swiped at them, the blood leaving streaky tracks.

Still, the Hecate ordered her. *It's a memory of the land, Petunia. It can't touch you. Gods were born and gods died, and their corpses and their afterbirth became grave things. Other things*, the Hecate whispered in her ear. The earth rippled under Pete's boots, and from far below she heard a scream, expressed more as an earthquake than a sound.

They spilled their blood on the earth, and they gave their seed to heroes, and some of us birthed mages and monsters and some of us birthed your dreams, the Hecate said. Pete saw the clouds descend toward the ground, a clinging black mist that withered wherever it touched. A fat white sheep grazing the hillside tried to escape and was instantly reduced to a pile of bloated entrails.

Only one gave death, rather than birth. Pete saw a figure step out of the fog, not a spirit but a whole man, clad in black, fingers extraordinarily long, with black, oil-fed flames dancing across his black, fathomless eyes.

He killed what he touched. The ground where he stood turned to salt, and the cities he visited turned to ashes. The Hecate's voice was no longer a reverent whisper, but scornful. She bit off each word and spat it at the figure. *We spilled his blood, but we did not know what we'd done. When we cut him down, stopped his march across the face of the Black toward the living world, he gave us his revenge—a child.*

The ground rattled again, and Pete lost her footing, going hard onto her hands and knees. A stone cut her palm, and the figure in the valley swiveled, elongated nostrils flaring. Pete met its eyes and clapped her bloody hand over her mouth to stifle a scream. It was like pressing hot needles into her brain, directly through her eye sockets. The thing below wasn't simply wreathed in black magic—he was the source of it. The ground zero of the wave of malice that coated the valley, turning it into an abattoir for anything living.

The god of plague giving birth to the one thing that no god or demon could slay. The Hecate removed her hand from Pete. *Irony is not lost on gods, Petunia. And the men trying to free the child from its bonds do not realize what will happen if it becomes so.*

Pete stayed where she was, sitting back on her heels, trying to quell the wave of nausea and pain. The clouds rolled past, and the bloody rain dried on her skin, and it was as if nothing had happened to the valley at all.

And the Hag, said the Hecate, *is no better. She is power hungry, and she will use the child to spread the armies of Death to the daylight world. And then, because she is arrogant and grasping, she will inevitably lose control, and the child will become as his father.* She smoothed her hands over her dress. *Nergal was slain before the world, but he has tried*

*to return before. If the Morrigan weakens the Black,
he will succeed.*

"So that's his name," Pete said softly. "I wondered."

A name, the Hecate said. *There are many more
for what he is.*

"Can't you stop her?" Pete said. "The Morrigan?
You're stronger. You walk the gateways."

*If the dragon crawls up out of its prison, I will per-
ish*, the Hecate said sadly. *The offspring of the plague
god can tread anywhere it wishes. It will shatter the
gateways. Nothing is older or stronger than death,
Petunia, and the Morrigan is death's maiden.*

"But in the Black . . ." Pete started. The Hecate
shook her head.

*There will be no Black, and no daylight world.
They will bleed, until all of the crossroads are in
flames, and when we are all gone to cinders, I wager
the demons will caper up from Hell to chew on our
bones.* She gave Pete a humorless smile. *Crafty little
creatures, demons. The only true survivors in this
wretched world.*

"So what can I do?" Pete said quietly. "What will
keep this . . . thing locked up?"

The owl woman sadly stroked a hand over Pete's
head where she crouched, her hand warm against
Pete's damp, bloody skin. *There is nothing to be done
now. If the dragon were still imprisoned, perhaps.
But he is awake, and soon he will be free. Death
comes for us all, Pete. Even gods.*

"I won't lie down," Pete told her. "I know I didn't
do what you asked of me, but I can still stop Jack.
Somewhere, he's still got to be Jack."

Hell changes a man, the Hecate said. *It molds
him into the worst obscenity of himself. He leaves*

shreds of his soul even if he is raised up again. The demon who claimed him is in him forever.

"You have to let me try," Pete said. "I can get Jack. And if I can get Jack I'll have the dragon's soul cage, and we can keep Nergal from running roughshod over everything." Maybe. If Jack hadn't abandoned her completely.

The Hecate touched Pete's cheek, and then shook her head. *You are so young, even for a human.*

"Please," Pete said, because it had worked once before. She never begged—begging was for the weak, Connor had taught his daughters. Hell, *asking* was for the weak most of the time. Real coppers—who smoked and drank and lived off their hunches and smacked a suspect in the gob if it'd get things moving—didn't ask anyone for anything. They didn't ask if it was all right to go on and die with less than six months' notice, and they didn't ask to go out and make things right.

You cannot do what is necessary, the Hecate sighed. *And so you'll stay here. Until the storm passes or I do.*

She began to walk down the hill to the motorway, and Pete rushed the words out.

"I'll do it."

The Hecate turned around and blinked once, slowly. She cocked her head and for a moment she was an owl, all downy feathers and silent wings. *You will do what, Weir?*

"It's Jack or the whole bloody world, right?" Pete said. "I'm not a fucking idealist. I'll do it. Let me out and I'll do it."

She held her breath, held every bit of herself absolutely still, and waited. A halfway decent Met detective could spot a liar, but Pete knew that she was an accomplished one, and also that the Hecate was about as far removed from human as England was from the moon.

If she'd really thought Jack would go through with ripping the Black to shreds, she wouldn't have lied. But it was Jack—*had* to still be Jack, somewhere deep inside the new skin Hell had hardened onto his old one. She'd pulled him back from the Bleak Gates. Pulling the man from the Morrigan's shadow couldn't be so much different. *Yeah, Caldecott, and a fucking complement of unicorns might march up and down outside Buckingham Palace when you do.*

Very well, the Hecate said. *Dispose of Winter and return the soul of Gerard Carver to my auspices and I will consider you in good standing.*

Pete laughed, short and sharp. "You were just rattling my cage. Put me in the in-between and let me sweat a bit." She tapped the Hecate on her breastbone. "I think you're more human than you let on."

The Hecate looked at her for a long moment before she blinked. *Return to the world, Petunia Caldecott. Remember your vow. And do not disobey me again.*

"Bloody gods," Pete said as she spun back into her body, still flopped on its side on Naughton's freezer floor.

CHAPTER 32

Ollie fussed over her until Pete managed to assure him, via repeated insistence and finally swatting at his hand, that she was all right.

"You were screamin' to wake the dead," Ollie said.

"Trust me, Ollie," Pete told him. "The dead don't need any help on that score."

"Scared the piss out of me," Ollie muttered. "I know we're in a bad way but don't do that again if you can help it, yeah?"

In a bizarre way, the pain and the psychic bombardment had cleared Pete's head. She was past the point of no return—in that zone beyond exhausted where everything becomes tunnel visions and knife edges. She'd lied to the Hecate, she hadn't delivered to Naughton, and she'd trusted the one person in the Black who could fuck her over properly the way no other could. Not to mention that Felix Patel would probably find a way to pin McCorkle's murder and Ollie's situation on her if he were given half a chance. If Pete were in Patel's shoes, she'd arrest her too.

"I'm fucked," Pete said out loud. "Properly."

"Your sunny optimism never fails to gird my loins and strengthen my bloody spirit, you know," Ollie said. "Don't unravel on me now, Caldecott."

"I've got bloody nothing in my hand," Pete said. "Except I either go out and murder someone in cold blood or we stay here until the Met digs up our skeletons in a few decades and we become a mystery program on Channel 1."

"Jesus," Ollie said. "And there you go reassuring me."

"I'm sorry," Pete sighed. She stood up and paced to each wall, just to have something to do. "I just needed to say that to someone, before I screamed some more."

"You know something?" Ollie said. "I hated you the first time I clapped eyes on you."

"Is this your idea of helpful?" Pete said. She had to get the fuck out of this freezer and find Jack. At least try to talk him out of handing Carver over, if he hadn't already.

"You were just some snot-nosed DC who had a famous da, clearly years too green for CID," Ollie said. "And you remember what the first thing you said to me was when I reluctantly rolled meself over to shake your hand?"

"'You've got kidney pie on your shirt,'" Pete muttered, glad it was dark so Ollie couldn't see her flush. She *had* been green, barely twenty-six and well aware that everyone in the CID room at Holborn had been staring a hole in her.

"Too right, kidney pie," Ollie said. "And I knew then that you were either even more of a little snot than I supposed or you had a pair of great brass ones." He shifted in the dark. "I'm glad it was the latter, Caldecott, because you've kept my arse on the straight and narrow these past years, and you were a good copper, and you're going to be all right now." He reached out in the dark, caught her hand, and squeezed. "Now leave off your whingeing and use that cracking wit to get us out of here, will you?"

"Survival," Pete said, Ollie's words sprouting a mad idea in her head. It was more than mad—it was fucking suicidal, and it was something that Jack would have smacked her into a wall for even contemplating. But it was that or kill him, and Pete's answer to that was still the same. Couldn't fucking do it.

"'S what I said," Ollie agreed.

Pete dug her lighter out again and flicked it on. "Open up these boxes. I need chalk, or paint—even a marker will do. Something to draw with."

Ollie's forehead crinkled, but he helped her, the rodent-chewed and broken-down cardboard coming apart in their hands. "Don't mind my stupid question," Ollie said, "but what d'you need to draw, anyway?"

"A circle," Pete told him. "There's someone that I need to talk to."

She unearthed chalk and a wealth of discarded candle stubs in one of the boxes, along with bills for a band that had played Naughton's club in 1989 and several Halloween decorations of the same vintage. Pete lit the candles, which guttered over the steel walls. "Stand back," she told Ollie, putting the black candle at the head and the white at the foot.

"You sure know what you're doing?" he said, backing up to the corner of the freezer.

"Yeah," Pete said as she chalked a crooked ring between the candles. "I'm a bloody expert in all matters of the occult." She didn't know all the markings that Jack did, didn't know the words his discipline had passed to him, but with this, all that mattered—really—was the name.

Pete drew another circle around herself, doubling it for safety. She sat, folding her hands over her knees, and looked back at Ollie. "No matter what happens, do *not* cross the chalk and do *not* break the circle, you understand me?"

Ollie's eyes were wide. "Pete, what exactly is about to happen here?"

Pete shut her eyes and tried to take a calming breath that only aggravated her rib. "Probably nothing good."

Jack would say that what she was doing was an obscenity. That it would probably kill her, and even if it didn't, that it would rip her soul away from her surely as wind snuffed a candle flame. "But you're not here," Pete murmured as she chalked a final word in front of her toes. "Are you?"

Jack had brought her here. Because she'd believed his lies, and she'd let herself think that he was the man who could save the world, if it came to that. She'd followed him too far down the rabbit hole, and now there was no way back, only through. The choices were down to one—fight or lie down and die. And Pete had known since long before she clapped eyes on Jack Winter that she wasn't the dying type.

She had to close the circle, imbue it with her will, and Pete pressed her thumbs into her forehead, trying to massage the twinge that rose when she reached down into herself and tried to push a little bit of talent into the chalk markings. Jack's magic looked like blue fire, so Pete clung to that image, seeing faint blue flame rising from the twin ring of chalk marks. Her headache worsened, and she felt something warm and wet trickle from her nostrils. A hum built in her back teeth, vibrating all through her skeleton, and Pete recognized it as the same impulse that had rushed through her when she'd flung the hexes, simply sustained. It hurt like sticking her fingers into a socket, and she dug her nails into her palm to take her mind off it. There was an incantation for these sorts of things, dozens of them, in as many languages, but Pete didn't know any by rote, so she used the name.

"Belial."

Nothing happened, except an increase in her headache, verging from uncomfortable into the territory of concussions and blackout hangovers.

Pete swallowed, her mouth dry as a wad of cotton, and tried again. "Belial. Prince of the demons of Hell. Pete Caldecott wants to talk to Belial."

The air shimmered before her, yawning into a black vortex, and Pete heard screaming and smelled the faint scent of fires, the sort of dirty smoke roiled by burning corpses.

"Belial?" Pete said, the power gathering behind her eyes making her skull throb. There was a time when the sight would have terrified her, but now she just sighed. "Come on, Belial, quit fucking about."

The theatrics ceased, and in their place stood a small man in a black suit and white shirt, immaculate tie pressed and done with a ruby stickpin. Belial smoothed his greasy hair out of his pure black eyes and grinned at her with shark's teeth. "Well, hello there, Pete. You wanted to see me?"

CHAPTER 33

Pete stood up. Belial wasn't tall, in the body he chose to wear like a flash little overcoat, and she could nearly look him in the eye. "Suppose I did."

Belial's tongue flicked out and wriggled, tasting the air. "Never thought I'd see the day, but awfully glad that I did."

Pete shot a glance at the circle. It was solid, but she started when she saw Ollie slumped unconscious against the wall. "What did you do to him?"

Belial shrugged. "You wanted to talk. Figured we should do it without that fat gobshite eavesdropping."

"You're a bloody bastard, you know?" Pete said.

His pointed teeth glowed in the guttering candlelight. "I am a demon, luv."

"I haven't forgotten," Pete assured him. Belial took a step toward her, and Pete took one back before she could stop herself. She stopped her foot before it rubbed out the chalk line. The demon laughed, sending cold dead fingers up and down her spine.

"So close and yet so far away. Jack's taught you a thing or two, hasn't he? Clever girl."

"You're going to have to at least work a little if you want out," Pete said. "It's not fancy, but it'll hold."

Belial shimmered, and when Pete blinked he was in front of her. He grabbed the back of her neck and drew them close enough to kiss. "You haven't got the stones to hold me, Petunia. I'm not a trained dog. I'm here because you interest me." He released her just as abruptly then fixed his tie. "Now why don't you smooth out that frown and tell me what you want, before I get bored and take myself off to the cinema?"

"If I'm so horrible at this, then why are you standing here?" Pete waved a hand. "There's the door. Go fly away, and open it for me while you're at it."

Belial chuckled again. "You may not have the finesse yet, but you've got bigger balls than Winter. He was crying and pissing blood when I came by his little summoning circle."

"Jack was dying," Pete snapped. "And I'm not afraid of you."

"Oh yes," Belial said. "You are." He pressed his cheek against hers, inhaled her scent. This close, Pete could sense a glimmering of the thing beneath the skin—writhing, many eyed, many-voiced, screaming and clawing to be free. "I knew there was a reason Winter liked you," Belial murmured. "You still smell sweet, no matter how many miles he puts on."

Pete shoved him back, hard. The demon only laughed. "What, are you embarrassed to admit you shagged a wrung-out junkie like Winter? I would be, too, were I a put-together little thing like you. I bet you keep your nightie on."

"Why don't you just simmer down before I knock

every one of those creepy teeth down your throat?" Pete suggested.

Belial frowned. "You just summoned me out of the blackest pits of Hell to chat, then?" He wagged a finger at her. "No, you're desperate. But not for the same reasons as Winter. Your reasons aren't petty and reeking of cowardice. 'S why I'm interested." He twitched his cuffs and examined the ruby ring on his left hand, breathing on it and rubbing it on his suit. "Spit it out, luv. I'm getting bored."

"About a dozen people want me dead, another dozen want Jack, and I've been locked in a fucking freezer by a pack of necromancers," Pete said. "That enough for you, you fucking bastard?"

Belial cocked his head. "Lot of trouble for one little woman to get into. Prolific Petunia, harbinger of death and destruction."

"I need help," Pete admitted. "I need the sort of help a demon can give."

"Surely you and Winter have a foolhardy little plan," the demon said. "Some last ditch attempt to save the day and send the guilty to their judgement and the righteous to their reward?"

"No," Pete said. "Besides, you know exactly what happened to Jack. You're the one who lost custody, after all."

"Winter licking the boots of the Hag and the rest of the Black beset by necromancy and terror?" Belial grinned. "Sounds like a Saturday night to me, Petunia. I don't think you're going to convince me otherwise." His black glass eyes flicked up and down her body. "'Less, of course, you want to use that fine firm mouth of yours for something other than talking."

"I thought demons loved a deal," Pete said. Her head hurt so much her vision was doubling, and her voice sounded unreasonably loud in her ears. She wasn't going to be able to hold the thin, slippery strings of power that girded the circle much longer. "I thought they loved bargains more than anything. I didn't think they were quite so interested in flesh."

"Me? I'm very interested," Belial said. "You know what Hell is, Petunia? It's fucking boring. We've got fleshpots and opium dens, torture chambers and souls to rip apart over and over again, to fuck and taste and deform to our pleasure." He sighed, and felt his body over as if it were quite new. "You don't have a fag, do you?"

"I'm out," Pete said. "And you wouldn't get one anyway."

"Pity," Belial said. "We have all of that, and I'm still bored out of my fucking skull. What I love is not the deal but when the deal comes due. And the sweeter the bargaining, the better it is for me. But you, Pete—you're entirely too good to make that kind of bargaining. Your lily-white soul is just going to wilt and die in Hell." He sniffed. "No fire in you. Just a misplaced need to run about playing savior." Belial yawned. "Snore. Think I'm going to push down your little spellwork here and head off. I am sorry if I cause you a brain aneurysm or something when I break the circle."

Pete wanted nothing so much as to punch Belial in his smug gob. She'd thought he would salivate at the idea of getting his hands on even the possibility of a bargain with her, and he was acting as if she were an unattractive girl in a chavvy nightclub. Fucking demons. "I'm not saving anything," she said. "I'm just trying to keep Nergal's fucking dragon in his place, so that all the Black, including your charming existence, can carry on."

He paused with his shiny black shoe just short of

the chalk, then turned to look at her. "What about a dragon?"

"Oh yeah, you know all about Nergal," Pete said. "The Hecate told me. The biggest, baddest bastard on the block, until the rest of you decided to take him down a peg. The Morrigan's after his child. She's aiming high."

Belial's grin was unconscious this time, pure sadistic joy spreading across his features. "Oh, *delicious*. The Hag was always the worst of them. Old gods. Old farts, you ask me. Barking over table scraps, what was left over when the daylight world moved on. But this—this actually shows some spine. Well *done*."

"Have we a bargain or not?" Pete demanded. Belial hadn't been wrong when he'd hissed at her that she was scared. She was terrified—anyone with sense was terrified of demons. Pete rather thought that if she were throwing her weight around with no trepidation whatsoever, she'd be a fucking idiot.

"Depends." Belial shrugged. "What wonders have you to entice me with, Petunia?"

"I don't have anything," Pete said softly. "Just myself."

"Mmhmm," Belial said. He tapped a forefinger against his own nose, once. "Tempting as that is, I think I'd rather have you in one piece, and willing to do something for me."

"I don't have a talent like Jack's," Pete said. "So unless you want me to go and fetch you takeaway . . ."

"I enjoy your sarcasm, Petunia, I really do," Belial told her. "But unless you want me to tear your throat out and paint myself in your entrails, shut the fuck up and let me finish."

Pete wondered if it was a measure of some kind

of madness to want to kick a demon square between the legs. A particularly smug and annoying bastard of a demon, but a demon all the same.

"Good girl," Belial said. "I don't want you used up and spent like a fiver at a strip club. I want you alive and vital, and ready to turn that quick mind and that pert little body of yours to my ends." He winked. "Having a favor with a Weir is never a poor life choice."

"You think I'm stupid?" Pete said. "An unspecified favor. For you. Sure, I was born fucking yesterday. Let's do it up."

"I think you wouldn't have called me if you were in a position to sass me," Belial said. "I'll help you smush your little plague lizard, and make the world safe for puppies, rainbows, and small children cavorting and licking lollipops, and in exchange, when I say it, you'll do me one favor. It's a very good deal, Petunia." His fingers slipped into her hair, smoothed it back from her face. "You don't even have to touch me."

Pete stared at the demon, and Belial stared back, that infuriating smile playing at the corners of his narrow lips. He had her backed against a wall, and he knew it.

"Right," she said. "If we're walking that road, I want something just as vague and abusive from you."

His nostrils flared. "I'd jump at the chance to abuse you, Petunia. Say what it is you want."

"You want a favor from me, you do what I ask to help me, until such a time as we've put the Morrigan's nasty little plan to rest or I'm dead," Petunia said. "In which case you'll drag me to Hell anyway, so it won't matter."

Belial shook his head at her. "Look at you, brokering deals like any streetwise black magic hustler. I think Winter's taught you a thing or two about the dark side, Petunia."

"And another thing," Pete told him. "My name's not fucking Petunia."

"Duly noted," the demon purred. "I'll be your obedient pet monster, and you'll be my card up the sleeve." He stepped forward and extended his hand in a businesslike fashion. "I've made a deal, Petunia Grace Caldecott, of my own will and you of yours. And you, Petunia Grace Caldecott, of London, child of Connor Caldecott of Galway and Juniper Morrow of Salisbury, freely bargain with me, Belial, a Named demon of Hell and Prince therein. So be it."

Pete grabbed the demon's hand before she could hesitate, lose her nerve, and run screaming for the hills. Belial might as well have been reciting daily specials in a café for all the effort he put into the phrase, but the enormous power it carried landed on Pete like a sack of sand.

This was a deal with a demon. This was the point she couldn't turn back from. *No turning back. Only through.*

"So be it, Belial."

He held her hand fast, and with his free digit tilted her head to stare into her eyes. "This is one of the sweetest days of my long and varied life, make no mistake. Getting the crow-mage, that was fantastic, don't get me wrong. Like having Ursula Andress in her prime suck your cock while being serenaded by a live performance of the entire *Hunky Dory* album. But this . . ." He grinned at Pete. "This is just a little sweeter."

"I agreed," Pete reminded him. "You can shut your gob now."

"Well, then," Belial said. "Consider it a bargain, freely made and freely worked. You've officially dabbled in the deviant side of magic, Pete. Does it give you a naughty tingle?"

Pete moved as far from him as she could within the confines of the circle, letting the power trickle away. Belial had her now. He wouldn't hurt her simply for sport. "Can you just open up the door and get us out of here?"

"Giving orders already. Good woman." Belial gestured at the door and it flew off the hinges and clear across the kitchen.

Pete ignored his showing off, and bent down next to Ollie to tweak him on the earlobe. "Wake up, Heath."

Ollie groaned. "Jesus, me head." He saw the demon and blinked. "Who the fuck is that? Am I having that bloody dream again with the funeral director and the parrot?"

"Oh, he's funny, the fat man," Belial said. "I think I'll enjoy him a great deal."

"Says the bloke dressed like he's trying out for a Duran Duran cover band," Ollie muttered.

"*Ollie*," Pete said. Ollie caught on, thankfully, and shut up.

Belial walked over to the door, which had crushed Sean, who stared up at him with bulging eyes, legs trapped under the steel. "Never understood necromancy," Belial said. "Mucking about with dead things. Got plenty of the dead in Hell, and I don't go about fondling them. Disgusting."

Pete cleared her throat and pointed behind the demon, where more of the pasty thugs that clung to

Naughton like maggots on a corpse had appeared in the narrow back hall.

"How the fuck did they get out?" the first asked.

"You didn't lock the fucking door, did you?" the other said.

"Gents." Belial spread his hands. "You can go, or you can die. Shouldn't be too hard, even for a brain trust such as yourselves."

The necromancers considered for a moment, and the first shook his head. "Ain't worth it, mate. That's a fucking demon."

"Fuck off," the second said. "That's not a demon. Just a git in an undertaker suit."

Belial smiled, and showed them his teeth. The second said, "Oh, shit."

"Forget it," said the first. "I'd go back to hustling in Tower Hamlets. 'Least I'd be alive."

He turned tail and ran, leaving the other standing alone, his eyes growing steadily larger as the demon advanced on him. Belial grabbed the necromancer by the front of his black windcheater and lifted him off his feet. The demon wasn't much larger than Pete, but he moved with the speed and sharpness of a veldt predator, hands with their long black nails puncturing through the necromancer's jacket and into his flesh.

The man let out a scream, and Belial shoved him up and back, the way Pete would knock aside an errant insect that had flown into her face. He carried the necromancer, hand reaching deep inside the man's sternum, until he crashed through the door at the end of the hall and into the club proper. Belial tossed the body aside and picked up a neatly folded napkin on the nearest table, gingerly dabbing blood off his hand.

Pete looked behind her at Ollie, who'd gone white, spots of crimson on either cheek. "This is not on," he muttered, his Adam's apple working.

"He had it coming," Pete said. "Trust me."

Shouting echoed off the low soundproofed ceiling of the club, and Naughton rushed in, backed up by the big lug who'd busted into Pete's apartment.

Belial turned to him and tilted his head. "Ah, one who's not a complete chav. You must be the boss."

Naughton stopped dead, stumbling over his own feet. "Oh, fuck me."

"Just back off, Nicholas," Pete told him. "We're leaving, and I don't want a fuss."

She expected Naughton to throw a curse, or possibly, if he was less of a bastard than she'd calculated, break down and piss himself, but she hadn't expected him to laugh. "I never took you for the type who bargains with Hell, Petunia. Never in a million years."

"You don't know everything," Pete told him. "Now step, 'fore I have the demon pull out your spine and use it for a percussion instrument."

"Go ahead." Naughton gestured her toward the door. "You can't stop what's coming. Not you, and not that black beastie you've called up out of the pit."

"There's no need to get shirty," Belial said. "I'm a bit more than a beastie. You can tell, else you wouldn't be keeping your distance and"—his nostrils flared—"sweating that sweet, coppery mess into the air like a virgin on her wedding night."

"You keep away from me," Naughton told him. "I serve something much worse than a demon on a vacation from the pit."

"Yeah, you and Nergal can circle-jerk until the

end of days," Belial said. "But you're still not going to tangle with me, are you?"

"No," Naughton said. "I'm not." He pointed them to the door. "Go," he said. "The son of Nergal still rises. The ashes of this world will still fertilize the soil of the next. The dragon of my god will see to it. I've done my duty. Who raises him is inconsequential."

"Let's get out of here," Pete told Belial. "You let him, he'll talk for hours. Loves the sound of his own voice."

"It's not going to work out the way you think, Nicky boy," Belial told him. He examined the cuff of his shirt, which bore a halo of blood. "But yes. I'll leave you for now. I do enjoy living things to play with."

Pete helped Ollie outside, although his weight combined with her own wasn't helping her stay upright. It was nearly morning: dampness on the cobbles, and a cold bite to the air that would vanish when the sun rose higher.

Belial inhaled deeply. "Smoke and piss and death. Smells just like home."

*   *   *

Pete settled Ollie on the curb. "You all right?"

Ollie nodded, swiping sweat droplets off his pudgy jaw. "I'll live. Feel a bit like puking my guts out in the nearest drain, though." He looked between Pete and the demon. "*You* all right? And who's this tosser? Don't like his look."

"But I like you a great deal, fat man." Belial grinned. "You'd look so very pretty turning on a spit with a poker shoved up your bum."

"You," Pete told Belial, "shut it. You"—she pointed

at Ollie—"get yourself home, and take a few days off."

Ollie didn't move his stare from Belial. He'd be feeling it, his lizard brain screaming at the intrusion of a predator into the fold, but he wouldn't allow himself to quite answer his own question. "What am I supposed to tell Patel about falling off the map the night after me partner got himself sliced up and coming back looking like I've been bloody tenderized?"

"You'll think of something," Pete told him. "Now please, Ollie. Go home. If anything else happens to you, it can't be because of me."

Ollie narrowed his eyes, but he nodded. "Anything you need, Pete, you call me, all right? Fuck Patel and the rest."

Pete patted his broad shoulder. "You're a good man, Ollie. Go on now."

"Sentimental git," Belial said after Ollie walked away toward the main road.

Pete glared. "Nobody asked you."

The demon sniffed the air, nostrils flaring white. "I'm famished. Everything smells so . . . so much. All grease and oil and digestive juices. I'd eat for days."

"You expect me to believe you eat food?" Pete said. She walked a little way, settling against one of the orange columns that marked the way through Southwark to the Tate Gallery on the bank. She didn't intend to stay long, just take some of the weight off her bruises and try to curb the dizziness and nausea that had become her constant minders.

"'Course I do," Belial said. "What, did you think I gnawed on babies or summat? I like food." He inhaled again, shutting his eyes and turning his face to the weak sunlight. "I like food, and the cinema, and feeling rain on my face. I'm not so different from a human, Pete."

"You're fucking miles from human," Pete told it. "And don't try to lull me into thinking otherwise."

Belial shrugged. "It was worth a try."

"I'd rather give Nicholas Naughton a deep tongue kiss," Pete said.

"That's rather harsh," Belial said. "At least I'm not a necrophiliac like your little friend back there." He walked out to the center of the street and turned in a slow circle. "I love this city. I can't understand what humans find so terrible about their world that they try to destroy everything in it."

"People aren't famous for thinking in the long term," Pete said. "'Sides, Naughton's just arrogant enough to think he'll be some kind of king of the apocalypse if his dead gods come out ahead."

"It's almost tempting to let Nergal chew him and spit him out," Belial said. "But if Nergal returns, there won't really be much left for me to enjoy in this world or any other, so how about you find Winter so I can gently persuade him to stop being a twat?"

Pete dug her thumbs into the corners of her eyes. "Give me a minute, all right?"

Belial shrugged, leaning against the column next to her. "Sure. Just stand here as long as you like. Nergal will wait patiently while you pull your shit together."

Pete saw a tightness in Belial's frame she'd never witnessed before. She'd hated him, sure he'd tricked Jack somehow, sure that the pleasure he took in pulling Jack into Hell was entirely sadistic. Now she was sure of nothing. Jack could have bargained with the demon freely, could have known exactly what he was getting into. And Belial wasn't human. The bargain was sacred to a demon. Belial had never actually broken his bargain with Jack. He'd tortured him, yes, but only after he'd given Jack his allotted thirteen years.

Pete decided she really must be beyond exhaustion. She was considering trusting a demon. "You're really piss-scared of Nergal, aren't you?" she said. "He's got your cage good and rattled."

"Like you're any different," Belial said. For once his tone wasn't the slick sneer that made Pete want to fetch him a smack. "You're scared, because you've got sense. Nergal's been around since the beginning of before the beginning. He's a force, a thing. Mesopotamians named him, made him the god of all ills. The Christians gave him a starring role and cribbed all the best bits for the devil. That's a PG-rated version of what he really is, though."

Belial watched a pigeon land on the column above. "I've seen him, in the plague pits and the camps. In the mass graves and the suicide bombings. Plagues don't have to be microscopic, Petunia. Black magic and violence and suffering and murder. Those are plagues of the soul, and they're Nergal's favorite kind, because there's no cure. The ancients got him nearly right," Belial said. "The adversary. The bringer of ill wind."

"Sounds like a barrel of laughs." Pete lifted herself away from the column. "I don't know where Jack is and I don't know how to find him. The one place he'd go that I know about, he won't be there now." Lawrence would never allow Jack back into the fold now. He was a good friend, but he had limits.

"I'm sorry Winter broke your heart," Belial said. "But you're the one who called me, and I'm holding up my end of the bargain." Belial put his hand over Pete's. "He fucked you. Get over it. Screw your head on and stop him from being the weak little cunt I always knew him to be."

"Don't play with me," Pete said, slapping his hand away. "You're not sorry. You're prince of a race of serial killers. You don't care how I'm feeling any more than you'd care about a cockroach crawling into the path of a lorry."

"I don't feel," Belial said. "But I understand. I understand loss and desire. It's the fabric of the bargains we make. It's what knits a human soul together—pain, too, and agony, and ecstasy, and love. It's such a fragile thing. You shouldn't work, but you do. I suppose I'm interested in how it came to this, you being here with me and Winter being gone."

"Like you're interested in the cinema," Pete said.

Belial nodded. "Has there been a Bond flick on? I do like that new bloke they've got doing the part."

"We can go to my flat and I can see if I can figure out where he might have gone to ground," Pete said.

"Won't work, but all right," Belial said.

"Then don't come," Pete snapped, "because it's the only idea I've got."

Belial followed her after a moment. They walked in silence. The only other humans in evidence were the street cleaners and the trashmen, going about their business in their neon slickers.

The area around Naughton's club wasn't made for daytime, and the street was gray and depressing in the light of the sun, weathered storefronts and pitted streets choked with garbage that sluiced away under the hissing hoses of the street cleaners. Pete realized they were being followed as they passed the entrance to the Tate and turned along the river, but she waited until they'd gone nearly a block before she turned around. She was reasonably certain it wasn't a ghost or something like the zombie—she hadn't felt the prickle of the Black that clung to those who'd crossed over from it.

"Hold up," she told Belial. He stopped, and his black shark's eyes scanned the street.

"It's something alive," he said. "Breath, blood, heartbeat. Want me to pull its limbs off until it tells us why it's here?"

Pete crinkled her lip. "I was thinking I'd ask them what they want first." She cupped her hands and shouted at the street. "We know you're there. You might as well come out."

After a few heartbeats, a shaggy black head leaned from the alley, followed by a lanky male body in a black leather coat and black jeans that clung like rot to the boy's skin. He walked with the shuffling, stumbling gate of a user, staring at her warily from eyes rimmed in blue, sleepless bruises. His cheek twitched. "You Pete Caldecott?"

"I might be," Pete allowed. The junkie looked at Belial.

"Who's that?"

"My fucking butler," Pete said. "Who are you?"

"Got a message to pass on," the boy said. "Guy on the ward paid me twenty quid and hooked me up with his connection on the outside if I'd take it to this bird named Pete Caldecott." He shoved a flat piece of flexible plastic at Pete. "Told me you might be here. Now I'm done."

"Wait just a bloody minute," Pete said as he started to turn away. "What ward? Who's the bloke?"

"Dunno," the boy shrugged. "Bad dye job, blue eyes, old, but he was tasty." He rolled his shoulders. "I wouldn't've charged him full price off the street."

"Jack?" Pete said. "Was his name Jack?"

"Sweetheart," said the boy, "in my line of work, they're all named Jack."

"Hey!" Pete shouted at the boy as he started to slump away. "What am I supposed to do with this?"

The boy walked backward for a moment. "He said come find him," he called. "Said you'd figure out the rest."

Pete looked back at the bracelet. LAVEY, GERALD was typed crookedly at the top, and a fat blue stripe warned Pete RESTRICTED PATIENT. Pete examined the hospital logo. St. Bernadette's, a hospital near the city, as gray and unassuming as the rest of London's postwar construction.

"What's Jack got himself into now?" Belial asked.

"Fake name on a psych ward, far as I can tell," Pete said. "Gerald Gardner and Anton LaVey— Jack's idea of a joke." She rubbed the strip between her fingers like rosary beads she used to count while she was waiting for mass to end as a girl, until her father hissed at her to stop the clicking. "He's at the hospital that gave him this." She held the bracelet, stripe out, to the demon's view. "And apparently they think he's gone insane."

CHAPTER 34

St. Bernadette's was doing a brisk business in the A&E when Pete and Belial arrived. A youth with a stab wound was screaming on a gurney while his hysterical mother shouted at the attending doctor in Polish and a pair of uniformed Met officers shouted at her in a counterpoint of Geordie and cockney accents.

"You stay here," Pete told Belial. "If Jack sees you, he's liable to blow a hole straight through the roof of this place."

"Winter was always such a sensitive boy," the demon purred, but he took a seat obediently in a salmon-pink chair bolted to the wall and picked up an ancient copy of *Tattler*.

Pete avoided the check-in desk, walking with the determined stride that told any observers she knew exactly where she was going and didn't brook interference. With any luck, the nurses would assume she was with the pair of coppers dealing with the stab victim.

She skirted the curtains that contained patients deeper into their trauma than the boy in the entry, most lying quietly, many smelling of old lager and newer vomit. A glance at the floor map once she'd gotten past the gatekeepers told Pete that the psychiatric unit was on the fourth floor, and she got in the elevator, nodding to an orderly who got on at the same time. They rode in silence, and Pete disembarked into a low hall lit with flickering tube lights. A charge nurse sat behind a desk, and she looked up for less than a second when Pete approached.

"Visiting hours are posted in the lobby."

"I'm not here for a visit," Pete said. "Here about a patient of yours."

The nurse sighed and reluctantly made eye contact. "What's this regarding?"

"Gerald LaVey," Pete said. "He was admitted . . ." Another Connor trick. Human beings were inclined to fill in relevant information. The nurse didn't bite.

"If you're a copper or a social worker, let's see some ID and I'll see about getting someone up here to unlock him."

"Look," Pete said. "I need to see him. What's it going to cost me?"

The nurse regarded Pete as if she were something slimy and still moving that the woman had stepped in. "It's gonna cost you a trip to the local station now." She picked up the phone and punched an extension.

Pete reached out and slammed her finger on the disconnect button. The nurse jerked the phone from her. "Oi! How dare you?"

"I'm sorry," Pete told her, stepping back and holding her hands up. "I'm very, very sorry."

"You should be," the nurse said. "And you're

gonna be sorrier when I get your arse hauled off to jail."

"My dear woman." Belial appeared at Pete's shoulder, as if out of thin air. "I assure you that our intentions toward your patient benefit you as well as him." He reached out and put his hand over the nurse's, as she grabbed for the telephone receiver again. "It's all right," Belial told her, thumb stroking across the woman's knuckles. "I know. I know the bills aren't being paid, even though you've been working shifts back to back. I know about young Ned and his trouble at school, about those boys who held him down and took photos down his pants and posted them all over the net." Belial leaned in. Pete watched as the nurse's face went slack. "I know that every day since your husband left, you think about walking into this place with his skeet rifle and doing as many as you can before you cram a handful of those pills you feed the crazies down your gullet."

The nurse stared at Belial, her jaw slack. One tear worked its way down her face, running into the furrow next to her nose. Her lips worked, lax and rubbery, and a pathetic sound came from her throat.

"I know how to make it all go away," Belial said. "I think you do, too."

Pete wanted to move, to tell Belial to stop, but she felt as rooted as the nurse. The demon's power wasn't like being touched by cold—it simply curled up and lived in her mind, as if it had always been there, whispering to her. It was like sinking under with a handful of the pills Belial had talked about. Warm, soft, a slowing heartbeat, and a flow of euphoria that made everything around Pete—the smell of the ward and the screams of the patients and the ding of the PA—matter very little.

Belial cut his eyes to her and mouthed *Go*.

"Don't hurt her," Pete said. She backed up a step, which lessened the thrall of Belial's power, but not enough to completely stem the tide of fascination. She wanted him to speak to her, to touch her and read her like he was reading the nurse.

"I want you to do it right now," Belial said, ignoring Pete completely. "Get up and do it."

The nurse stood, gathered her purse and coat from behind her desk, and left the ward without a backward look. Pete watched her go, until the doors swished shut behind her ample rear.

"What did you do?" she said. Belial took up a seat behind the desk, putting his feet up.

"Convinced her she wants to be somewhere else. She's going to go out there, empty her checking account, buy a ticket to Leeds, and look up the girl she was in love with at university. Of course, that one's married with two girls and actually straight, but it'll keep her out of our business."

Pete snatched the charge list away from him and ran her finger down to Gerard LaVey. "You're enjoying this."

"Of course I am." Belial laced his fingers behind his head. "People are so simple most of the time. Give them permission to do what they really like and they behave like animals, blood running in the streets."

Pete threw the charge list back at him and grabbed up the nurse's keycard, going to the third locked room on the ward. She swiped the card and waited for the slow progress of the electronic door.

Jack's room was bereft of furniture, except for a steel bedframe propped on end against the far wall. He sat in the center of the painted cement, naked, knees drawn up to his chest. "There you are," Pete said softly. She made a move to step inside, but Jack spoke.

"Don't come in."

Pete glanced around the cell-sized space, and saw that every inch of wall and floor, save a small spot for Jack to sit, was painted with ritual symbols. He'd started in marker, black ink jagged and done in shaking hands, and as the symbols flowed toward the center of the floor, they became blood, sticky and gleaming from long exposure to the air.

"Fuck me," Pete said. "What have you done?"

"Don't come inside," Jack said. "Don't come any closer."

"You'd hurt me?" Pete said. She stuck an arm out and caught the doorframe. The Black flowing through the writing on the cell walls was like being smacked across the face, and left her skull ringing.

"They're not for you," Jack said. "Now go away."

Pete took a step inside instead, and when nothing happened, sat next to Jack on the clear patch of floor, drawing her own legs up. "Been here long, then?"

"I was going to go and start the ritual and give the raven woman Carver," Jack said. "Then I went back by the flat to get a few things. You were gone." He put his forehead on the knobby points of his knees. "Didn't know if you'd chucked me or Naughton had taken you. But I turned around and I checked into hospital. Figured some anti-psychotics would keep the sight down, thick steel walls. I fucked everyone I know to do this thing and I couldn't even follow through on that."

Pete realized that now that she was inside the cell, the Black had gone softer, as if they were behind thick stone walls muting a rush of traffic on the other side.

"I'm a waste," Jack said. "Eventually she'll find

me, and I won't go back to Hell. I'll go to the Underworld, and then even Nicholas fucking Naughton can't fetch me back." He breathed deeply, back quivering. "Then it'll be done."

"Yeah, well," Pete told him, lifting his face so she could look at him. "I'm not about lying down and dying, so you better snap the fuck out of it and get on with helping me."

Jack put his hand over Pete's, and tangled his fingers tight enough to bruise her. "What the fuck," he snarled, "ever made you have such blind faith in me?"

"I don't," Pete said. "I have no faith in you, Jack. That's over, and that's between you and me." She removed her hand from him. "Now, you promised Carver to the Morrigan?"

"You know I did," Jack mumbled.

Pete stood, smudging her foot in a wide circle across as many of the symbols as she could. "Then I think it's time we give her what she wants."

CHAPTER 35

Jack started to shout at Pete, scrambling up and trying to grab her, but she twisted away from him and smeared at the walls with her hands, ink and blood coating her palms.

He screamed at her, but Pete soon lost the sound amid the wild rushing of wings, hundreds of wings and thousands of feathers, wind across an endless, empty place as the Black convulsed and shifted around them.

She'd seen the Morrigan before, once, when she'd appeared to take Algernon Treadwell's soul back to the Underworld. Just a glimpse, and that had been enough. The raven woman had feathers for hair and black coals for eyes. Her skin was the skin of a corpse and her fingers dipped to run down Jack's spine.

I knew you'd come, she whispered, and Jack let out a quiet sob.

"He's not the one you're dealing with," Pete told

her. The Morrigan turned her eyes on Pete, and staring at her, Pete felt her talent writhe, filled with the same empty, sharp feeling as when she'd come to the hospital for the last time—not to say goodbye to Connor, but to collect his things after the nurses had cleaned out his bed and packed them up.

The room, devoid of oxygen machines and heart monitors, the crisp pink spread and all of the flowers she and his friends from the Met had brought thrown away. Empty. Nothing.

You think you're a hero, the Morrigan whispered. *A bright soul that will outshine the dark.* She put her clawed hands on either side of Pete's face, and brought their lips so close they nearly brushed, sharing the air. *The dark is greater than all of you. And I've lived in it for so long, Weir. It's time the rest of you do as well.*

"I know I'm not a hero," Pete said. "But I wasn't stupid enough to come alone."

Belial stepped from the doorway and raised a hand. "Why, look at you. Out in the daylight and everything. Mind your tan."

The Morrigan hissed, baring her teeth. Her canines were sharp as needles. Belial answered with his shark's grin. "I like things the way they are," he said. "The dead should stay dead. So why don't you hop on your broomstick and leave the world as it is?"

Pete crouched next to Jack, pulling him to his feet. "Come on," she said. "We're going."

The Morrigan turned on them, and Pete put her body between the raven woman and Jack. *This changes nothing,* the Morrigan snarled. *You think I fear a maggot feasting on the flesh of lost souls? I am*

*death. I am the maiden of war and the bride of blood
since Nergal's dragon first crept forth from the old
places, the lost places. You won't stop me.*

Belial moved, but the Morrigan was quicker, and
she raised her arms. Behind her, Pete saw the great
wings rise, the wings that carried souls to the Underworld, and death from it.

The demon flew back into the corridor and
slammed the wall. The body he rode let off a small
wheeze, and Belial curled into a ball, blood coming
from between his lips. Fat drops landed on the gray
tile.

The Morrigan stretched out her hand to Jack.
*Give him to me. Or you go back to how I found you,
alone and in Hell. And I will take your Weir to the
Bleak Gates, and I will ensure she never sees the
daylight world again, until everything goes to ashes.*

Jack grabbed his skull, moaning, and then quickly
as he'd convulsed, he went limp. Pete saw the symbols on the walls of the cell blur, fall away as the
Black pushed through. Gerard Carver's spirit stood
before her, and behind him Pete saw the London of
the in-between, burnt and blacked, its back broken.

The shadow she'd seen with the Hecate unfurled,
and she became aware the Morrigan was speaking,
and that this wasn't the Black, but somewhere else.
Older, buried down deep before the first human or
thing that would become human had ever drawn
breath.

*Son of Nergal, serpent of the world. Eater of
death and life, darkness and day, be free.* The Morrigan didn't raise her hands, or even chant. Her lips
barely moved as she watched, reverent.

The dragon wasn't a dragon in the sense of scales,

but a shadow that wrapped London around and around, spilling forth from the place Gerard Carver's ghost connected the hospital cell with. Pete felt it unfurl, saw that it was a prison, this place where the dragon had lain, and heard it scream as it came barreling toward Gerard Carver.

Pete tried to reach for Jack, but she wasn't near him any longer, wasn't anywhere. The dragon came, and it swallowed Carver, jerked as the soul cage tugged at it, pulling it down and holding over the burning city, as the spotlights roaming the sky winked out one by one.

Go, child, the Morrigan whispered to it. _You have come to me, and because you have come, I offer you the chance to be free._

The dragon howled again, and the Morrigan passed her hand across Jack's face. _He will lead the way. And you will lead the dead, the armies of the Underworld, and the Black will be clean and new._ She stroked his hair, ran her claws through it, and Jack shivered under her touch, leaning into it. _None of the throbbing masses. None of the filth and sweat and blood. Clean and cold and free of what troubles you. You, crow-mage. You brought this dawn, and I thank you._

Pete watched as Jack stood, and the Morrigan drew something from her great dress of feathers and blackness. She handed Jack a black blade, and pressed her thumb to his forehead. All over Jack's naked form new markings blossomed, tattoos that painted themselves onto his skin, burst to the surface like shattered veins. Jack screamed, going to his knees, clutching the blade so that blood flowed from his palms.

Belial was not stirring, and Pete tried to reach for him, but the Black was whirling, colliding with the daylight world. The London outside was burning, and Pete could hear screams and klaxons.

The dragon fed. Unwinding, devouring Carver's soul, it fed and Pete felt the swell of all the things Belial had spoken of—the plagues of rage and greed and base human nature.

Give them permission to do what they like, and they're like animals.

Jack's ink became wings, claws, agonized faces of spirits frozen against his skin. He stood before the Morrigan naked, blood flowing over his hands, and watched as the dragon laid its coils over the city, a darkness so complete not even sound could pierce it.

"Jack," Pete said. "Please don't. Remember why you came here."

"I am," Jack mumured. "It's like I told you, Pete. I did it so you could be safe. Aren't you glad now?"

Come. The Morrigan folded him beneath her wings, pressed their lips together. Blood dribbled from their kiss, down the Morrigan's chin, where she lapped it up.

Pete looked to Belial again, and saw his eyes open, cloudy and staring. She followed his gaze and saw the owl, sitting on the sill beyond the mesh and bars, amid the rain of ash.

"Jack," she tried, one last time. He wouldn't look at her, locked in the embrace of the Morrigan.

"This is what has to happen, Pete," he said. "You can't stop it. Nothing can stop it. Worlds have to die for a new world to be born."

"A world of more death?" Pete whispered.

"I'm a part of it," Jack said. "You never accepted it, but it's always been that way. I'm one of the dead, Pete. I just didn't know it until now."

Pete felt the Morrigan's death sense replaced with something else. It was the knowing, the truth she couldn't lie her way out of.

The owl watched her. Behind it, Pete saw something larger rise, something beyond the dragon, older and larger, a vast intelligence without form, an ill wind blowing the ashes of the old London, the one she'd thought was real until she met Jack, before it.

She took a step toward Jack, then another. Reached out and put her hand on his shoulder. She shook, fingers vibrating, tears flowing thick down her face, running to the corners of her lips, salt in her mouth.

The Morrigan hissed, but Pete pulled Jack to face her. "I know," she said. "I do. I know what you are, Jack."

She gripped his wrists, and they were close enough to share a heartbeat. "That's why I'm sorry," Pete whispered.

Jack grabbed the back of her neck, pulled them so their foreheads touched. "Don't be," he said. Pete kissed him, and tasted his blood on her tongue. She let herself take just a moment, an extra heartbeat, to remember him. His scent, his warmth, the firmness of his hands and the feel of his palm against hers. Then she turned the black blade of the Morrigan, and drove it into Jack's chest.

The Morrigan screamed, and all around them, in this burning London, thousands of crows took flight.

Do you have any idea, the Morrigan screamed at her, *any idea what you've done?*

Pete saw the owl take flight, join the crows. She

felt nothing. Not like screaming, not like weeping, nothing. Jack was gone. Jack had always been gone. Touched by death, his presence in her life was a reprieve, not a certainty. And she'd fought, and refused to let go. Now there was nothing to hold at all, just ashes, and plagues, and the taste of blood in her mouth.

She met the Morrigan's black, burning eyes, like oil burning on black water. "What I had to," she whispered.

Beyond the window, the thing retreated, the prison doors rolling shut. The dragon gave a scream that shook the city to its foundations. The crows circled and then shot east, a great flock that could blot out ten suns, straight to the Bleak Gates.

Pete hoped Jack's soul was among them, borne on to a place that would be, if not better than the one he'd found here, at least a place that wasn't Hell.

Mark my words, Weir, the Morrigan snarled. *You cannot cheat death. You cannot stop it or placate it or bargain with it. You and I, we know this. And someday, you'll be at the Gates yourself.*

Pete let the blade slip from her grasp. It landed by her feet with a dull thunk. "Until that day comes?" she told the Morrigan. "You can fuck right off."

Tired beyond all reason, battered by the Black like driftwood, Pete felt herself slipping. Back from the Bleak Gates, back from the disturbance caused by the Morrigan, back into the cold, hard edges of the daylight world.

The Morrigan took flight, joining her crows, and the fires in the east winked out.

Pete heard rushing feet, the snap of surgical gloves, the thud of bodies. Shouts.

This one's conscious!

Check the one in the hall—looks like bloody roadkill.

The fuck's happening? Who is this git?

She lay on the ground. Jack lay a few feet away, a single long line in his abdomen, straight and thin, trailing surprisingly little blood. A pair of orderlies in white jumpsuits worked over him, bag on his face while the other prepped a defibrillator.

"Clear!" he shouted, and Jack's body jumped. His new ink covered nearly every inch of him, from neck to feet, and he was still, and pale, and dead.

Pete choked, and that was all she could give. She was too wrung to cry, too spent to even try. A doctor in pink scrubs loomed over her, flashed a light in her eyes, checked her neck.

"You hurt, love?" she said. Pete managed to shake her head. The doctor helped her up.

"Let's get you down to A&E," she said. "Stand up, there's a good girl. The hospital's going to have some forms it'll want you to sign about the patient who got out."

An orderly came up on her left side and took her arm. "I'll escort Miss Caldecott, Doctor. You tend the wounded."

The doctor ran back inside the cell, where the other orderly shocked Jack again. She leaned over his chest and then shook her head. "Jolt him again. He's not going to bleed out just yet, but it won't do a bit of good if he's brain-dead, will it?"

Psychic death. Would stop your heart surely as plunging onto concrete. Pete tugged against the orderly's grasp, trying to be somewhere she didn't have to look.

Don't be.

He'd told her to. Told her to let him go. Pete saw

the owl again, on the sill as if it had never left, gray and unremarkable in the sun. "Leave me alone," she whispered. "I did what you wanted. Tell your bitch that."

He was gone this time. Gone, to the land of the dead. She would never see him, talk to him, touch him. He was gone, and she was still here, and he wasn't coming back.

The owl blinked, tilted its head, then took flight, as if it had suddenly remembered there was no need to hang about.

In the next moment, one of the machines working over Jack pipped. "I've got a rhythm," the orderly shouted. The doctor took over the bag and pointed out the cell door. "Call trauma and get a surgery prepped. Get me some blood and a fucking surgeon. Fucking git, tries to kill two people and kick himself off. Doesn't bloody deserve the fuss."

Pete did sag then, against the orderly who grabbed her. "Best we be going," Belial said in her ear.

"You're all right," she said as he dragged her to the lift. She was flat. Jack was alive. At least for the moment, and she was being dragged from the hospital by a demon.

"I've had better days," Belial said. "Bitch walloped me a good one, tried to push me right out of my skin and back to the pit like a tube of toothpaste. But fortunately she's only good at swanning about and looking terrifying. Piss-poor exorcist." The demon cackled.

"I saw him," Pete said, as they wound through the packed A&E lobby. "Nergal. I saw the dragon."

They came out the door, and the scent of smoke went up Pete's nose and choked her. She saw a motor accident in the street, ambulance versus taxi, and people sitting on the sidewalk, staring, some walking in circles. She heard screams over the klaxons that were no longer in her imagination. Saw two youths in hoodies pick up a rolling garbage can and toss it through a shop window, grabbing handfuls of pocket cameras and MP3 players.

"What the fuck . . ." Pete started. She was having a hard time standing, her eyes going unfocused in slow, rolling waves.

"The dragon," Belial said. "Creeping up through the layers. It'll die down." He put her off and stood at arm's length, looking at her. "It's been fun, Petunia Caldecott," he said. "And I'll be dropping by, sooner or later, to collect my end. But until then . . ." Belial dropped her a wink. "You and Winter have a nice little life."

"You're not . . ." Pete breathed in, out, tried to keep on her feet. "You won't try for Jack?"

"Winter gave me his soul," Belial said. "I lost it because I was a stupid twat, and that winged bitch is stronger. For now." He tipped his head back at the hospital. "Not to worry. I'll have another try at the crow-mage's soul, Petunia. You just wait and see."

Belial faded away into the roiling crowd, and Pete sat down on the curb, holding her head. Jack was alive. The dragon was free, but Nergal was still in whatever hole the old gods had stuffed him in. The Black was shredded—she could feel it rolling and pulsing in her skull even now. She still owed Naughton, Ethan, still had McCorkle's death hanging over her head.

It was a bad world, sooty and broken and hard. Full of nothing but trouble, if you listened to Jack. But Jack didn't speak for her.

Pete stood up, and started for the tube. Whatever world she was in now, she reasoned, she would adapt and so would Jack. They would be survivors, together. The way it should be.

EPILOGUE

GHOSTS

Still they come up to me
With a different name but the
  same old face
I can see the connection
With another time and a different place

—The Stiff Little Fingers

CHAPTER 36

Nearly three weeks later, Pete met Felix Patel at the Dogstar on Coldharbour Lane. She watched him check the bar from the door, eyes scanning the entire room before he made his way to the two-top where she sat beneathed the arched window. The sun hit the blue paint on the bar's exterior walls and reflected harsh silver light across Patel's face.

"What is it?" He didn't even take his coat off, just sat and folded his hands as if he were in the interrogation room rather than a bar.

Patel had deep grooves under his eyes, and Pete detected stubble on his formerly pristine jawline. London to the north had settled down, the isolated riots, murder, car accidents, and random acts of mayhem wrapped up, but London to the south was still evacuated in wide swaths, the British army running backup to the Met. Ollie had gone back to work the week before and declared the entire city, "A fuckin' mess from top to fuckin' bottom."

Pete didn't bother even trying to explain. The

cataclysm that had rolled outward from the Black was gone, but the twilight world was even worse off than the daylight one. Lawrence had become a virtual hermit. Pete hadn't even tried to go to the Lament and check in with Mosswood—she figured if the Green Knight was ever going to speak to her again, it would be on his own terms. She wasn't going to force the issue.

"You look tired, Felix," she said. "Can I buy you a pint?"

"I'm on duty," Patel said. "And I haven't ruled you out in the McCorkle matter, Ms. Caldecott. If that's what you brought me here to ask."

"McCorkle and Gerard Carver were schoolmates," Pete said. "Ask Ollie for the details from his case file, but Carver was caging artifacts from his job and selling them on the black market. He sold McCorkle a reliquary, Babylonian. Carver'd promised that particular item gratis to a bloke named Nicholas Naughton."

Patel narrowed his eyes. "This means what to me?"

"Naughton is wanted in Devon for the murder of his brother Danny," Pete said. "He killed McCorkle, and Carver, and I wager if you wander down the lane to Southwark, you'll find some talkative mates of his in a club called Motor."

Patel stood up, chair shoving back with a screech of wood on wood. "Caldecott, I don't like you. I don't trust you, and I don't believe a word of that shit you spout to Heath. Until I say otherwise, you're still a suspect."

"But you'll look into it?" Pete said. "You'll talk to Heath about Carver?"

"'Course I bloody will," Patel snapped. "Unlike you, I'm a good fucking police detective."

Pete stood as well and put a tenner on the table for her drink. "That's all that matters, then."

Patel pointed a finger at her. "Don't cross paths with me again, Petunia. Unless you want me to get a lot more interested in your business than is comfortable."

"When you find Naughton, Sergeant, do me a favor," Pete said. Patel held the door for her as they left the Dogstar.

"And what's that?"

"Tell him to enjoy it while it lasts."

She watched until she was sure Patel was in his unmarked and driving back down the lane toward the Lambeth station before she walked back to McCorkle's flat.

Naughton wouldn't last in prison. He'd been unseated as the baddest man on the block. He might skate on McCorkle's murder, but not on Carver's. And if the other inmates of Pentonville didn't get him, sooner or later an angry ghost he'd had a hand in creating would. Without his protection hexes and thugs in their matched suits, Naughton was just another sad bastard grasping at magic. He'd get sent on soon enough. What was waiting for him in the thin spaces was worse than anything Pete could wish on him while he was alive.

She waited on McCorkle's steps until one of his neighbors came out, and slipped through the door. The third floor was still taped off, but Pete ducked under it and stood in McCorkle's living room. No one had bothered to clear away the blood, and the room was musty and stank faintly of rotted things. Flies buzzed around the bin in the kitchen, and the taps dripped out of sync.

Pete found it behind the kitchen wall—a patch

of plaster half-covered by a cheap generic poster of Tower Bridge, curling at the edges. The plaster had been painted, but the patching was rough. She searched McCorkle's drawers until she found a tenderizing hammer, and smashed the plaster in three short blows.

Nergal's reliquary was smaller than she'd imagined. A stone jar, rough and round, chipped into a circle by hand, covered in incantations and covered over with a bronze seal that had oxidized from the thousands of years it had lain untouched.

The magic crawled around it, faint but there, holding a tiny snip of the essence she'd felt from the thing that had followed the dragon out of the pit.

Pete rolled it in a tea towel, put the tea towel in her bag, and left, not bothering to lock the door behind her. While she rode to Regent's Park, she went over all the reasons this was a terrible idea. And all the reasons she had to do it no matter what.

Dreisden answered the door at the Order, and looked her up and down before he stepped aside without a word. Juniper was in the sitting room, reading with her feet tucked under her. Pete tried to sneak by, but Juniper saw her and jumped up.

"Oh, Petunia. I was so worried. So many awful things have been happening."

"Yeah," Pete said. "Couldn't agree more." She moved toward Morningstar's study again, but Juniper stopped her.

"Pete." She chewed on her lip, a mirror of Pete's own nervous gesture. "I know you hate me," Juniper said.

"I don't hate you, Mum." Pete held up her hands. "I don't want to reminisce and forgive. I just want to talk to Ethan and then leave and never see any of you ever again."

"I made a mistake," Juniper said. "When I left. I had to leave your father, but I thought that meant leaving you girls, too, and I was wrong. And I wouldn't have seen that without the Order, because the people I was with before didn't give a toss about family or any of it. So hate me if you want, Pete, but please stop thinking the Order is the reason for it."

"Mum," Pete said. "You and I never got along. We are never going to get along. And that is truly the least of my worries right now." She knocked on Ethan's door. "Don't give it another thought on my account, please."

"Pete . . ." Juniper started, then stopped. "It's all right. I hope you'll believe me. In your own time."

"Give me sixteen years or so, and I just might," Pete said.

Morningstar opened the door to his study, and looked at her for a moment, eyebrow cocked. "Do you have something for me?"

"We talk in private?" Pete said. Morningstar stood aside, and shut and latched the door after her.

"I don't see anyone with you. Anyone responsible. Why is that, Petunia?"

"Because I gave him to the cops," Pete said. Morningstar's face went red, and he started for her, hands balling into fists.

"I warned you. I warned you and I wasn't fucking playing games, you stupid little girl."

Pete pulled the reliquary from her bag. "I did bring someone, though. Maybe not the hand holding the knife, but the responsible party nonetheless."

Morningstar stared at the thing, not moving, not

blinking. A tremor passed through him. Pete knew instinctively that this was the closest she'd ever see Ethan Morningstar to fear. "Fuck me," he said softly.

Pete dropped the thing into his hand. "Can't think of a better bunch of nannies for the reliquary of Nergal."

Morningstar turned it in his hands. His face was pale and his fingers were quivering. "I didn't want this," he whispered.

"Well, it wants you," Pete said. She shouldered her bag. "And I'll assume that makes us fucking square."

Morningstar still clutched the reliquary, as if he couldn't decide between throwing it or embracing it. "The Order considers this a service," he said. "If you need anything in the future, you can call on me."

"Yeah." Pete stopped with her hand on the doorknob. "You can do me a favor, Ethan."

"Anything," he said.

"Never bloody come near me or anyone I know again," Pete said. "And this isn't a request, just advice—stop wearing that stupid fucking hat."

CHAPTER 37

Jack was still in hospital. Lawrence had moved him closer to their flat, but the stab wound had been deep and he'd been in and out of the ICU with complications. Pete felt rude checking her watch while Dr. Abouhd was drawing her blood, but all he did was raise an eyebrow.

"Visiting hours," she explained.

"I see," he said. "Anyone special?"

"Nobody you know," Pete said. Abouhd filled the vial and handed it off to a nurse. She'd had as many visits in three weeks, and repeated this process before. The third try didn't fill her with much hope that Abouhd would actually find anything.

"Still dizzy?" he asked her. "Still feeling sick?"

"Ever since a couple of days before I came in," she said. Abouhd looked inside her file, shut it, and faced her, rolling his stool back and forth a bit with one foot.

"Let me ask you, Pete—when was the last time you had a period?"

Pete held up her hands, fighting the urge to leap up, since she was in a backless paper gown, panties, and not a great deal else. "No," she said. "No, that's not . . . I mean, that can't have anything to do with this. I think I may be anemic."

Abouhd gave her a regretful half-smile. "Your results were positive. I'll do another test, of course, to double-check, but I wanted to tell you in person." He took out his pen and scratched on his prescription pad. "If I can ask—you're not married, are you?"

"No." Pete could hear her heart beating, but nothing else. A baby. Jack's baby. But not Jack's fault. That one was on her.

Abouhd said something, and then rolled closer and tapped her on the knee when she didn't answer.

"Eh?" Pete said. She should have known. Should have been careful, cautious Petunia. Especially since she knew Jack, and knew his typical MO when it came to women. Should have at least glanced at a bloody calendar.

"I said, do you have any idea what you're going to do?" Abouhd said. "There's several lovely people you can speak to if you need help with the decision . . ."

"No," Pete said. "I know who I need to speak to."

"All right." Abouhd handed her the scrip. "I wrote you up for vitamins and a few other prenatal goodies, but Pete . . ." He sighed and then stood. "I'm telling you this as someone who's known you a while, not as your doctor. Don't let anyone tell you what to do here. I know you'll be fine."

"That makes one of us," Pete told him. Abouhd put a hand on her shoulder.

"Good luck, Petunia. You can get dressed."

Pete took her time, now hoping she'd miss visiting hours. But when she'd made a follow-up appointment and waited through two full lifts, there were still ten minutes on the clock.

All right, Caldecott. Stop being a fucking coward. Go upstairs, tell him, and take care of your business.

The traitorous part of her whispered that Jack never needed to know. She was barely a month along. *Nobody* would ever need to know. She couldn't deal with being pregnant, never mind having a baby. What sort of mother would she make? She'd be shit, even more shit than Juniper.

But then she'd have to look at Jack and wonder what he or she would have looked like. The Hecate had given her a chance.

She was at the door to Jack's room, and his eyes fluttered open. They'd taken him off the heavy opiates as soon as possible. Former junkies didn't get morphine drips. Jack winced as he tried to sit up, but he grinned at her.

"You're a sight for sore eyes, luv."

Pete sat in the hard plastic chair next to the bed, and gently pushed him back to his pillows. "None of that," she said. "You pop your incision, you're going to be in here another month."

"Incision," Jack said. "Is that what we're calling it now?"

"Why?" Pete said. "You can do better?"

"I'm calling it the great bloody hole in my guts where my girlfriend stabbed me with a fucking knife," Jack said. "I think it's catching on."

Pete didn't smile, and Jack's mouth turned down. "What?" he said. "I didn't bloody do it, whatever it is. I can't get out of bed without taking a header, so I swear, I'm innocent."

"I want to tell you," Pete said. "But I'm . . . well." She rubbed her forehead. "I'm scared, Jack."

"Luv." Jack sat up, then grabbed at his abdomen. "Fuck. Come over here before they have to operate on me again, will you?"

Pete stood, and sat on the very edge of his mattress. Jack tugged her closer, and even though she knew it wasn't the time, Pete put her head down on his chest. She could hear his heart beating, steady and strong despite the weight he'd lost and the paleness in his face.

"I know we haven't talked about it," Jack said quietly. "But I don't ever want to fucking talk about it, and I don't have the fortitude to *make* myself do it right now, so please don't look at me like that." He passed his fingers through her hair before wrapping them around her shoulder. "I'm fucked. I went down the rabbit hole and I know it. I can't believe you're even here." He sighed, chest jumping. "You have every right to bloody hate me."

"Jack." Pete sat up, and looked at him. "Stop it. Right now."

His eyebrows drew in. "What?"

"The fucking pity party," Pete said. "We've all been desperate, Jack. Yes, you fucked up. But that doesn't give you the right to decide whether I hate you or not. That's for me. And I don't. So change the fucking record."

Jack stared at her for a moment, then pulled her into a kiss, harder and longer than she would have thought him capable of in this state. "What the fuck did I ever do to deserve you?" he mumbled against her lips.

"Shit," Pete said, and did smile then. "You're just fucking lucky." Jack let her go, stroked her face.

"Tell me what's wrong then, luv. I'm here. I'm not going. I want to talk, about you at least."

Pete put her hand over his, curled their fingers, held them in her lap. She allowed herself to contemplate for one moment if this turned out all right. She could have a baby, and have Jack. Have him accept what had happened and stay, rather than pulling his usual act of vanishing when things got the slightest whiff of a commitment about them. They might not be in love, or even on firm ground with one another, but they could work this one thing out. The third time could be the fucking charm.

Or he could run off as usual, leave her alone and pregnant with the Black growing around London by the day, and her bargain with Belial hanging above her head like a crushing weight. He could call her a slag or a whore, he could shout, and tell her it was all her fault.

She could have the baby and be no better than Juniper and Connor, one disappeared and the other so present he nearly suffocated her.

Jack could relapse and use, and be the same junkie father she'd seen a dozen times over on the Met: sad-eyed kids, no money, no sort of life.

She and Jack could be a lot of things, Pete realized. But she wasn't psychic, and she couldn't see the future, and she didn't bloody want to. It would be her stupid choice, and Connor had at least given her that much. She could step up, and she could make it when it counted.

Pete squeezed Jack's hand and moved closer to him on the bed. "Good," she told him. "Because we've got lots to talk about."

Don't miss these novels in Caitlin Kittredge's
extraordinary Nocturne City series

DAEMON'S MARK
ISBN: 978-0-312-94366-0

WITCH CRAFT
ISBN: 978-0-312-94362-2

SECOND SKIN
ISBN: 978-0-312-94831-3

PURE BLOOD
ISBN: 978-0-312-94830-6

NIGHT LIFE
ISBN: 978-0-312-94829-0

Available from St. Martin's Paperbacks